EXCALIBUR
Reclaims Her King

ANGELICA HARRIS   COREY BLAKE

EXCALIBUR RECLAIMS HER KING

By Angelica Harris and Corey Blake

© Angelica Harris 2008
Writers of the Round Table Inc

ISBN Hardcover: 978-0-9822206-1-0
ISBN Paperback: 978-0-9822206-2-7
Library of Congress Control Number: 2009921477

Published By:

1670 Valencia Way
Mundelein, IL 60060
Phone: 224.475.0392
www.writersoftheroundtable.com

Cover Illustration by:
Hyunsang Michael Cho

Cover Design and Interior Layout by:
Nathan Brown
Writers of the Round Table Inc

Yet some men say in many parts of England that King Arthur is not dead, But had by the will of our lord Jesu into another place; and men say that he shall come again and he shall win the Holy Cross. I will not say that this shall be so but rather I will say, here in this world he changed his life. But many men say that there is written upon his tomb this verse; HIC IACET AUTHURUS REX QUONDAM REXQUE FUTURUS.[1]

—*Le Morte d'Arthur* by Thomas Malory

[1]Here lies Arthur, once king and king to be.

TABLE OF CONTENTS

Acknowledgements

I met Corey Blake online five years ago at the inception of my book *Excalibur Reclaims Her King*. What started with a few e-mails blossomed into a lifetime friendship and partnership. I began to send Corey sample chapters. He loved the premise of the story but wanted more, knowing that I had the potential to turn what was a good tale into a great epic. I wrote a foot — Corey wanted a yard. But that was not enough. Corey demanded excellence, that I myself emulated. He called for an acre, again, yet this time when I delivered it, my friend commanded from me an entire countryside. When I faulted, he raised me from the trenches. For that, I am truly thankful. Corey envisioned the world that I was creating and with his direction, it became a magical universe. He became my Merlin.

To my husband John, you are my Jack. Like Arianna and Jack, we have had good times. The hard times were sometimes unimaginable, yet you have been there through my tears and anxiety, so that I could see this book to its completion. I love you so very much.

To John my son, you are the real Joseph; the boy I feared would never see manhood. You are my knight, the man I hoped that my faith would come to see. I love you.

For my daughter Andrea, my Alexis, you, my child, have been my strength when our road as a family was tested repeatedly. On days when I had no one to turn to, you were there with your gleaming smile and warm embrace. I love you, my daughter. I dedicate this book to you, and to all women who search for the grail within themselves, those who search for the road to empowerment. May we, all of us, find our Holy Grail and the weapon to battle what lies ahead.

Thanks Dad for always telling me to write it down. Love you!

I wish to thank the Tourette Syndrome Association and their social workers, Emily Kelman-Bravo and Evan Michaels. When my family was in its darkest times dealing with Tourette syndrome and the co-morbidities of the disorder, you were there to listen, help us fight the battles from within, and keep us whole. Thank you from the bottom of my heart. At TSA I found Kevin Josephson, my Cavyn; you are so much like Joseph, and I thank you, young man, for modeling the character for me.

I wish to thank Lilli and Carl Haiken for their friendship and advice in the writing of this book. To the Society for Creative Anachronism, your friendship and support of my work mean so very much to me.

To Sue Publicover, thanks for all the times I bent your ear about the progress of the book and about the angst of life in general. You listened and gave sisterly advice, put my feet on the path I am to walk, and showed me the light at the end of the tunnel.

Mostly, I thank Jesus Christ with my whole heart and soul for giving the world his Holy Grail, and for giving me his love and the strength to tackle each day. Without Him, I could not write this book. In addition, to the Mother Earth: may she always shelter us, and may we look to her wondrous face for peace and inspiration.

COREY BLAKE WOULD LIKE TO THANK...

First and foremost, Angelica Harris for her incredible tenacity, her tireless researching, her willingness to dive into my repeated requests for rewrites, and her patience in dealing with my constant barrage of editorial commentary. She truly is Arianna, yielding her pen like a sword and fighting for her place in this world. To my blessed wife who has continually provided emotional support and brilliant business advice throughout all of my creative endeavors, I thank you with all my heart. To my business partner David Cohen, I appreciate you for being an exceptional sounding board and friend. To my parents and sister, I thank you for always supporting my addiction to dreaming. To Sue Publicover, I thank you for being so reliable and taking care of Writers of the Round Table so that I could dedicate the time necessary to complete *Excalibur*.

⬤◆⬤

Both authors would like to thank Nathan Brown: we bow to his design genius. To Rita Hess, we thank you for taking this book from good to great.

To all the loyal fans of Arthurian folklore and fantasy, who have waited patiently for this book, it is with deep gratitude and pleasure that we give to you *Excalibur Reclaims Her King*. Let the magic begin!

CHAPTER ONE

A Fever Rages

A bone-chilling cry emanated from Merlin's room as though his body were being pulled apart by the king's strongest horses. He cried out again but this time in words, "Get away from me, witch!"

Hearing his screams, Nimue ran to her husband's side from the hall. She reached for him and clutched him in her arms rocking him. "He is burning up!"

"What else can be done?" shouted Galahad as he charged into the room behind her. He reached for Merlin, and tried to take him from Nimue. "You have been caring for him night and day. You're exhausted. Let me help you."

Nimue hesitated, but surrendering to her fatigue, she allowed him to take Merlin from her. Feeling the burden of her husband's weight leave her, she leaned on the bed for support.

Nimue was the daughter of Lord Ardent and Lady Gandalwynn of Cornwall. She was raised Christian, but learned the ways of the Goddess through her mother's friend, Lady Viviane, who also introduced her to the Wizard Merlin. Eventually they courted and married under Druid ritual. The church was not pleased with Merlin's unwillingness to convert to Christianity, and they excommunicated Nimue. She never let her undying faith waver, though, knowing that neither God nor the Goddess would abandon her.

"This illness is far beyond my understanding," said Galahad standing nearby. "I have called upon my royal physicians from Warwick. They come with aid for Merlin."

Nimue rested quietly for a moment, trying to push back the fear that stabbed her in the belly like a hot blade.

"Give him some of that tisane," recommended Galahad as he lifted Merlin's head from the pillow and helped him sip the tea that Nimue fed him with a wooden spoon. Merlin's chest heaved with labored breath. "His heart is racing like a stag from its predator. Nimue, this is good—he tries to ward off the fever."

She placed her hand on Merlin's chest and looked up at Galahad for answers. "My God, what is this poison?" She felt tears fill her eyes.

Galahad placed Merlin back down upon the soft sheets, and Nimue rested a cool cloth on her husband's chest. Her eyes shed the tears they held, and Galahad reached over to hold her trembling hand. She allowed his touch to comfort her.

"I am afraid that after forty-five years of marriage I will lose my sweet man."

"We will pray to our lord."

Nimue grasped Galahad's hand and held it to her face. "Where is Arianna? She should be here."

"She should have been here a week ago," said Galahad. "When something is wrong with either one of them, the situation is always linked like a puzzle."

She agreed, "It was certainly that way when Merlin found Arianna and brought her back here to aid Arthur in his final hours." Nimue caressed her husband's face, he was wet and clammy, she searched his features for answers. "Merlin gave her a jewel before she left. He told me the jewel held a piece of her destiny and that soon she would return." Her clenched fingers held tight to the yoke of her dress and she sobbed, "I want my Merlin back."

"I have sent for Lady Viviane. She can help us."

Nimue felt her face blanch with worry as she sat exhausted from the past week. The relentless task of trying to break Merlin's fever was becoming a heavy undertaking for her in her crones years. She loved her husband so very much but in the past, when either of them was ill, youth was the leader in giving both of them the strength to overcome hurdles.

She thought back to years ago, when she and Merlin wanted children of their own. Nimue miscarried two and had a stillborn child. Her inability to bear children hurt them so. They were both people of strength and conviction and found that their mutual faith and love for each other healed their grief. What they also found was that a young King Arthur and his knights became all the family they could ever want and need. This was who they were, a fortress of love, strength and honor.

A playful whistling came from down the hall and Nimue knew it to be Prince John and that his lessons were over for the day.

"My lady, may I come in?"

His lighthearted noises turned to sadness as Nimue looked at his face. "Oh John, please come stand next to me."

She watched as he looked down upon his dear uncle. Like most fifteen-year-old boys, Nimue always knew that sickness confused him, yet somehow she also understood that the young prince was aware of the rather desperate nature of the situation. As his eyes fell upon his hero in so much pain, she witnessed a single tear streaming down his cheek.

"If Merlin were awake, he would have loved to hear about my lesson this morning."

Nimue eyed the young prince from head to toe. Since John was a babe, Merlin always wished to hear the daily report of the boy's development. He loved this young man so very much. John was taking on Galahad's strong features, and Merlin knew that the future of Camelot was in the promise of his tutelage towards serving a better England. John walked to the windows and opened the curtain. "Uncle Merlin loves the sun. Maybe he'll wake up if he feels it on his face."

The sun's rays spread about the room and the crystals that hung from the windows threw the colors of the rainbow upon the walls. The light caught the dust particles in the air as they danced upon the furniture.

If Merlin were up and about, he'd be waving his hand through them. Merlin enjoyed the art of hand-fasting, a slight of hand he employed to play with one elemental particle of dust and turn it into anything that the young Prince desired.

Nimue was lost in thought, looking around the room. Merlin's walking staff sat lonely in the corner as it waited for its master to take it in hand. The staff, given to him by his father Medwynn, was hune from the oakwood that grew on the Isle of Glastonbury. It was painted cherry, with oak leaves delicately carved into the wood. Crowning the staff was a brass dragon, with two ruby red eyes that ignited wildly in the sunlight. From his head protruded five spikes, with four more extending down the back of his neck. One of his talons curved around the throat of the staff, the other held a scroll tight in its grip.

Her eyes drifted to a painting that Merlin was working on that sat patiently waiting for its artist's brilliant strokes of color; and then to his brown cloak hanging over the chair near the low burning fireplace where Merlin always left it because he knew that it annoyed his wife.

"Ariannnnnna!" cried Merlin in his sleep. His head tossed back and forth on his pillow. His face began to sweat. "Ariannnna!" again he cried this time louder.

"Why isn't she here?" yelled Nimue. "Merlin needs her right now."

"Arianna!" Merlin cried out again.

"Uncle Merlin!" John yelled out noticeably shaking in his boots.

"Arianna!" Merlin moaned. His voice sounded like it came from the bottom of an empty barrel.

"Uncle Merlin, wake up you are scaring me!" John reached for Merlin's fingers. "Uncle Merlin's hand is like ice, he's going to die I know it!"

Nimue left her husband's side stroking the back of John's head. "He's calling for Arianna, where is she?" Nimue asked as she saw Galahad's eyes fill with concern for not only Merlin but now for his son as well.

Sobbing cries came from John as he tried to speak. "Where is grandmother? I want my grandmother."

Nimue placed her arms around John. "We don't know my love. It is scaring all of us."

Galahad placed his hand on his son's shoulder as though it was all he could do.

A knock on the door startled them both. Nimue turned her head as the Guard opened it. "Oh Viviane, thank God it is you!"

A rush of their history together flooded Nimue's mind. Viviane was her long time friend and the High Druid Priestess—The Lady of the Lake. Nimue had a hard time befriending the lady at first; Viviane did not trust Nimue's Christian heritage and was afraid that Nimue would turn Merlin against his people. Eventually she found that all she wanted was Merlin's love.

As time passed and Merlin and Nimue were looking to create a family, Viviane helped heal Nimue from the bleeding of her courses that caused her miscarriages and it was Viviane and Merlin who forged the relic sword Excalibur at the lake of Avalon. Could she forge a miracle today?

Viviane kissed Nimue on the cheek and bent low and placed her hand over Merlin's head, feeling for the raging heat of his fever. She placed her hand on his chest and put her ear to his left breast to listen to his heart. Merlin groaned with the weight of Vivian's head upon him. "His heart is beating fast, but his lungs are clear of sound."

"What is causing this?" Nimue felt the knife twisting within her again.

Viviane removed the covers from Merlin's body, examining him further. Nimue watched as her friend probed his chest, his arms and legs.

"I cannot see any evidence of rash or wound that should bring on such a fever of this magnitude."

Without warning, the fire in the hearth exploded into the room and as suddenly was sucked back towards the brick wall and up through the chimney, painting the room in a canvas of darkness.

Nimue stumbled over the edge of the bed in the absence of light.

Falling to the floor, she screamed out, "What is happening?"

"Everyone be still," Galahad cried from somewhere nearby. Using the embers from the fire pit, he must have lit the wall torch and reignited the fire pit because the room filled with dim light. He reached for a shaking Nimue, and gave her his hand. She received it, holding firm to his grip as he assisted her to a chair.

Viviane was reaching for a goblet of water for Nimue when, out from the hearth, came a moan that shook the walls with bated breath. All heads turned as a black form rose from the fire.

"Avert your eyes!" shouted Galahad, "the devil is upon us!"

CHAPTER TWO

Museum of Kings

2010 AD

———◆———

Arianna Lawrence was rummaging through the chests in the tack shed behind the barn. Her marriage was in turmoil, and she had just lost a precious, rare jewel. She looked down, and the place was a mess: boots, saddle straps, stirrups and under-saddle blankets were sprawled all over the floor. She brushed the dust from her black lace blouse and Levis and stepped outside to take a cleansing breath. She rested at the entry side causeway of the barn where the horses ran out to the gated pasture, and her eyes found their way to the rose garden behind the Museum of Kings. As she climbed up the stairs alongside the rambling roses, she noticed that the light was on in the Artifacts office. The sound of her boot heels pounded with each step, revealing the urgency of her search.

She arrived on the landing and could see from the window that her friend and comrade, George Wells, was at his desk working on a museum project. She opened the door quietly and tip-toed to the Artifacts closet. In this oak paneled room, the remains of King Arthur Pendragon and the Wizard Merlin rested. Again she searched the shelves of the twenty-foot by-twenty-foot room, but to no avail.

Before checking her desk, she draped her brown rider's jacket over her chair.

"Good afternoon, George."

"Shush," he replied with fervor.

On George's mahogany desk was a cedar box from the sixth century. From the box, he had removed a small brown pouch, and the once velvet material was crumbling in his hands. There were brown ties on the purse, and George—with great effort—unraveled the sinews. As the sack bounced on the table, a jiggling sound emitted from within.

Arianna pinched her brows with curiosity.

Ties loosened, George gently opened the pouch, his hands shaking with enthusiasm.

George, Duke Wells of Wiltshire, was the lord of the land on which he lived. He was the son of Lord Randolph Wells, a member of the Queen's court and of Parliament. His background stated that he was the great, great, etc. and so forth, grandson of Galahad du Lac, King of Britain, and son of Sir Lancelot and Lady Elaine of Astolate.

George grew up in the cottage where he now lived, a ten-bedroom modest-sized mansion built for the comforts of his mother Edwina, a woman who preferred living in the countryside as opposed to the oppression of the large city of London. George, due to his family lineage, was raised to continue the history of his family and that of King Arthur. He was dubbed Duke ten years ago and given the procurator duties of the Museum of Kings, as it was his pleasure to bring the folklore of the king to the modern public.

Arianna and George came to work with each other five years ago when George and his daughter Cynthia invited the Lawrence family to live with them. Arianna was named the entrusted guardian of the sword Excalibur and the adopted mother to Galahad. She had traveled back in time twice, and through her journeys, she and the Wizard Merlin formed a unique relationship based on the cause of King Arthur. She was trained by the high priest in the ways of the Goddess. Arianna and George were now working closely together for the cause of the revered king and his country.

George poured the contents of the sack on the table as Arianna quietly looked over his shoulder at the new found treasure neatly arranged on the desk. In his hand, he held a magnifying glass, and he concentrated as he examined each piece. Arianna kept her silence as she heard George whisper to himself what he was reading on his find: "Providentiae AVVG, with an engraved campgate." He pulled the desk lamp over the piece, and the light glared hard into Arianna's eyes. She could not make out what he was reading.

"The Providence of the Roman Empire?" George asked himself with adulation. "With a campgate to guard the Empire. How intriguing."

Arianna pulled her long brown highlighted hair back in a ponytail and dug through her own desk.

"I've had a most unusual find," whispered George.

"Not my husband's missing affection by chance, is it?"

George snickered quietly under his breath.

"My brooch is missing, George."

"Your brooch?"

She looked up at him, but George was still staring intently at his find.

"Is it that important that you search for it right now?"

Arianna placed her hands about her lithe waist, looking around the room. "It was a gift from Merlin, you ass!"

"These items will need to be displayed by tonight before the members of Parliament arrive tomorrow."

"I have my own to do list, George."

"These dignitaries are looking to see how well their money is being spent, Arianna."

Arianna held her hands as though in prayer, taking a moment to collect her thoughts. "Alright, let me see what you have."

George threw a coin to Arianna, who caught it with ease. "I just found these."

"You found patinas?" Arianna held them up to the light. "These don't look familiar, George."

"They're Roman," he said as he looked at the others. "Look at the intricacy of the design and how each piece is adorned with two turrets and no doors. On the bottom are the letters GSIS, the letters of GLORIA EXERCITVS, a double crescent moon, and a star above the gate. On the other side there is a face, Arianna!"

She could hear the shear excitement that he held for his work. "The names have worn off, George." Arianna studied the details. "The crescent moon was revered then. How wonderful!"

George smiled. "It was."

"Look at these, George!" She pulled up a seat at his table.

George's rather large hands made Arianna's look like those of a child as he snatched the coins from her. He laid them under the light and placed the monocular to his right eyeglass lens so that he could see the faces more clearly. The device was nearly part of George, as Arianna had seen him use it so many times to bring images into better view.

"Look. Arianna, the face is that of a man. His head is diademed at a right angle and his hair, cropped short in the Roman style, adorned with the braided ropes of his status."

"Who is this?"

"Give me a minute." George placed the coins under the raised magnifying tray for Arianna and him to see.

Arianna felt a hint of a smile as she read the letters aloud. "CONSTANTINVS AVG."

George nodded his head. "When Arthur traveled to Rome to fight the Holy Wars he visited the shrines of the Emperor Constantine and the High Empress Helena to look for answers as to where the titulus of Christ was."

"I know Arthur was always in search of the cross of Christ," followed Arianna.

"Yes, the high king, just like the high emperor here, searched for the true meaning of that cross and the essence of the man called the Christ." George cleaned the coin with a chamois. "This is the face of Constantine."

"The first Christian Emperor!" Arianna grabbed the monocular from George to examine the coin herself. She traced her finger over the intricately engraved face. "He looks like a man that I would not want to have misgivings with."

"Constantine had an aura of power around him that made both enemy and friend admire him."

Arianna looked up at the portrait on the wall of King Arthur. "Reminds me of a king we knew." Arianna felt her expression turn to that of deep thought. "George, do you know how Arthur came to possess these coins?"

"It is said that at the foot of Helena's shrine, a woman of great beauty gave the sack to Arthur, telling him that the coins held the key to his future."

She picked up the magnifying glass for another look and continued to admire the details on the coins.

"This isn't possible." Arianna watched as George's hands franticly flipped one coin over several times and he looked at it even more closely. "This must be the Emperor's son, Crispis. These coins were supposed to have been melted down."

"Explain!" Arianna was immediate in her desire for information.

"Crispis was executed for treason against his father. Anything that bore the crest or likeness of Augustus Crispis was to be destroyed."

Arianna plucked the coin from George's hand. "Treason? Do you know what the charge was?"

"He was accused of trying to seduce his stepmother Fausta, High Empress of Rome and wife to Constantine."

Arianna laughed and broke the tension. "So it goes back all the way to Rome that sons play games at their father's expense?"

George stole the coin back from Arianna. "Fausta secured the lie to make way for her son, Constantius, as the next High Emperor of Rome. When Constantine heard what his son did and Crispis could not defend himself, Constantine ordered his son's execution."

"I hope that the Emperor found out what his Empress did and reattributed his son's death."

"Constantine was actually not the culprit who had Fausta killed.

Someone else did. History has no idea who, but she was found dead in her bed, her skin scalded like a hot prune."

Arianna was overcome with anxiety again.

"Tell me about the brooch," said George.

Arianna made her way over to the larger box on the table across the room. "When I was in Camelot six months ago, Merlin gave me a brooch." Arianna continued to sift through the box. "I need to find it."

"Are you sure it's not in your room?"

"I ransacked my room, my saddlebag, and the barn this morning. It's not anywhere."

"What does it look like?" he asked.

"It's a red crescent moon with the entwined triangle of the Goddess engraved in gold in the center. On the back is an intricate sword that looks like Gwydion."

"Why is it important?"

Arianna was throwing articles everywhere again. "When Merlin placed it on my dress, I had a feeling that I was connected to it." She closed her eyes contemplating. "I am supposed to be wearing it right now."

George put his coins down. "Anything that comes from the wizard is not to be taken lightly—where can we look?"

"If you'll rummage through that closet," she replied, "I'll check the back room."

Arianna peered back into the storage room and opened the wooden strongbox that held King Arthur's artifacts. She rummaged through its contents, and her heart raced as she raised his black and red cloak from out of the box. This was the garment that Galahad had asked her to wear at the *Ceremony of the Robes,* when the young King Galahad and Arianna adopted one another as mother and son, before he left to find the Holy Grail.

Arianna's mind drifted back to the day of the Ceremony when Merlin placed it over her shoulders before they walked into the church. Galahad and his knights were outfitted with the Robes of the Grail

Quest and she, in front of the whole of Camelot, was blessed and made adoptive mother to the then younger king and grandmother to Galahad's son Prince John Arthur. What a day of bittersweet pride it was for her. How she wished to be with them again!

She draped the cloak over the box, admiring the beautiful gold pendragon embroidered on the back and the Celtic cross sewn on the left chest. Arianna was surprised that the years had not deteriorated the material. She wrapped herself in it, feeling the security of Arthur cradle her. The soft satin lining caressed her skin as she came to a cold sweat remembering that five years had passed since Draco told her of Arthur's coming. The prophecy had not yet been fulfilled.

She opened the door of the verandah, walked out to the gaping wall and lifted her eyes to the hills of Avalon where Arthur was buried. Staring at the gravesite, she wrapped herself more tightly in the robe. "Arthur, you would look better in your own garment than I do."

"Arianna! I found the brooch!"

Arianna turned to see George fumbling onto the verandah. He placed the pin in her eager hands.

"Oh, George. Thank you so much." She pressed it to her heart. "Merlin told me that it holds a secret to my destiny."

"What do you mean?"

"George, you know the High Druid Priest. Every good lesson he gives is told in riddles. It's the way he taught King Arthur and the way he continues to teach me." She held the jewel in front of both of them. "I wish I knew who this woman is engraved on the back of the crescent moon."

"Another riddle to conquer."

Arianna placed the pin on her blouse under the cloak, feeling resolved, and stared out into the forest that surrounded the Museum of Kings. It was late noon and the sun was sparkling on the leaves as the wind rocked the trees like a baby in its arms. She inhaled the aroma of the fresh cut grass and let it intoxicate her.

"Can you remember any moment in the past when I may have had ill will against the Goddess?"

"Never have I heard you speak in any ill manner towards the Goddess," said a flabbergasted George. "Why are you asking me this?"

"It's been years since the prophecy was foretold to me, and there is no recourse to my future." Arianna felt a peculiar chill about her. "You realize that there is an irony here. A woman tells Arthur that his future lies within the coins and Merlin tells me that this pin has something to do with my destiny. Neither have been revealed."

George placed his hand on Arianna's shoulder and she felt his supportive friendship. "Arianna, maybe what you need to do is leave here and go home for a while."

Arianna cocked her head to one side. "There is so much work to do here, and Jack is in New York on business."

"Merlin and the Mother gave you a great gift. Make use of it more often."

Arianna studied the tree line of the hill, remembering the words with which Merlin taught her to open the wall. "It would be good to visit with Merlin for a while."

CHAPTER THREE

Arianna Leaves for Camelot

Arianna was just finishing the cleanup of the tack shed. She wanted to straighten up the damage she wrought earlier that morning looking for her brooch. She could hear George as he came down the back steps. He must have just set the alarms on the doors and windows, part of his usual closing rounds at the museum. It was his duty to lock the displays and put the important artifacts away in the safe. He was now proceeding to the barn to feed and brush his horses, which he also did nightly.

Appearing from the tack shed, she watched as he saddled up Titan and Sir Brach to ready them for the ride up the hill. A short whinny came from across the barn. It was Alana, prancing around wanting out of her stall.

"Ahy my girl, not tonight," said George. "You and Mystic can take a long beauty sleep."

The horses were prize-winning stallions and fillies. Titan, Alana and Mystic came from the thoroughbred line of the mustangs in America. Sir Brach came from a line of wild pony in northern England, a larger version of the Shetland steeds used in the Roman arena for chariot races. Titan was a black stallion, his mane dark as midnight. He had amber green eyes and a white diamond mark right between them. Sir Brach had a body of mahogany, highlighted with streaks of red, like the color of good wine. He wore a long black mane that ran down his neck and back with a long thick tail to match. His chest was white like snow and shaped like a shield, and his ebony eyes sparkled with gold flecks.

Arianna came to Brach and gave him some apple bits. She was dressed in her travel clothes, a brown, full-length skirt and a blouse laced up the back. The blouse was adorned with long bell sleeves, each tied at the shoulder so that the strings would hang at either side of her arms. She wore tan knee-high boots laced tight at the knee. A silver chain belt wrapped around her waist and with it, the black and silver sheath belt. She was armed with her sword, Gwydion, and over her shoulders rested a hunter green rider's cloak.

Arianna hung her saddlebag on the back of her saddle and George helped her mount Sir Brach. George climbed onto Titan, and they were out the barn door.

It was dark and clear and crisp. A crescent moon decorated the sky, and the stars twinkled in the dome of the night. This night was different from others, and Arianna felt a peculiar chill. She silently swore that the ancients were winding their souls around her as though trying to channel their energy through her. George shivered and Arianna took notice.

"There is a strangeness in the air, my lady."

They rode through the vast trees and flowers of the forest. There were different types of trees, mostly oak and maple, tall and climbing into the darkness. Species of every flower grew here, especially red roses and purple jasmine. After a short ride, George and Arianna arrived at the hilltop.

Arianna checked the area to make sure that no one was either riding or walking through the forest at this time of night. George rode a bit away from the sight to make sure that all was clear.

"I think that it is safe!" said George, reassuringly.

Her heart pounded in her chest as it always did before she uttered the words that would open the wall to the other world.

George lifted Arianna's hand, kissing it gently. "Please convey my good wishes to His Majesty and Merlin."

"I shall, my good friend."

Arianna and Brach stood between a pair of twin oaks. These trees were monstrously tall with branches that climbed up into the canopy. She positioned herself in the center under an L-shaped branch to the right and a U-shaped branch to the left. It was there in the middle of these branches that she commanded the elements of Mother Earth.

She looked to the moon and withdrew Gwydion from her sheath. She raised the hilt and touched it to her forehead, meditating on the stone of Avalon, the blue stone of the Mother. As always, a burning sensation fell upon her brow as the power surged within her. She pointed the hilt of Gwydion forward and with all her might shouted, "I, Lady Arianna Lawrence Pendragon, guardian of Excalibur, ask the God of Heaven and the Goddess Mother of the planet earth to reveal her most precious secrets!"

A bolt of lightning crackled down from the crescent of the moon. A refracted light shattered in the darkness between the two large oak trees, conducting itself on the L- and the U-shaped branches. The wall was opening.

The atmospheric pressure was changing. Arianna pointed Gwydion into the refracted light to assist the wall to open. The shattered light cracked as Arianna waited for the breeze to pick up around her and for the fragrant aroma of the mists of Avalon to tickle her nose. She waited for the veil to show itself so that she might point Gwydion into it and walk Sir Brach to the other side. The white veil came like a frosted glass, and the aroma of roses exploded around them. The fragrance intoxicated her, and she pushed Gwydion through.

"Goodbye, my friend!" she shouted to George as she and Brach were about to make their way into the mists. The distorted light pulled Brach and Arianna through.

Suddenly, Brach came up on his hind legs, kicking at the refracted light around the mists as it cracked down upon his mane.

"Whoa, Brach!" Arianna screamed, holding on tightly as she was almost knocked from him. She grabbed Brach's pommel as Gwydion fell to the ground with a hard thud.

George rode Titan towards them and reached for Brach's bridal. As though trying to control the beast, he backed them away from the portal.

"Whoa, boy!"

Brach pranced Arianna around in a circle completely out of control. George held Brach tighter, guiding Titan to pull the horse away from the trees.

Arianna reached down and held onto Brach's neck for dear life. They were both breathing hard, and she felt as though the earth was spinning. She caught the stench of burned hair as she pulled herself up, checking to see if Brach was alright. Arianna felt a jolt through her saddle as the trees grumbled, and the last of the refracted light disappeared into the indigo of the forest background. The door had closed.

She looked down at Brach. His beautiful black mane and neck were burned by a mark shaped like a crack in an hourglass. She dismounted him and, shaken, she reached into her saddlebag, removed the canteen, and poured out some water to wash down the burn. Brach whinnied in pain.

"There now, my friend," she said as she caressed her companion. "What in bloody hell just happened?" she screamed.

"I don't know, Arianna." George seemed just as confused. "Maybe it's the moon phase."

Arianna picked up Gwydion from the ground, holding her with both hands, examining the sword. "I don't understand. Brach is burned, and yet Gwydion isn't even warm."

She looked at the moon, wondering if maybe she held Gwydion the wrong way and the light had refracted out of its boundaries. "Maybe it was the moon, indeed," Arianna said with a morose inflection to her voice.

"Try it again," said George with confidence. "You are saying the right words—speak it again."

Sheathing Gwydion, she dashed back over to Sir Brach, examining his neck. "Not tonight, George." She held Brach's face to her own, caressing his neck and kissing his nose. "Come on, Brach. Let's get you away from this place."

CHAPTER FOUR

A Distressing Problem

———◆———

Alexis Lawrence opened the living room door, holding her plate of grilled chicken salad and buttered biscuits, hoping for a bit of quiet while she ate and watched television. She looked at her mother, who was sitting on the royal blue upholstered chair in front of the unlit fireplace, a half-filled glass of wine on the side table. Her mother was in deep concentration, palliating the blue stone on her sword that lay in her lap. Alexis took careful note that Arianna was in her travel clothes for the sixth century.

"Are you going somewhere?"

Arianna turned to Alexis and by the ruddy look of her features, distress was showing clearly on her face. "I should have been home enjoying Merlin's company right now."

"I don't understand," said Alexis as she placed her plate on the table.

Arianna stood from the chair. "I had planned to go home for a few days to visit with Merlin and the boys."

"That would have been a good idea. Lately you've been a bit tense."

Arianna's hand clenched Gwydion's hilt, "Bollix—well, now I am more than a bit tense."

"Did something change your mind about leaving?"

"The damned wall wouldn't open for me."

Alexis was stunned. "What do you mean the wall wouldn't open for you?"

"The wall wouldn't open, Lexy. I spoke the words, did everything I normally do and it just bloody hell wouldn't stay open!"

"Are you alright?"

"Poor Brach is in the barn with a bad burn on his neck."

"Rewind and tell me what happened."

Arianna stepped towards the table, still holding the sword. "I spoke the words and meditated on the stone. The light refracted as always, and the portal cracked open. When I placed Gwydion's blade through the light and nudged Brach to go through, the light jolted back, burning Brach and the tree."

"Is he okay?"

"George and I medicated him and put a bandage on the wound." Tears showed in Arianna's eyes.

Alexis was completely confused. "This has never happened. Are you sure that the moon and the blade were in the proper positions?"

"Everything was in its place." Arianna wiped the corners of her eyes and Alexis knew that she was trying to compose herself. "If you can spare some time from your studies, we can use some help researching the books tonight."

Alexis looked at her mother. "What do you mean by *we*?"

"George was with me when this happened. He pulled Brach and me to safety."

Alexis lifted her plate and started quickly eating her dinner. "My thesis is not due until next week. I can help."

"Thanks, honey."

"I know something is really wrong when you start cussing up a storm." When things got crazy, Arianna's tongue flared up horribly, something Alexis recognized that Arianna did not like about herself. "Dad said that he'll be back at the end of the week. Business meetings are taking more time than he thought."

Alexis caught a hard glare from her mother.

"I guess that will have to do." Arianna poured herself another glass of wine, leaving it on the table. "When George comes down with the books, tell him I went up to change."

Alexis watched her mother leave the room. She could tell by the way Arianna held Gwydion that she was ready for battle.

CHAPTER FIVE

History Tells Tall Tales

———◆———

When Arianna was in the sixth century keeping careful watch on Camelot for His Majesty Galahad, time passed too slowly for Alexis' comfort in the twenty-first century. Because Arianna traveled back in time and influenced the past, the history books were constantly being rewritten. To comfort herself, Alexis would continually reread the books to find answers as to how her mother was affecting the course of history.

The books told Alexis that Galahad and his knights had returned from the Forest of Fire with the Holy Grail in hand—only to find Sir Frederick Garris holding his own session of court to have Merlin cast out of Camelot. The Lady Arianna Lawrence stood proxy, defending the king's position for the aging wizard, but Frederick Garris was a very persuasive orator and was turning the court in his own favor.

Galahad, with Grail in hand, interceded and in the court, the following was published: *Galahad, King of Britain and son of Lancelot du Lac, resided over his court, taking account of his Christian knights' testimony over the Merlin and his Pagan worship. Galahad, with the command of his kingship, acquitted the Merlin of all charges of devil worship and Black Magic. "It shall be written upon this day, that I, Galahad, give all honors of council to the high priest of the Druids, Merlin; for he shall take seat at my table of the round."*

Alexis sat in her chair, contemplating that nine months ago in the Twenty-First century, Arianna had returned to New York to be with Alexis' father, trying to patch up their already rocky marriage. She had confided in Alexis that Galahad and the boys were leaving for Rome. Galahad had been summoned by Gregory I, Rome's patriarch. The situation was grim, as the church was verbally outspoken against the Druids of England. This was the beginning of a crusade against Pagan idolatry, and the church wanted all Christian countries to join with them against the worship of idols other than the *One God*. Apparently, Sir Frederick Garris was going about his business again, preaching his opinions against the Druids and bringing up old accusations against Merlin. Frederick, who was one of the Liaisons to the Catholic Church of Camelot, reported to the head office in Rome that a Druid high priest was living in the Christian home of Camelot.

From New York, Arianna desperately needed to know how her boys were faring and what would happen to Merlin and his fellow Druids. She had gone to the library where she read to Alexis about Galahad du Lac and his crusades for Merlin and his people.

Alexis remembered her mother reading from those books and telling her that Galahad, King of Britain and successor of King Arthur, traveled to Rome with his knights—Sir Peter, Sir Luke and Sir Joseph— to meet with Gregory I. It was at this meeting that Galahad and this patriarch, who was the successor of the Apostle Peter, the first Bishop of the Catholic Church, spoke about the conversion of the Druids in England. Gregory knew of Galahad's history with King Arthur and the man called Merlin and of the Holy Grail quest. Bishop Gregory felt that God had hand chosen this Galahad of the Lake for a special purpose. The Patriarch Gregory wanted Galahad to bring Merlin and the Pagans of Britain to the altar of Christ to be reconciled and converted to the cloth. During the meeting, His Majesty Galahad defended the Druids and told Gregory about his adopted mother Arianna who, like King Arthur, was both Pagan and Christian.

The patriarch did not appreciate Galahad's comments in defense of these Pagans and warned Galahad, "No other God or Goddess would stand before the one God." Galahad tried to explain that the Druids in his homeland were good and decent people, but Gregory would listen to nothing of reason. He told Galahad that he must crusade to avenge Christ, who died on the cross, and that he must abolish Paganism in Britain. Galahad left Rome that day a very confused and saddened king, for he was being forced to either disobey the church or confront Merlin and his adopted mother as well as the legacy of King Arthur; not a decision he could easily make.

Alexis could feel her mother's heartache in the library that day; it was the wish of King Arthur, Merlin and Arianna that both the Christian and Pagan houses would someday find peace with one another and live side by side.

———◆———

Today, Alexis hoped to find some clarity in the books once again, fearing that Frederick might have stirred up some trouble that barred Arianna from the past, or even worse, that Galahad had made his decision and banished her from the city.

Arianna came down the stairs dressed in her robe. George had already arrived and prepared several volumes on the table. Alexis was rummaging through a book called *The Medieval Doctrines,* looking for any changes that might have occurred recently in the text. The book was a chronicle of the British kings who came before King Arthur and the ones who ruled after him.

"Every time I see your name or your initials in these books, I get chills up and down my entire body." Alexis felt her mother lean on her shoulder as she read her name. By the way she pinched her arm, Alexis knew how hard it was for Arianna to comprehend the attention that came from having such celebrity in the history books. "Look, here you are again." She read it aloud, "And Merlin and the Lady of the Lake told Lady Arianna that it was of her choosing whom the heir of Excalibur would be."

"Let's pass my name over, shall we? We have much more important matters here to dig for," said Arianna.

Alexis looked at George and both nodded their heads in agreement.

"Mom, are you sure that you said the words in the right order?"

She could see her mother's jaw tighten. "Lexy, I said them just as I always have."

Alexis rummaged through the books looking for any clues possible. She darted back into the library to find another and upon returning said, "Why is it that in all of these books we never really see anything about Merlin's past?"

Suddenly the trio was interrupted as Alexis' friend Cynthia entered the room.

Lady Cynthia Wells, a young and attractive woman in her early thirties was the daughter of Lord George Wells. Following in her father's footsteps, she held many degrees in history and in archeology. The Lady Wells had married Professor Robert Gains, a fellow archeologist; however, constant controversy over family and politics caused a rift in their marriage which subsequently ended in divorce. She remained true to her family's cause and close to the museum and the historic treasures held within.

Arianna continued the conversation. "Merlin never really had an accountable past. He was raised by poor means and became the wizard that he is after he was given powers by the Goddess."

"He was poor? Isn't he a high priest?" chimed Cynthia.

"Just because Merlin is a high priest doesn't mean he is wealthy. Remember, Druid priests give up worldly goods when they elevate their powers of healing to high statuses."

"But Mom, wasn't Merlin's mother a high priestess of great power?" asked Alexis. "Didn't you tell me she was an evil witch or something?"

Arianna stared at Alexis with an expression of great fear.

"Mom, are you alright? All the color just drained out of your face."

Arianna caught hold of her chest. "Please, can we change the conversation? I do not want to talk about the woman who is responsible for Mordred's madness and the death of my King Arthur."

"Arianna, the young lady is just looking for some answers."

"George, I need answers about tonight!"

Alexis was stunned with her mother's outburst of anger. "Mom, you can't tell me that just saying her name brings bad karma."

Arianna slammed the book she was holding onto the table. "Alexis, you weren't there when Arthur was killed, and you have never seen a bloody battlefield the likes that I have. That woman should rot in hell."

Still in shock over her mother's blatant show of rage, Alexis watched as George hurried over to Arianna, taking her by the arm. "My dear, Queen Mab is gone. She has no power here. You are vexed at this point over today. Leave it be."

Arianna yanked her arm away from George. "Don't ever say her name around me again."

Trying to comprehend this scene of events, Alexis looked to Cynthia.

"Mom, would you like some tea?"

The notion made Arianna smile. "I would love a cup of tea."

"Come on Cyn, you can help me."

Alexis led the way, and as Cynthia reached the kitchen door, she yelled, "Bollix!"

"What's wrong?" asked Alexis.

"Your mother is not going to like what I am about to show her. Prepare that tea, and I'll meet you back in the drawing room in two minutes."

CHAPTER SIX

A Letter of Evil

Arianna was beginning to enjoy her cup of tea, when Cynthia walked into the room. Immediately curious as to the aged scroll Cynthia held, Arianna grabbed it and unrolled it. As she did, the fine hairs on her arm stood at attention, anticipating the worst. She saw flashes of her memory, standing at the lake watching Arthur and Mordred in the heat of battle, slashing at each other mercilessly, trying not to trip over severed hands still clutching their swords and nearly dead soldiers crawling in the bloody puddles of mud around them. She stared at the words on the scroll now, not reading them, but rather engulfed in her vision of Mordred attacking his father with a heavy branch, striking him at the back. Arthur writhed in pain, and Arianna closed her eyes—hearing Mordred laugh mercilessly at the pain he had wrought on the king. Arthur was trying not to strike back, but Mordred kept on with his attack, and the two wrangled long and hard. The battle was not over territory but over the evil madness of Mordred and the love held for him by his father.

Now bloodied by the hand of his son, feeling his last moments upon him and seeing the dead of both armies lying all around, Arthur knew he had to stop Mordred's treachery and ran him through with Excalibur. Mordred fell to his knees as his life poured from him, keeled over and died.

Seconds later, Arthur fell, giving into his own gushing wounds. Merlin sprinted to his aid; taking his foster son in his arms, he rocked him to silence.

Tears came to Arianna as she returned to the present moment and felt the parchment in her hands. A dead calm filled the room. With courage in her heart, she read the words.

My Dearest Merlin,

You love Arthur more than you love your mother. You think that following these Christians will save you from me? They will never trust you. Side with your mother. Human kind looks to power, not to love and kindness. Arthur's destiny is weak. You cannot place him on the throne again. The Christians will banish you. Join me. I will reign again as high priestess.

Ebbyn woo zyll senfynn maga amnen Myrddin efwwar dah!!!

No sword, son, or Gatekeeper of Avalon will take my place. Come to my side or I will be the future of your despair.

Mab
Σ

Cynthia, why did you not show this letter to me when you found it?" Arianna asked, displeased.

"I was just rummaging through some of Merlin's artifacts, and I came across it. I didn't consider that you hadn't seen it until tonight."

"Mom, what are these words *Ebbyn woo*....I can't pronounce them."

Arianna looked at Alexis, remembering as a youth when her own mother said words of hate to her that could never be taken back.

"Daughter, they are words that no loving mother should say to her child." Arianna sauntered over to Alexis and kissed her on the cheek.

"So what do they mean?" Alexis inquired again.

Staring at her daughter Arianna said, "Let us let sleeping dogs lie for a while."

Alexis understood. "Ah the black magic effect, I get you!"

Arianna smiled at her daughter.

"Forgive my ignorance, but didn't Mab die sometime after Mordred's death?" asked Cynthia.

"I do not believe that history ever recorded her demise," said Arianna scanning the letter again. "She just ceased to exist after Arthur's death and Galahad's ascension. I don't think that Merlin ever knew where she disappeared to."

"Mom, can this be related to your not being able to open the wall?"

Arianna shrugged her shoulders, "I cannot say."

"Maybe it is something that you should consider," George responded.

"I have always felt that my being able to pass through time and substance has been a miracle of faith." Arianna read the words once again in silence. "Tomorrow we will go and feel the circle talk to us."

CHAPTER SEVEN

The Avalon Cemetery

———◆◆◆———

"Mom, come on. George is in the barn already!"

"I'll be down in a few minutes!"

Alexis and Cynthia made their way out of the kitchen door and toward the barn. A crisp cool morning greeted them as they opened the barn doors. Titan, Mystic, Allana, and Sir Brach whinnied their good mornings, and George was preparing their feed bags with oats and alfalfa for breakfast. Titan snorted as George fastened the feed bag to the hooks on the belt around his mouth. Alexis could hear him chew down on his food as though he hadn't eaten in weeks.

George laughed. "Ahy Titan, you eat your food with as much gusto as I do!"

Sir Brach greeted Alexis with a snort and a nudge at the shoulder.

"Okay, my lord. Your feed is here," said Alexis as George helped her fasten Sir Brach's bag. The horse neighed with delight, digging into his oats. "You deserve that after what you've been through."

Mystic and Allana were prime looking Fillies and somewhat more dignified in receiving their feed bags. Mystic only whinnied softly, and Allana swung her bag back and forth a bit before giving into her hunger and chewing down on her meal.

"Good morning, Father," said Cynthia as she kissed George sweetly on the cheek. Mystic pushed her way into the middle of the father-

31

daughter pair, stirring them all to laugh. Allana made herself known to Alexis with a loud snort, and Alexis strolled over to her and caressed her neck. She loved her filly, and the horse reciprocated with a bob of her head.

"Okay girls, let's get to work," said George.

Alexis and Cynthia joined George in grabbing the brushes from the shelf and starting to groom their horses. Alexis watched George brush Titan with generous downward strokes, tending to his black midnight mane.

George looked up at his daughter, who was smiling as she watched him take care of his horse. Alexis knew the look. Cynthia always admired how her father cared for his steeds.

Alexis and Cynthia strolled into the tack shed, taking Mystic's and Allana's blankets and saddles off the rail and outfitting the horses. Mystic snorted loudly in protest, and Cynthia patted him on the neck. "Yes, I know we are in our lazy mood today, but that will make you a fat old girl."

Snort, snort and one a loud neigh was Mystic's answer.

"Is your mother on her way up?" asked a pondering George.

"She was in the hall putting on her jacket when I left." Alexis looked back towards the house. "Careful, she is not herself today."

George shook his head, affirming. "I do not doubt it, lassie," he said as he prepared Sir Brach with his gear. Brach was always ready for a run, but Alexis noted that he did not take too kindly to his saddle this morning. She turned to see her mother enter the barn like a lion ready to devour her prey.

"George, that saddle is too heavy." Arianna walked straight to the tack shed and came back with a change of saddle from a Western style to the lighter English. Just as the nurturing mother she always was, Arianna checked the wound on Brach's neck. By the loud neigh he gave out, it was clear that Brach was still in a bit of pain. Alexis helped her mother remove the bandage.

"How do you think he is, Mom?"

Arianna took a moment to check the wound. "The burn is not as irritated as it was yesterday." She stopped and stared for a moment. "George, I want you to see this—I woke up with this thought on the tip of my tongue this morning, but convinced myself I was wrong. I wasn't—Brach wasn't just burned, he was branded. The shape of his burn is the same as the symbol on that letter below Mab's signature."

George looked at the wound with the girls staring over his shoulder. "We will find our answers soon."

With the help of Alexis, Arianna put a fresh bandage on her horse. She rested Brach's head on her shoulder, hugging him, reminding Alexis of how her mother would nurture her when she was hurt or sick. Brach pushed his head into her shoulder, sharing the affection. Alexis smiled; her mother always found peace with Brach.

Arianna kissed him on the snout. "Sir Brach, my friend, today we will see another adventure unfold."

Alexis thought she saw a hint of a smile crease her mother's face as the horse caressed Arianna's cheek. He was ready for the task at hand. Arianna put her helmet on and mounted her steed. It was Alexis' clue to mount Allana. The others followed her lead and rode out the barn door.

———◆———

The morning sun bathed its riders in warm rays of light. Arianna guided the way. She was distant, moving ahead of the riding party, taking on the solitary mood that she generally exuded when the answers to problems seemed so unresolved. Alexis figured she was looking around at the land that once held the blood of her faithful friends. On the day when Arianna returned home from Camelot, she had told Alexis that all she wanted to do was ride away and never come back. Alexis knew from her mother's anger and anxiety that she felt this way again today. That reckless emotion surfaced again as she was being held back from the one place that kept her sane.

Alexis watched as her mother looked back at her and the others, who were trailing about half a block's length behind. She led the way to the cemetery at Avalon and they met up with her at the iron gate.

With her left foot, Arianna kicked the latch of the cemetery gate open, swinging it hard. The black gate shook, vibrating with her arrival. Alexis and the other riders followed her through.

"Mom, why are we stopping here?"

"I need to visit with Arthur."

Alexis shook her head, saying nothing to her mother. She knew that when it came to King Arthur, only God stood before him. This was always hard for Alexis. She loved her father so very much, yet her dad was not the husband that a woman like her mother needed at her side. Jack Lawrence was a good man, but his illness and depression made him a bitter person—one who could be quite difficult to live with. King Arthur, on the other hand was a warrior and a man of strong faith and conviction, one who fought hard for his people and his home. He was Arianna's equal in all ways, and Alexis knew that their friendship made her father jealous.

Arianna dismounted Sir Brach and led the riders to Arthur's grave. As always, she respectfully knelt down on one knee, making the Sign of the Cross and bowing her head in silent prayer. It hurt Alexis to watch her as she pulled at the blades of grass with frustration before standing up and looking about the cemetery. Alexis caught site of her mounting tears as Arianna leaned on Arthur's tombstone for support.

"I need your help today, Arthur," she overheard her mother say.

Alexis began to dismount, but Cynthia held her back. "Give your mother some privacy." Alexis recoiled and kept to her mount. George signaled to the women to let Arianna be. Alexis nodded and the two gave their horses a light kick in the direction of the gate and exited the cemetery only a few feet away. Alexis stayed close to listen to George speak to Arianna and tried to make sense of it all.

"Maybe it's your apprehension that is holding the wall closed to you."

"Leave me alone, George."

"Maybe they don't want your anxiety."

"It's easy to sit on that horse and tell me what my problems are, isn't it? *You don't have enough bullshit to deal with, Arianna, so let me pile on some more!*" Arianna stood there sneering. "Why was I chosen for this prophecy, George?" Her voice was piercing, and Alexis watched as birds fled from the tree above the grave.

"I'll check on the girls," said George turning his horse around and heading out of the cemetery. He made a gesture to leave, but Alexis chose to stay by the gate.

Arianna removed her helmet, letting it drop to the ground. Tears rolled down her cheeks as she fell upon the grave, her eyes focused on the words inscribed upon it. With her finger, she traced over King Arthur's name and the word *Excalibur* beneath it. She rose, kicked a stone across the field, and seized the cross around her neck that Alexis knew held Arthur's bloodstain. Her hands were shaking as they gripped the precious cross. The gold carried a blemish on it from Mordred's sword; the one thrust to cause the fatal wound that bled out and left the dying king upon the grass.

Alexis watched as Arianna wrenched off her ring, looking deeply into the pendragon signet. It was Arthur's ring, his royal seal. Arianna closed her eyes and Alexis felt something was definitely not right. She stuck close by her mother as Arianna spoke to Arthur—something she often did in times of trouble.

"Arthur, can you hear me? Remember the day I came home to Camelot? I told you that I was lost. I am lost again and having trouble finding the way back." Arianna looked out at the lake across the field of Avalon. "I remember Lady Viviane's ship, berthing quietly there in the other world." Alexis heard a hushed sob as Arianna pulled a rose from the bush. "Arthur, put your hand on my shoulder and guide me. Please, I beg you, guide me home once more."

Cynthia rejoined Alexis as she kept watch from the gate. "This is lame—can we go now?"

"My mother is tired. Can't you see that?" Alexis dismounted Allana and headed towards her mother. "Mom…"

Arianna looked up at Alexis. "Please leave me alone."

"You know I love you, Mom, but enough already. I know you're angry, but heck, so are we, and we're on your side, remember?" Arianna walked away from her. "Mom, I'll leave if you don't talk to me!"

Arianna closed her eyes and reached for Alexis, who gripped her mother's hand. "Mom, tell me how you felt when Merlin and Galahad showed you the words inscribed on the tomb."

Arianna inhaled deeply before speaking. "There was hope that day. Not only for Arthur's return but that Galahad would find the Grail."

"Wasn't Galahad angry that you would not tell him the meaning of the words?"

"He was mortified." Arianna leaned her back on the tombstone, relaxing a bit. "I've told you before that should I have revealed to him the meaning of the words, the Grail quest would be lost to him." Arianna laughed, "What I never told you, though, was that we fought each other right over there." She pointed to a nearby tree. "Galahad was acting like your brother Joseph. He was so outraged with me that in a fit of anger, he slashed my arm open." A cold breeze whipped around the grave. "I never told any of you." Arianna rolled up her sleeve, and Alexis glanced at her mother's left forearm.

"I never knew that you fought Galahad!"

Arianna nodded her head. "Excalibur and I did some damage that day. When Galahad cut me, I saw Arthur's spirit at a tree that used to stand right here."

Alexis' eyes opened wide with delight. "You fought Galahad with Excalibur?"

Arianna was holding fast to the lapels on her jacket. "On that day, the sword showed my son who to listen to."

"That's cool."

"I really never thought I'd see him with that kind of temper."

Alexis shook her head. She had grown up with a temperamental Joseph. "Please remind me never to anger Galahad."

Arianna smiled. "More poignant here is to never anger me." Alexis laughed and Arianna joined her in a hug before walking around the tomb. "George, please part the roses for me!"

Alexis looked for her uncle, who was nowhere to be found.

"Oh, I pissed off Uncle George," laughed Arianna.

Alexis helped part the roses and her mother read the words aloud. "*Hic Iacet Arthurus Rex Quondam RexQue Futurus!*"

"And why couldn't you tell Galahad what these words meant?" asked Alexis.

"If Galahad knew that heaven was planning to raise Arthur in the future, he might have given up his quest."

"But was it not his birthright to find the Grail?"

"Galahad would have sacrificed the Grail for Arthur. That is the kind of love he had for his king, his uncle."

Arianna breathed deeply as she reached over and placed her hands upon Alexis' shoulders and smiled with delight. "Let's go to Stonehenge," she said to her daughter. "Perhaps there are more answers there."

CHAPTER EIGHT

The Stone Circle

The sarsen stones stood massive as they accepted their guests, guarding them and allowing for the ancient spirits to gather them into the fold of their fortress. A cool breeze and warm sunshine welcomed the girls as they rode quickly up the Avenue of the Henge.

"I win!" Arianna heard Cynthia shout as she broadsided Alexis. The two waited for George to dismount and open the protective gate around the Henge. The metallic barrier was built within the moat around Stonehenge, and it detracted from the natural beauty of the circle. But building it was unavoidable because many in the past came to deface the wonder of the ancients, especially those of Christian doctrine who thought it was something evil because it was carved by Druids. George opened the entryway, and they all rode over the land bridge; only the caretakers of the Henge had access to this bridge.

"You were born on that horse, that's your excuse!" said Alexis breathing hard as she dismounted Allana. Cynthia straddled her right leg over Mystic's saddle and jumped down off her horse. Arianna watched from a distance as both horses and riders panted together exhausted. Alexis grabbed for her canteen, taking a long refreshing drink, as Cynthia rifled through her saddlebag for a towel and dried the perspiration from her face.

"Me thinks you need a little more practice to outrun Cynthia!"

commented Arianna, who entered the circle with George.

"You don't have to rub it in, Mom."

Arianna and Sir Brach walked through the gate and around the perimeter of the circle, passing each sarsen stone as though inspecting a soldier standing in line. They came to rest near the Altar stone; the stone that had split through the years, falling to the ground. In the times of Merlin, the Altar stone appeared blue in color, but now it was a pale green micaceous sandstone with traces of garnet running through its ridges.

Arianna stared at the stone, looking at the symbols now eroded with years. She knelt down, tracing her finger into the sun and moon symbols. Around the sun were thirty rays pointing to each space between the tall sarsens. Within the broken corners of the stone, Arianna could see what remained of the North Star. She knew these symbols well. The great wizard had shown them to her. In the time of Merlin, this was the point of axis for worshipping the sun and moon phases and the seasons. Arianna's eyes rose up to the trilithons. These were not signs of the Trinity or the entwined triangle of the Mother but monoliths standing side by side carrying lintels, guarding the secrets of the cosmos and the doors of heaven.

George dismounted Titan. It was evident to Arianna by his expression of awe that he felt the enormity of the circle. Alexis and Cynthia walked outside the stones. To them, the circle was not the glorified ring that Arianna and George felt it was.

Arianna unexpectedly felt uneasiness fill her stomach; it was as though someone or something came and robbed her comfort levels for the day. Taking heed of the warning, she reached for Gwydion, her faithful sword, but today it was not with her. The wind gusted around. *Was that the sound of laughter?* Her skin prickled as she asked George, "Did you hear that?"

"Hear what, Arianna?"

Arianna listened to the sound of the wind. "Did you hear someone laughing?"

George looked at her disbelievingly. "No. I did not."

Again, the wind whipped around the stones—only this time the laughter was louder. It rung in her ears, surging a chill to her nerve endings. "Tell me you didn't hear that." She was becoming more frantic.

"I am sorry, but I heard nothing."

Arianna reached for the tightness in her stomach and held on. She carefully looked around. "Cynthia! Alexis! Did you hear someone laughing?"

The girls were far at the other side of the circle goofing around. Alexis yelled, "No, Mom."

Cynthia chimed in, "We didn't hear anything."

"Someone is mocking me," Arianna whispered. The air around her became cold. Her legs stiffened and her blood quickened its pumping through her veins. Her eyes scanned the circle.

"What is it?" George whispered.

"Do you remember me telling you how I felt after Lord Gresham threatened Joseph and me behind the knights hall in Camelot?"

"Refresh my memory."

"Gresham was one of Mordred's men. He did not want Galahad on the throne. Seeing Joseph was my son, he wanted to train him outside of Galahad's army. He had a purse for him, but I would not trade my son for coins. When I threw the sack of money to the ground, Gresham threatened Joseph's life." Arianna kept her eyes on the stones. "That night, I was in the archery yard with Prince John. I heard fallen leaves behind the outside wall being crushed. It was dusk and no one but John and I were there, except for the guard by the door." There was a restlessness growing within her like a snake slowly slithering its way through her belly. "I knew someone was there, but the dark blinded me. It's not dark now George, but something is here, and I am now blind again."

"What are you feeling that reminds you of that day?" asked George.

Arianna held onto her side. "That day I was not armed with Excalibur. That was the day Gresham acted on his threat, came from behind the wall and impaled me..." Arianna reached for the scar on her left shoulder where Gresham's blade ran her through. "Today I am not armed with Gwydion, and I am feeling those same warnings."

Arianna took a deep breath. "Something evil is here." The wind gusted again, and again she heard the laughter. Arianna clenched her fists. She could feel the blood drain from her face.

Alexis came to her. "Mom, when I see that face I know enough to be scared—something is not right here."

The cold sensation returned, and Arianna wrapped her arms around herself trying to keep warm, her body shivering in the sunlight. She backed away from Alexis and felt the stones, running her fingers over the gritty surface of each, walking around the circle leaving none untouched or unstudied.

She turned, looked at George who was visibly uncomfortable and said, "Let's come away from here. We can return tomorrow. Perhaps the stones will reveal their secrets then."

Cynthia had made her way over. "What's going on?"

Alexis grabbed her by the hand and led her from the rocks. "We're leaving."

Arianna nodded her head. "Yes. Let's return to the cottage." Slowly, she backed away from the stones.

The four mounted their steeds and rode away from the circle.

CHAPTER NINE

Insomnia by Nightmare

<hr />

Arianna was lying awake again for the third time this week. Soft music she had turned on to calm herself played in the background. Her body was nestled comfortably in her bed under the warm covers—yet sleep would not come.

"Ariannnnna!" she heard weaving through the soothing notes of the music. She suddenly felt the night chill slide under her blankets and creep over her like a thousand spiders marching up her body. "Ariannna!" she again heard her name called to her.

"Merlin?" she whispered as she looked about her room. There was no answer. She pulled the covers tightly around her. The temperature in the room seemed to drop below zero and she could see her breath before her. Daring to push the covers off, she climbed out of bed and snatched her robe from off the chair, wrapping herself in it. She turned on the light and looked about the room. Everything was in its place: the curtains were drawn on the windows, her family pictures sat undisturbed on her dresser, the doors to the closet were closed, and the room smelled of fragrant rose oil as it always did.

Arianna's gaze fell upon the mirror, and she stared at the reflection of the room. She could see the crucifix hanging above the window, and as she looked at the Body of Christ, she raised her hand to Arthur's cross that hung around her neck. When her eyes lifted from the symbol, they caught a movement in the bed behind her. Merlin lay there, raising his hand towards her.

She turned in shock to look at the bed, but saw nothing. Again through the darkness, a voice cried out, "Ariannnna!"

She shouted out into the night. "Merlin, what is it?" A frigid breeze wrapped around her and, in the draft, the sweet smell of jasmine caught her nose. She gazed back at his image in the mirror. "What is it, wizard? Show me what I need to know."

The fireplace on the east side of the room suddenly raged with fire, blazing light around her. Arianna held tight to her bed to balance herself. The sound of the fire was deafening. Moans of evil, groans of anger, and screams of agony crackled into the glow of the orange light that was cast about the room as black shadows danced upon the walls.

An explosion of fire blew from the hearth, hurling its bolt towards the mirror and leaving an image of the stone circle on the glass. Within the image, a vision came to life. Arianna slowly crept towards the mirror, holding her arms high to block her eyes from the blinding light of the fire. She could see movement in the mirror, but her eyes had not yet adjusted to the light. It looked as though someone were digging. *Was it burying? Was that the Altar stone?*

Again, she heard her name called out, but this time it was carried by the fire. "Arianna!" It was followed with a hush—a hush that allowed the coldness of death to seep into her chambers. The vision vanished, and the fire blew itself out like a back draft as quickly as it had started.

Arianna gripped tightly to the bedpost. All she could think about was the last line in the prayer *The Act of Contrition*: "Save me from the fires of hell!"

She rose and dressed quickly in her jeans and warm clothing, put her black knee-high boots on and, without a measure of doubt, pulled her sheath belt on and slid Gwydion, her faithful sword, into it.

Opening her door and carefully taking note that all were asleep, Arianna ran down the stairs and out the door. Heading straight to the barn, she heard Sir Brach awaken at the sound of her boot heels pounding the wood floor. He whinnied long and loud that he was ready, and Arianna mounted her steed.

"To the circle my friend. Make haste!"

———◆———

Driving up the causeway, Jack saw his wife leaving. He looked at his watch. It was three o'clock in the morning. *Where the hell is she going at this hour?* Jack turned the car around and headed off to follow Arianna.

CHAPTER TEN

Jack Lawrence

Jack Lawrence slammed his foot on the gas of his modern station wagon and followed his wife up Wiltshire road, following her towards Salsbury Plain and the Avenue of Stonehenge. His hands curled tight around the wheel to the point of numbing his fingers. Here she was, his wife, the gatekeeper of the time portal, on her horse Sir Brach—horse and rider, an inseparable pair. She'd kill for that steed—the two were linked together since the day she met Brach at the Warwick Riding Academy so many years ago. She left Jack that day at the Dalton hotel with the kids while she enjoyed a horseback riding expedition to the ruins of Camelot. That was the day she unearthed Excalibur and was made the gatekeeper of time. Since then, life had been a living nightmare for Jack, one he planned to end as soon as he could pack. This was it, the last straw; leaving his home in Queens, New York, five years ago to live out his wife's fairy tale in England—something about a future quest—was one thing, but he wouldn't tolerate her leaving in the middle of the night again. "Yeah, okay, I'm done Arianna!"

From the road, Jack caught her in his sights as she arrived at the monolith. He hit the brake and stopped short to sit in the car and watch his wife. His anger swelled. Sweat came to his brow. He shook his head repeatedly, holding onto his steering wheel as though he could crush it. *I have had enough of King Arthur and his band of holier-than-thou friends.*

She finds a sword, opens a portal, and makes friends with a dead king? She's told in some century that I don't even care about that she has a quest with this hero?

He kept the headlights of the car off so that he could spy without worry; the road lamplights provided enough of a dim glow. Arianna jumped off of Brach and made for her saddlebag. She removed something and then opened the entryway, leading Sir Brach halfway over the land bridge before returning to lock the gate behind her. Jack laughed to himself. *Yes Ari, the circle must be secured,* he thought. She straddled Brach and off they gallopped. Jack started the car and drove on until he could only see a glimpse of her; the circle was always dark at night.

CHAPTER ELEVEN

A Circle of Evil

———◆———

Arianna and Sir Brach rode up to the massive ruins of Stonehenge, the half moon of the night guiding them towards the circle. Arianna dismounted Brach and grasped Gwydion's hilt, securing her position in case of foul play, before moving quickly to the altar stone. She reached into her saddlebag and pulled out a small hoe and flashlight she brought from home.

Arianna knelt on the ground and tunnelled. A gust of wind wrapped around the soil. She paused. The wind was mocking her again. Arianna sat up and, with caution, grabbed hold of Gwydion again. *Sword of the Mother, aid me now!*

The wind quieted itself, but Arianna's heart raced. The tall stones morphed into a different shape this night, one that made her skin crawl. She fell back to the dirt digging quickly. It was so dark and difficult to see what she was doing, even with a flashlight. She pushed the soil away from the hole that was already about half an arm's length deep and shoved the hoe further into the soil and clay. Again, the wind was accompanied by laughter, but now the sound bounced off the stones, echoing throughout the circle.

"What is it you want?" she cried into the night. Her chest heaved. Looking down at the ground, the earth shook under her feet as though the circle was swaying back and forth. Nausea overcame her. Arianna placed the hoe into the now two foot-deep hole and dug with all her might. Something was in her sights. She reached for the flashlight, but the wind came hard and pushed the small beam from her hand as the darkness below the ground pulled her down hard. Her face hit the dirt, and pain seared through her as though a spear had punctured her cheek. She tried to pull back, but the force that held her was strong and her arm felt like it might be torn from her body. Arianna attempted desperately to get her legs beneath her, but the force was too strong.

With the toes of her boots, she finally dug into the dirt, trying to establish some resistance. Her legs finally planted firmly, she pulled back with all of her strength, then propped herself on her knees for leverage. With a huge heave, she pulled her arm from the hole. Attached to her wrist was a black-gloved hand extending from beneath the ground and gripping her like a clamp. In a swift attack, Arianna grabbed for Gwydion with her free hand and sliced right through the blackness. With great force, she flew back from the hole, dropping her sword and landing on her hind parts. In her left hand was a soiled white sack, but now hanging from her wrist was a black mummified hand, parched and riddled with age.

Arianna's stomach rolled over with fear. She took a deep breath and swallowed hard, trying not to purge on the site. She grabbed at her wrist that was seething with pain and cautiously pulled the gloved hand— only to see it disintegrate into the wind.

For a moment, she sat still, exhausted, before opening the bag. Within it was a piece of parchment.

Arianna fished it out and tried reading it, but in this darkness, she could not see the words. She mounted Brach and rode up the avenue towards home with a quickness of stride.

CHAPTER TWELVE

Merlin's Desperate Hour

Arianna dismounted Sir Brach and reached into her saddlebag, taking her canteen out and drinking the cool water down as fast as she could. She checked behind her, paranoid she might have been followed home by some demon. Leading Sir Brach up the ramp into the barn, she removed his saddle and tack and hung them in the shed next to the horses' compartments.

Carefully, she reached into the saddlebag, taking out the soiled white sack, tearing away at its strings and removing the parchment from within its confines.

Dearest Arianna,

I am the bearer of urgent news. My mother is upon us again. The day of Arthur's resurrection must be at hand, as her magic is holding the wall between our worlds closed. I fear it will be your task to find retribution for her evil.

Arianna, she has already poisoned

me. Help me before my soul seeks the
path to the afterlife and my eyes will
never look upon your face again.

Merlin

Arianna scanned the letter again and stared out of the open door of the tack shed. It was already dawn. She looked at the shadows of the open road as she remembered the wind laughing at and mocking her. She unsheathed Gwydion and, gazing upon the blue stone of Avalon, remembered the day that Merlin graced her with this weapon of beauty and strength. Merlin had told her to whisper the sword's name upon the stone. From that day on, the sword would sing its powers only for her.

Arianna and Merlin met years ago when she came to England to rest after being ill. At the advice of the hotel concierge, she purchased a slot on a horseback riding expedition to the ruins of Camelot, where a man named Edmund showed her the ruins. It was on that day that she unearthed Excalibur, and the sword whisked her away to the sixth century. Her arrival in clothing that was very unfamiliar to medieval eyes surprised the citizens, and she immediately stood trial in Arthur's court for witchcraft.

It was there that Edmund revealed himself to be the Wizard Merlin and came to her defense. With his aid, Arianna was acquitted of all charges and befriended King Arthur. The three became inseparable for the cause of Camelot and the Holy Grail. Arianna witnessed Arthur's death on the battlefield as he died in Merlin's loving arms. From that day on, she was named the guardian of the sword, and she and Merlin became kindred for the cause of Arthur, his Camelot, and her future. After Arthur's death, Merlin taught her the rituals and magic of his faith. He knew she had a destiny, but what it was had yet to be revealed to either of them.

Unending, unimaginable tears flowed down Arianna's face as she reread the letter. If she could not fight and kill Mab, her death seemed imminent. Merlin would die and Arthur's life would be in danger again even before he came to existence once more.

She remembered Mab's words: *I am the future of your despair.*

"So Mab, you think your laughter scares me?" Arianna held her head high, rolled up the parchment and placed it carefully into the inside pocket of her jacket. She quietly closed the barn doors and read the time on her watch. It was already six o'clock in the morning. As she walked up the short causeway towards the cottage, she noticed Jack's car parked in the carport. *Be nice to me, Jack, or you're in for a nightmare of your own.* She proceeded to the kitchen to make herself a very strong cup of coffee.

Chapter Thirteen
Jack's Guilt Ridden Arrow

———◆———

Arianna unlocked the back door to the kitchen, took off her jacket, and hung it on the chair. She ambled over to the sink and turned on the faucet to wash her face and hands. The cool water felt good as it rinsed some of the fear away. She splashed the water on her face again and pulled a few squares of toweling from the paper towel trolley to dry her face and hands. Reaching into her pocket, she unrolled the letter and read it again carefully. Her heart quickened with grief. She wished she could comfort Merlin and tried to catch her breath as she sobbed with sorrow. Arianna closed her eyes. Concentrating on the wizard, she tried to send him a message telepathically. *Merlin can you hear me? Send me more signs.*

Arianna's adrenaline was lowering, and the stress was now catching up to her. She stood from her chair and pulled the coffeepot off the shelf, filling it with water and grinds. She placed the plug into the wall socket, hoping that by the time the coffee was made, George would be down for his morning ritual.

The churning sound of the coffee maker and the smell of freshly brewed coffee permeated the house. Arianna opened the curtain and let the morning light flow into the kitchen. She removed her boots and put them on the mat near the door.

The Wells' home was a simple country cottage, the home she had wanted from the time she was a girl. She always wanted to live in the country. Back when they were in New York, Jack was adamant that he never wanted a long commute between his job in the city and the doctors he needed for his health issues, so city life was what she endured until they moved to England.

The rooms in the cottage were airy and filled with Victorian splendor. The windows were dressed with lace curtains, and silk scarves decorated the furniture. Flowers of every species surrounded the outside and inside alike. It may have been the home of an English dignitary, but it was comfortable and inviting.

She could hear George coming down the stairs behind her. It must have been six thirty.

"I see you are ready for an early ride this morning."

Arianna turned to find George in his denims and flannel shirt, eager to drink his coffee and take care of his horses. He looked long at Arianna, with a questioning expression.

"Actually, my friend, I have already been out for a very early ride."

"You are pale and your eyes are swollen...how early is early?"

"About three-in-the-morning early."

"I didn't hear you leave," replied George.

Arianna placed the parchment in his hand.

"What's this?" he asked.

"Open it and read."

George unrolled the parchment, reading the letter carefully. He looked up at Arianna and shook his head. "Merlin is poisoned in the other world by Mab?" He looked up from the page and directly into Arianna's eyes. "So the Queen of Darkness comes out of hiding."

Arianna stared out the window. She leaned on the shelf and banged it with her fist. "It seems it is I who will finally see Mab to her end."

"How has this come into your hands?"

She placed a cup in front of him. "Sit down and drink your coffee."

53

Jack sat quiet as a mouse atop the stairs, listening to why Arianna left on her late night escapade.

"Last night Merlin came to me. In my sleep, I heard his voice calling me. I woke up, stood in front of my mirror, and saw him reaching to me from the bed. In the mirror, he showed me a vision that he had buried something near the altar stone at Stonehenge."

"You rode out to the circle alone in the middle of the night?" Jack heard the ill contempt in George's voice as it resounded from the stairwell. "Are you daft, woman? Why did you not wake me up? I would have surely joined you!"

Jack came strutting down the stairs, his feet pounding with annoyance as he hit the board of each step. He made his way into the kitchen.

"Good morning, Jack. How was your trip?" asked Arianna as she poured herself a cup of coffee.

"Don't *Jack* me—I agree completely with George."

Arianna pursed her lips at him in that way he hated. "What do you mean?"

"I came home at three o'clock this morning and followed you to that *place* you call the circle."

"What?" she retaliated. "If you were so curious as to what I was doing, why did you not get out of your car and come see what I was up to?"

Jack became incensed. "I don't have a key! Remember? Not to mention I was tired. All I wanted to see was what my wife was up to at that ungodly hour."

Arianna briefly recoiled, and Jack knew he had gotten to her. "So what did you see?"

"I saw nothing. It was too dark."

"You're a liar," barked Arianna. "You were spying on me!"

"Spying? Yes! I was spying. I'm tired of your childish fairytales, Ari!"

"If you were so concerned about my well-being, you would have gotten out of your damned car to see what was going on. I could have used your help!"

Jack stood there stewing in his temper.

"Can't think of anything to say?"

Jack knew she was pushing him hard.

"Or do you know that I'm right?"

Jack stood there, his eyes burning in their sockets. "You are my wife. You are my partner. We have a family here that you are neglecting." He knew his voice was coarse and sarcastic.

The crease on Arianna's forehead was evidence of the guilt-ridden arrow that Jack had fired at her. He stood there and watched as she grabbed her jacket and boots and walked out the back door. She ran back to the barn barefoot, turned, and waved her jacket in the air, yelling back at him."I will fight a thousand Queen Mab's before I fight my husband any longer."

Moments later he watched Arianna ride away on her horse. "Don't say anything, George. I've had enough with all of you!" Jack poured himself a cup of coffee as Alexis entered the kitchen.

"Hey, Dad!" said a cheerful Alexis.

"Hi honey," responded Jack with a big smile.

Alexis gave her father a huge hug. His daughter always had a way of putting him in a cheerful mood. "Did you have a good flight coming home?"

"It was alright. I'm sure glad to be back! Are we going to go shopping this morning—I think I owe you a trip to the mall."

"That sounds awesome," she answered. "Can we do it in about an hour?"

"We'll go after breakfast."

"Good morning George, where's Mom?" asked Alexis as she grabbed a banana.

Jack sat back in his chair, a bit reluctant to get involved. "Go ahead and tell her. I don't really care."

Alexis looked hard at her father. "What, already!"

Jack waved his hand to George, giving him the floor.

"Your mother had a vision last night and spent the night at the circle."

"Didn't you go with her?" asked Alexis.

"No. She went by herself."

"I don't get it—what do you mean she was by herself?"

"What Uncle George means, Lexy, is that Mom took a ride in the middle of the night without telling anyone."

Alexis shrugged her shoulders at her father and poured a cup of coffee. "Mom's always having some sort of vision. What's the big deal?"

Jack said nothing, but looked at Arianna's empty coffee cup still sitting on the table.

"Where is she now, Dad?"

Jack looked out the window. "I got mad at her, and she stormed off."

"Cool! You and George have a nice breakfast—I'm going to the office to work with Cynthia. We'll go shopping after you take a shower."

"You're not worried about your mother?"

"Dad, chill already. You know Mom's just being Mom."

Jack caught George's expression, as he obviously agreed with Alexis. "I just don't get all of you."

George seemed unable to contain himself. "It's none of my business, but you're not going after your wife?"

"Nope. I'm going to sit here and have a quiet breakfast, and then I'm going to take my daughter shopping."

"As usual, it's up to me to clean up your mess," smiled George.

"It's your ball game, my friend."

CHAPTER FOURTEEN

George's Witch Hunt

When visiting the circle, Arianna always made sure that from where she stood, she was hidden by the stones so that none of the drivers on the road could see her. She, George, Cynthia and Alexis were the only people who held keys to the circle gates—and none of them needed curious, uninvited guests.

She took rest under the four sarsens that still were crowned by their lintels. Titan neighed loudly in the distance. Turning and seeing George on his steed, she knew deep down that he was there to support her. Arianna felt badly that she and Jack had another fight. This was not easy for Jack to understand, but why could he not learn from George? This man who believed in her from the day they met in the museum, when Merlin presented her to him. There was no contest—she was Arianna Lawrence the gatekeeper and guardian of Excalibur, and that was all George needed to know. But Jack was always doubtful, and it was a growing thorn in her side, one she knew had to be cast out before she could truly move on.

The sound of laughter brought Arianna back to the task at hand and she stood and scanned the circle. She unsheathed Gwydion, meditating on the blue stone. "Mother Goddess, I ask thee for the power to fight this evil that has been placed before me." Again, the laughter echoed off the stones. "Come out, Mab, and show me your face!" Nothing but the whisper of the wind answered her plea. Arianna scanned each stone. The laughter mocked her and again Arianna dared to call her out. "Where are you, Mab?"

Thunder filled the air, booming its sound all through Wiltshire. From behind one of the stones rose a black and ghostly figure. Arianna raised Gwydion in the direction of the apparition. "Sword of Avalon, do not forsake me."

"Arianna!" yelled George from the rider's path, pointing to the figure. She watched as he and Titan raced to aid her. Arianna felt a burning jolt pass her—a flash of red light headed right towards Titan. Horse and rider were thrown to the ground; the bolt set up some kind of force field. George and Titan lay writhing in the dirt with light fragments flowing through them. Titan neighed with pain, his body visibly shaking as he swayed and shot back up to his feet. Arianna ran towards George, but the energy from the force field kept her at bay. From a distance, she was forced to watch George struggle on the ground, attempting to gain his whereabouts.

"George!" she screamed.

The figure came closer to Arianna, passing around her. She could feel a cold hand brush across her face. The chill reached through her. "So this is the poison you put upon your son. *Witch*, I call you. A murdering, thieving witch."

The figure hovered around Arianna like a dense fog cloaks the morning on a cold damp day. She heard the wind whisper in her head. "History will repeat itself, Christian. Excalibur, Gwydion and Prince John will be mine for the taking." Arianna shivered. "A Pagan daughter!" Mab laughed loudly.

Thoughts of Alexis entered Arianna's mind.

"Alexis. What a sweet name." Mab stroked Arianna's face again.

"Leave my daughter alone."

Arianna struck at the figure. Gwydion ripped through the dark wraith, who screamed a hideous shriek and turned red before igniting into flames, turning Gwydion's hilt so cold that frost spread like vapor up Arianna's arm. Arianna dropped her sword with a thud, and she and the smoldering apparition backed away from one another.

Arianna was the first to speak. "Mab, I will be here at the first sign of the new moon."

A final clap of thunder filled the morning, and Mab's voice bounced around the circle. "At first sign of the new moon, we will battle to the death."

With that, Stonehenge ushered in a deafening quiet. Arianna's heart raced and her skin crawled. She screamed, "Domh Ringr, temple of Merlin and the Mother! I ask thee this day, give Gwydion and the daughter of Avalon powers as deep and as black as Mab herself! I am the Lady Arianna Lawrence Pendragon, and I will see to Mab's demise!"

The blue stone on Arianna's hilt glowed as radiant as the sky.

Chapter Fifteen

The Chapel Avalon

———◆———

Arianna mounted Sir Brach. She felt jittery, as though her body would break if she shifted the wrong way. She approached the avenue gates to where George and Titan had retreated. They were hobbling around together, still shaking from the pain of the jolt. George called to her and she recoiled. "Get away from me!" Arianna put her hand up in front of her face.

"We need your help," he called after her, but Arianna had already disregarded George and kicked Sir Brach, causing him to neigh long and loud before trotting out the gates. As she passed the causeway up to the museum, her eyes caught sight of the Chapel Avalon. She and Brach paused their canter, and she sat there wondering if she should go inside to pray or lock herself in the office upstairs in the museum to hide from everyone until she could calm herself.

Her breathing labored, as she could still feel Mab's cold hand reaching through her. A chill ran down her back, and a sweat emerged from her pores. She led Brach up the hill towards the small building in the middle of the trees, where she dismounted.

Sir Brach whinnied loudly at her as she tried to wrap his bridle around a low hanging branch. She was having problems controlling him. He again snorted at her. "What is your problem, Brach?" she pulled hard on his reigns. Brach was obviously ill at ease. Arianna rubbed his side.

"Please dear friend, forgive me, for I know not what I do right now."

Arianna looked around to see if the priest's car was in the driveway, but she saw only the custodial manager's vehicle, which was parked there every day from nine in the morning until four in the afternoon. She made her way up the entry path and opened the door to the chapel.

As she stood in the small foyer, her eyes found the crucifix that hung from the ceiling, suspended by old, thick gold ropes. The cross, at least six feet long and four feet wide, was painted birch. To Arianna, it looked like the inside skin of a tree after it shed its bark. It was pale and lifeless. On the cross was an intricately carved body of Christ. Wrapped around His midsection was a white linen cloth covering His groin. On His head rested the crown of thorns, and His long brown hair was soaked with blood as it dripped down His eyes, nose and mouth. The nails that pierced His hands and feet extruded red upon his limbs. Her stomach tightened, as she ought not look upon the cross so closely. She sought refuge in the pew to the right of the altar, looking upon the stained glass windows. The sun shone wonderfully through them, making the resurrected Jesus look as though He were in the room. The six-foot angel stood so majestically between the windows that she dared not go to the base stone it stood upon. She wanted to touch it, calling on the secret that it held to help her unleash the evil that had touched her.

Arianna felt unworthy, so unworthy that she considered running from the church. Such a bone stiffening fear came over her that she thought her feet had become cemented to the stone beneath her. She pulled the lapels of her jacket tight to her chest. As she turned to make her way back to the pew, her eyes fell upon Saint Helena; a three-foot high statue that stood on a white marble base. Helena was a beautiful woman who became a saint when she helped her son Constantine find the origin of Christ and convert Rome to a Christian state. She was, by birth, a Pagan high priestess but a Christian by choice, even though she never disavowed her Pagan heritage.

"Arianna!" said a voice from the Sanctuary.

She jumped—not expecting to hear anyone in the chapel. "Father,

I'm surprised you're here this time of day."

Father Wallace walked down the short aisle and stood a foot from Arianna. "Are you ill, my dear?"

Arianna wanted nothing to do with priests this day. All she wanted was some solace in this place of peace...no speeches about how God plans these things and certainly no pity from a priest who wanted nothing to do with her Pagan roots.

"I am fine, Father."

Father Wallace was looking at her strangely, adding to her agitation. "Forgive me, madam, but you seem out of sorts this day."

Arianna's head pounded as she tried to hold herself from screaming at this respected man of the cloth. She cleared her throat. "It has been a long day, Father, and I was hoping that I could find some solace for awhile."

Again, she felt him look at her, and his eyes were piercing her the wrong way. "Arianna, your face is so rigid from whatever is troubling you that you look as though you have seen a ghost."

Arianna tried to calm her features, but she could not. He reached for her arm, but she looked on the priest with contempt.

"You are so tense. Please, is something wrong?"

She pushed his hand off her forearm. "I ask you to leave me alone here while I pray." Her voice croaked in her throat.

Father Wallace stood there and shook his head disapprovingly at her. "I will respect your wishes, madam. As your friend, I am here if you need me."

Arianna retreated to her pew, saying nothing to the priest. She followed Father Wallace with her eyes as he left the church through the sanctuary side door. She sat back on the pew, her hands shaking, unable to rid herself of the coldness. Her body felt as though spring had turned to winter overnight and she was sitting on a snow bank without the protection of a warm coat. Arianna knelt on the kneeler, folding her head in her arms as to hide from Christ on the cross.

"What is it you want with me?" she asked aloud with a melancholy voice. "I have done enough for you." The flow of Arianna's blood pounded in her skull. She stood and walked despondently around the square of the chapel, looking upon the symbolism of the church. Her eyes laid upon the cross, and the statue of Mary, the mother of Jesus, and the stone angel behind the altar. She laughed morosely and her lip quivered with hate for the church. No matter what happened to her in life, her shame and her sacrifice were the only bloody things that God wanted from her. Arianna walked over to the angel, looking straight into its eyes. "So you wish to take my Merlin's life, no?" She shook her head. "Take mine. That's all any of you want, isn't it?" She turned and held onto the altar, gazing upon the gold unicorn embroidered on the white fabric. "Resurrection, my bloody ass! You know that I love Arthur with all my heart, and that's why you selfishly keep him with you."

Arianna unsheathed Gwydion. She remembered the words that the wizard told her and the day that she named Gwydion. *Before you raise your sword, dear one, you must name her or nary, she will not defend thee.* Tears fell down her cheeks. "Merlin," she whispered.

As she kneeled down on the floor, shamefully prostrating herself, she looked up to the cross. "Please, God, don't take Merlin from me. He is the only person who truly knows me."

After a moment of silence, Arianna stood on her feet and walked over to the statue of Saint Helena. She pulled from under her blouse a pentacle, a silver one that Alexis had brought back to her from Salem, Massachusetts. Holding it with a nervous hand, she looked at the statue. "Why did you give up your Pagan roots so easily? Did you forget who you were? Who we are?" Arianna ripped the pentacle from her neck and drew Gwydion from her sheath. "You're a high priestess, not this statue they perceive as a saint."

"Arianna!" Father Wallace's voice bellowed at her from the back of the chapel.

Arianna turned and looked shamelessly at him. "You think you are so perfect because you're a priest! Ha! You hide your feelings behind that black robe of yours."

Father Wallace folded his arms looking livid at the attack. "Please, my lady, let me help you. Your soul is in danger!"

Arianna lifted up Gwydion as though to strike the priest, but then sheathed the sword and quickly ran from the church. She hastily mounted Brach and led him straight up the hill towards the time gate.

"I, Lady Arianna Lawrence Pendragon, daughter of Avalon, ask the God of heaven and the Goddess Mother of the planet earth to reveal her most precious secrets." Arianna slashed at the wall, trying to open it, stabbing at the empty air, screaming, "Why won't you open for me?"

She turned to the sound of Titan's hooves as he and George were galloping up the hill. He rode up to them and quickly pulled her off Sir Brach and onto Titan. Allowing Gwydion to fall to the ground, she wept in George's arms.

"Dear lady." His manly hands stroked her hair. "What has been done to you?"

Shaking, Arianna could feel George's pulse soar as he held her. He yelled to the heavens, "I promise God that if anything else happens to my lady, I will burn your chapel to the ground."

Arianna wrapped her arms around George's neck, feeling the security of his body steady her. He carefully dismounted Titan, holding her firmly in his grip. Her feet touched the ground, and he helped her stand firmly. Her legs shook from under her as George let go of her and reached into his saddlebag, removing a canteen of water. Her body warmed again. He gave Arianna the canteen, and she drank the water down quickly, cleansing the bitter taste of Mab's touch.

"Please, I beg you to tell me what evil should make you behave so."

Arianna looked upon the stillness of the hill, laboring to breathe. "I feel her evil within me."

George stepped from her and rummaged through Sir Brach's saddlebag. In his hands, Arianna saw her compact mirror. "Mab has marked you more than you think my lady." George opened the mirror and showed Arianna her image. Her fingers brushed through her hair. She pulled some strands out towards her shoulder to see it for herself.

Her soft brown hair had become a thick black mane. It had taken on the color of the raven with all the texture of the bird's feathers.

"Dear God, George. What will I do?"

CHAPTER SIXTEEN

Blaise and Aaron are Called to Camelot

———◆◆◆———

"Arianna! Where are you?" Merlin screamed in agony as he raised his hand and swung it through the air as though submerged in water and trying to pull himself to the surface. His chest heaved with labored breath, and his fever transported him to the height of delirium. Today marked ten days straight that Merlin had been plagued with the unknown fever. "Ariannnnnnnnnnnnna!" Merlin's arms reached out into the darkness.

Nimue ran straight to her husband's side, taking a cloth and soaking it with cold water that was laced with willow bark root to bring down the fever. The cool cloth turned hot in Nimue's hand as Merlin's chest throbbed, and his body toiled to fight the raging temperature. She picked up his hands and held them to her.

"Galahad, it always enamors me, the enduring strength of my best friend," said Viviane as she gave Nimue another moist cloth.

Nimue stood at Merlin's bedside, silent in her thoughts and beguiled by what this fever meant. She knew that everything humanly possible had been executed under the law of Christian and Pagan medicine, as Viviane had done all that she could according to her Druid beliefs and the ordinances of herbal laws—and yet her husband remained imprisoned by this unknown illness. Viviane procured the cloth from her and stood over Merlin, reprieving Nimue, who walked over to the window looking out upon a cloudy sky and towards heaven, asking God to send a sign.

"Daniel." Nimue was pulled from her meditation as Galahad beckoned to the young squire.

"My lord, what is it you wish?"

"Go tell my brother I seek his company in Merlin's chambers."

Daniel left the room in haste. Here was another of Arthur's young men, merely a boy when his father Sir Percival Montgomery died in battle with Arthur. Nimue was so proud of Daniel, as he was about to step up and become a knight—now in Galahad's court.

Nimue turned her ear to Merlin, who kept calling out the names of those he knew, yet they did not come. The fever seemed to be a memory inducer as Merlin called upon the ghosts of his past.

"Will no one answer his delusions!" asked Nimue, weeping into a cloth she had used to bathe Merlin. Viviane came to her aid, holding onto her. Nimue pushed her away and again started to care for Merlin. She looked up at her friend and said, "I am sorry."

Viviane reached for another cloth, saying nothing, and the two women washed and gave Merlin the tisane that Viviane mixed to keep the fever at bay.

"Brother, you sent for me," said Joseph as he hurriedly entered the room. The son of Arianna, Joseph was the boy who came to them when Arianna returned home many years ago. He came to them a reckless, ill-educated half-wit. Galahad and the boy bonded, and the king adopted him as his brother. With the help of Peter and Merlin, here now stood a man of great distinction, a Knight of the Round Table, and someone Nimue and Merlin had come to love as their own son.

Viviane spooned the tea into Merlin's mouth while Nimue held his head and listened to the men converse.

"Joseph, I need you to leave Camelot for awhile."

Joseph's face was puzzled. "To where do you send me, my brother?"

"To the Forest of Fire."

Nimue could see Joseph's pores swell with perspiration. His face flushed of color, leaving him white as a sheet and, from the way he cupped his hands in front of his lips and blew moist breath on them, she could see that he was chilled with anxiety.

"I want you to go and bring back the Druid priests. I believe they are the last hope that Merlin has."

Joseph saluted his brother with a closed fist to his chest. "And whence do I leave, my lord?"

"Before another moon rises in the north sky."

"I will make haste to prepare." Joseph beamed with pride.

Galahad placed both his hands on his brother's shoulders. "Choose whatever men you need for the journey."

Joseph left the room to prepare for his travels. Galahad reached over, taking Nimue away from Merlin. She paused slightly and allowed Galahad to lead her. "Please, my lady, sit down."

Nimue felt befuddled at the request but, in her exhausted state, obeyed and sat down on the chair across from Merlin's bed. "What is so important in the Forest of Fire that you send Joseph and give him free reign to choose his riding partners?"

Galahad lifted her hand. "Do you remember when we came home from the Grail quest?"

"What does your homecoming have to do with Merlin?"

"Do you remember the boys and me telling you about two very special Druid high priests who cared for us before we were allowed to cross the Grail Gates?"

Nimue held her hands to her abdomen, trying to tame the uneasiness growing in her belly. "I remember when you returned with the Grail, you told us how after you slew the demons of the forest, these priests who lived there brought you in, tended to your wounds and healed you from your long journey to reach the Grail."

Nimue sought out Galahad's eyes for some recourse, for she was becoming fragile—not only from her husband's illness but from her age, as time had found its way with her.

"Were they not named Blaise and Aaron, my lord?" asked Viviane.

Galahad smiled responding, "Yes, High Priestess. Those are truly their names."

Nimue raised her head, "And what about them, my lord?"

He spoke with certainty, "They will know the medicine that we have not the knowledge of."

Nimue held tight to Galahad's hands and placed them to her face, cradling in his strength. Galahad stroked her cheek, and she bathed in his warmth.

"For the love of the Mother herself, two priests of my own faith will be brought here to Camelot," said Viviane. Nimue saw a smile on her friend's face. "My lord, I am a priestess of the arts. Blaise was the one who taught Merlin the healing potions that saved many of Arthur's men on the battlefields in Rome and Germania. When you were a boy, and Camelot was plagued with fever, it was Blaise and Merlin's tonics that saved all of us." She placed her hands in prayer. "I could learn so much from them."

A knock on the door interrupted their conversation and Joseph entered, heading straight towards Galahad, his king.

"What say you, my brother?"

"I have gathered my men, and they make ready to leave in a few hours by the first light of morn, my lord."

"Who have you chosen for the journey?"

"Sir Luke, Sir Michael, and two squires will join me, Sire."

"Take thee rest, my brother, for your journey will have need of it."

Joseph crossed the floor, his walk carrying a stride of command. He stopped in front of Viviane. "My lady, whence we journeyed for the Grail, you gave us your vessel for a safe passage into unknown waters."

"My lord Joseph, take her and do us honor again. Her North Star will guide your way."

"Thank you." Joseph kissed Viviane on the hand. "I take my leave. Brother, please tell my betrothed that I will return shortly."

Galahad embraced his brother. Joseph reached for Nimue and kissed her on the cheek before exiting.

"Arianna would be so proud of her son," she said.

CHAPTER SEVENTEEN

Gwydion the Hostage

Arianna and George approached the museum from the less utilized south entrance. George halted his canter with Titan before dismounting. Arianna gave him Brach's bridal, and he led Arianna and the horses up the back causeway. As he unlocked the door of the tack shed, Arianna looked toward the house; the light was on in the kitchen. She, Brach, George, and Titan walked through the shed and into the barn.

Arianna dismounted Sir Brach and, as usual, removed his gear. Brach gave a snort, relieved by the removal of weight.

"There, there now, my friend. You must be tired and hungry after what I have put you through this day."

Brach turned his head and whinnied in agreement. Hearing Titan chime in with a snort of his own, Arianna sauntered over and stroked him on his neck. "I thank you, too, my friend." Titan whinnied an appreciative response.

George gave Arianna Brach's feedbag and they both watched the horses chomp down on the oats, enjoying their savory meal.

"Eat hardy. You deserve this nourishment today," said George as Arianna looked at herself in the rectangular oak-framed, beveled mirror nailed to the post of the barn. It was there so that guests could see how well they were attired before they left for the daily tour. Arianna was stroking her hair, her light olive complexion blanch against the now ebony contrast of her mane. She felt George watching her and followed his gaze as it landed on the can of kerosene fluid used for the patio lamps. "Would you really burn the chapel down for me?"

"I would, Arianna."

She saw a hint of a smirk come over his expression. "I can't imagine you doing such a thing."

George laughed morosely. "I would do it without mercy, my lady."

Arianna turned away from the mirror and walked to the door.

"Are you ready to go in?" asked her apprehensive friend.

From the exit, Arianna stole one more look at herself in the mirror, thought of her husband and said, "Let's get this over with."

Exiting the barn, Arianna started walking towards the museum. "I need some time in the office upstairs. I want to read those letters again."

"Are you of good mind to do so?" asked George. "Come with me to the kitchen and have something to eat before you search for your answers."

Arianna shook her head in agreement and allowed George to lead the way back to the cottage for food and drink. George opened the door and they both walked through.

<hr />

Jack was sitting, reading the paper and drinking his iced tea. When he saw Arianna enter the kitchen, he stood from the table. "Good evening."

"Mom, I was worried," said Alexis as she ran over to her mother and gave her a kiss on the cheek. Jack could see a note of confusion pass his daughter's face as Arianna pulled away from her. Alexis folded her arms and looked at him, then again at Arianna with a perplexed expression worthy of a sour grape.

It was evident to Jack by the look on his daughter's face and by the way Arianna put her hand to her mouth that she was asking Alexis for her silence. Alexis shook her head, heeding the gesture. She snatched a cookie out of the jar and bit down on it. Jack looked at Alexis and at Arianna from the top of his glasses, knowing something was amiss. He coughed loud and long and saw Arianna try to crack her neck. He smirked.

"Alexis, may I see you in the hall for a moment?" asked George.

"Yeah. Mom and Dad could use some private time together."

Jack pulled his glasses off and bit down on their metal frame as he watched George take Alexis out of the kitchen. *Yeah, you got the idea, George,* he thought. Arianna still had not made eye contact with Jack, but he listened to her sigh as though she were trying not to stir up a fight. She kept to the counter and made herself a scone with cream cheese, then shimmied over to the refrigerator. Still not giving Jack an eye of attention, Arianna grabbed a glass from the dish rack and poured some wine, placing the bottle next to her scone as she took a sip.

Jack just shook his head. *So we're playing that game?* She removed her riding jacket and sheath belt, hanging both on the chair. He rose from his seat, walked around the table and pulled Gwydion out of her sheath. Arianna said nothing, and continued to eat her meal.

Giving a sarcastic, low, caught-in-the-throat laugh, Jack mocked the sword while staring into the blue stone on the hilt. By the way Arianna tapped her nails on the butcher block wood of the counter, he knew her silence would break eventually. She again bit into her scone and rubbed her throat with her fingers. Jack sensed she was about to blow but could not stop himself, playing with the sword, swishing it around a bit. This was the sacred sword of Avalon and the sister sword of Excalibur. "Is this how those knights of yours wield their swords?" Jack knew his words were course and rude and it actually invigorated him.

Arianna put her wine glass down. "Please give me my sword, Jack."

He was not about to hand it over.

"Jack, give me Gwydion now!"

"Gwydion? Is that what you call this thing?"

"Give me Gwydion," demanded Arianna. "Now!"

"I'll give you this thing after you pack your bags and we are home in New York."

"Don't do this. Give me the sword."

"Give me what I want."

Arianna stared at her husband. Slowly, she repositioned her five-foot nine-inch frame closer to his broad frame, which towered over her by exactly four and a quarter inches.

"Jack, I am not kidding."

The sun was shining through the curtains, and the rays cast a blue light on what was now her black mane. Jack looked at his wife, feeling his eyes open wide.

"That's what is different! Take that ugly wig off, woman!"

Arianna ran her fingers through her hair, showing Jack that she could not remove "the wig."

"What the hell do you think you're doing, Ari? Have you gone completely crazy?" Jack stepped closer to Arianna but held the sword at bay so that his wife could not reach for it.

"Give me the sword, Jack."

"Heck! I'm glad your king is dead!"

Arianna screamed, "Have some respect!"

"You look like a witch!"

"A witch you say?" Arianna put her hand to her brow, as if he her head was going to explode. "The word is Wicca, Jack!" Arianna folded her hands in prayer. The stoic look in her eyes spoke volumes to Jack and cast upon him an eerie chill.

In that instant, a gust of wind shot through the window and whipped Jack around. He felt a coldness surge within him and course though his body. Again the wind wrapped around him—only now it ran down his neck and into the hand that held Gwydion. His hand became so icy that he lost his grip and dropped the weapon. Gwydion hit the floor with a hard resonating clang.

Arianna grabbed her sword from the floor before thrusting her face within an inch of his. "Now leave me alone!" She turned and walked out the kitchen door and up towards the museum.

Chapter Eighteen

A Vision of Strange Sight!

——◆——

George ran after Arianna, calling out, "Arianna, please let me help you!"

Arianna was shaking, "This is none of your business, George." He reached for her arm but she pushed him away. "Leave me alone."

Arianna opened the side door and climbed the steps that led to her office. She turned at the landing as she heard George run up behind her, his voice declaring, "If you were not sworn to King Arthur, I would take you to my bed and make you my wife."

She stopped in her tracks, turned, and calmly walked down two of the steps. "Excuse me?"

"You deserve a man who cares for you and treats you well."

"Yes, I do, George. But make no mistake. Though I hate Jack at times for his inability to understand me...though he can be the ultimate jackass and a complete fool...he is my husband. Please don't forget that." She turned and made her way up to the artifacts room, leaving George standing alone.

Angry tears befell her as she dropped to her knees, sobbing. She yanked Arthur's cloak from the box and wrapped herself in it, holding tight to the beautiful satin and envisioning Arthur's arms around her. Her heart, her body cried out in silence for her friend. "Arthur, please...I cannot go on without you. What else is there for me to do?" She choked for air and closed her eyes, remembering the words on Arthur's Tomb. *HIC IACET ARTHURUS, REX QUONDAM REXQUE FUTURUS.* She ran her fingers over the cloak, stroking the satin, as she thought to herself, *Arianna, if you want your Arthur back, you must fight and you must win. The game is in your court—no other's!* She sat on the floor a few moments to calm herself.

Feeling a bit resolved, she moved to her desk. Opening the drawer, she took out her glasses and placed them on her face before picking up the keys and opening the strong box where the letters from Merlin and Mab were carefully hidden away. She brought them over to her desk, draping the tails of the cloak around her legs as she sat. With Gwydion securely next to her near the chair, Arianna grabbed the hilt of the sword. "Gwydion, sword of the Mother, no one will ever take you from me again. This I promise you!"

She unrolled the parchments, reading Mab's harsh words one more time and sneering as she read the word *Myrddin.* Then she read the curse that Mab wrote to her son. *Ebbyn woo zyll senfynn maga amnen Myrddin efwwar dah!* She read the words again, this time repeating them in her own tongue, *"The ebbing moon of evil elves shall poison the earth around Myrddin. Fear death!*

Arianna placed the parchment on the desk and unrolled the letter that Merlin had managed to write before Mab's curse imprisoned him, reading the last line. *Help me before my soul seeks the path to the afterlife and my eyes will never look upon your face again.*

"Merlin," Arianna said aloud, "hold on. Our day is coming." Closing her eyes, she rubbed her temples. The day's events were taking their toll. Having barely touched her wine glass before she and Jack fought, she felt the desire for a drink to relax her—or at least ward off her nervousness.

Walking over to the private bar where George kept his special aperitifs for when dignitaries visited the museum, she opened the side drawer of her desk and brought the keys to the cabinet. As she removed the keys for the lock, she heard a dull ping hit the floor and looked down. It was a coin. Arianna picked it up—it was definitely a gold coin, but it was quite tarnished. She grabbed a chamois from the drawer and cleaned some of the green discoloration from it. On the coin was a woman, a striking woman with an olive wreath wrapped around her beautiful curled hair. Arianna's heart raced as she started to read the lady's name. *Augusta Helena* and on the bottom of the coin was *S.P.Q.R.* The mark of the High Legion.

She kissed the face of Helena. Here was the Empress of Rome. Nobody truly knew who Helena was; the true nature of the woman was hidden from the history books. She was Élan by birth and renamed Helena; Pagan by birth and converted to Christianity. They shared that hidden history, though Arianna was baptized Catholic and now embraced the Pagan faith. She yearned to learn more from this woman who, like her, was Christian and Pagan, who believed in the Father in Heaven and his bride the Goddess, the Mother Earth.

"Oh, High Priestess, your daughter Arianna needs your help." Arianna kissed the coin and placed it to her brow. "I beseech thee, High Priestess. How do I fight this madness?"

A blue light, so bright, shot from the coin, and Arianna dropped it to the floor. The beam found its way to the wall, drawing the crescent moon in an otherwise darkened room. Rainbow rays of color painted the wall and, within the crescent moon, an image of Arthur in his pendragon armor appeared. From behind him grew the image of Helena, who came forward to stand next to Arthur. She was dressed in the blue robes of the sisterhood of Avalon, her brow adorned by the crescent moon tattoo.

Arianna bowed to the lady in blue. "Élan, High Priestess of Avalon, I am your servant."

"You honor me, my child. I have not heard my birth name in many years." Élan floated from off the wall into the room. "Arianna, stand. You are the high priestess of the present. You must acknowledge your powers and use them well."

Arthur reached through the light towards Arianna, who in turn reached for him, her hand moving through his hand like dust passing through a sunbeam; they could not touch.

"I will be with you soon, my dear," said Arthur.

Tears streamed down Arianna's face. "I am here, my King. Your will be done."

"Pick up your sword," commanded Élan, and Arianna did as she was told. "Look within the eye of the stone." Again, Arianna obeyed the high priestess and saw an image of herself with Arthur in another time—not of theirs nor of the present. "Arianna," interrupted Élan, pointing towards the window where Arianna witnessed another vision; it was a battle at Stonehenge. Her sword glowed with boundless power.

"Look for the coming of Draconian. He will guide you."

With that, the visions of both Helena and Arthur pulled back into the grain of the wall, leaving Arianna with a dreaded sense of loneliness.

CHAPTER NINETEEN

I Take Thee, Gwydion, to My Breast

Cloaked in Arthur's cape, Arianna kept to her office for the remainder of the day, feeling secure from the turbulence that life had so generously thrust upon her of late. At dusk, she opened the verandah door and stood on the portico near the gaping wall that faced Avalon and Arthur's tomb. The red sunset cast a shadow upon the cemetery, which reflected its radiance in the distance.

She folded her hands and prayed to the Goddess. "Mother, forgive me this day for my anger. My mind is clouded by many things." Her eyes looked upon the trees and the roses that graced the area around the museum and the cottage. The wind blew and was fragrant with the Mother Earth. Arianna took solace with its perfume and allowed it to relax her.

Concentrating on the vision of her and Arthur that Élan had bestowed upon her, she fixed her eyes in the direction of Arthur's tomb. Holding Gwydion under her cloak, she said softly, "I take thee, Gwydion, to my breast for the love of Camelot, Arthur, Merlin, God, and the Mother Goddess."

Lightening streaked the sky and a bolt shot down towards Arthur's tomb.

"Arthur!" she felt herself screaming, fearful that his tomb had been obliterated. Frightened, she ran out the back door, mounted Brach bareback and rode to the gates of the cemetery to find that the grave was untouched. The lightning had parted the roses, which—along with some of the beautiful green leaves—were now ablaze. Arianna could see a hole in the ground, as though it lay open and bleeding beneath a pile of smoldering dirt.

Using the tails of Arthur's cloak, she put the fire out, burning the edges of the fabric on the embers. With caution, she picked up some of the burned soil and found that it had turned to ash. Within the ash was a single digit from a dragon's claw resting in the roots of the rose bush. She knew that it was a dragon's claw by the way it curved like the crescent moon and because it was hard like the rib bone of a bull. It bore a spiked design around the edge of its outer half-circle and was razor sharp at the point to rip into its prey. Wrapped around the thickest part of the claw was a red parchment with the initial *D* burned into the golden seal. She looked around before breaking the seal and unwrapping the parchment.

Lady Arianna Pendragon,

*The hour of Arthur is at hand. Heed to this:
Gwydion and Excalibur are in danger. For the
Black One to rein again, she needs the Sisters of
the Lake to do her bidding.*

*Take thee wisdom,
Draconian*

Arianna shook the cloak, now charred at the ends, and draped it over the tombstone. She traced her finger upon the intricately woven gold and red pendragon embroidered on the back and then stood away from the stone.

Holding the crescent part of the claw firmly she seized the talon and cut a gash the shape of the crescent moon around her forearm, letting her blood drip onto the blades of grass that grew on Arthur's grave. Feeling the chill of the night consume her body, she read the words on the tomb. *"HIC IACET ARTHURUS REX QUONDAM REXQUE FUTURUS."*

Raising Gwydion with both hands, feeling the heat of her blood pour down her arm, she screamed into the night, "I, Lady Arianna Lawrence Pendragon, give my blood to the Mother, for I am the High Priestess of Avalon, and no one claims my right!"

Chapter Twenty

The Arrival of
Blaise and Aaron

The sea was calm as the sailors led by Sir Joseph and his entourage were guided by the North Star on the sail of Lady Viviane's ship. They had journeyed from the Forest of Fire, passed quietly by the shores of Glastonbury and now entered the waters of Avalon, where they were met by a small clipper ship at the mouth of the isle. Viviane had sent a group of young fishermen from the nearby village to join with their vessel and bring them safely through the marshes that would lead them back to Camelot.

The Isle of Glastonbury, also known as Ynys-Witrin, the Island of Glass, was a peninsula with waters that encircled a cluster of hills surrounded by marshes as thick as wet sand. This is where the land and sea met and led into the secret and enchanted Isle of Avalon. Where Lady Viviane resided, and where a lake had formed. Viviane's cottage stood majestically on a hill that was nestled in the valley. The isle was named after the Welsh god Avalloc, who ruled the underworld. Here is where the dead met and the point where they passed into the afterlife; where Gwyn ap Nudd lived—the lord and master of the underworld— and where Arthur's soul would have gone to wait until the ruler picked him up in his arms and brought him to Elysium.

Sir Joseph Lawrence stood at the bow of the ship, feeling the sea winds brush through his hair. Gavin, Marc and Michael were busy as they strung the towing ropes down to the awaiting clipper. The lady's vessel, with the North Star embroidered on the mast, was now being tugged home.

The tree-lined horizon of the city was nothing short of a gift, a sheer delight for the eye to behold. This passage was hidden from onlookers, as Avalon's passageway was only for those who were chosen either by birth or by invitation of the Lady of the Lake.

A bell in the abbey tower that was hidden by the vast arboretum rang six times, letting the friars and nuns know that it was the call to vespers. To Joseph, it was the sound of England welcoming him home, which was surely a delight.

As the ship passed through the marsh, the gold cross atop the cathedral high on the hill was revealed through the trees. Joseph made the sign of the cross over his heart and said a silent prayer, thanking God that he and his men made a safe journey, free from incident and danger.

"My lord, what would you have me do?" asked the young squire, Gavin.

"Gavin, rest the sails taut on the rigger. The winds of Avalon greet us home."

Gavin did as he was commanded and Joseph heard him whistle, glad to be returning.

"Joseph, our king and brother will be most proud of us this day," said Sir Luke as he aided Gavin in resting the sails.

Joseph yelled up the pole, "I agree, but your father will insist on a full account as soon as we walk our sorry butts into the castle."

Both the young knights and their squires laughed together as Joseph thought of Luke's father, Sir Gawain, standing in the hall waiting anxiously for his report.

Luke finished resting the sails and joined Joseph at the bow.

"Remember when we returned with Galahad from the Grail find? Father was not happy that we waited almost a week before we presented the details."

"I remember it well. He pulled you, Peter and me into the Round Table room and sat us down, giving us his speech about the importance of such descriptions." Joseph imitated the voice of the older knight. "Being Knights of the Round Table is a responsibility, one never to make light of." Joseph wrapped up snugly in his cloak, as the breeze coming off the isle was a bit cold.

Luke spoke again. "I can still see my father sitting with King Arthur at the table when I was a boy. He would read from his personal journal the reports of a battle or a meeting with a dignitary from another country." Luke stroked his goatee, and Joseph could see him ponder the memory. "My father is a proud knight—as I am, Joseph."

"As *we* are, Luke. I will be so glad to see your father tonight and recount to him the story of our journey."

Joseph stood at the helm with a sense of self-respect. He had come a long way in his life, and it was a great feeling to carry the pride and dignity of a man who had worked hard to earn his keep. Here he was, a soldier of twenty-five years, who at the age of nine was diagnosed with a neurological disorder that alienated him from family and friends. Problems in school learning, embarrassed him, made him the subject of much ridicule and taunting at the hands of other students. He remembered one particular day when he received his report card, which revealed that he had failed every class. His mother had done everything in her power to procure help from the medical and educational fields to aid him, but Joseph was not responding to the programs. He could see the shame on his mother's face as his teachers told her how badly he had behaved in school and how they felt nothing more could be done for him.

Yet his mother never gave up. She kissed him on the cheek that day and Joseph made up his mind that he would make her proud. He worked hard from then on, passed all his grades and finally graduated.

A smile came over Joseph's face as he savored the memory of his graduation day. He was the keynote speaker, and his mother was aglow for her son. She had brought him to manhood with all her faith. Joseph found odd jobs to bring in an income, but he always struggled to find his way in life. So by faith or fate, Joseph Lawrence was brought to England in the sixth century, and somehow every bad fortune that had befallen him was righted here. Was it Galahad who showed him the true way of manhood? The king trained him in weaponry and sent him on errands to far off lands with the other squires and knights for the sake of the kingdom. Was it when his mother almost died when he had to go forward in time to where he came from—to bring his father and sister back to Camelot? Was it the bravery that made him a man? Was it when Sir Gawain, Sir Martin and Sir William saw potential in him and gave him duties to prove himself? Was it when he fought hard in the battle against the Saxons that he finally knew what responsibility truly was? Was it his mother's boundless faith for her son? Was it God or the Goddess? Joseph cared not for the questions—only that he had become a man, one who worked hard in Galahad's court, learning the ways of Camelot and earning enough respect from the elders to be dubbed a knight and earn the right to be invited by Galahad to find the Holy Grail. Soon he would be married to Lady Leonora, Luke's younger sister and daughter to Sir Gawain, and her joy would become his new mission.

The sound of wind chimes interrupted Joseph's thoughts as Marcus, the young squire, rang them to announce that High Priest Blaise and his assistant Aaron were about to make their way onto the deck.

Blaise and Aaron came up from the under-deck dressed in the finest of their priestly vestments. The High Priest Blaise placed his foot upon the deck, and Marcus rang the chimes long and loud. Joseph turned and walked over to the priests, examining the intricate design of their attire. Blaise wore a dark blue velvet shirt with wide bell sleeves. He wore black suede pants with black knee-high boots. A gold and blue long over-tunic adorned his torso with a gold and red braided belt worn about his waist. Hanging from the belt were the blue stone beads of the Mother.

The outfit was finished with a dark blue and gold cloak that carried the Long Hood of the Druids and the white crescent moon, the marks of his priestly vows.

Aaron was attired in much the same way except that his colors were beige and brown. He, too, wore the blue beads of the Mother, but his belt was silver and his cloak was brown and purple. His hood was not as long as Blaise's nor was the crescent moon white—it was yellow, because he had not yet taken the last of his vows as a high Druid priest.

Joseph bowed to Blaise and Aaron, respecting the status of their vestments.

"We prepared an offering to the Mother in our cabins before we arrived," said Aaron. Joseph smiled at the priests anticipating what was to come.

"Make ready your gift," announced Joseph.

"Please come, brothers of our Mother," said Blaise with an inviting sound to his voice. "Come take part in our prayer of thanksgiving."

Joseph, Luke, Gavin and Marcus joined the priests. Joseph stood back and watched in awe as he did with his mother when she prepared her rituals. Blaise pulled out the wooden censer that had been primed already with hot stones and placed onto them the fragrant leaves of oak, mistletoe, St. Johnswort, wild rose and fern. He poured the oil of the rose over the leaves and closed the censer, and Aaron placed it in the mesh basket. As the stones started to burn the herbs, the ship took on the scent of the Mother's gifts and the smoke from the container floated into the breeze.

Performing the ritualistic act of the alter server, Joseph came to Aaron with the censor. The young priest lifted the rope and rocked it back and forth and in triangular motions, making the sign of the pentacle—the five pointed star that signified the four elements of the earth headed by the spirit or the soul. He shifted to a circular pattern, making the disc or shape of the moon for which the Mother's symbol rested. To Joseph, it was like watching his own Catholic priests in high prayer, letting the smoke rise, symbolic of prayers rising to the heavens.

Blaise procured from his pocket the blue stones of the Mother Earth, rubbing them in his hand. He placed the stones in the shape of a triangle, and Aaron rested the censer in the center. As the smoke from the metal ball rose to Blaise's height, he waved his hands, gesturing for all to come within it and take of its fragrance.

Blaise and Aaron started to chant in long rhythmic sounds. Taking a deep breath, the High Priest Blaise uttered these words in thanks, "*A Elffyntodd Dwyr Sinddyn Duw Cerrig Yr FFerllurg Nwyn; Os Syraiaeth Ech Saffaer Tu Fewr Echlyn Mor, Necrombor Llun.*"

They again raised the censer and blessed the ship, thanking her for all the shelter and comforts she had given them during their journey. As the ship sailed closer to its berth, Aaron took the censer and held it taut over the point of the bow, blessing the water and the land.

"Gavin, ring the bell. Let all know that we have returned!" cried Luke as the ship approached its port. Gavin ran and introduced the hammer to the brass, letting her ring tidings to all who would hear her on the Isle of Avalon.

"We are home!!" shouted Joseph.

<hr />

Lady Viviane heard the bell from the cottage near the Sea of Affalon. She grabbed her cloak from its hanger, threw it over her shoulders, and ran to greet the travelers. Her novices followed her to port.

Viviane, with increased anticipation, stood out of breath on the stone dock, watching the small clipper guide the travelers back to the Motherland. She was filled with bittersweet joy. The anticipated honored priests were there not for glad tiding but to aid her in healing the Old Man of the Forest. Viviane stretched on her tiptoes trying to see the high priests as the ship came to rest at the dock. From the bow of the ship, Viviane heard, "Marc, lower the anchor!" It was the voice of Joseph.

Marc did as instructed, allowing the ship to finally take rest. From the port, Viviane could hear the anchor hit the water and splash upon the sands of Avalon. She clapped her hands in silent prayer, thanking the Goddess for bringing her ship and her mates home safely. The loud creaking of old wood interrupted her prayer as the side hatch of the ship was opened and Marc, the stable boy, led the horses out to the dock.

"My lady," said Gavin as he walked upon the sand.

"It is good to see you home safely, Squire," said Viviane.

"Tis good to be home."

Vivian stroked Gavin's cheek and he smiled back. The cousin of Peter, who was schooling him in the ways of knighthood, Gavin had come to live in Camelot after his mother died. He became a squire a year ago and he already was showing that his knighthood would soon follow.

Viviane continued her watch for the high priests. She removed the veil from her brow to reveal the crescent moon tattoo so that the priests could see that she was in the service of the Goddess and a High Priestess of the Lake. She remained steadfast near the landing, looking into the ship for the two men.

A faint hint of incense caught hold of Viviane's senses. From the caverns of the ship, she heard the voices of her priests chanting greetings as they blessed the ship and the soil of Avalon.

"*Elffyntodd Dwyr Sinddyn Duw!*" Viviane heard the chant and joined voices with them "*Cerrig yr FFerllurg Nwyn; Os Syraiaeth ech Saffer tu fewr Echlyn mor, Necrombor Llun.*" She bowed to the priests as they sanctified her with the censer.

"I am honored by your blessing," said a humbled Viviane.

"Please Viviane, Lady of the Lake and mother to Avalon, it is we who are honored to be in thy presence." Emotion welled up in Viviane as the High Priest Blaise raised her hand to his lips and kissed it gently. "I am Blaise, and this is Aaron, my successor when nature sees fit to make it so." Aaron showed the same respect to the lady, kissing her gently on the hand.

"What news have you of Merlin?" asked a worried Joseph.

"He is not well, my lord. The fever continues to ravage him," said Viviane turning and gesturing to her novices. "My ladies have prepared food and drink, and then we will travel to Camelot."

Joseph looked around at the Isle of Avalon. He turned to ask, "Lady, what news of my mother?"

Viviane felt her excited expression withdraw as she placed her eyes on Joseph.

"She is not here?" he asked.

Viviane reached for his forearm. "We will find the answers."

Joseph managed to give Viviane a hint of a smile and turned and jogged towards the ship to start unloading her cargo. "Michael and Luke!"

"My lord, what is it you wish?" bowed Luke.

"Assist the lady and our guests to the cottage. I will join them soon. Go and tell the king we are home."

Both Michael and Luke bowed their heads to Joseph and carried the priests' belongings on horseback, leading them up to the grassy knoll of the isle.

CHAPTER TWENTY-ONE

A Pantry of Healing

◄──◆──►

"My lady, I thank thee for such a fine feast," said Blaise to Viviane. She was proud of her home and took pleasure in serving guests. Blaise walked around the room and as he examined the adornments, Viviane's eyes followed to each place that Blaise was looking. She felt pride in the feminine design of her domain. Columns at least two feet in diameter and ten feet tall saw fit to hold the ceiling high above their heads. It was painted white and carved within the molding were the birds that flew on the Isle of Avalon. "I see you fancy birds of prey, my lady."

"I do, my lord priest. As you can see, the falcon is king in my home." She stretched out her arm, and a falcon flew from the column shelf and landed on her. She pet him with generous strokes. "The ravens and crows etched in the mortar are his subjects."

Blaise smiled at her and attempted to pet the falcon who screeched. Viviane warned him, "Evyn does not take to strangers."

Blaise backed away towards the sitting area where he made himself comfortable. Viviane's furniture was cream painted wood with fine silk cushions. Scarves of deep jeweled tones adorned the room. Flowers of every species hung from the rails and borders. Mixed with the aroma of the food on the table was the lingering fragrance of jasmine and lavender oil; a mixture of Viviane's making to intoxicate her guests into peacefulness. She was glad to welcome anyone who graced her home.

"My lord priest, these are the ladies that you should thank for this feast. It is they who created these delicacies."

Blaise turned to Viviane's novitiates, who she smiled on with motherly pride. "Students of the isle, you have learned well the harvest feast of the Mother. We thank you for sharing her food with us."

The Ladies bowed to Blaise and left to clean the table and prepare the herbs and oils for evening meditation.

"It has been many seasons since we have dined in the adornments of a cottage."

"I understand, Aaron, that you are men of the woods."

Aaron looked at Viviane, "I am glad that you know the rites of the order."

Viviane gently bowed her head again. "I would not be the High Priestess of the Lake if I were not knowledgeable in my faith or in the Mother."

One of the novitiates entered the room. "Excuse me, my lady, but Sir Joseph has arrived and is anxious to leave for the castle."

Sir Joseph walked into Viviane's dining room. She could see his weariness in his slowness of pace.

"Anna, please set a plate for Joseph." Anna bowed and left for the kitchen.

Joseph addressed the priest. "Master Blaise, I would like to be underway as soon as possible. My lord Galahad awaits and is most anxious for your arrival."

"My lady, please show to me the cabinet where you keep your herbs," requested Blaise as he and Aaron rose from their chairs. "It is most urgent that I know what your pantry holds."

"Come, Blaise. It is on the other side of this wall."

Blaise and Viviane left the room and walked over to the herb pantry. Viviane proudly opened the door as she knew that her pantry was in line with the ordinances and councils of the rites of the Druids.

Blaise walked into the pantry, looked around and inhaled the aromatics of the closet. On the wall hung black willow bark, valerian root, mugwort, sage, mandrake and Echinacea. Chamomile sat in wooden bowls drying on the shelf. Thyme and myrrh were housed in a silver cup to keep their oils from being absorbed into the wood. Rose and lavender petals were soaked in safflower oil to absorb the aroma of the flowers. Fennel seeds were sitting on fine linens drying, and in clay jars was fresh honey harvested from the hives on the shores of Avalon. On the wall was the pentacle, and around the pentacle were etched the symbols of the Druid calendar, marking the seasons, the holidays and the times of the year when the moon was at its highest phases. On the side wall were the tools that Viviane used. Every tool was made from the Mother Earth herself: the wooden hoe, rakes, shovels and picks to dig the proper holes for fencing in the herbs.

Blaise turned to Viviane. "My dear High Priestess, never have I seen a pantry so properly fit such as I would have in my own hut."

Viviane smiled with pride. She had studied the laws of her faith well and knew the rights and respects of herbal law.

"What herbs have you used on Merlin?"

Viviane pulled the black willow bark from the wall, and grabbed the Echinacea, chamomile and valerian root.

"And how were these mixed?"

"I used two husks of willow bark. Chopping them in small pieces, I brewed them into a tisane to bring down the fever, which only worked for a short time. I mixed it in the chamomile, using only a spoon of the powdered tea leaves, and I added a pinch of valerian root when Merlin showed signs of pain." Viviane placed some of the tea leaves in Blaise's hand.

"And what of the Echinacea? Did that not ward off the infection to fight the fever?"

Viviane shook her head and took a deep breath. "Little I have done in the past two weeks has brought any comfort to Merlin." She dropped her head and sighed.

"My lady, thank you for such a fine meal," said Joseph as he made his way to the pantry. "Please, I have asked two of your novitiates to bring the priests' horses and your steed around. We must make haste to Camelot."

Viviane ran quickly and snatched her rider's cloak from the hook outside the pantry door. Without delay, she and her revered guests left for Merlin's side.

Chapter Twenty-Two

The Plight to an Ailing Merlin

The Lady Viviane and her riding party departed for the castle of Galahad with Joseph leading the way in silence. It was plain to Viviane that his mind was focused on making sure that Blaise and Aaron arrived in Camelot safe and in one piece. Viviane was joined by Luke, who had been commanded to remain behind and guard the others.

"My lady, please tell me more about what you have done for Merlin," requested Blaise.

Viviane turned to answer as they rode. "Priest, I have done everything humanly possible, but Merlin does not heed to my medicines."

"His chest is clear?"

"Yes, it is, Aaron."

"There is not one sign of a wound on the skin?"

"No. Not one opened sore." She closed her eyes, taking assessment. "Nothing, my master."

Viviane could see the wheels of thought turning behind his eyes. "And what of mandragora? Could it be a dark spell?"

Viviane felt despair overtake her. "I do not know." She dared to tell Blaise, "Even the Christian priests tried using their medicines on Merlin."

Blaise shot her a sneer of distain. "Do not tell me that they used their crosses and holy waters on the Druid."

"My lord priest, they said their prayers over him at the request of Nimue and Galahad."

"I fully understand that Merlin married out of his faith and that Nimue is a Christian." He gave Viviane a look of contempt. "It pains me to know that we Pagans respect these Christians for who they have become." His look of disgust turned to a cautionary glare as Viviane took watch and sighted Camelot city ahead. "Aaron, be warned that these Catholic priests will do everything in their power to convert us."

"So you have told me many times before."

"Please, I beg you!" said Viviane with advice on her tongue. "His Majesty Galahad, as did King Arthur, respects the creeds of all who enter his castle. The church has been made to stay clear of his politics."

Blaise's tone relaxed a bit. "I will thank His Majesty when I see him for the respect he has shown my fellow man of oak. But know this, my lady: I will not have these priests defile my vows. I come in peace in the name of the Goddess, and any Christians should return that harmony for the sake of the Merlin."

Joseph turned and Viviane caught sight as he waved his hand to Luke, who was still with her. It was the signal to advance as he hurried the group to the castle. Joseph yelled back, "Luke, make haste. Camelot awaits us no longer!"

CHAPTER TWENTY-THREE

Galahad Greets the Druid Priests

———◆———

A soldier of Camelot stood on the fort wall looking out to the horizon just before dusk as the sun was beginning to fade in the sky. He was ordered by Galahad to sound the horn and blare it loud from the tower as soon as he sighted Sir Joseph's riding party. Galahad wanted his brother's homecoming announced with joy, for he was so proud to call him 'brother.'

A group of riders approached the castle grounds. Looking at the two men leading the group, the soldier tried to discern the garments they were wearing and what appeared to be a banner flying above one of the riders. The wind blew hard, and he could not determine what insignia they flew. What he could see was that they were attired in blue-grey rider's cloaks, their heads covered to keep away the chill of night. They were outfitted with black knee-high boots, and as they came closer, the squire saw that they were armed.

"Man your stations!" he sounded the warning to his fellow guards, never taking his eyes off the forthcoming party. As they drew closer, the Celtic cross and the crescent moon of Camelot came into view. It was the crest of the knights of Galahad. Sir Joseph and Sir Luke led this group, followed closely by Lady Viviane, one squire and two unknown men.

"He has returned with aid for Merlin," the young soldier said aloud. "Raise the gates! Sir Joseph returns!"

Hearing the fanfare announcing them, Joseph looked up and saw the young man tooting his horn as the gates were lifted. He smiled, as he would be most proud to bring his report to Sir Gawain and see his betrothed, the Lady Leonora Agavene. He and his riders were met with cheers as they rode though the gates.

"Your brother is quite anxious to see you!" yelled Viviane over the horn's blare.

Joseph took a deep breath as he rode through the entrance of the village square towards the castle steps. He looked up and—with the aid of the torches held by pages—he saw his brother standing at the top landing of the castle keep waiting for him with Sir Michael. Joseph's horse arrived at the bottom of the steps, and Galahad ran down to greet him.

Joseph dismounted and Galahad embraced him before he could say a word. "Thank God you have returned!"

There was a great deal of angst in that embrace, and Joseph removed his hood and looked into his brothers aching blue eyes. Galahad held firm to Joseph's forearm as Blaise, Aaron, and Viviane dismounted their steeds.

"Blaise and Aaron are here, my lord," said Sir Luke as he joined Joseph in bowing his head to respect their king.

"I am glad that you are home, Luke!" said Galahad as he reached for Luke's shoulder. Although Joseph was tired from his journey, he could see that Galahad's knuckles had turned pale from the grasp he held on Luke. Galahad was in obvious need of his honored guests and turned to look upon the priests and Viviane. There was a hint of relief on his face yet he never let go of Luke's shoulder or Joseph's arm. Joseph felt his forearm cramp from the hold before Galahad discreetly allowed him to lead them all in greeting the priests.

"My lord, I give you Blaise and Aaron!"

The high priests and Viviane had already started to make their way towards the steps. Blaise and Aaron approached the king with a firm bow of their heads. Galahad released his grip from Joseph and Luke, and allowed Blaise to show his respects by taking the king's hand and kissing his signet ring. Aaron followed suit with the same gesture. Galahad embraced the Druids in a bear hug, as though they were long lost relatives.

"Lady Viviane, your presence here is always a joy." Galahad kissed the woman on the hand after releasing the priests.

She smiled at Joseph with a look that told him she was ready for anything. After her greeting, she quickly made her way into the castle. "I will go to Nimue and await you in her chambers."

Viviane ran through the open door of the castle, and the riding party and their king were escorted towards the drawing room by a young page.

Joseph removed his cloak and placed it on a nearby chair upon their arrival. His eyes quickly scanned the accoutrements of the room: a fireplace, comfortable upholstered armchairs, arched framed windows. He wanted so much to go to Leonora, but his duties came first and he would see them to their end.

"My lord, my men are tired. May I dismiss them?"

Galahad waved his hand, and Joseph commenced relieving his crew.

"My lord Luke," said Joseph, "please tell your father and Leonora, that I will speak with them later this evening."

"My lord!" said Luke with a clenched fist to his chest. He left to see his father.

"My lord Michael, take rest this evening. In the morning take Gavin and see to the cargo on the ship. Prepare the inventory and the report for Lady Viviane."

Sir Michael, too, saluted Joseph, and left the drawing room.

"I trust that you have been fed," said Galahad continuing the protocol of his castle for his guests.

Blaise nodded his head. "Lady Viviane has been most gracious." Joseph read Galahad's smile as one of relief, hearing that the Druids had been cared for. "My lord, what have you to say on Merlin's behalf?"

continued Blaise.

"I trust that my brother has informed you well," said the king as he turned his head towards Joseph.

"He has been a true leader on this journey," replied Blaise.

Joseph's eyes caught sight of Merlin's pipe and tobacco pouch sitting in the ashtray on the mantle, waiting for the wizard to partake of its pleasures.

Aaron spoke up, "My lord, please. What can we do for the wizard?"

"My priest, he is very ill. The fever rages in him without mercy, I fear if you do not have aid for him, the wizard will die."

Blaise pursed his lips, replying, "Do you have enough faith in the Mother's medicine to allow Aaron, Lady Viviane and me to do our work to save the Druid?"

Joseph watched as Galahad held his cross under his tunic; he did this often when his faith was tested, and Joseph knew that his brother would have to disavow his Christian faith and allow these Druids to practice their Pagan laws in his home for Merlin to live.

Galahad approached the Druid and placed his hand on Blaise's shoulder. "My lord priest, do what your ordinances allow for healing. It is not only the will of the Mother that I seek, but I am beseeching the will of my God to grant Merlin his life."

"I am glad to be in your presence, Your Majesty. Let the will of both the Goddess and your God seek out Merlin's renewed health."

It was Joseph's honor to witness, this day, the joining of his brother, the king, and the Druid priests as they bowed heads to one another respecting each other's station.

"Come, let us go to Merlin," requested Galahad. Joseph was about to follow when Galahad raised his hand. "Joseph, stay and take thee rest, then go to Leonora." Joseph joyfully gave the reins back to his brother as the young page lit the hand torch with the fire from the fireplace before leading his king and his guests out of the room and up the stairs to Merlin's chambers.

Joseph raised Merlin's pipe; he could still smell the cherry tobacco and a hint of linden flowers in the bowl. He closed his eyes and hoped to God that all would be well.

CHAPTER TWENTY-FOUR

The Priests Examine Merlin

———◆———

Nimue sat in the chair across from Merlin's bed, having fallen asleep, exhausted from the toils of caring for her husband. She awakened startled by a sudden knock on the door and rose from the chair with great difficulty. To her surprise, it was not just Galahad who stood on the other side of the door but a group of people, two of whom she did not know.

She heard footsteps in back of her and turned to see Viviane, who must have entered the room to care for Merlin while Nimue slept.

Viviane spoke, "Sister, you may rest now. We bring you Blaise and Aaron."

Nimue tried to focus on the two tall Druid men, but the haze of her stuper clouded her mind. Galahad took her hand and introduced the strangers.

"My lady Nimue, spouse of Merlin and daughter of Lord Ardent, I give you Blaise and Aaron, high Druid priests and fellow men of oak to heal your husband, Merlin."

Nimue stared at the men. Fatigue would not allow the words to come.

Blaise extended his hand in greeting. Nimue followed his lead and extended her own. Blaise kissed it gently. "My lady Nimue, it is an honor to meet the wife of our revered friend."

Nimue looked over her shoulder to her husband who lay in such a deep sleep. "Reverence is a kind gesture, Priest, but the only reverence now would be to bring him back to health. Do you have this kind of regard for him?"

"My lady, may we examine your husband?"

Nimue looked upon Galahad for approval. Galahad broke a small smile and looked over to Merlin with an assuring nod of the head.

Nimue took a quiet breath, "Go, please, and give my husband aid."

Blaise and Aaron walked across the room to Merlin's side. Nimue stood at the foot of the bed, and Blaise put out his hand as though feeling the heat of Merlin's body. Merlin tossed violently back and forth on his pillow, the muscles on his face tensing in spasm. His features twisted and his mouth opened wide as though he would scream, but not a word came from the silent rage.

Nimue held hard to the bed post. "What has happened to my sweet beloved?"

"For the love of the Goddess, my lady," commented Blaise. "How has the wizard been able to endure this kind of heat?" Blaise placed his hand on Merlin's head and chest. "What kind of infection has caused such an illness?"

"I know not, but I fear that it will be his death."

Merlin growled in his sleep, and his eyes suddenly popped opened and he looked around the room. Nimue felt frightened, as this was a new behavior in the mix of the fever. Galahad stepped to her side, taking hold of her hand. Nimue turned away and felt time slow as she looked at all the faces—contorted, confused, and horrified—staring down upon her husband.

Aaron urgently made his way to the table where the medicines were kept. "Are these, Lady Viviane, the herbs you have used from your pantry?"

Viviane rushed to his side. "Yes, as you can see we dispensed willow bark, valerian mixed with linden flowers we had picked just this morning, chamomile for brewing and Echinacea.

"My lady, quickly, how long have you been using these medicines?" asked Aaron.

Nimue turned to Aaron, taking over and blurting out, "Two weeks now and there is no recourse for my husband."

"May we proceed with our medicines, Majesty?"

Nimue looked to Galahad. Her apprehension was growing but so was the urgency for care.

"Good priest, your answer lies with the Lady Nimue," answered Galahad.

Nimue shouted to Galahad over the constant groaning of her husband. "My lord, you told me that these are the men who healed you and led you to the gates of the Holy Grail."

Galahad grabbed Nimue by the shoulders. She was trembling and accompanied by his touch, she felt a growing anxiety. "My lady, these are Blaise and Aaron, and they did show us the way to the Holy Grail."

Nimue quickly made the sign of the cross on herself. "If these men led you to the Grail, by the will of God let them lead my husband home to me."

"By the ordinances of our Druid faith and the Mother Goddess, we will practice every law allowed to bring our brother home to you..." Blaise turned and looked at Merlin. "If it is the will of the Mother that he be healed, he will be healed."

Aaron stepped between Merlin and the group. "My lord, we ask that all leave the room."

No more words were said. Everyone in the room rushed to exit so that the priests could do their work.

"May I stay?" asked Nimue, turning by the door, her voice cracking.

Viviane assumed the lead. "Sister, let me heal you of your toils so that you may regain your own strength."

Nimue ran back to her husband, kissing him gently on the cheek before allowing Viviane to lead her out of the room.

CHAPTER TWENTY-FIVE

Merlin's Fight for Life

"Nimue, my wife, don't leave me!" Merlin cried out in his fever, but no one seemed to hear him. His voice was trapped in his chest and so he screamed again, "Nimue!" Searching for her, his eyes opened again, but he could not control them, and they rolled around in his head.

The door slammed closed, and in his delusionary state, it echoed and resonated as though through a tunnel. "Don't leave me!" he yelled at Nimue, but again his voice would not pass from his throat.

Strange voices uttered over him, voices that sounded like the muddled, squeaking rats that made their homes in the infested dungeons under the castle.

"Who's there?" he tried to call out frantically.

Eyes open again, but covered in a haze of gray, Merlin saw the black shadow of a man walk around him and come to his side with a lit torch. Suddenly flames were licking towards him, engulfing him in his bed. He tried to pull away, but the heat still seared into his legs, his face, his shoulders, his hands. In a moment, he was running down a series of passages in a cave, but the fire was following him, the sound of the crackling flames echoing through the narrow corridor. At the mouth of the cavern was a figure coming towards him, choking on a hideous laugh.

"What is it you want? Leave me alone!!" he yelled as he tried to find cover behind the gray mortared wall.

Just as suddenly as he had found himself in the cave, he was back in bed in his room, hands upon him, pawing uncontrollably at him, ripping at his clothing. He pushed away at his assailants, but the hands kept coming, touching him, pulling at him, seeming to pierce his skin and pull at his organs as his body temperature dropped from raging hot to frigid cold. "Cover me—somebody cover me!!!" he screamed, but no one came to his rescue.

⸻◆⸻

Blaise looked upon his friend, taking mental note as to how the years had deteriorated his body. Here lay a man who was once firm from head to toe. In his day, Merlin's chest was that of a god's, strong and taut; now the muscles sagged with age, and only the shadow of the young man lay before them.

Placing his head on the wizard's chest, his cheek absorbed the heat from the fever. He listened to him breathe and to the beat of his heart; its beats were rapid warding off the fever but strong as they pounded at the muscle in his breast bone and his lungs were as clear as a calm flowing lake.

Blaise stood back, stroking his beard, scanning every inch of Merlin. He picked up the wizard's arms, checking for bruises and wounds. Only scars from injuries of days gone by remained. He checked his legs for the same. There were none. Turning Merlin on his side, they checked his back. Merlin started to moan again.

Blaise turned him back over and redressed him before covering him under the blankets. "Aaron, prepare the room for meditation."

Aaron opened the velvet grey bag that Blaise had brought with them from their forest. Removing a piece of wood within which a pentacle was carved, he placed the pentacle on the floor, picked up a gold braided rope and encircled the star within it. Under it, he placed a white rune with the crescent moon burned into it and right above the pentacle a gold rune which was cut in the round and spiked at the edges, imitating the rays of the sun.

He opened his medicine satchel removing a wooden bowl, blue-green petals and three large reddish brown husks. A small pouch was removed from the bag and placed on the table. Out from the pouch came three black stones, and Aaron placed them in the fireplace, tossing them around in the embers. When the stones turned red, he moved them with a wooden spoon to the wooden bowl. Tearing off small pieces of the husk, he placed these over the hot rocks, which turned them to ash, releasing their fragrance into the air.

Aaron circled his hands around in the vapors that now wafted from the bowl and a strong scent of cedar enveloped the room. Placing the bowl on top of the pentacle, he allowed the star to bless the herbs that the bowl held. Blaise joined Aaron near the fire, and they chanted vowel and syllabic sounds that filled the quiet of the room. Standing atop the fire and holding his hands high, Blaise prayed, "We ask thee, oh Mother Goddess, aid in the healing of our brother Merlin." The fire growled in the hearth as the mixture of the Goddess burned and created a fog that spread throughout the room. "Mother, we beseech your knowledge of all that is good in this world and ask you to find favor with us in this, our hour of need." The fire bellowed even louder. "*Ciariac saffer ech mor to lun*," prayed Blaise.

He and Aaron stood beside Merlin's bed, one at the right, the other on the left. They joined hands making an arch over the wizard. "Goddess Mother, here lies Merlin, your most cherished high priest and holy servant to your cause. Grant him renewed health at this most urgent of moments." Merlin started to writhe in his bed, his fever raging harder as the priests' prayer filled the room.

For a brief moment, Merlin was an apparition, floating on the waters of the lake of Avalon. It was as though he was on a raft, and the waters were carrying him under the trees that lined the lake. He felt pressure on his chest, heavy as an anvil and in an instant, he sank in the waters, as though drowning pool. He tried to raise his arms to push through the raging current, but felt paralyzed. "Help me!" he yelled and in return, his ears filled with tribal chanting.

"*Inogan mendor Mammeah sool.* Mother Goddess, I give you the pentacle, your elements of earth, air, water and fire. Bless thy spirit and return Merlin to us."

Merlin fought against the water, releasing a cry, but this time sound exploded from his chest like a thundering herd of bulls running on the ground.

"Yes, Merlin, come, we hear you. Come home to us!" cried the voice. "Keep chanting, Aaron!"

"*Mammeah mendorian sool vorgin dah*!!"

"Merlin, come on, you must control yourself...Aaron restrain him...I beseech the Goddess, bless her symbols and heal thy servant."

Merlin screamed again, feeling as though his chest would burst apart from the crushing pain that surged through his ribs. He felt the desire to flail, but his hands and feet were held by slithering snakes.

"Hurry, Aaron, he hears you! Toss the herbs of the mother into the fireplace."

"Blessed Goddess, prepare the instruments I give to thee. Here are your leaves of eucalyptus, petals of the sage bush and the willow bark of your mighty trees. Their fragrance will cleanse and heal."

<hr>

Blaise watched as Merlin coughed hard at the scent of the mixture entering his breathing passages. He choked again as though in his sleep, he knew the problem and this was not the answer. Through the cough, Merlin wailed long and hard. "Ariaaaanna!" he groaned bringing her name forth.

Aaron looked down at Merlin. "He speaks."

"What did he say?" asked Blaise.

"I do not know, sir."

Merlin moaned again—this time louder. Out from this pain came what sounded like a word: "Ariaaaaaanna!" He labored to breath.

"Aaron, soak some linens in that water over there." Aaron obeyed the order, going over to the table and soaking the cloths. Blaise seized them and washed Merlin down at the face and chest.

Merlin screamed in pain as the cold water poured onto his hot body. "Arianna! Arianna!" he cried, tears rolling down his face.

Blaise was beside himself. "How can I heal an illness I cannot see?"

"Arianna," Merlin whispered under his breath. This time he reached out, but there was still no comfort.

After a moment of perplexing silence, finally Blaise spoke. "Aaron, go. Find Galahad. We must know what this Arianna is."

CHAPTER TWENTY-SIX

An Urgent Prayer

Galahad came running up the back stairs from the galley where he and Joseph were catching up on family affairs. Aaron opened the door for him, and Galahad ran into Merlin's smoke-filled but well lit room. There in the middle of the floor was the Druid star encircled by stones with symbols etched into them. The aroma in the room brought memories back to Galahad, as this was the scent used in aid for his own healing. He felt for his cross that was hidden beneath his shirt. *God of my fathers, aid us.* He looked upon Merlin, whose face was even more pallid than before, and he gasped at the sight of the ecru colored window cords that were tied to Merlin's bedposts, restraining his hands and feet. "What in the name of God have you done to him?"

Blaise looked up at Galahad from where he was sitting across from Merlin. The priest looked completely devoid of energy, as though it had been siphoned from his body. "Majesty, I wish I could give you answers, but I fear I have them not. I can tell you that whatever this fever is, it is causing my fellow priest to act in ways that are not his own"

"I do not understand, Blaise. Why is my mentor tied to the bed?"

Blaise wobbled as he stood and stepped back to Merlin's side. Taking the cup from the table next to Merlin's bed, he placed some of the chamomile tisane within it and mixed a spoon of dried valerian root into the tea. "Your Majesty, while we examined and prayed over the wizard, he became violent, thrashing his legs and arms, striking at us." Blaise picked up Merlin's head and slowly poured the mixture down his throat. "At any time before we came, did this maddening behavior show itself?"

"No, master, never did he once abuse any of us in his illness."

Merlin fought to swallow the tea, the majority of which ran down the side of his face. Blaise massaged his throat so that the liquid would settle. He looked hard at Galahad, "Does anyone wish ill will to the wizard?"

Galahad looked back at Blaise. "What do you mean by *ill will*, master?"

Blaise's eyes opened wide. "Is there someone here who Merlin has some argument with? Someone who would wish harm to him?"

Galahad laughed morosely, "Master, the only two people who Merlin argues with are Nimue and Viviane."

Blaise pinched his eyebrows, listening. "There is no one else?"

Galahad pushed the curtains aside and looked out the window thinking. He shook his head. "Master, there are days that we have fought, but the quarrels are only in the name of love—not in hate or ill will."

Merlin moaned again, and the cry pierced through Galahad's heart. He rushed towards the wizard. Uncomfortable with the ropes attached to the bed, he undid them and brought the ties back to the window and retied the dressing. "I do not want Nimue to see this. She has enough to bear."

Galahad stepped back to Merlin's side, picked up a cloth and dried the wizard's beard. The gray hairs felt course, and the strands were a bit mangled from Merlin being bedridden for so long.

Blaise asked again, "You are sure that there is no one here or in his travels that has wished this man," he pointed to Merlin, "ill will?"

"Travels? He walks the grounds these days, master. He and Nimue stay close to home."

Blaise and Aaron looked at each other. It was evident to Galahad that they were at a loss. Blaise walked over to the wall. Taking Merlin's walking stick, he held it firmly and looked up at Galahad. "Is there something called 'arianna' in these parts?"

Galahad nearly choked. "Arianna! Yes, there most certainly is someone in his life named Arianna." He looked at the priest. "Why do you ask about this woman?"

"I never heard of such a woman," said Blaise.

Galahad closed his eyes. These men, though high priests of their faith, had no knowledge of the mystery of Arianna. "The Lady Arianna Lawrence Pendragon is my adopted mother, the birth mother of Sir Joseph, the guardian of Excalibur, and a close and faithful friend of Merlin and King Arthur."

Blaise looked at Galahad, his expression was blank. "Say her name again, please."

"Arianna," Galahad said. "Why are you asking this question?"

"Merlin kept moaning her name in his rage."

Galahad played with the ring on his hand, the ring he and his mother formed a promise on years ago. "Come, Master Blaise. I can show you who Arianna is."

CHAPTER TWENTY-SEVEN

A Portrait Transcending Time

———◦◆◦———

Galahad and Blaise walked down the stairs and through the back hall towards the Round Table room. Galahad's guards stood at the head and foot of the corridor, keeping sentry watch over their king.

Galahad brought Blaise through the passageway of history. The Druid was faced with the portraits of King Uther Pendragon and Lady Igraine of Cornwall, King Arthur's father and mother. To his right was the image of Sir Mordred Pendragon, King Arthur's son and nephew, birthed by his sister Morgaine. Hanging to his left was a picture of Sir Lancelot and Lady Elaine of Astolate, Galahad's biological parents. Mounted high on the wall atop the entrance doors to the Round Table room was the portrait of King Arthur himself, standing majestically in his pendragon cloak and holding his precious Excalibur. Blaise placed his hand over his heart as he stared at the portrait of the dead king. The long wavy brown hair, blue eyes and strongly chiseled features showed the powerful character that this man carried through his life. Blaise bowed his head in respect and reverence to the memory of the man who was loved and cherished by all. Galahad took a breath at the gesture and he, too, bowed to his uncle.

At the entryway to the Round Table room, two well-armed guards stood at attention when Galahad made his appearance. Directly outside the room was the painting of Lady Miriam Dougray—wife of Galahad,

Queen of Camelot and mother to John Arthur du Lac, the prince and heir to Camelot. Galahad placed a kiss on his finger and touched the kiss to her lips.

"Your heart still beats for her," commented Blaise.

"Even in death, love holds me captive for my Miriam. There will be no other who can fill her place."

Hanging about a foot away from Miriam was John Arthur's portrait. Galahad smiled as he looked at his son's whimsical expression in the painting. From there, he turned to the other side of the hallway. "Here she is, Blaise. This is Lady Arianna." Galahad stood back and watched the Priest ogle the portrait.

"She is a beautiful lady, sire."

Galahad stared at the picture and replied, "Yes, she is."

"I see she wears the ring of Arthur."

"She does, sir." Galahad smiled, remembering the time he gave it to her.

"And Merlin sits next to her."

"Separating their portraits would be an act of treachery."

Blaise ambled over to study Arianna's painting. "Who, sire, is the artist?"

"I am, Blaise."

"Your attention to each brushstroke and your use of color to shadow the light to enhance the portrait is impressive."

<hr />

Blaise placed his finger on a brushstroke of Arianna's hair, running it down the shape of her shoulder. A chill passed through him. He turned away from the painting and down in the caverns of the hall he saw a woman dressed in the garments of another place. Standing near a body of water, she held a dirt-encrusted Excalibur in her hands. Merlin was nearby, but he, too, was dressed in clothing unlike anything the priest had ever seen before. He reached for Galahad.

"Are you ill, master?"

He looked down the hall again, breathing heavily. The vision vanished, and his eyes found their way back to the portrait. While simultaneously experiencing a heaviness of his physical being, he felt his spirit rising from his body. Blaise approached the painting and touched it again. Visions filled his head, like the oils on the canvas. He saw Arianna atop a hill, being accosted by two knights. Then she was standing in Arthur's court with her hands bound, knights screaming at her. "Witch!" Blaise held onto the painting, his eyes scanning her face, sweat pouring down his own.

"Sir, are you alright?" asked Galahad as he came to touch him. Blaise saw his king, but could not feel his touch and instead stood there bound to the painting.

"You, guard, go to Merlin's room," Blaise heard Galahad say. "Tell Aaron he is needed here."

Blaise's eyes were entranced. His body was in the hall, but his mind was in the forest at the lake in Avalon. He saw Arianna on her knees, submerging Excalibur into the lake from which she was forged. Arianna was delicately washing the sword, and when she lifted the blade from the water, Excalibur sang for her. The song rang in Blaise's ears.

From his periphery in the hall, Blaise heard Galahad's Excalibur sing in her sheath. He turned to the song and smiled.

"Excalibur has not sung for me like that in ages," said Galahad. "What is going on, Blaise?"

He could not answer as he was watching Arianna in a new vision. She stood between two trees by the water's edge. In front of her, Arthur was in high battle with his son. The young prince slashed at Arthur's chest plate, the blade squealing as it pierced his ribs and then withdrew from his body. Arthur ran Mordred through with Excalibur, and the young man fell to the ground slain. Arthur died in Merlin's arms, his own wounds gushing his life onto the Mother Earth.

"Arthur, no!" Arianna screamed as tears fell from the eyes of Blaise.

"Aaron, what is wrong with Blaise?" he heard Galahad ask his fellow Priest.

"My lord, Blaise is with the Mother right now. She gives him the sight."

He cried out, "Arthur!" and pushed away from the painting, running off down the hallway. When he arrived at the doors of the Round Table room, he thrust them open and stood staring at the infamous Round Table now engulfed in flames. Arthur was on his funeral pyre, his body burning.

Blaise fell to his knees crying, "No, no, you did not burn him!"

He felt his eyes wide open, moving back and forth quickly, trying to focus, but unable. A gust of wind ran through the Round Table room—its breeze flared the burning fire in the hollow center of the table. Voices from the past filled the room as Blaise walked around touching the chairs and listening to the voices of days gone by.

He saw a woman in a dress stained by the crimson of battle, carrying a bloody Excalibur to King Arthur's chair.

"Arianna, who will be the heir to Excalibur?" Blaise heard the question coming from the walls.

"I choose Galahad," the woman answered as Blaise saw her lock eyes with Merlin.

He reached for his chest, struggling to stand.

"No, my lord Galahad, you must not touch him," he heard Aaron yell. "This must not be stopped. The high priest must finish the sight."

Blaise's eyes fell upon the wall over Galahad's chair. The stones opened into another world, one he was not privy to. A woman in traveler's clothing sat on her horse, her voice commanding, "I, Arianna, Lady Lawrence Pendragon, daughter of Avalon, ask the God of heaven and the Goddess Mother of the planet earth to reveal her most precious secrets!"

A hideous black apparition interrupted his vision. He tried to avert his eyes but the spirit pushed his hand away.

"She will die! Merlin will die!" The dark wraith was screaming at him. Blaise stood there stunned, staring at the shadow.

"Be gone, spirit!" he suddenly screamed, but the spirit hovered over the room laughing viciously.

"It is a spell that holds Merlin hostage," yelled Blaise.

The spirit laughed louder. "No. It is I, Priest, who holds my son hostage." The voice was hoarse and arrogant.

"Mab! If it is you, show yourself!" screamed Blaise towards the vision.

"Look to Stonehenge, where the high priestess will die!"

The dark evil disappeared into the fire, and Blaise was left staring at the flame burning brightly on the table.

"Arianna," he yelled. "Yes, I know who Arianna is!"

Chapter Twenty-Eight

The Secret that is Arianna

———◆———

Blaise collapsed on the floor. Galahad ran quickly to him along with Aaron. The two men knelt near the high priest, and Aaron removed his tunic and placed it under Blaise's head.

"Bring water!" yelled Galahad to a young page who stood outside the door. The boy returned within moments carrying a bowl of water and a cloth. Aaron moistened the fabric and dabbed the cool water on the Druid's head. Several moments passed in quiet, but he finally came around.

"Master, are you alright?"

"I am," said Blaise to Galahad. "Now please get me off this cold floor."

Both Galahad and Aaron assisted the elderly priest to a nearby chair. Galahad poured Blaise a mug of ale to help calm him.

Aaron stood by his mentor. "Is there anything I can do?"

Blaise drank down his ale. "Do you remember the prophecy of Élan?"

Aaron looked at his mentor. "I do."

"If this is the time of the prophecy, we have much work to do. Go and tell the Lady Viviane that I need her immediately."

Aaron bowed his head to his mentor and to Galahad and left the room with the guard following, leaving Galahad more confused than before.

Blaise remained in his chair and poured ale for Galahad. He handed him the mug and gestured, "My lord, please sit down. There is something you must know about this Arianna."

Galahad sipped his ale. He could hardly swallow it and felt a cold sweat forming in his pores. "Please tell me everything."

"Is Arianna a woman of this presence of time?"

Galahad was cautious. "If I answer you honestly, might you think of her as an entity who should have never been here in the first place?"

Blaise shot a stern expression to Galahad. "I am a man of my faith. The world is one vast puzzle, and we are the players. If the Goddess sees to place us in the presence of time that serves her and her precious planet, I shall surely not question her motives."

Galahad returned the honor. "As you are faithful to your Goddess, I am faithful to my God."

Blaise extended his arm, and the high priest of the Druids and the high lord of Camelot and finder of the Holy Grail grasped hands.

"Your mother has endured many reincarnations on the way to her final destiny."

"Reincarnations?" questioned Galahad.

"They occur when a single soul needs to live the journey of many lives in order to fulfill its destiny. The soul continues the cycle of birth, death and rebirth until it finally reaches its highest reward in the Elysium, our version of your heaven."

The guard opened the door and Viviane walked through. "My lords, what is the urgency?" she asked as she walked across the large room towards the two seated men.

"My lady, please sit down," Galahad offered her a chair next to his own.

"I am confident that Merlin is being held hostage by a dark spell," said Blaise.

Viviane grabbed at Galahad's shoulder and sat forward in her chair with an expression of pure attention. "What is it you wish from me?"

"Do you know the ordinances of exorcism?"

Viviane immediately stood. Galahad saw her hand tremble and her cheeks flush at the thought of such a ritual. "I do indeed, master."

Blaise clutched Viviane's hand and she curled her fingers around his. "Please make haste and bring back mandragora, black cohash and wolf bain for tonight. We pray in the ordinance of the Mother."

Viviane bowed to Galahad and to Blaise. Taking the folds of her skirts in her hands, she walked out the door.

Blaise turned to Galahad, "Do you want to know who Arianna really is?"

Chapter Twenty-Nine

The Holy One

———◆———

Galahad stood from his chair and walked the perimeter of the room, silent for a few moments. He looked up to the sentry post above him. There was a secret panel on the wall that led to the wizard's chambers. He closed his eyes trying to quiet the sound of Merlin's screams that could still be heard throughout the castle.

"Blaise, what you are about to tell me had better be for the good of that man suffering up there." Galahad saw a hint of a smile pass Blaise's face. "I know who my mother is and what she means to Merlin. What can you say that I do not know?"

Blaise sat back in his chair and began. "Arianna, as you call her, is named Aryanyn. Her name means *Holy One*," explained the priest.

"Holy One, you say?" remarked Galahad.

"In the years after Constantine, when the world became Christian, our people were being persecuted for their belief in the Goddess. Élan, who the Romans called Helena, gave up her faith as a high priestess and followed her son Constantine."

"I know the tale," interrupted Galahad. "She was the wife of his father Emperor Constantious. She was a Pagan and converted to Christianity when her son Constantine embraced the faith and declared Rome a Christian state. What is this prophecy?"

"Élan was a member of the sisterhood. When the first Merlin was in my position, he had a sister named Aryanyn who was known to be pure of heart and soul." Blaise brought together his hands as though in prayer. "When Aryanyn was given her crescent moon tattoo on the day that she gave her final vows to the Goddess, Élan had a vision about her."

"Like the sight that you and Merlin are gifted with?"

"That is exactly what I mean."

"What was Élan privileged to see, Master Blaise?"

"Élan saw Aryanyn in the form of several women—women whose fatal flaw was the willingness to sacrifice themselves for others."

Galahad held tight to the leather vestment over his heart.

"Only the true Aryanyn can open the gates of other worlds, and if this Arianna can open portals to both her world and others, then she is Aryanyn, the Holy One, and the prophecy of Élan is about to unfold."

Galahad felt a solemnity pass though him as he tried to internalize what this priest was saying. "Please, tell me the rest of your tale."

Blaise reached for Galahad's hand. "Sire, Élan saw the High King Constantine and King Arthur the Great Bear, who were both born of Pagan faith and adopted Christianity as their own. Arthur and Constantine were both steadfast in their quest for the Grail and the wood of the cross. In her sight, Élan saw Arthur and Constantine standing with Aryanyn, who brought them together for the good of both religions. It is those three—who are of both faiths—who will complete the quest for unity in our worlds."

Galahad retreated a moment, thinking. "Are you saying that Arthur Maximus Pendragon and Augusts Flavius Constantine are both going to show us the true nature of the cross and the Mother?"

Blaise clasped his hands in prayer. "You speak of truths lost in the realms of time."

"Priest, can you tell me what my precious Uncle Arthur was to find?"

"In his youth, he was to bring back the titulus of Christ. So that when you, the blood sake of the Arimathea, found the Grail, both the Grail and the titulus would unite the two worlds. But Arthur was delayed in his quest by an untimely death."

"Not to impugn your tale, sir, but these are Christian symbols—not Pagan."

"They are indeed, but for the world to be joined, a man and a woman of both houses must complete this quest for the truth." Blaise clenched one hand and folded it in the other. "The Father and the Mother must be represented for this cause." Blaise's voice was firm. "Arthur Pendragon and Aryanyn of the Isle are children of both houses, and therefore, it is their birthrights that this quest be seen to its completion."

"And what of Constantine?"

"Constantine has his role to play in securing the titulus. The titulus is the root to the Mother. Its body is bound to the Mother as Constantine is to his own mother, Élan. It is the figurative branches of this titulus that were intended to reach out to connect all of us to the Father, and the Father's bride the Goddess, the Mother Earth.

"Understand that Élan means *tree* and Aryanyn means *Holy One*. It is the women who will connect the men in time, and their unity will lead the way to unity for all. However, if Aryanyn cannot reach the ears of Constantine, he will disavow the Mother Earth and adopt Christianity as the only faith of Rome. If this should come to pass, the possibility of unity among the two houses will end.

Galahad wanted to believe this tale, but his nobility and faith told him to beware of false profits. "Priest, I ask you now, if this is true, what visions did your sight give you to claim this tale?"

Blaise closed his eyes, calling back the visions. "Tell me, sire, did she not lift Excalibur from the soil in her time? Did she not suffer under pain of trial in this very court before she was accepted into this world? Did she not wear Arthur's blood on her dress?"

Galahad sat motionless.

Blaise opened his eyes. "The high king, whose tomb states that he is the future king, must be joined together with the Holy One of the Isle for the good of all of us."

Galahad looked into the face of the high priest. "It has been told by Draco that this prophecy will take place."

"Draconian?" Blaise asked.

"Draco, as Lady Arianna calls him, is the dragon lord of all constellations. It is he who foretold of Arthur's coming to Lady Arianna and I at the grave of King Arthur."

Blaise stared into the fire on the table, then closed his eyes and replied, "So Draconian and even the stars are prepared for this union." Blaise smiled earnestly. "Let us join today for the journey at hand."

"But Master Blaise, you have not revealed to me how this unity will be possible. Why, if Arthur was to complete this quest, is he dead?"

"My lord, Arthur's murder was untimely. He must be raised."

CHAPTER THIRTY

Jack and Arianna

———◆———

Arianna hid in the office for a few days. She was sleeping on the couch and only leaving the safety of the museum to take a shower and grab some food when Jack left for the office. Today she sat quietly in the kitchen eating her breakfast. Her stomach tightened as her body received the nutrition. On her hand were both her wedding band and Arthur's signet ring, and she was playing with both of them. She looked out the window, and remembered the day when the rainbow was sent to her by Viviane: the signal to return to Camelot. How glorious the rainbow looked at Rockaway Beach in New York, as it arched its colors in the sky over the ocean and how wonderfully crazy one hundred geese looked flying in the shape of a sword through the rainbow. This was the way that Arianna, Lady Viviane, Merlin and Galahad had agreed that she would know that it was time to come home to Camelot.

Arianna played with her spoon, nervously tapping it on the table, knowing that Jack would be home from work in a few hours. She marched back to her room, decided to write him a note, and left it taped to the computer on his desk.

Dearest Jack,
I know that lately we have been angry with one another.
I hate being upset with you. We need to talk. Please

meet me by the lake near the old maple tree.
I love you,
Arianna

Going back to the office to do some work, before she knew it, it was time to leave for the lake. In the barn she outfitted Brach for his ride, reached for her rider's helmet that hung on the post near the mirror, and caught her reflection. Her fingers brushed through the raven color of her hair. Her chest heaved with anxiety. *So this is what price I pay for having faith in the Goddess.* She looked up towards the skylight and into the blue ceiling of the Mother Earth. *Is this your punishment for that faith?* Placing her helmet on her head, she mounted Brach, and led him out of the barn.

"Ha!" she yelled giving Brach a light kick on his side. Horse and rider galloped long and hard in the direction of the lake. Arianna cantered quickly through the trees. The warm wind on her face and the fragrance of the trees gave her courage, feeling the power of the Mother around her.

Arriving at the lake, she dismounted Brach and tied his reins to a tree near the water. Taking her helmet off and hanging it on the pommel of the saddle, Arianna turned to the bridge, and to the beautiful monument that Parliament had commissioned above the water near the bridge gate. It was a marble sculpture of Merlin receiving Excalibur from the Lady of the Lake, all enshrined in a massive seashell. It was breathtaking to see the great wizard and her good friend immortalized in such a manner. She laughed, though. *Immortalized in marble. What a way to be remembered.* Arianna cocked her head to the side. *Viviane, my friend, I can't remember you being that endowed. You would have a great laugh at this.*

Crossing the bridge, Arianna read the poem that stood in testimony of the history and folklore.

See
The Lady of the Lake
Throw a Pence
And make her wake
Make a wish
Wish it well
Maybe Merlin
Will cast a spell!

She laughed at the poem and pulled a penny from her pocket. Tossing it around for a moment, she threw it into the lake. "For old time's sake, my friends."

Arianna rolled up the cuff of her jacket to look at her watch. It was five in the evening. *I guess that Jack decided not to come.* Her gaze drifted to the lake and the statue of her friends and she decided to stay and enjoy the gifts of the Mother.

Returning to Brach, she grabbed the canteen from her saddlebag and drank the cool water before hanging the canteen on her belt. Arianna's purple Wicca sack caught her eye. The black velvet strings were hanging out of her bag. She pulled out the sack, untied it, laid the purple cloth on the ground and sat on the grass near the water. Pointing Gwydion's blade to the lake and the monument, she rested the sword on the blanket beside her.

Now removing some of the runes from her bag, Arianna placed the crescent moon at the right of the blade, and the sun to the left. She drew the pentacle on the soil, and placed her palm down upon it. Taking a long breath, she chanted, calling the high priestess within her to join with the Mother. She folded her hands in prayer, raising them over her head. "*Saffier Ciarac lun, f*or I am your humble servant. *Saffier Ciarac manon* for it is I who seeks the truth."

Lifting Gwydion, she placed the blue stone of the hilt to her forehead, meditating on it. *Saffier Ebbyn mor ciarac hulyn.* "I am ready, Mother. Reveal your power force and rage its might in my blood." She lowered Gwydion, holding her hilt with both hands, and rested the blade between the fold of her lotus position, concentrating on the stone.

A gust of wind wrapped around Arianna, entrancing her. Her body felt as though it was floating above the water, and she could feel no pain. She sat there meditating on the forthcoming battle, chanting over and over again, "*Saffier Ebbyn mor ciarac hulyn.* Quiet hails the power force within me."

Gwydion's blue stone glowed as Arianna was joining with her guardian in prayer and service. *Quiet hails the power force within me. Quiet hails the power force within me.*

"Arianna, what the heck are you doing?" Jack's voice sounded like it came in a dream, disturbing her concentration. "Is that your sword that is glowing? Arianna, what are you doing?" he yelled again yanking her out of her trance.

She jumped to her feet, but her head was caught in a fog; even her vision was blurred. "I thought you weren't coming." Arianna looked down at her altar. "I was praying."

"That didn't look like praying to me," Jack's face was befuddled.

A surge of heat flowed through her, "Merlin taught me to pray to the Mother this way." Arianna closed her eyes trying to stifle the powers in her body that were building towards a climax.

"I never saw you pray like that before."

Her heart was pulsating in her chest, and she could feel the blood in her arteries flowing rapidly. Every ounce of her being was attuned to the Mother Earth, and she was having massive problems controlling the arousal of her spirit. "It is a private prayer."

"What happened to the quiet Catholic girl I married a long time ago."

She was losing the battle to keep herself contained. "I am still a Christian, Jack, and still believe in Jesus with all my heart, but when I pray like this, I am heightened by my spirituality."

"Spirituality? It's a bunch of nonsense." His face was twisting in knots.

"I didn't ask you here to start another fight. We need to talk about us and things that are changing history right now."

Jack looked at the stones on the ground. He was cracking his knuckles, and watching him, she felt the pleasure that had permeated her body, all surging into her chest, mounting towards an explosion. "Could you please get rid of those?"

"I won't do that, Jack. These are a part of me."

He was visibly uncomfortable and could not look at the arrangement at her feet. "They bother me."

Incapable of stopping herself, Arianna lifted the stones from off the ground and thrust them into his face. "They are just stones." Jack turned his body away from her. Arianna placed them back on the blanket as Jack walked a few steps away from her.

She picked up Gwydion from the ground, kissed her blade and sheathed her, then started towards her husband.

Jack looked over to her. She could have started a war in defense of her new found spirituality. He knew that. He placed his hands in his pockets and let out a long clearing of the throat sound before speaking. "Ari."

Arianna looked at him. "Yes, Jack."

He again cleared his throat. "Listen, I was a real jackass the other day taking that sword from you like that."

She stood there with that distant stare of hers. "You know how important this sword is to me. You disrespected me." There was a chill in the air, but Jack noticed that his wife was sweating; her cheeks were red as though the sun beat down on her. She removed her jacket and hung it on a branch.

"I'm not you. I can't figure things out like you do, nor do I have your strength to battle problems head on without dwelling on them." He took a breath. "It's not me." Jack noticed the four-by-four bandage on her left forearm. "What happened to your arm?"

Taking hold of her hand, he felt that she was unusually hot. She pulled away and grabbed hold of her belt buckle in that boyish stance of hers. The size of her bandage distressed him.

"Tell me what happened, Ari."

"After we fought and I took refuge in the museum, I had one of my visions."

Jack felt quick to jump down her throat. "Arianna, these visions are driving me crazy!"

She held tight to her buckle reminding him of a cowgirl ready for a parlay. "Please, Jack, just listen."

"Fine," he said reluctantly.

"My vision came near Arthur's tomb, and it came from Draco."

"I don't know who Draco is."

"Draco—his real name is Draconian—is the King of the Dominion of Constellations. The one who foretold of Arthur's coming when we were home in Camelot."

He looked up towards heaven. "God help us." He was trying to hold his temper. "What does this have to do with your arm?" Jack folded his own arms in front of him.

As Arianna brought forth from her pocket the dragon's claw, giving it to Jack. He looked it over, "What is this, Ari?"

"It's Draco's claw. It was sent to me by Draco himself with a note wrapped around it."

How could he believe his wife? "What are you trying to tell me?"

"That Arthur's coming is upon us. Draco sent this to warn me to prepare."

"You're talking in riddles. What are you preparing for?" Jack said curtly.

"I, Arianna, Lady Lawrence Pendragon, wife of Jack Lawrence, sister to Avalon, confidant of Merlin and loyal friend of King Arthur, take my new quest in blood for the love of my family and for Camelot."

Her chest heaved in proud adulation and it sickened him. Jack reached for Arianna's arm and he could tell that she was trying not to show him that it hurt, but she winced and he heard it. "Did you do this to yourself?" he screamed.

"Yes, with this claw, and I will do it again if it means protecting the people I love." Jack felt contempt and fear cloak his every sense. Arianna stared back at him keeping a calm voice. "Please, Jack, I love you." She pulled down on him, reaching for him to look at her, her eyes were filling with tears. "Just listen to me. Please!"

He had to push her away, "Listen to you!" His temperature must have risen ten degrees. "I don't know who you are anymore!"

Her cheeks were getting red again, and there was a strange spark in her eye. "I asked you to come here so that I could explain what is going on in my life right now. If you don't care to know, then leave!"

"Leave? Leave now? Oh no. Ari, this is getting so good. For once, I have the ammunition on *my* side. If it means putting you in a mental ward for observation, I will!" he yelled, scaring away the birds.

"I brought you here to tell you that Merlin is in grave danger and that he needs me."

"Merlin's in grave danger?" Jack laughed morosely. "He should see his protégée!" Jack again reached for Arianna. He grabbed at her injured arm, but she pulled away from him.

"Don't touch me!" She reached into her belt purse and gave Jack the letters that Mab and Merlin and Draco wrote. "Read these and maybe you'll understand."

Jack ripped the letters from her and unrolled them. "What game is this, Ari? These look like artifacts from the museum." His eyes scanned the page of one. "This isn't even English. I can't read this."

"It's old Druid, Jack, and it's a curse on Merlin."

"I've heard enough!" Again he reached for his wife, tugging at her wounded arm and dragging her towards the car. Arianna yanked herself away and pushed him hard, almost knocking him over. He watched as she started walking up to the bridge. "Ari, your arm is bleeding!"

She turned and snarled hard at him, her eyes transfixed on his. She unsheathed Gwydion, and—taking her in both hands—she lifted the sword and struck the marble model of Excalibur. "What am I, some fallacy you call a wife?" She held onto Gwydion so hard that the muscles in her arm contorted, and her blood streamed down onto the bridge slats.

"A wife? I may not know who you are any more, but I know you are not my wife!"

"If I am not your wife, I'll remain here with my friends!" She turned and held tight to the sculpture of Excalibur. Her blood smeared onto the cream colored marble and streamed through the slats on the bridge, dripping down into the lake.

The lake reacted, as though it was receiving her offering, rippling her blood as tides in the sea. The earth rocked under Jack's feet, and from the background, he heard Brach whinny.

"Arianna!" Jack called as he ran up to help his wife. He reached for her but the bridge was shaking, swaying back and forth as though its bronze supports had turned to mud.

Jack tightened the muscles of his legs to support him from falling off the bridge. "Arianna! Reach. Come on!" he screamed, but she was holding on tightly to the statue. Her sword fell from her, and as though in slow motion, Jack saw Arianna's blood soak the hilt as the sword plunged into the water, blade first. The sound of the steel spearing the water rang in Jack's ears like the bell on Glastonbury Tower and echoed through the trees and into the valley of Avalon.

A golden light as bright as the sun sprung from the lake, and Jack averted his eyes for a moment. Looking back, he watched as the light carried the sword Gwydion, hovering safely in its rays. Jack felt aghast as he realized that the sword was singing.

Gwydion sang loud her song, and Jack saw joyful tears stream down Arianna's face as she reached out with her blood soaked arm.

"I, Arianna, Lady Lawrence Pendragon, take thee Gwydion as my sword of power today and till the end of time!"

Sweet singing pushed through the rays, and Jack's bewildered eyes followed the sword as it came to rest in the hands of its guardian. The blue stone shone on Arianna. She was the High Priestess of Avalon.

Jack stood there, recognizing that his jaw must have looked like it hit the dirt, not knowing what to think or say.

Gwydion sang softly as the light in the lake retreated, and Arianna kissed the stone and held the sword close to her heart. The last particles of light beamed down into the lake, and the water's edge returned to its once peaceful state. Jack was still frozen, taking deep breaths as though there wasn't enough air for him to breathe.

"Jack, are you alright?" He felt his face twist in contortion. "Jack, tell me you're okay."

He reached for Arianna, trying to find his balance. Arianna helped him stand firm. As Jack grabbed her bad arm, catching some of her blood, he looked at her wound, shaking his head. "Did I just see a vision?"

Arianna laughed, "I believe you did." Laughter came again, and the release of her joy made Jack feel nothing short of patronized. She laughed so hard, in fact, her jocularity caused her to hold her stomach and double over a bit. Her forearm was still bleeding, and Jack was distraught that his wife's lovely beige blouse and brown pants were highly stained with her blood.

"That really needs attention," Jack's voice was shaking.

"I have a first aid kit in my saddlebag," Arianna replied as she turned and walked to her horse. "Oh, Brach, are you alright?" Brach neighed and Jack watched Arianna caress his snout. "You're always here for me, my friend." Brach shook his head up and down, and Arianna withdrew the kit from her bag.

Jack came to her aid, helping her clean the wound with peroxide. Arianna clenched her hand as the disinfectant stung. He put some cream on it and wrapped it, but the blood quickly soaked through.

"This needs a doctor," said Jack as he looked at his wife straight in the eyes. "Are you really a high priestess?"

Arianna wet her lips and swallowed hard. "Yes, my husband. I am a high priestess by the order of Merlin and the High Lady of the Lake." Arianna unsheathed her sword. "Here, take her." Jack was reluctant, but put out his hands. "Gwydion is the sister of Excalibur. Both were forged in these waters by Viviane and Merlin."

"How has this happened to you?"

Arianna bit down on her lip, "I don't really know how or why, Jack, but this land chose me to aid it in a cause. A cause I am honored and privileged to take on."

Jack put his head down. "I guess I never really tried to hear you. I thought this was all your imagination. I feel like a fool."

She pressed her fingers to his lips. Her touch was soft. "You are not a fool, my husband. Never the fool."

He felt despondent as he tried to put together the pieces of the puzzle.

Arianna reached for him and he looked at her. She snickered, "I love you, Jack." He took a breath and entered her gentle embrace as his wife tenderly pulled his face to hers and placed a sweet kiss on his lips. She held him for a while, and he felt a bit resolved.

"Where are the letters?" she asked. Jack reached into his back pocket, thinking that he put them there when the ground started to shake.

"They're over there!" he said. "Near the rose bush by the gate."

Arianna ran over picked them up cautiously, they were fragile with age.

"You must read these carefully. They will help you understand."

Jack looked at the letters.

"I know how lost you must feel." She grabbed for his hand, and he held her tight.

"Come, we will sit over here." Arianna led him to the tree stump sitting ever so lonely one hundred yards from the lake, and together, they sat on the large remains of the tree. He looked at her as she closed her eyes. "What an irony this is. This is where I found Excalibur."

Jack's stare could not move from his wife's face. It was like looking at her for the first time. "Right here?" He saw a light in Arianna's eyes.

"Right here, hon. And it is here that you find out who I am."

Jack accepted the letters from Arianna and handled them much more tenderly than before. He read the first letter.

"What does *Ebbyn woo zyll senfynninyh...* What language is this?"

"It's old Druid." Arianna gently requested the letters back from him. "I will read this to you, and then I will explain." She grasped Jack's hand feeling confidence in his touch.

"*Ebbyn woo zyll senfynn mega amnen Myrddin efwwar dah!*"

Jack was staring again. "I would think you were another person reading that."

Arianna looked down at the letters. "I don't know how I know this language. When I read the books, it was like I was born with it on my tongue."

Jack sat motionless for a moment. "So what does it mean?"

Arianna hesitated. "The ebbing tides of evil elves have poisoned the earth around Merlin. Fear Death."

"That doesn't clarify anything for me," Jack felt overwhelming emotions surge through him.

"Merlin's mother didn't die after Mordred's death. She simply disappeared without a trace until now. Merlin received this letter from her. Read this one," she said as she passed him another letter.

Jack read some of the words. "I fear it will be your task to find retribution for her evil." He knew his face was hot and flushed with fear. "Merlin doesn't mean you, does he?"

"Yes Jack. The letter is addressed to me."

That matter-of-fact sound in her voice made him feel as though the world just crushed him. "So this is the beginning of the new quest?" his voice became hoarse.

"Yes it is," Arianna said with a calm conviction.

"Tell me what the hell is going on?" Desperation was taking him over now and he knew he could not fight it.

"The words that Mab wrote are a curse."

He had to walk away from her. "What the heck does this have to do with my wife?"

"Jack, I still don't know what this quest is or what my part is in it. All

I know is that Mab is holding the wall to the other world closed so that I cannot pass through."

He shook his head. "Hon, this is really scaring me." Taking Arianna by her good hand, he felt a strength in her that he wanted to embrace but was afraid to.

"What you are about to learn concerns the safety of you and Alexis and Joseph and of all the people in the other world who are in desperate need of my help." He felt himself trembling and she was holding onto him tightly. "What I am trying to explain will be hard to understand. I will guide you through it." Jack was listening intensely, trying to connect with her and draw strength from her touch. "At the first new moon I will meet Mab at Stonehenge, and we will battle."

Jack shook his head. "This is too much for me." He started to walk away again.

"Jack, she is the reason for the color of my hair!" Arianna screamed so loud that Brach retaliated with a whinny and Jack's heart skipped ten beats.

"Come on, Ari! You're putting your family in danger." The fear he was fighting coursed through his entire body. "You're fighting with swords and sorcery. This is insane."

Arianna looked at Jack with the eyes of a warrior, and her intensity silenced him. "This bitch of a witch came to me in the guise of a black spirit and won't leave me alone. She threatened my family, Jack. You know me. Nothing threatens my family!"

"Why do you have to do this? Why is this your responsibility?"

"Jack, I know that we have been on delicate grounds in the past and present over me being here and you having to put up with me waiting for a dead king to rise." She paused. "If I were you, I would act the same way. I don't know why this has happened to me. What I do know is that all my life, I have understood things that others have not, have felt things that others could not imagine, and have seen and lived through things that I wish to God I never had to live through. But I am still here, and I need to face whatever my life is about to bring me." She covered her face with her hands. He pulled them away to look at her. Blood, soil and tears dripped down her beautiful olive complexion. "Do you believe in me, Jack?"

He stared at her, fear swelling in his chest. "You know that I do. If it weren't for you, I'd be dead today myself."

"Trust me, Jack. I will fight and I will win!"

He reached for his wife, held her tight in his arms, and kissed her deeply, as though it was the last kiss that they would ever share.

CHAPTER THIRTY-ONE

Arianna calls for Assistance

She kissed him again, and he felt an energy flow through him, one that seemed to trickle all the way down into his toes and back up to her touch. He looked at her. She was so different to him now.

"It feels wonderful that I no longer have to hide my identity from you. I can finally be myself, and you can understand the nature of who I am."

Jack stood next to his car, looking at the lake and eventually at her again. "That arm is not good, Ari. We need to get home."

Arianna and Jack left the lake site, she on Brach and he in his car. He followed her up to the riders' path, then drove on home.

About an hour later, they met each other near the carport. Jack kissed Arianna outside of the house before they walked towards the door.

Breaking their embrace, he saw Alexis reading a book on the porch swing. They approached and she looked at her father. Her expression was precious, and he realized how long it must have been since he and Arianna actually held hands and exhibited romantic feelings for each other. His daughter's "What's up?" look made him snicker with delight.

"Mom, what happened to your arm? It is bleeding into that bandage."

"Your mother cut her arm a few days ago, and it didn't heal well.

Will you please call Dr. Marcus and let him know that we are on our way?"

"Jack, please, I would rather have Dr. Marcus come here." Jack looked at his wife's arm and hesitated to answer her. "Please, hon, I'll feel more comfortable in my own surroundings."

He nodded his head in agreement. "Lexy please ask the doctor to come here to tend to your mother."

"I'll call him right away."

A few moments later, Alexis returned to the kitchen, and Jack waited for an answer as she placed the phone on its receiver.

"Dad, the answering service took the call and said that the office was closed for the day."

Arianna spoke. "Okay, honey, please go up to my office, and bring my cell off the desk. Dr. Marcus' number is logged on that phone. I'll call him directly."

"Okay, Mom. I'll be right back."

Arianna pulled up a seat to rest. "The good doctor will be here soon enough."

Jack shook his head in amazement. "How can you be so calm?"

"It's just another battle wound." She shrugged her shoulders. "That's all."

Jack felt himself grow weak in the knees. Everything about his wife seemed strange. "You're very sexy as a high priestess."

"Jack!" She swatted him away. "You're gonna get me all flushed!" She kissed him sweetly, and he savored the moment.

"Mom, here's your phone," said Alexis as she placed it on the table. "What is going on with you two?"

"Nothing," said Arianna. "Your father and I haven't seen each other in a long time."

"You guys are acting weird," said Alexis as she backed out of the kitchen. "Just take care of your arm." Alexis grabbed her jacket from the back of the chair. "I'm meeting some friends at the airport. I'll be back soon. Stay out of trouble."

"Friends?" asked Jack, looking back at his daughter. "What friends?"

"Jeremy and Gerard are flying in from New York." Alexis opened the back door of the kitchen. "Love you!" yelled Arianna as her daughter ran out to the car.

Jack returned his eyes to Arianna, who smiled at him. "Where were we, kind sir?"

"You were about to call the doctor!"

Arianna smiled back coyly and picked up her cell phone. She pushed the code for Dr. Marcus' number, pressed the speaker phone option and set the phone on the table. Jack could hear it as it rang. A friendly voice finally said, "William Marcus here. How may I help you?"

"Hello, Dr. Marcus!" said Arianna.

"My lady, how good to hear from you."

Arianna rose from where she had seated herself and paced around the kitchen. "Doc, I had a small accident. I could use your assistance if you have a moment to spare."

"Do you need hospital?" he asked in the traditional English tradition.

Arianna bit down on her lip before answering. "To be honest, I probably do at this point, but I would much rather you came here if you could."

"What was the accident?"

Jack walked up behind her and spoke over her shoulder. "It's a really bad cut on her left arm and it needs immediate attention."

"This sounds strikingly similar to something we have been through before," the doctor replied.

"My friend, that is only the half of it," said Arianna.

Jack could hear a tapping sound from the other end before he heard the doctor reply, "I can be there in an hour."

The High Priestess and the Druid Doctor

Arianna and Jack seated themselves on the bench outside the cottage, and Jack nuzzled close to her. He threw a blanket over the two of them, wrapped his arms around her, pulled his left hand out from under the blanket, and looked at his watch "Where is he?"

"He said he would be an hour."

Jack looked at the bandage on his wife's arm and replied, "I knew I should have taken you right in."

"Relax, Jack."

"Relax!" Jack stood from the bench, sauntered over to the patio rail and leaned on it. He again looked at his wife, feeling fear creep over him. He kept his hands in his pockets trying hard not to show how they were shaking. "How in the hell can I relax, knowing who you are right now? Just a few hours ago you were the woman I married, but now you're this powerful priestess who has to fight a mad-assed evil bitch."

Arianna seemed incapable of stopping herself from laughing at him.

He pulled from the rail. "What? This is funny? I love you, damn it! I don't know how to face this with you!"

She reached for Jack's forearm, calm to his growing anxiety, and he resented her for it.

"I am not afraid to fight Mab or any other demon that comes to face me." Arianna's eyes sparkled when she spoke. "I will shed myself on the stones of the circle to save my Merlin. I have no fear."

Jack looked at his wife, shaking his head. "I'm not going to be able to handle all of this."

Arianna leaned in closer to him. "I just need you to be here for me when it's over."

With those words, Dr. Marcus' car made its way down the road, and Arianna scurried from the porch to greet her friend.

"My lady, 'tis good to see you," said the doctor, setting his feet upon the gravel pathway.

Arianna extended her hand, and the two friends embraced each other.

Jack stood on the patio watching the two, recalling the day that he and his wife met the doctor in the hospital in London years ago—and later when they sought his medical aid for Arianna's shoulder after they returned from Camelot.

Knowing that Ari was about to tell Dr. Marcus what had really happened, Jack felt a wetness come over palms as they approached the cottage. Remembering that the doctor was a confidant of his wife, Jack sank a bit, as though he suddenly filled up less space in the universe. It dawned on him that his wife, the modern day High Priestess of Avalon, was about to tell her friend of her new quest, and the reality would be set in stone—like the sword that set all of this in motion.

"Jack, good man, how are you these days?" asked Dr. Marcus as he greeted him with a pat on the shoulder.

Jack looked at the doctor through what felt like a haze. "I'm hanging in there, Doc." He scratched the tension from the back of his neck. "I guess."

"Good man," he replied. "Now what am I here for?" Arianna took her jacket off on the patio and showed the blood-stained bandage to her friend, who replied, "Let's have a look, shall we?"

The three moved inside and headed right to the kitchen, the best lit room in the house. Dr. Marcus placed his backpack on the table. When the bag hit the wood, Jack's heart jumped. The doctor stepped to the sink to wash his hands as Jack handed him a few paper towels to dry them before he pulled his latex gloves on and proceeded to remove the bandage.

Jack was a bit relieved to see that the wound had already started to close itself, but the skin was still red and seeping blood into the newly formed scab. Dr. Marcus placed a sterile sheet on the table, removed his antiseptics and cleaned the wound so that he could see how deep the gash was. Jack took careful note that Arianna did not move; the peroxide should have made her jump as it stung her skin, but she didn't bat an eyelash.

The doctor examined the wound more closely. "What nasty bugger did this?"

Arianna remained silent for a moment. With powerful conviction she calmly said, "I am the bugger who did the deed."

Dr. Marcus smiled. "Enlighten my curiosity."

"Will you listen to me as my friend and not my doctor?"

His wife's stoic eyes stared down the doctor—a look that sent chills down Jack's back. As he pulled up a chair and sat down next to her, the doctor urged her to continue. "Go on, I'm listening."

Arianna sat back in her chair. "Do you remember awhile back? You asked me if I were a Priestess of the Isle?"

"I do indeed."

Arianna stood from her chair and asked Jack, "Would you please see if there is a bottle of wine in that cabinet. And some glasses, too?"

"You need wine at a time like this?"

"Please, hon, you will understand why soon enough."

Jack ambled over to the cupboard above the sink and found a bottle of Merlot. He brought three glasses from the dish rack, opened the wine and watched as Arianna poured it into the glasses, handing one to him and one to the doctor, keeping one for herself. She drank a sip of the wine and fingered the bowl of the glass.

"The Druid in me is reading a sense of magic in the air," said the doctor, putting Jack more ill at ease.

Arianna took a moment. Jack sat taut in his chair, and the doctor folded his hands on the table and eyed Jack's wife like a child anticipating a show. Arianna closed her eyes. "*Saffier ech mor.* For I am the seer of light and darkness." Again Arianna played with the bowl of her glass and placed her finger into the liquid. Pulling it out, she allowed the wine to drip off her, pooling onto the surface of the table. She then let some drip from the glass. This time, as the wine hit the wood, it sizzled like hot steam. Arianna waved her hand counterclockwise over the vapors, and the puddle on the table swirled as though it were a small tornado lifting from the wood. Within this funnel, Jack and the doctor witnessed the vision of Arianna cutting herself at the tomb of Arthur and taking her sword Gwydion high above her head. *I, Arianna, Lady Lawrence Pendragon, give my blood to the Mother. For I am the High Priestess of Avalon and no one claims my right!*

Jack's eyes absorbed the vision. He folded his arms in front of him as though he were caving in, and he grabbed for his own bicep and nearly dug his nails into the muscle. In a flash, Arianna waved her hand, and the vision vanished, leaving the trio sitting in the silent room.

The doctor was the first to speak, and he did so in a low whisper. "So your powers have come to you."

Jack shook his head in awe of his wife, so uncomfortable with all of this.

"I have come to know the powers that be, my friend."

Jack was going crazy inside. "I am glad for you, Ari, but let the doctor do what he came for." He knew he was being rude, but the wound on his wife's arm was still bleeding, and all he wanted was to see the damned thing cared for.

Arianna gave the doctor her arm, and he again cleansed it and started applying a butterfly stitch to the bottom of the cut. She was not moving, though Jack knew she hurt.

"Doc, there is something you must know."

"I am listening," he replied as he placed the next stitch to the wound.

"Merlin and I have become inseparable. He has taught me, as you just witnessed, about the ways of the Druids. In many ways, he has taken me under his wing like a younger sister."

The doctor continued his work. "I am well aware of your relationship with the wizard."

Arianna pulled back a bit as he placed the third stitch on the deepest part of the wound. She placed her hand over his, stopping him from applying another.

"Merlin is very ill in the other world," she told him. "Mab has poisoned him. I must fight her to save him."

Jack watched as Dr. Marcus placed the last stitch on Arianna's arm and wrapped a white gauze bandage around it.

"Lady, please forgive my ignorance, but why must you fight this Mab?"

"Doc, can you please talk some sense into her?" begged Jack.

Arianna opened her leather sporran and removed the letters, giving them to Dr. Marcus to read.

The doctor looked over the parchments, reading the words once and carefully reading them again. Jack had hoped that the doctor would have some sane advice for his wife. Instead, Dr. Marcus gently placed the letters on the table, then lifted Arianna's hand and kissed it gently. "Please know that I am ready to assist you in all ways possible."

Arianna smiled and replied, "Please be here at high dusk on the first sign of the new moon. I may need you after the battle."

Arianna toasted her glass of wine with his, and the alliance was formed.

Jack abruptly left the room, unable to listen to another word.

Chapter Thirty-Three

Sir Peter Returns from Rome

———◆———

"Peter, 'tis good to see you!" greeted Galahad as he embraced his first knight and dear friend home from his journey.

Peter handed his riders cloak to the page. "Bring wine to the table, young Cavyn, for I am parched." Cavyn left in haste to obey the order.

"How goes it in Rome?" asked Galahad as the guards opened the door to the Round Table room.

"Rome!" Peter shook his head, "I would rather cut my throat than have one more audience with the pope and his conclave of cardinals."

"So our pope still has no regard for the Druids here in England?"

"For a man of the cloth, all I see is blood in his eyes for his Pagan brethren. He speaks of Christianity with one voice and of Satan with the other."

Galahad beckoned Cavyn to come in with the carafe of wine and two silver goblets he had fetched and to pour the wine for Galahad and Sir Peter.

Peter stole a sip and placed the goblet on the table. He eyed Galahad with what looked like underlying anger and stated, "When we accepted the Holy Grail from the hands of our Lord and drank the wine from its bowl, I did not hear Jesus telling us to kill the Pagans. All he asked from us was to love one another." He paused. "I am sick of war." His voice boomed off the walls.

"Then the news about Merlin was one more burden for your heart to bear?"

Peter stood from his chair, taking his wine with him. "How is the wizard?"

"Even the Druid priests have not the cure."

"There is no recourse for him?"

Galahad remained silent and watched as Peter paced around the court, rolling his wine cup back and forth in his hands, as though trying to figure out the matters of the day.

"Where is Lady Arianna? She is always here to greet me." Peter took his chair next to Galahad and grabbed his brother's shoulder. "Your silence tells me something is wrong. Is my lady alright?"

"No, Brother. Merlin and Mother are in grave danger. Mab has poisoned Merlin and closed the wall to Arianna."

Peter again filled his wine cup. "Arthur's coming is at hand then. "Is the council ready to reconvene?"

"I have heard from the messengers that the courtiers will arrive as early as tomorrow at noon."

"We have much to plan, my lord."

"Indeed!"

"And Joseph?" asked Peter.

"Actually, I was waiting for your company before I told him," replied Galahad as he walked away from his chair.

"Does he know that I am here?"

"I told him of your coming earlier this day and invited him to dinner tonight."

"Will Blaise be joining us as well?" asked Peter, his eyes raised over the sentry wall to where Merlin's chambers were located down the hall.

"He will my friend. Blaise has much to tell Joseph about the lady and her destinies."

"I understand. Allow me to refresh myself and pay my respects to Nimue and Merlin."

"Go, Brother, and ask God in his mercy to aid us in our endeavors!"

CHAPTER THIRTY-FOUR

His Mother's Destiny

Sir Joseph ran down the hallway. He was late for dinner and did not like being tardy. Stopping by the private dining room of his king, he adjusted his clothing, which was in shambles, and it was not in his personality to appear untidy. Joseph raised his hand and the guard opened the door. Walking through the small foyer and entering a well lit room, Joseph recognized that this was to be a private dinner by the silver plates and goblets set on the table—the finery used when Galahad held his high dinners for political dignitaries.

Galahad and Blaise were already seated at the long rectangular table, and he felt their eyes were immediately upon him. He quickly noticed that the window dressings had been drawn, as was customary when Galahad and those of high position had meetings that were to be undisturbed. A chill ran through Joseph as his eyes fell upon Blaise, who stared back at him.

"John and I were practicing in the archery yard, and I lost myself in the games."

Galahad walked over to Joseph and kissed him on both cheeks. "Blaise, I give you Joseph, son of Lady Arianna."

Blaise stood and walked over to Joseph. "It is an honor to know you."

Joseph looked hard into Galahad's brilliant blue eyes. He turned to Blaise, feeling confused. "You have known me a while. Why is it suddenly an honor?"

Galahad ushered him to a chair, "Please, Brother, sit down, as we have urgent news."

Joseph's legs gave way as he sat quickly down and picked up a cup of wine from the table.

"Is my mother alright?" asked Joseph feeling his face drain of color.

"Why this question?" asked Blaise.

"Mother should have been here at the first sign of the half moon. She has not arrived yet, and the moon is three quarters hence."

"You suspect that something is wrong?" asked the priest.

Joseph nervously played with the knife on the table. "Master, your being here is enough to tell me that all is not well in either this world or my mother's. It is something I have suspected, especially since Merlin is not yet healed."

Blaise pulled at the piece of bread in his hands and passed a piece to Joseph, who ate it but felt as though the dough was catching in his throat. "What has brought you to this conclusion?"

"The wizard and my mother are joined in body, mind and spirit. If there is a problem with Mother, then goes the same with Merlin."

"Can you be certain of this?" asked Blaise.

"Master, the wizard keeps calling out for my mother in his fever. He calls for her incessantly. When I lived in my mother's world and life was chaotic, she would fall asleep and call out for Merlin."

Blaise looked upon Joseph. He grabbed hold of his shoulder and said, "On the ship, I felt an entity within you. I could not understand what I was sensing. As with your mother, you, too, are part of the fabric of time."

"You are correct."

The guard opened the door, startling Joseph and Peter strode into the room. Joseph stood as Peter came to him. "Please tell me that your arrival here is not to deliver the news of my mother's death."

Galahad placed his hands on Joseph's shoulders, holding him firm.

"Joseph, I assure you that she lives."

"Thank God!" Joseph said as he closed his eyes and sat down quickly. "Then why are we here?"

"Joseph, your mother is absent because the time gate has been closed to her," said Blaise. Joseph looked at the priest and felt his brown eyes frozen in their glance. "Before we continue, I need you to tell me something of your childhood."

"What does my childhood have to do with my mother at this present time?"

"Please, Joseph, do as Blaise asks," intervened Galahad. "We will explain later."

Joseph felt his rage coming to him. He could not understand the interrogation. "Are you asking me this as my king or as my brother right now?" Joseph stared at Galahad with contempt.

"I am asking you this as both your king and your brother. Mother needs our help. You must answer the questions asked of you."

Joseph briefly made eye contact with Peter, who came to sit next to him. The mere presence of his best friend gave Joseph the support he needed. "What do you want to know about my past?" Joseph asked in protest.

"I need you to tell me what sort of boy you were," said Blaise.

Joseph felt lightheaded, the same way he felt in school as a boy when he could not understand what his teachers were trying to teach him. He felt his focal points begin to wax and wane.

"My lord, do you realize how hard it is for me to remember that child?" Joseph's heart was racing. He threw back his chair, rose from the table and stepped to the window. Opening the curtain, he looked out into the dusk of the evening, trying to find something in the night sky to focus on, something tangible to ground him. He found it over the rail, where an auburn hue hovered above the horizon right before the sun set behind the forest. Slowly, he spoke. "When I was a boy, I was very ill, both mentally and physically. My illness caused my mother many sacrifices." Joseph stole one more look at the gloaming and returned to the table to drink down his wine.

"Go on, Joseph," prompted Blaise.

"I knew that my mother loved me, but I used that love as a weapon against her."

"How did you come to be here and a knight in Galahad's army?" asked Blaise.

"When I was a boy of ten, my mother found Excalibur in the ground in my time. Excalibur brought her here to Camelot where she and King Arthur became close friends before Mordred killed him."

Peter poured Joseph another cup of wine.

"Mother and Merlin became so close while she was here that they bound as kindred souls. When mother had to leave to go home to our time, Merlin and the Lady Viviane bestowed upon her the ability to reopen the time gate to come back when His Majesty had need of her."

"Where do you enter the story?"

"Before Mother left Camelot, she and Galahad made a promise to one another—that he would keep her in his heart."

Joseph felt Blaise's eyes leave him and focus on the king. "And Your Majesty, what was your promise to Arianna?"

Galahad answered him, "I asked Arianna to bring Joseph back with her when she received the signal to return."

"Why did you wish Joseph to return with the lady?"

Galahad looked to Joseph with forlorn eyes. "I was eighteen when I became king. Lady Catherine and Lady Nimue raised me and I loved them for it." He paused and Joseph felt his sadness. "In the short time that Arianna was here, she became the mother I lost when I was a boy. She wanted to stay here and never go back to her time. I would have given my right arm to have her remain. I needed her to help me nurture my new kingship." Joseph looked at him, feeling a strong sense of remorse fill his boots. "I knew the kind of boy that Joseph was by what Arianna had told me, and I was afraid that Joseph would end up like Mordred if she had not returned to raise him well."

Joseph looked at Peter, admitting, "If Mother had not brought me here, I surely would have killed her." He paused. "Maybe not of body but of heart and soul."

"Honestly, Brother, I wanted you here to see what I sacrificed in sending our mother back to you. What I did not realize was that the fates were aligned to bring me a brother, one I cherish every day."

Joseph felt not only proud but resolved in their telling Blaise the truth.

Blaise shook his head. "It was both your destinies that brought you here."

"Destiny?" Again Joseph looked to Peter, who he knew was there as his silent comrade. "I don't understand. What about this destiny, and what do you want with me?"

"Do you believe in reincarnation?"

Joseph nearly gasped. "Yes, I have heard of reincarnation. It can be the answer to our destiny; we have to listen for the signs."

"What I am about to tell you is your mother's destiny, and she needs her son to be strong for her so that she can complete it."

"Is Arthur's return part of this providence?"

"You are astute, my young knight."

"My Priest, Mother has told me that she had a quest in her future—that even though she knows not the reason for her mission, she is ready to take it on."

"Everything your mother told you growing up is about to unfold. First thing you must know is that your mother's real name is Aryanyn the Holy One. She is the sister of the first Merlin and the one who must accompany Arthur on a quest to save both worlds."

"Aryanyn?" Joseph asked. "How do you write this name?"

Galahad pulled his quill from the tablet and spelled it out for Joseph. *Aryanyn.*

Joseph lowered his wine cup. "When I was a child and we returned from England, Mother asked my sister and I if we knew anyone by that name. She wrote it over and over again and claimed not to know why." Joseph took a deep breath, asking, "If my mother is this Aryanyn, who is she really and why is she not here to find out what her true destiny is?"

"Please, sit down," urged Galahad.

Joseph felt himself weaken in the knees but held his ground. "Answer my questions."

Blaise stood. "It was prophesized years ago by Élan, the mother of Constantine, that she would accompany the high king to find the titulus of Christ."

"The titulus of Christ?" Joseph again felt confused.

Galahad stepped in. "The titulus, Joseph, is the written sign that headed the cross of Christ on the day of his Crucifixion."

Joseph felt enlightened. "You speak of the letters I N R I scribed on the wood above his head?"

"Yes, that is exactly correct, Brother."

Joseph looked at his wine cup, a simple pewter goblet embossed with the pendragon symbol on it, and up to Galahad. "Are you saying that we did not find the whole of the Holy Grail and that my mother has been chosen to find its companion?"

"How do you know this?" asked Blaise.

Joseph lifted his wine cup from the table. He opened the curtains and walked out to the verandah, followed by the others in the room. The auburn hue had turned indigo, and the sky was illuminated with twinkling jewels. "Do you see that hill over there?" Joseph pointed near the mountains of Camlann. "I have had a recurring dream in the past month of our mother and a king—both dressed in blue and red, riding down that hill holding the wood you speak of." Joseph gazed again at the pendragon on his cup. "Tell me, is the king in my dreams King Arthur, and is it his coming that is endangering my mother and Merlin?"

"We fear that Mab will try to kill your mother before Arthur is raised."

Joseph placed his wine cup on the verandah ledge so as not to spill it.

"You should know that Aryanyn had a son named Jared in her third world, and who, as you, gave her nothing but grief as a child. He was mentally ill until Élan cured him."

"Her third world?"

"Aryanyn is not of two worlds," answered Blaise. "She is of three."

"Then I am truly a part of mother's reincarnation."

Blaise smiled with Joseph's understanding; "You most certainly are, Sir Joseph, son of Aryanyn."

Joseph laughed, releasing his angst. He raised his hand and pushed his wine cup from the rail. The wine spilled on the tiles of the verandah. He looked at the wine as it hissed like a snake on the cold tile floor. Both he and Blaise knelt down watching the phenomenon, and Blaise raised his hand over the wine and waved it in the shape of a rainbow.

Suddenly and with force, Blaise grabbed Joseph's face and held it between his hands. As though he were examining his soul, Blaise's eyes pierced through Joseph as he announced to the room, "The priestess battles Mab at Domh Ringr at the first sight of the new moon."

CHAPTER THIRTY-FIVE

Galahad Leads His Court

The Lord of Camelot, King Galahad stood at the guard's post right above the Round Table room, looking down on all who entered the court. He was assessing which of the hand-selected members he thought would come to the aid of the High Druid, Merlin. His Majesty held tight to the pommel of Excalibur as he wondered how the coming caucus might play out.

He kneeled and reached for the tapestry that hung beneath him. His hand gently ran over the soft velvet that held the symbol of the pendragon. A distant stare came over him as he remembered the days of his boyhood, standing right there secretly listening to his uncle and the knights of that time. His heart quickened as he thought about the gentle King Arthur walking these halls again. He looked to Excalibur's pommel. *I must return you to Arthur. I have no claim to you.*

"My lord," Sir Peter interrupted Galahad's thoughts. "Blaise and Aaron are waiting for you in the knights' hall."

"I will be there shortly."

"You seem to be in deep thought, sire."

"My mind is on Mother and Merlin."

"As it should be right now."

"Peter, Nimue was so glad to see you last night."

"I know, my lord. She is tired. I ask God to aid us today as we convene with our courtiers."

Galahad noticed his pages preparing the Round Table for his guests. "Do you remember spying on Uncle Arthur and his men when we were children?"

"Yes, and when they caught us, oh, it was surely hell to pay," Peter laughed. "I can remember my father pulling me away from this very spot by the ear." Peter rubbed his left ear lobe, remembering the disparity of the pain.

"Uncle Arthur almost pulled my arm out of its socket dragging me down the stairs." Galahad grabbed his shoulder. They shared a hardy laugh, remembering their childhood, before Galahad returned to the seriousness of the moment at hand. "Come, let us appease these people."

Galahad and Peter made their way down the side stairwell that led to the knights' hallway. There, Blaise and Aaron awaited, and the two bowed to Galahad. He acknowledged their greeting with a nod of the head.

"Master Blaise, Aaron, I beseech you. Wait for me to signal your entrance, as these Christians do not understand the plight of your visit here."

Blaise snickered, "Majesty, is the world so small that even these warriors cannot see who and what we are without digging deep into the flesh?"

Galahad stared into the Druid's eyes. "My good priests, some of these men are open of mind and soul, but some have minds as tight as a steel trap. Listen closely and tell me who is friend and who is foe."

Blaise stroked his handsome beard. "You speak the wisdom of one who taught you well, my King—the High Druid Merlin."

Galahad gripped Excalibur and said, "I will forever be in Merlin's debt for the lessons he has bestowed on me. The Great Man of the Forest told me to listen to the words that men speak. If they look at you straight in the eye, they speak from their heart and their soul. If they cast their eyes away and lean back from you, know that somewhere in the depths of their minds, they are hiding some truth and cannot be trusted."

"Look, Brother! Gawain and Martin arrive!" said a grateful Peter. Galahad turned and took note of their entrance from the side door of the hallway.

"Come, let us greet the knights of King Arthur," said Galahad as he and Peter made their entrance into the court unannounced.

"Majesty!" said the guard as he stood at attention.

Galahad, followed by Peter, strode over to the two elder knights, Martin and Gawain, greeting them with a warm embrace. By the standards of court, the knights bowed their heads to their king.

"Is there news of my father's arrival?" asked Peter.

"William will be here, my lord," replied Gawain. "His ship has been detained by the storm that rolled in last night."

"It does not surprise me that my younger brother should arrive fashionably late as usual," said Martin.

Galahad laughed at the comment and it caught on as Peter, Gawain and Martin, too, cackled at William's expense.

Sir Joseph, Sir Luke, and Sir Michael made their entrance into the court. Luke bowed to Galahad and approached his father, Sir Gawain, greeting him. "Is mother with you?"

"Yes, my son. Your mother joined Lady Viviane and Nimue in Merlin's chambers just minutes ago."

"I am glad the Lady Catherine accompanied you, sir," said Galahad. "Nimue needs all of our love and support right now."

"Ahy, sire, when she heard the news I could not keep her from packing her bags."

"Are you holding up well, my brother?" asked Galahad turning to Joseph.

"As well as can be expected, sire."

"Sit at my left and Peter to my right," demanded Galahad, to which Joseph bowed his head. "Come fellow Pendragons. Call to orders, commence."

Galahad felt the eyes of the knights of the old days and of the present on him as he and Peter and Joseph circled the room. They all stood at attention as Galahad strolled to his seat and unsheathed Excalibur. Watching for his knights and courtiers to follow his lead and take to their respective seats, he raised Excalibur and saluted Arthur's pendragon symbol by striking the hilt of the precious sword to his left breast. Then he placed the sword on the table in front of him, the tip of the blade facing the center. His knights followed suit. It was the tradition of Arthur that each man at the Round Table would salute one another and place their sword on the table at bay in front of them. The points of each sword should face the centerpiece of the table, the five-pointed cinquefoil intricately carved into the wood, to show that each man came in peace to serve his king and his country.

The knights' shouted *"Dues le Volt,"* and placed their swords down.

Galahad fully assessed who was now sitting in his court, taking account of the empty chairs of knights of old that were no longer with them in body but who, by the hand of God or by the spoils of war, had been taken to their peaceful reward. He looked up to heaven and asked them for guidance.

Only two of the three remaining Brothers of the Order of Pendragon were seated amongst them: Sir Gawain, King Arthur's cousin and protector of Camelot when Arthur left for battle; and Sir Martin, King Arthur's oldest and wisest knight and the one who aided Lady Arianna in both this world and her own. Missing today was Sir William, Martin's youngest brother, one of the liaisons to the church in Rome.

Sir Frederick pushed through the side door to the Round Table room from the knight's hallway. With a tankard of ale in hand, he meandered drunkenly towards Galahad, saluted his king, dropped his sword on the table in front of his seat, drank a long swig of ale and sat himself while the others still stood.

It was Frederick who witnessed Arthur's murder on the field of battle that fateful day, and since, Galahad thought he had seen a steady decline in the old knight's behavior.

Behind Frederick, the aging Christian priests, Father Thomas and Friar James, walked into the court dressed in the albs of their vows. It was they who blessed Arthur's' body for burial and ordained Galahad as king and Lord of Camelot. Like Frederick, they had since lost their respect for the court of the king.

Galahad took his seat, and the Knights of the Round Table followed suit.

"Friar Thomas, a prayer please."

The good priest lifted his arm and said, "*In nomine Patri et Fillii et Spiritu Sancti. Amen.*" Each man followed the arm gesture of the priest; as he made the sign of the cross over the table, they, too, crossed themselves with the symbol of Christ.

"Lord God, through the intervention of your Son, our Lord Jesus Christ, we ask for your blessing on this court. It is by your will that we are gathered here today." Thomas again blessed the table. "The Lord be with you."

"*Et cum spiritu tuo,*" the gathered knights replied.

The guard opened the main doors to the room, and Galahad looked up to see Sir William enter. He walked to the edge of the table and saluted Galahad, who gestured to an anxious Peter that he could leave the table and go to his father. Peter left his chair to embrace him.

"Forgive me, Majesty, for my presence of late," offered Sir William.

Galahad rose and embraced the man who helped Arthur raise him. "No apologies, William. We are glad that you have arrived safely. Please take your seat, as we have much to discuss."

Cavyn, Galahad's personal page of the Round Table, walked in with a tray of goblets. Behind him, another page entered with a keg of ale, while two others carried in a roasted boar—head and all—and placed it on a side table. Cavyn set the mugs on the table. Galahad smiled at the young page as Cavyn poured a cup of ale for each man, leaving one at the space where Merlin would have been seated. At the spot where Arianna would have placed Gwydion, he placed a red rose. Galahad was pleased with the boy.

"My lord, I am sure that all who are seated know of Merlin's peril, but should not the Lady Arianna be present for this most grievous of affairs?" asked Sir Frederick, with a tone of sarcasm in his voice.

Galahad turned, looking straight into Joseph's brown eyes, nodding to his brother to answer the maturing knight.

"My mother, Sir Frederick, is not here due to unforeseen circumstances surrounding the wizard."

"We know that the lady can open the walls to the worlds. Why can she not be here for the wizard? Are they not kindred to the cause of Camelot?"

"Mother is being held hostage by a force surrounding the portal," replied Joseph. "The force is linked to Merlin's illness."

Friar Thomas spoke up with doubt in his inflection. "What force should cast such a shadow on the portal?"

Galahad motioned to his brother to stand down as he handled his court. "Good Priest, the force is named Queen Mab."

"Mab!" Commotion erupted.

"She is dead!" declared Frederick. "She died after Mordred was killed."

"Did she?" asked Galahad. "Did you see her body on the battle field? Can you remember seeing her body burning on the funeral pyres of Avalon?"

Thomas commented, his voice catching in his throat, "No, sire, I cannot say that I was witness to such a burning."

"Mab did not die. It appears that she hid away, lurking, waiting for the perfect time to return."

"And what makes this the *perfect time*?" asked Friar James, the Christian priest.

"Do you remember the words written upon our King Arthur's tomb?" asked Galahad to all of his court.

The priest glared at him. Galahad knew that neither James nor Thomas appreciated being tested. "We do indeed, sire."

"Speak them to me, Thomas." Galahad requested.

Thomas bit down on his lip and answered, "*Hic Iacet Arthurus Rex Quondam Rexque Futurus.*"

Galahad struck his chest as he heard the words. "And their meaning, good priest."

Thomas played with the rosary beads that hung from his rope belt before sneering at Galahad. "Here lies Arthur, once king and king to be."

"From the day I saw those words, I felt that Satan had written them with his own hand," proclaimed Father James.

From across the table, Sir Frederick stood. "No one can be raised from the dead. Only Christ has such powers from his father."

Galahad snickered. "So, my priests, you who are men of the cloth cannot fathom that King Arthur will return to us. What you are about to hear may change your faith or despair it."

Thomas retorted. "My faith is strong in my God. Perhaps it is yours that is weak."

"How dare you speak to your king in that tone!" shouted Peter rising in Galahad's defense.

"I have but one king and he is my Lord and Savior Jesus Christ," fought back the priest.

Galahad sat back in his chair and allowed the men to argue for a moment longer as he sipped his ale. Raising his hand to the guard at the door, he beckoned him to open it and Blaise and Aaron entered the room.

His knights looked upon the strangers making their entrance in his court. Galahad rose to his feet and greeted them with clenched forearms. "My lords, I give you Masters Blaise and Aaron, High Druid Priests of the Forest of Fire."

"Druid priests! This is absurd!" screamed Thomas. "You bring worshippers of the devil into your castle?"

Galahad grasped Excalibur's hilt as she rested at the table. "Father, it is these two priests who cured and prepared us for the Grail gates."

"Druids, how dare they call themselves priests," boomed Frederick's voice over the room.

"They are priests of their own faith, Frederick," Sir Martin retaliated.

"Priests, you say!" said Father Thomas. "All I see here are two men who wear the signs of Pagan idolatry. I don't see priests here at all."

"Thomas, is that your name?" questioned Blaise. "You wear the symbol of the man who sacrificed himself for the very things we argue over now."

"How dare you speak blaspheme against Christ!"

"No, sir, it is you who creates evil!" shouted Aaron.

James and Thomas looked at Galahad and at Aaron. "How could these Pagan priests have been part of such a Christian undertaking as the Grail find?" asked James.

"Enough!" shouted Galahad. "I understand the arguments at this table, but if these good men of oak are evil—" Galahad placed his hand on the shoulders of both Blaise and Aaron before continuing. "—why were they chosen by God to heal us and prepare us to find the Holy Grail?"

He searched the expressions of all in the room who had fallen silent for a brief moment.

"And thank God for them," proclaimed Gawain. "My son Luke would not be here if it wasn't for Blaise and Aaron."

Galahad beckoned Cavyn to assist the Druid priests as they took the seats of Sir John and Sir Percival, two knights who had fallen with Arthur.

William stood from his chair. "We are honored by your presence here, good sirs. I am the father of Peter. He spoke highly of you upon his return."

Picking up his ale tankard, Galahad stated, "Here here, good men of the Round Table. We welcome our guests, that they may find friendship in these halls."

"Here here!" shouted all the knights of the realm as they picked up their cups in revelry—all but one. Frederick sat silently with arms folded in front of him, staring at Galahad, who returned his glare.

Galahad placed his hand firmly on Joseph's shoulder and said, "I bring news of grave heart. Not only Arianna has felt the wrath of Mab.

Merlin, our brother, is taken hostage by the dark poison of his mother."

"Dear God, I thought we were rid of the demon," shouted an angered Gawain.

"What does she want with Merlin and Arianna?" asked Frederick, his voice course and demanding.

Galahad seized control of the room. "Blaise, I implore you to appease these men with your tale."

Blaise rose from his chair and joined Galahad at the crescent of the table, where Galahad gestured with his hand that the court was his.

"The words on His Majesty's grave are a prophecy made years hence before any of us were light upon this earth. In the time before Constantine, a woman named Élan was a high priestess here in the Isle of Avalon. She was as revered as the nuns are here in the abbey. She was a seer, gifted with sight beyond her comprehension. Élan knew a woman named Aryanyn. She was a fellow priestess who was also gifted as she, but by the grace of the Goddess was given a gift that no other woman has ever had until now. Aryanyn could not only see into the future, but she could open the walls to other worlds." "Who is this Aryanyn?" asked a humbled Thomas.

"She is the sister of the first Merlin."

"The name Merlin is inherited?" asked James.

"It is given to those who the elder Druids deem worthy of elevating to their higest status. Our Merlin was chosen for his commitment to the Mother and his selfless acts as a spiritual leader, doctor and wizard."

William entered the conversation. "I heard that after Constantine converted Rome from Paganism to Christianity, some of the Pagan rituals were brought forth to our faith as well."

"Your Pagan brothers of the cloth were the first to choose chastity to heighten their spirituality."

"But Merlin is married to Nimue?" rebuked Thomas.

"He is not forced to be chaste as you are."

Thomas snickered with sarcasm. "Get to the point, sir!"

"Who is this Aryanyn and what does she have to do with us?" inquired the younger Christian priest, James.

"My brother will answer that for you," said Galahad.

Joseph stood. "Aryanyn is my mother. It is she who will accompany Arthur on the quest for the cross of Christ."

"Accompany Arthur!" yelled Thomas. "How can your mother accompany a dead king?" He laughed at the notion.

Blaise rose from across the table. "It is by the will of God and the Goddess that Aryanyn the Holy One and Arthur the High King of the Cross, quest for the titulus of Christ."

"How can the finder of the Holy Grail dabble in such evil?" questioned Frederick, throwing up his hands.

Galahad stood, "Blaise show these good people who Aryanyn is."

Blaise quietly removed his cloak and placed it on the Round Table. The crescent moon and the sun symbol were evident on the cloth.

Brushing his hand over the moon symbol he chanted. "*Saffier Echlin mor.* I ask the Goddess to show us the way." The room was as quiet as a tomb.

Blaise waved his hands over the cloak, and a cool breeze blew through the room, whipping around the table. At the center appeared a vision of Arianna and Brach at the portal. Arianna spoke the words that opened the time gate, pointing Gwydion into the dark of the black hole. The wall opened before them, and a white veil appeared over the time gate. Suddenly, Brach rose up on his hind legs as a bolt of the refracted light cracked upon him. The two were pushed back out of the time gate as another rider dressed in clothing from a different time came forward and pulled Arianna and Brach from the closing wall.

"Lady Arianna has never been locked out of our world," whispered William under his breath.

"Mab poisoned Merlin and closed the portal to Arianna," said Aaron. "She wants to prevent Arthur, Merlin and the Lady Arianna from uniting and allowing the prophecy of Élan to come to pass."

"Please explain. What is this prophecy, good priest?" requested Gawain.

"Aryanyn of the Isle and Arthur the High King of the Cross must quest for the titulus of Christ. The wood of the Father and the Grail of the Mother must be united for the two houses to become one."

"We burned Arthur's body. How can he be raised to fulfill a prophecy?" asked a bewildered Martin.

Blaise replied, "The answers lie on the field at Stonehenge as Arianna and Mab prepare for battle. For Arianna to claim her right as High Priestess of the Isle and to raise Arthur from his sleep, she must first defeat the witch."

Martin rose from his chair. "Are you saying that Arianna fights to the death at Stonehenge?" The blood in his face drained, leaving him pale.

Galahad turned to see Joseph rise in horror. "Please, good men of Arthur, help us. I do not want to see my mother die like this."

Martin could not hold his tongue. "Priest, I ask you, what is it you wish with us?"

"Arthur will need his men to surround him whence he is awakened from his slumber. His Majesty will need strength from you to fulfill his destiny."

"And what is the secret to his resurrection?" asked Frederick, moving over to the side table, pulling the apple from the mouth of the roasted boar and taking a bite from it, the juice from the fruit dripping down into his beard.

"Arianna carries the secret. Whence Mab is killed and the wall is opened, the poison should cease in Merlin. It is up to the high Druid to tell his sister Aryanyn who she is and to lead her in the raising of Arthur."

"Master Blaise, I, Sir Martin Borwell, knight of Arthur Pendragon and of Galahad, will be here for the love of Arthur and our sister Arianna, High Priestess of the Isle." He looked straight to Galahad and Galahad to him. Turning to the table, he asked, "Who is with me?"

"For my mother, I will go to battle," shouted Joseph.

"I am with you as well!" followed William.

"And I," said Gawain as he pounded his hand on the table.

"Here! Here!" shouted Peter with the rest of the younger knights as Luke and Michael came to his side. "And we shall join for the sake of the prophecy."

Galahad seized Excalibur from the table and held her high to Arthur's pendragon, saluting him. The other knights followed their king and raised their swords together.

At the height of the revelry, Sir Frederick threw his half-eaten apple at the pendragon symbol hanging above Galahad's head. The apple exploded showering its bits upon the court as Frederick hastily made his way towards the door, pushed it open and exited the room, followed by the two Christian priests who had entered with him.

CHAPTER THIRTY-SIX

Connecting with the Mother

---◆---

"Brach, hold still while I brush you," ordered Arianna. She tried to see how well Brach's wound had healed, but he was moving so much that she was having a hard time controlling him. She caressed his beautiful mane, which calmed him just enough for her to check where he was hurt. "I see the medicine and these gentle strokes helped your hair grow back well, my friend." She kissed Brach where the light struck him, but he pulled away from her and pointed his snout towards the barn doors. "Yes, we will go for our ride later today," said Arianna. Brach snorted back to his mistress. "I wish that I could go for a ride this morning," she continued, "but if I am to be victorious at Stonehenge, I must connect with the Mother and prepare for battle."

Arianna finished brushing Brach and reached over to the oats in the manger to fill his feed bag. She hooked it to his bridal, and Brach chewed down on his meal as she caressed the horse on his neck. "We know each other a long time, you and I," she whispered to him as he ate. Brach neighed through his chewing, bobbing his head up and down. Arianna gently rested her head on Brach's side, feeling for the rhythm of his heartbeat and trying to calm her own racing pulse. "Brach, I am so afraid of this woman." Arianna's hands shook, and she pressed them to her chest to control their quivering. She stared at her sheath belt hanging on the pole. Anxiety consumed her as she walked over to the mirror, sighting her reflection, and ran her fingers through her long black hair. *Dear God, what else might she do?*

Arianna looked outside into the quiet of the day. It was just before daybreak, and the green hue of the first sunlight cast it's aura over the canopy. Within the trees, she thought she saw an image: Mab's sword crashing down on her. She grabbed onto Brach's bridal, holding hard to her friend. "What if I am dead, Brach? Who will save Merlin?"

Fear pulsed through her as she fell to her knees and held onto her stomach.

"Are you in here, Arianna?"

Startled by her husband's voice, she rose up and tersely responded, "I'm back here, near Brach."

Jack stood by the tack shed entrance of the barn wearing his pajamas. "I turned over in bed and noticed you were gone. Your boots were not in the corner. Ari, its four-forty-five in the morning. This is early—for even you." He approached Arianna, kissing her good morning. "Are you alright? You seem out of sorts."

"I'm fine, Jack. Really I am."

"You know you're pale? Ari, please, this pending battle is worrying me."

"Was there something that you needed?" asked Arianna, crossing her arms over her chest.

"Yeah, to know that my wife is going to live. That's what I need."

Arianna placed herself in Jack's embrace. "Kiss me like you did last night."

She pressed her lips to his, and he kissed her back long and hard. Placing her head on his chest, she held on to him for a moment before pushing away.

"I can use some time with Brach, and I must exercise in a little while. A girl has to keep fit these days." She was trying to smile.

"Are you sure it's alright to leave you?" asked Jack reaching for her.

"Jack, you know me. I think things through better when I am alone."

He cupped his hand on Arianna's cheek, looking into her eyes, and she appreciated his tender touch. Jack took his wife's hand and kissed it gently before he broke from her and left the barn.

Okay Arianna, time to get a grip! She removed her Wicca sack from her saddlebag and hurried outside to the twin maples. It was daybreak, the blue sky was aflame with the rising sun coming over the hills and the arboretum. Arianna smiled, *the Mother's eye is on me.* Unfolding the purple blanket on the ground, she filled her censor with dried jasmine and rose oil, lighting it with a wooden match. She placed the runes down near the censor and, sitting in the center of the blanket, allowed the Mother to fill her with the nature that surrounded her.

"Quiet hails the power force within me." Arianna stretched her body flat on the blanket, allowing the fragrance to relax her mind and her muscles. She took a long deep breath and stood upright. She bent low to the ground, contouring her body so that her frame looked like an upside down V, and then she slid her torso down to the blanket and practiced her cobra and her cat forms while aligning them with the breath she was inhaling. Arianna shifted to a squatted pose before she gently stood, drawing air within her, placing her hands above her head and forming a triangle with her fingers. Pulling the air into her diaphragm and up into her lungs, she chanted, "Mother Earth, fill my body with your energy, surge thy grace within me, and give the power of thy planet to my veins."

Feeling her breath burn within her, she exhaled, bringing her hands down and forming them as though in prayer. She sat on the ground, folded her legs in the lotus position and placed her hands on her knees, breathing in the Hatha style of the Hindus. Arianna rested her hands, one over the other, atop the lower part of her abdomen, and took in deep breaths allowing her core to fill and release the fear that her stomach had harbored earlier that morning. Remaining in that pose, she allowed the stance to quiet her before she stretched out and laid down flat on the blanket gazing into the blue of the sky. The breeze shook the trees above her and she lay there for a short time, enjoying the Mother's voice as she whispered into the rustle of the leaves. Bird song filled the air as the sunrise announced the new day.

Arianna stood and rolled up her blanket, looking north near the cusp of Avalon. Families of deer were eating grass atop the hill. Arianna smiled. Life was around her. "Mother Earth, thank you for all that you bring to me this day." She picked up her blanket. Time for some hot oatmeal and coffee.

CHAPTER THIRTY-SEVEN

Preparing for Battle

A bowl of hot oatmeal and cinnamon coffee was her favorite breakfast, and Arianna savored it this morning with a small group of Alexis' friends who had risen early. Upon finishing her meal, she decided to return to the barn. George was with the horses, beginning his usual morning routine. He was speaking directly to Brach, and there was something in his voice that spooked her as she approached the tack shed.

"Stay close to Arianna when she fights this witch. She needs all the protection you can muster for her."

Arianna stood there for a moment, staring at the bale of hay in the corner, then pulled a piece of the alfalfa, placed it between her teeth and playfully walked into the barn.

"Arianna, were you out early meditating this morning?"

She placed her Wicca sack back in her saddlebag. "I was, my friend. The cool breeze of the morning helps me unite with the Mother." She removed her sweatshirt and stood there in her red silk blouse. "George, how long has it been since you used your sword?"

George smiled and replied, "Awhile. Why do you ask?"

Arianna looked deep into her friend's eyes. "I need someone with skill of the blade to ready me."

George stood proud. "I will be most happy to accommodate you."

"Prepare your weapon."

George made his way to the tack shed and to the cabinet at the far wall where he kept some of his fencing gear locked in the closet. He opened the latch and hauled out an old broadsword that was showing visible signs of aging. "Ahy, now isn't she a beauty? I purchased this lassie from the weapons dealer in Winchester ten years ago."

Arianna looked at the blade as George continued his story.

"The sword belonged to a knight who fought in the Crusades. Look, Arianna, on the pommel is the crest of a lion, the symbol that the knight had taken as his own in battle."

Arianna was itching to hold the weapon, but she saw how excited George was as he described the blade. "See how the hilt is adorned with black leather and tied with copper wiring. On the tang is the knight's templar cross, and on either side is a delicate copper *fleur de lis* representing the purity of the knight." George studied the sword and played with the blade in front of Arianna, honing in on his skills. He swung it around, and the blade made a whooshing sound as it cut through the air in the barn. "Knight of the templar, give me the wisdom to aid my lady in her hour of need."

"He will help me and so will you!" She stood tall and pounded her boot heels on the wooden floorboards. By the way George jumped, she knew that she was getting his heart pumping. "May I?" she asked, reaching for the weapon. George placed the sword in her hands, and she fingered the steel. "You will unleash my rage, good blade." She kissed the weapon and handed it back to George. "Are thee ready to battle my friend?"

"To the death, my love," George bowed with a grin, never taking his eyes off his new opponent.

She reached for the pole near Brach, grabbed her sheath that held Gwydion and girded her belt taut to her waist. She felt the weight of the blade near her left hip and the power of her weapon about her. "During breakfast, I asked Jeremy to join us in practice."

"Jeremy?" George was perplexed. "Alexis' friend is skilled with a blade?"

"He has won many awards with his weapons."

George was hesitant. "My lady, does this young man know enough about you?"

Arianna approached George and stepped within a couple of inches of his face, staring at his mouth, willfully playing into his attraction for her. "Jeremy knows what Alexis wants him to know. He can be trusted." Letting her breath linger on his lips, she backed away and unsheathed Gwydion, looking into the blue stone on the hilt. "I need Jeremy to represent the mental diversion that Mab will undoubtedly create at the circle. I asked him to join the battle in progress when he sees fit to distract me." Arianna grabbed George's hand. It was evident that he was fighting a fear that was spreading within him. "Please, dear friend, do not hide your thoughts from me. I know you are worried, and you have not been forthcoming with me."

George looked down at his sword. "My lady, have you looked at the moon these days? The position tells me that the battle is three days away." He paused and squeezed her hand. "Three days is an eternity to wait for the future to cast its lot upon my friend."

"We must hurry and prepare, for the new moon hastens us."

"There is a fire in your eyes, one I have never seen before," said George as he lifted his sword and held the blade high.

"Come. Let us see who knows better the ways of the warrior."

CHAPTER THIRTY-EIGHT

A Joust of Wills

The sun was raging its heat upon the grass and Arianna's light olive skin absorbed the rays as her raven hair reflected the blue of the bird's feathers for which it took its color.

George and Arianna stood ten feet away from one another, both holding the tips of their weapons to the ground. Arianna placed her feet in first position, giving George the signal to do the same. The warm wind wrapped around them. Arianna's eyes connected with George's, and she enjoyed the way his chest was throbbing with excitement.

She saluted her friend who stood before her. "En guard!" she screamed before she advanced into him, their blades banging hard against the quiet of the day. Her feet scampered quickly away from George's counter attack.

"Did you say that you needed to sharpen your prowess, High Priestess?" George was trying to joke with her, but Arianna was consumed and would not let words come between her union with Gwydion.

George parried into Gwydion's offence and his sword sounded like a steel pole clashing against an electric rod. It pierced her ears with that annoying crackling sound the elements make when matter and energy collide.

Arianna reposted from George veering away from him. He lurched in her direction, turning sharply and trying to volley into Arianna's next blow, but Arianna foiled his move using the tang of her sword as a block to George's strike. By the stunned expression on his face, she knew that she was more capable than he had anticipated.

He yelled, "AHA!" parrying into her again, clashing into Gwydion. Arianna used the sun as a weapon, reflecting it from her blade into George's eyes. He squinted at her and in his blindness, she rammed the hilt of Gwydion into his shoulder.

"So you want to play dirty!" said George with a bit of playful anger. He retaliated, raising his blade and swinging it hard at Gwydion. She sounded like a brass bell as she absorbed the blow, vibrating in Arianna's hand.

Arianna counter-swung at him, her eyes focused on his moves. George reposted the spar, diverting her. The move was quick. Arianna fell to the ground on her right hip, and from her peripheral vision, she saw Alexis, Cynthia and Gerard running down the side causeway to witness the swordplay.

"Yah!" screamed Jeremy as his tall, six-foot four-inch frame came from her left side and crashed down on the unguarded Arianna. She rolled onto her side, avoiding the blow, and quickly leapt to her feet. Jeremy attacked her again, clashing his sword into hers. Arianna was shocked to see a Scottish long sword in Jeremy's hand. The blade struck at her with full force and Arianna, with everything she had, advanced back at Jeremy, crashing into him.

The two advanced and retreated into the other's parry. What began as a game of swordplay now looked like a force of wills. Their steel rang through the barn walls, frightening the horses.

Swinging Gwydion back and forth, Arianna tried to pry Jeremy's sword from his hands, but his young skills forced Arianna's Gwydion to the ground—and her with it.

He lunged at her, but she quickly hopped up on her knees and retrieved her sword. She knew he was surprised at how fast she moved. He attacked her on her knees, bringing down his blade upon her and nearly cutting her hand off. Arianna rotated clockwise, forcing his body forward into her parry. Jeremy reposted and counter-struck into her, banging his sword to her blade once again.

She felt the combination of sweat and dirt pouring down her face. The red of her silk blouse looked like blood as it soaked up the perspiration from her body.

As she was preparing for another move on Jeremy, George advanced his spar. Arianna cut him off, slashing her blade into his advance, engaging her sword high into his parry. The two exchanged blows in a volley. George used his tall frame against the medium height of the priestess. Arianna prayed aloud, "Quiet hails the power force within me, raging in my blood," as Jeremy came in for the kill.

"You want blood, I'll show you some!" he shouted through the hail of steel on steel.

Jeremy was baiting her and she enjoyed it. George came in and tried to divert her from Jeremy, and she turned to her tall adversary and adopted the stance of the falcon, holding her sword high above her, the blade taking on the plume that crowns the bird's head. Jeremy thrust into her, and she swung her sword to her right and to her left as both men came to her quickly. One parried as the other volleyed into her next move. Arianna stood fast and again held Gwydion in the stance of the falcon. She swung the blade to and fro, and the three swords struck at each other, ringing in the air.

Arianna screamed as she took control of the swordplay. George was losing strength; she could see that with every strike, his steel lowered further to the ground. He disengaged, and his fatigue caused him to drop his weapon onto the soil beneath them. The blade clanged hard and he followed it, exhausted.

Arianna raised her sights from George to Jeremy, baiting him, and he hurried towards her. Their swords bounced off one another, but quickly she swerved into him again, forcing them both to the ground. Jeremy's sword fell as his large body hit the grass. Arianna stood fast and pointed Gwydion to his chest as he lay there motionless.

Alexis and Cynthia both leapt towards the pair.

"Mother...don't—"

"Arianna, wait!"

Arianna looked up at the girls and back down at her fallen prey.

With terror in his eyes, Jeremy spoke hoarsely. "If I didn't know any better, I might think that you would kill me."

Arianna disengaged her sword from his chest and rammed it into the ground beside him. She offered each of her opponents her hand, helping them to their feet, first George and then Jeremy. They were all breathing hard, and Arianna felt as though her lungs were burning. The warm air filled them quickly.

"My age has caught up to me," said George.

"I think not, Father," said Cynthia admiring her dad. "You fight like a lion."

Arianna bent forward as she tried to relax and looked up at Alexis as her daughter punched Jeremy on the shoulder, surprising him with the gesture.

"What was that for?" he asked as he reached for his arm.

"For being you, that's all," Alexis said with a smile.

"Thank you," said Arianna as she extended her hand to Jeremy.

"From what Alexis told me, which was very little, I knew that this was not a game. But I have to admit that I am humbled. I almost thought that I was about to breathe my last breath. I am certainly curious to know more about you."

"Jeremy, you have gained my trust by your honor and your skill." Arianna looked into Alexis' brown eyes. "Daughter, take them to the museum and tell them the whole of the matter."

Jeremy bowed to her and took his leave with the girls and Gerard.

"I am glad that they will know the truth," said George.

Arianna pulled Gwydion from the ground. "If my death is the will of the Goddess, my daughter needs her friends to support her in her hour of condolence." She could tell by the way that George grabbed his throat that he swallowed hard with her words of death. "Promise me that you will do me this favor?" Arianna requested.

George looked at his friend, sweat pouring down his face. "Anything my lady wishes," he replied as he wiped his forehead with his sleeve.

"Please tell Father Wallace everything about me."

George was stunned. "Why would you want a Catholic priest to know your secrets?"

Arianna pulled a cloth from her pocket and wiped her own face dry. She placed Gwydion's point to the ground again and leaned on her. "I was disrespectful to him in a fit of fear and rage that he did not deserve. He is not a stupid man, George. I fear he has already figured out some pieces of this puzzle."

"Arianna, I know you well enough. Your reasoning goes deeper than what you are revealing."

Arianna rocked Gwydion back and forth on the soil. "Promise me that if I die in battle, the good priest will give me Extreme Unction."

Concern replaced George's previous look of determination. "So you fear that your death will be imminent?"

"I do not fear the physical death, my friend. It's my soul that I worry about." Arianna lifted Gwydion, clashing her blade on the metal gate where the horses grazed. "Promise me on Gwydion that you will do as I request."

George's blue eyes stared hard at the sword as Arianna presented her to him with both hands. George placed his fingers on the blade and said, "As you wish."

CHAPTER THIRTY-NINE

Three Days to Domh Ringi

Arianna came down the stairs, refreshed from her sparring session with George and Jeremy, to find her family and guests already seated at the table, waiting for her to start the evening meal.

"I thought you got lost in the shower," remarked Alexis.

Arianna smiled, "After the workout that George and Jeremy gave me, a hot shower did feel good." Arianna took her seat at the table. Alexis and Cynthia had prepared a wonderful roast beef dinner with all the trimmings: mashed potatoes, corn with creamery butter, dinner scones and spinach salad. The aroma in the room heightened Arianna's appetite for the feast.

Jack stood and served while George poured wine for everyone at the table.

Arianna lifted her glass and inhaled the aperitif, taking in the fragrance before sipping it and allowing the grapes of the Mother to relax her as she enjoyed the company of her family.

Jeremy and Gerard sat at the end of the table with Alexis. Arianna looked at Jeremy and raised her wine cup. "To a very worthy opponent." Jeremy blushed a bit and raised his glass in return.

"To a woman who can kick ass with me any day."

Jack looked at Arianna with a questionable expression.

"Jeremy sparred with me this afternoon. He possesses the skill of a knight."

"Yes, Alexis told me of his many trophies," said Jack as he cut himself a bite of meat.

"My lady, I admit that I have won many trophies, but comparing me to a knight?" he shook his head. "They can fight their own battles. Leave me the heck out of it."

"A peace loving man, I see," replied Arianna.

"Jeremy would rather use words to argue," remarked Gerard.

"And you? What is your preference?" questioned Arianna.

Gerard smiled at the baited question. "I'd run the other way." Everyone at the table laughed.

"Come on, Gerard, you've won a lot of debates in college," said Alexis, coming to his defense.

Gerard turned to his friend. "I'll debate any subject, but fight someone to the death?" He poured himself a glass of soda. "They can have it."

Jeremy and Gerard were two young men that had found their way into Alexis' heart during her adolescent years. Alexis found them to be her true confidants in every way. Arianna was glad that they were here at what may be one of her daughter's most lonely of moments.

Jack looked at Arianna from across the table, and she connected with him. She sensed some fear in his glare.

Gerard seized the moment. "Priestess, what is it like to be around men like Galahad and Arthur?"

Arianna sat back in her chair, fiddling with the pendragon ring she wore on her right hand forefinger. "Gerard, life is so different there. These knights live to fight for king and country every day without thinking of danger."

"I feel the danger every time I raise my sword," responded Jeremy.

"You have to understand that they welcome an opportunity to demonstrate their loyalty and their honor. It has been bred into them from birth."

"People of such integrity are rare and hard to find," remarked Jack.

Arianna stared back at her husband. His comment made her feel so good. She looked upon him, a man whose bed she shared for many years now in a marriage that suffered many blows and created as much love.

Alexis was a product of that love and a child of which no mother could be more proud. Arianna thanked God for her every day.

Arianna looked at Joseph's picture on the credenza, opposite the table. Here was the boy who tugged at every ounce of her being and the reason for her running away from home. *Was Joseph the key to her being there? Would she witness his marriage to Leonora?*

And what of George and Cynthia? How in the name of all that is holy did this friendship form—a friendship that only the essence of time and the boundaries of faith could sculpt into being.

Arianna again found her eyes on Jack. *Would he stay here or go home to New York and remain alone there? Would he stay with his daughter and find strength in their father-daughter relationship? Could he find a friendship with George after all the strain?*

Arianna tugged off the ring of Arthur and held it tight in her hand, overwhelmed with emotion. This would be her last supper with her family. She suddenly felt the need to be alone, to concentrate and take solace without the distraction of love or friendship.

Jack was distressed by her decision, but he knew that it was in his wife's best interest that she endure the solitary road now. He had asked her to wait until after dinner to go into seclusion, and Arianna had honored her husband's request. She gazed at the clock on the wall. A peculiar chill ran through her before she felt a burning sensation coming from the brooch she wore. She rubbed her chest under her blouse.

"Are you alright, Mom?" asked Alexis.

Arianna held tight to her pin. "I'm not sure. This is burning my chest."

"Take it off," suggested Jack as he rose from his chair.

Arianna pulled at the brooch, "I'm sure it's just a nervous twinge."

"Hon, why don't you go inside and listen to some music for a while?" he suggested.

"I promised you that I would stay until we finished dinner," replied Arianna. She hunched her left shoulder as the burning sensation ran up to the bone, then she grabbed the brooch under her blouse, trying to isolate the pin from her skin. The metal bar vibrated in her hand.

"Are you sure you are alright, hon?" asked Jack.

"Please excuse me for a while as I take my husband's suggestion." Arianna looked across the table.

"Go ahead, Mom," added Alexis. "We'll clean up."

Arianna lifted her wine cup and left for the drawing room. Walking through the hall, the pin was burning her hand. *Is this part of the riddle, Merlin?*

CHAPTER FORTY

The Riddle Begins

---◆◆◆---

Arianna entered the drawing room and flicked the switch to light the chandelier. She placed her glass on the coffee table, removed the pin, and opened her blouse to see if there was any sign of irritation. There was nothing there but the soft cream color of her skin. Running her fingers over the metal and the intricate details of the design, Arianna silently wondered, *What on earth was so important about wearing this brooch?*

She placed it on the table near her wine cup, strolled over to the entertainment center and pulled out her Mozart CD, placing it in the machine. The music started and Arianna sat in the recliner to rest her mind for awhile.

Mozart had a strange affect on her. The percussion of the piano keys mixed with the soft violin strings was intoxicating. Her eyes fell upon the room. She wondered if these would be her last days and prayed that Father Wallace accepted what George was going to tell him—that he would be there to grant her what her soul wished for.

Seeing a pen and paper, Arianna took them up and wrote.

I, Aryanyn Lady Lawrence Pendragon, decree my last will and testimony to my family and friends.

The prelude began and soft piano notes filled the room.

I ask that before you take of my gifts, cremate my body on a pyre on the hill from whence I came. Let the fires burn me to dust. Call to the wind and let the breath of the Mother take me into the ages of time.

A flute danced, its melancholy melody spilling notes of harmony into the air.

I leave to you my undying love and affection. Take what you have learned from me and share it with one another.

Deep notes of the cello were taking over.

I leave my legacy to you all. Separate the material things amongst yourselves and only take what you know you will enjoy in the future. Whatever is left, cast it to the Seas of Affalon and let them sink into the deep, for time will see fit with their remains.

Violins whispered their sweet strokes into the chambers of the minuet.

Jack, I, your wife, have loved you through every bright road and dark alley our lives have shared. The years have seen to bring out the worst and the best in us. I don't know what I would have done without you. You have been a good husband and father, and I have cherished each year of our ever growing love. Please remember our most loving moments and hold them to your heart.

As the other instruments floated into the distance, the clarinet sang its song of joy.

Alexis, my sweet daughter, you are my diamond. When you feel the need for my presence in your life, remember when I held you as a babe in my arms, loving you and nurturing you. I will come to you in sleep and together we will dance in your dreams.

The snare drum beat hard and fast as its rhythm overpowered the notes of the players.

Joseph, my heart-song. What turmoil have our lives shared together and what blessings have this life bestowed on us? Know that through the caverns of time, I will always be with you. You are strong and you are good. Forever feel my belief in you.

A trumpet blew its fanfare as the drums and the violin mixed in harmony beneath it.

Galahad, oh son of my heart. Thank you for showing me that my life had meaning beyond the measure of love and desire. Be there at the gates of heaven, and welcome me in my Lord and King.

Cymbals crashed like swords in revelry.

Merlin, I will meet you in Elysium, and we will share in the cup of the afterlife. It is there that you and I will be joined for all eternity as our kindred souls fulfill their destinies. Merlin, it is you who showed me the essence of my soul and for that, I am eternally grateful.

A masculine choir of voices sang with deep baritone sounds that filled the room with power billowing over the drums. Cello strings joined with them like angels' wings fluttering through the room.

Arthur, what battles have we witnessed in our lives and what love have we managed to embrace deep in the caverns of our hearts? I wear your blood upon me every day-blood shed for the very love that your heart gave so generously to all whom you touched. Be with me, dear king, as I spill my blood on the circle of Stonehenge for the same cause. Arthur, if it is the will of our Lord Jesu that I die in the same manner did you, be with me on the battlefield, and lead my soul to the gates of heaven. Maybe there, we will finally be enlightened as to how two people from different worlds have been joined in such a cause.

The epitaph of the symphony reverberated around her. Drums rolled with thunderous percussion, leading the piano into its harmonic roar.

For all the rest, my dearest friends and loved ones, I leave you my eternal gratitude for being a part of my life and sharing with me the path that was laid before me.

For the love of the Goddess and the Mighty One above us, I leave the world in peace.

Arianna kissed the paper, tears flowing down her face onto the sheet.

Remember me,

I am Lady Aryanyn Lawrence Pendragon, guardian to Excalibur and Gwydion, and High Priestess of the Isle.

The music ended and Arianna held the will to her heart. Starting from the beginning, she read the letter over again.

Aryanyn. She felt her heartbeat pounding in her shoulders, in her ears, and in her hands as she read the name again. Why had she written it that way? She grabbed another piece of paper and wrote her name again only to find her hand write Aryanyn once more. Why would she write this name? *Merlin, what are you trying to tell me?*

The brooch vibrated on the table, and her hands shook as she grasped it. An odd tingle came to her brow as she looked at the image of the strange woman engraved on the back of the jewel.

Are you the Goddess?

CHAPTER FORTY-ONE

Mandragora and a Prayer to the Goddess

"Viviane, do something!" cried Nimue. "He's slipping away from me!"

Viviane grabbed Merlin by the shoulders, leaning over him. His face was white, and the veins under his skin were protruding to the surface in a web-like pattern of purple, black and blue. Placing her ear to his chest, she strained to hear his heartbeat; his chest sounded like a hollow can. She placed a mirror under his nose to see if the wizard was still breathing. The fragmented vapors showed themselves.

"Please, I beg you, don't let him die, Viviane," said a mournful Nimue.

She ran over to the priests. "Blaise, if there is something else you can do, do it now!"

Viviane looked over to her friend. Nimue had a grasp on Blaise, a grip that showed she wasn't only begging for her Merlin's life; she was begging for her own.

"Hold on," Viviane whispered under her breath to Merlin. Nimue stood there, clutching the priest. Her horrified expression echoed what was in the hearts of everyone present.

Blaise assisted Nimue over to Merlin where she took her husband's hand and held it tight. Viviane shot a look at Blaise as she held her tongue. In her opinion, Nimue was distracting them from preparing Merlin for his medicines. Viviane looked at Catherine, who had helped her earlier in the day. "Please take Nimue out of here, and let the priests and I get on with our work."

"No, no, I cannot leave him!" shouted Nimue. "If he dies, I must be with him."

Galahad entered Merlin's chambers and grabbed Nimue by the hand. "Please, dear woman, Merlin does not want his fair lady to suffer any longer."

Viviane looked Catherine squarely in the eye, sending her over to Nimue as Galahad placed the emotional woman in Catherine's care. With courage, Nimue left the room with Catherine at her side.

"Galahad, please, I implore you, leave with them," requested Viviane.

Galahad was reluctant. The fear in his expression told her what was in the good king's heart.

"My lord—" began Blaise.

Galahad put his hand up blocking the Druid's words. "Please, you do not have to beg me." Viviane knew that the rope of His Majesty's patience was just a thread away from breaking. He looked at the priest and at her, then left the room.

"Lady, fix your potion," said Aaron with desperation.

Viviane mixed the dark green mandragora leaves in a bowl along with a spoon of black cohash and another of wolf bain. She poured a cup of boiling water into the herbs and stirred the concoction before removing a cup of the liquid and placing it on the side table near Merlin. Finally, she added a touch of arrowroot to what remained in the bowl to thicken the rest of the potion.

Aaron stepped over to Merlin, removing the blankets from him. Viviane lifted her head to see the wizard. His heated body writhed as the coolness of the room washed over him.

"Look at him," said Aaron. "He has laid so long that his chest muscles are sinking into his flesh."

Viviane mixed the medicine in the bowl until it was thick enough to use as a mudpack on his skin. Fragrant aromatics gave themselves to the room, leaving a scent like a forest in the night with a hint of burnt leaves in the air.

She moved to Merlin's side where Blaise accepted the bowl from her, allowing her to do her work. She spooned some of the medicine from the cup she had left on the table, and Aaron held Merlin's head so that the tea would be ingested into his body. Merlin nearly gagged as his dry throat tried to swallow the tisane.

Viviane spooned the thicker matter from the bowl that Blaise was now holding and started rubbing it on Merlin's chest, massaging the lotion in circular motions. As his body absorbed the mixture, he bellowed in his sleep.

"Maaaabb!!" he stuttered. "Maaabbbb!!" his voice labored.

Blaise lifted his hands in prayer, "*Manon Echlin lun Saffier Cor dun mune.*"

Together, Blaise, Aaron and Viviane repeated the words, "*Manon Echlin lun Saffier Cor dun mune.*" They chanted louder, "*Manon Echlin lun Saffier Cor dun mune.*"

Viviane kneaded the muddy mixture into Merlin's body, hoping that the mandragora would alleviate the dark spell. "Aaron, give him another spoonful," she demanded. Aaron and Blaise lifted Merlin's head from the pillow and again slowly poured the tea down his throat. He gagged and in one short heave, the green liquid projected from his mouth onto Blaise's tunic. The vomit spewed with a foul stench, and Viviane nearly gagged.

Her spirit felt extinguished like darkness overcoming a dying flame. She backed away from the bed. "I cannot do any more." She wiped her hands clean of the medicine. "I place him in the hands of the Goddess now."

Blaise removed his tunic and laid it in the wooden washbasin on the floor. He lumbered over to Viviane and led her to a chair. "Go rest while we wash him. We will prepare his body for death."

"Is there nothing more that we can do?" said Viviane in a last call for hope, grabbing the alb of Blaise. "Please, you must know something that I do not." Blaise looked at Viviane with such intensity that she could feel his eyes spear through her. "You do know something. Please do it. Do it now!

"Viviane he is old. The spell could kill him."

"Kill him! Look at him—he already has one foot in death. If you know something, do it. Please, I beg you."

The priests looked at Merlin and at Viviane. Somewhere in her heart, she felt as though there was something yet to try, but what were they keeping from her?

Blaise turned to her. "Priestess, please sit and rest here a bit while we prepare our rituals." Blaise and Aaron washed down Merlin's chest. Viviane sat, staring, then looked to her long time friend. She knew that if the priests' plan failed, she would be standing next to a burning pyre the following afternoon saying the prayers to Gwyn ap Nudd, and Merlin would join Arthur in the afterlife.

The men laid their instruments on the table. Blaise stood in front of it, where she could not see what he was doing. He turned and in his hand was the carved pentacle he had used a few days prior to pray over the wizard. Aaron moved over to Merlin as Viviane sat there, concentrating on their ritual. The two priests lifted the star and laid it on Merlin's chest. Viviane stood from her chair and ambled over to the bed—her eyes nearly bulged from their sockets. The star—it was upside down.

"What black magic do you plan?"

"Have you ever heard of the Pentorium Morcarro?"

Terror leapt into Viviane's body like a lion clutching at the throat of its prey. "Yes, I have, and it is a dangerous dark spell." She looked at the upside down pentacle and put her hand over her eyes. "No, this goes against our edicts—what you plan can bring evil to this house." She looked at the pentacle quickly again and tried to push through Blaise and reach to take it off Merlin, but Blaise and Aaron stood between her and the wizard like a shield.

"Please, my lady, we know how dangerous this is, but if we don't try to align Merlin's soul with his body, he will surely die a death he does not deserve."

Viviane stood back for a moment. Every muscle in her body told her that this was wrong, yet what more was there to do? She looked at Blaise and at Aaron. "How can I explain this to Nimue?" She glanced at the door, then at Merlin lying motionless as if already dead. She rocked her head back and forth as she stared down Blaise. "Have you performed this before?"

"I have, twice in my service and it did work."

Viviane looked at both priests. "Do it then. Do it now!" She again found her eyes on the inverted pentagram. "I will pray over him, the prayers of the God of our Isle, to Avalloc to guide him."

Viviane watched as Blaise and Aaron stepped to either side of the bed. The two grabbed hands and arched them over Merlin. Blaise bent his head back and looked up towards the ceiling. He chanted, "*Mammeah, lorishna vorgin dool.*"

Aaron now did the same. "*Mammeah lorishna vorgin dah.*"

The two rocked their bodies back and forth and again vocalized in unison, "*Flyntha norswinda ech mor gliyntora.*"

Blaise let go and scampered to the table. Viviane continued her prayer to Avalloc as Blaise removed a small knife and a wooden bowl from the table.

"God of Avalon, oh mighty and powerful Avalloc, hold thy servant Merlin in your arms, and guide these priests to the service of the Mother."

She watched as Aaron removed the pentacle and placed it on Merlin's abdomen, before he added a spoon of sage to the bowl of leftover mandragora. Blaise positioned the bowl under Merlin's left wrist, clutched the knife and cut into the flesh of the wizard's hand, letting five drops of his blood mix into the potion in the bowl. He placed the pentacle back on Merlin's chest and turned it five times deosil in his hands, leaving it down in the right position where the star aligned with the form of the body.

"Mother, I give thee Merlin's blood for the sake of the spirit that is lost to his soul."

Blaise spooned the mandragora, sage and blood mixture onto his finger and traced it along the pentacle, starting at the head of the star and rubbing the now brownish red matter on its tip.

"Merlin, accept this potion and let it cleanse your soul," sung Blaise.

Viviane continued to chant quietly under her breath. "Avalloc hear us, take Merlin to your grace and heal him." Merlin's body shuddered under the covers. Holding her praying hands tightly, she said, "Mother, come to our aid, your son is in need of you."

Blaise raised his finger and in one movement, pushed it down the left leg of the star. His words rang through the room. "Merlin, take of the Mother's medicines. Let them burn into the fire of your being."

Viviane looked around. Something was in the air; there was a hum in the wind, one that seemed to be coming from under the wizard's bed.

Aaron reached for Blaise and joined a hand with the high priest. As the two scooped up a bit more of the mixture, Aaron spoke. "Merlin, release the poison from your lungs as the Mother fills your body with the air of her breath." The two ran their fingers up to the right point of the star.

"Cast out this poison!" shouted Blaise as he seized hold of Merlin's shoulder and shook him.

From deep in the wells of Merlin's chest came the sound of a thundering heartbeat. The noise filled the room, as though the tribal drums of the ancients had come to aid the wizard.

Viviane joined with them, "Cast out the poison that holds you bound."

The thump of his heartbeat grew louder, echoing off the walls, and Viviane's own heart beat with it. She grabbed for her chest as she felt pain surge through her body.

"Stop, you are going to kill us all!"

"The spell cannot be stopped," said Aaron.

Viviane knelt on the floor and held her face in her hands. "God of

Avalloc, hold us, forgive us our transgressions."

From the walls came a crackling sound as if they might implode. Viviane looked up over Aaron's shoulder. There above them, drips of crimson red fell from the ceiling. She was sickened, as opposite the wizard—near his staff—the walls were bleeding. They cracked like dried skin and bled out onto the floorboards.

Viviane looked under her feet. The blood was flowing towards them. She backed away but it ran over her shoes.

"Please!" she begged Blaise. "Stop this madness."

Aaron walked through the blood on the floor. He reaced for Viviane, who tried to push away from him. "You're evil, get out of here! God of Avalloc, hear me, help us!" she screamed.

Blaise ran to the wizard and again stirred the mixture, folding in the rest of the materials. He traced the pentacle one more time, in one continuous movement over the whole of the witch's foot. Going down the right leg of the star, he said, "*Ebbyn woo zyll senfynn maga Mammeah Eathera amnen Mab efwwar dah*!"

Merlin's body bounced up and down on his bed. The priests gripped the Druid star and spun it widdershins.

"*Mammeah*, cast out this poison!" chanted Blaise.

"Goddess Mother, Mother of Avalon, cast out this poison!" chanted Aaron.

Merlin's body was bouncing like a ball, contorting. Moaning with evil sounds, like the fury of the ocean when the seas are at war, he spewed up bile—and from out of his mouth rose a black wraith.

The doors opened, and the winds from the storms rumbled in the walls of the room, vibrating through the very foundations of the castle.

"You think you can cast me out, Blaise, but I am stronger than you," screamed the wind. Merlin's body was raised off the bed, where he levitated over the priests. Blaise and Aaron tried to reach for him, but his body hung like a marionette's puppet on strings, dangling and swinging.

From everywhere the voice boomed again, "I am Mab and no one takes what is mine."

"Show your face, Mab!" Viviane yelled, looking above her. Mab's black guise hovered like a shroud placed on the dead before burial. She was now holding Merlin's body like a rag doll, and she swung him around five times, thrusting the priests to the ground. In a final flash of anger, she threw Merlin across the room where he hit the wall and fell to the floor. When Viviane looked up again, the wraith was flying out through the open doors.

Merlin moaned from the corner. His body was contorted, crumpled like a lifeless heap of broken flesh. He sounded like a ghost, haunting the existence of his own life. From the dark caverns of his throat he bellowed, "Aryanyn!"

Blaise and Aaron rushed over to Merlin, picked him up ever so gently and placed him back on the bed. Blaise kneeled beside him, exhausted. "Fellow priest, you must choose now. Do you wait for your sister or do you go to the Goddess?"

"Please, Merlin, choose the Goddess. She will give your soul the peace it craves!" begged Aaron.

Merlin moaned louder "Aryannynnnnnnn!"

"Yes, Merlin, call her!" Viviane screamed in desperation. "Call her loud!"

Blaise prayed, "Goddess Mother, hear the plea of your humble priest. If it be your will, succor the greatness of your earth into the body of your daughter, Aryanyn. You, dear Mother, have saved her for this day. Grace her with your wisdom and your light, and grant her the destiny her soul has searched for." He knelt and bent his head. "Please, if it is your will, take Merlin into the great Elysium. He has nothing left to give."

CHAPTER FORTY-TWO

A Spouse is Distressed

"I have to go to her!" screamed Jack as he looked at the clock that read eight in the evening. The phase of the new moon would commence at nine. George and Alexis stood in front of the back doors holding Jack from exiting the kitchen while Gerard blocked the way up the stairs and Jeremy stood at the entrance to the hallway. "Let me out of here!" Jack turned and tried to run through the hall, but George cut him off. Jack stood just as tall as George, knowing that his hazel eyes showed the desperation of a man who was afraid that by nightfall he may very well be a widower.

George grabbed onto his shoulders, holding him. "Jack, please. I know that in the past you and I have not been on the friendliest of terms, but today you must listen to me."

Jack felt defensive as he looked at the clock on the wall. "Let go of me!" He threw George from him, but Jeremy—young and strong—grabbed hold of Jack, who kept fighting with all his might.

"Dad, for Mom's sake, you need to get a hold of yourself!" Alexis shouted.

Jack looked at his daughter's loving face, then at George and stopped struggling as the tears flowed. Alexis ran to him, throwing her arms around him.

"Mom knew that she needed to be away from us in order to

concentrate on this battle."

"I am her husband!" Jack sobbed at the top of his lungs as he watched his pain sting the others in the room. He felt George grab hold of his shoulder.

"Please, sir, let me be your friend today and help you share this anguish."

Jack yielded. "What will I do without my Arianna?"

Alexis held him close to her. "Dad, we must pray with all our faith."

He held onto Alexis and simply begged, "Stay with me. I am so afraid."

Jack paced to the kitchen door and watched for the light in the museum office to go on. Arianna would be dressing there. He closed his eyes and listened to Cynthia pray, "God of Arianna and all of us, look after our sister in her hour of need." The light in the office turned on.

CHAPTER FORTY-THREE

The High Priestess Dresses for Battle

———◆◆◆———

Arianna stood by her desk and took a set of keys out of the drawer. She opened the door to King Arthur's room and lit the electric torch that hung on the wall. There, His Majesty's portrait hung, and she bowed to her king and friend before removing the necklace that she and Arthur shared, remembering the day she gave it to him. Arthur had been standing on the steps of Camelot before he rode into battle. He had asked her for a favor, and she had given him her cross. Arianna placed it around his neck, and he kissed her sweetly on the cheek. Later, his blood stained the gold when Mordred's blade struck its fatal blow. Arianna rubbed the nick where his blood, still faded, marked the religious symbol. She closed her eyes, remembering the day Merlin gave it to her after Arthur's body was cremated. *Will my blood mix with yours, my friend?*

She opened the door to the museum's recreated Round Table room and flicked the switch. The chandelier light oppressed her vision so she turned it off, deciding to stand in the dark instead. Into the shadowy room, she screamed, "I, Lady Arianna Lawrence, choose Galahad as the heir to Excalibur." Images of Arthur's blood on her dress flashed through her mind. She walked over to Merlin's chair, sat down and held the arm tight. *Wizard, hold on. The power of the Mother hails in me this night.*

Arianna made her way up the stairs and opened the closet door where her travel clothes hung. Undressing from the clothes of the present time, she garmented herself in the clothes of her forebears; her blue dress laced with red ties on the front bodice and waist. Arianna grabbed for the rope laces and yanked at them, making sure the bones in the girdle formed around her ribs and waist to support her in battle. She placed her hand on her waist, sucked in air to fill her diaphragm, and released it to cleanse the tension in her abdomen. Pulling her hair back in a red and gold ribbon, she placed her pendragon cinquefoil around her neck.

Her censor was already primed, and she placed the petals of rose oil and jasmine on the hot stones. She covered the censor and allowed the room to fill with the fragrance of the flowers. Taking in the perfume, a calmness came over her.

Arianna stepped over to her desk and clutched her brown sheath belt in her hands. She girded it around her waist, making sure that the buckle would not give way in battle. Moving to the window, she watched as the hour of dusk waned from the day and the dark of the night sky took over.

"Gwydion, I call you by name. Come into my hands." Arianna raised her sword, kissing her on the pommel. "Thirst this night for blood. Wreak goodness upon the grass of the circle, and let time bury this evil there for eternity."

She placed the blue stone to her brow. "Quiet hails the power force within me, raging in my blood."

Arianna kissed Gwydion, then sheathed her. She was ready. Turning off the light, she descended the back stairwell to the barn where Sir Brach was waiting for her. He was ready to accommodate his mistress, already outfitted with saddle and Arianna's travel bags. She mounted her companion and out the barn door they rode.

CHAPTER FORTY-FOUR

Arianna's Confession

Arianna looked upon the moon in all her glory, shining brightly like the eye of the Goddess watching down on her daughter.

"Come Brach, to the chapel." Arianna pulled on the reins, and Brach headed for the Chapel Avalon. The chapel light was on, and Arianna followed it to the entrance, dismounting Brach. She quietly opened the doors, looked about the chapel and made the sign of the cross. It had been a while since she attended mass, and tears rolled down her cheeks. "Jesus, please forgive me. I have separated myself from you."

"My lady, it is the church who separated itself from you," said Father Wallace, walking into the chapel.

"Good evening, Father."

"George told me what was to transpire tonight. I had a feeling that you might come."

"Father, forgive my behavior of late. I have been overwhelmed with tonight's affairs." Arianna turned toward the altar.

"I know that God's earth is an endless bounty of miracles, but I do admit that this one is a bit hard for me to take."

"We come from two different worlds; mine is of the God in heaven and the Goddess."

"You speak her name in the house of our Lord?"

"She is the bride of our God."

"I am still from the traditional church."

"Is not the earth and her people all within the body of Christ? Are we not his bride then?" Arianna asked.

"I have never thought about it in such a manner."

"Hear it now with new faith," she said as she kneeled and kissed the ring of Father Wallace's priestly vows.

"What of Arthur? The words on his tomb?"

"The words, my priest," answered Arianna, "were written by the hand of God."

"But for what purpose?" asked the confused priest.

"It is for God to decide and for his will to be done, Father." Arianna reached for the door. "The time is at hand."

"I cannot support your thinking and these beliefs, but I do support you in your endeavors, whatever they may be."

"Please, Father, hear my confession."

Father Wallace removed his prayer stole from his pocket and placed it around his neck. He put his hands on Arianna's head and she began.

"In the name of the Father and of the Son and of the Holy spirit. It has been one year since my last confession."

"What sins do you wish to be absolved of, my child?"

Arianna held tight to her cross. "I ask God to forgive the anger I have held for my husband. And I ask him to forgive me of the evil that has held me hostage and prevented me from coming to him in the state of grace." Wallace placed the sign of the cross on her brow. She looked up to his face. "I ask Jesus to forgive me as I raise my sword in battle against a foe I plan to kill tonight."

Father Wallace stepped away from her and cupped the holy water from the font, returning to her and sprinkling it over Arianna's head. "Is this the evil that will take you from the state of grace when your soul returns to God?"

"Yes, good Father. I may taste the death I have feared the whole of my life."

"Why do you fear this, my child?" asked the priest.

"Good Father, I am undeserving of his love." Arianna took note of the expression of enlightenment on the priest's face.

"Stand, my child. Come to the altar with me."

Arianna stood and followed him.

"Kneel."

Arianna knelt on the altar step.

Father Wallace walked to the tabernacle, removed the consecrated host and wine and placed the cup on the altar. "I absolve you in the name of the Father and of the Son and of the Holy Spirit." He lifted the ciborium, removed the lid and received Jesus into his hands. "Know, Lady Arianna, that Jesus is with you this night and into all eternity."

Arianna raised her head and looked upon the host.

"The body of Christ," said the good priest.

"Amen," answered Arianna.

The Father placed the host in her mouth and her eyes lifted to the cross. Father Wallace raised the chalice of wine and covered the cup with his hand as he said the prayers of consecration before resting the cup in Arianna's hands.

"The blood of Christ," he said.

Arianna responded, "Amen," and bowed her head. She took of the cup and drank, the wine burning as it dripped down her throat—an uncomfortable feeling but one that she welcomed.

The priest turned and placed the host back in the tabernacle before speaking his last words, "Now go and free us."

Arianna stood and walked out of the chapel to where Brach was waiting for her. She climbed onto him and lifted her head to the moon, bathing herself in the light. She pulled on his reins. "Yah!" she screamed. Brach reared up on his hind legs before they broke into a run. "Brach my friend, tonight is a good night to die."

CHAPTER FORTY-FIVE

The Blood of the High Priestess

———◆———

"Mab, where are you, Mab?" screamed Arianna as she galloped up the avenue and into the sarsen stones. "Mab, come and face me!" She knew that from above, the monoliths were watching her as she arrived at the temple of the ancients. Arianna remained mounted on Brach, her eyes circling the area. She could feel her powers begin to course through her and again, she yelled, "Mab!" Drawing Gwydion, she struck the side of the altar stone with her blade, praying. "I call upon the ancients! Surge your powers upon me. I command the four ancestral guards! Fortress of the ancients, surge thy flames upon the circle. Bless me with the flame of your spirit. Quiet hails the power of fire within me.

Arianna dismounted Brach and guarded herself, holding the sword at bay, waiting for her enemy. "The sarsen stones call upon the Mother. She alone breathes life upon the keep. Stir your winds of wrath. I inhale them in my lungs. Quiet hails the power of air within me."

A droplet of water formed upon her brow, and Arianna took notice that lightning-filled storm clouds were slowly obscuring the moon, now locked in its phase and shining brightly in the night. "Come forth all ancient spirits. Baptize me with mighty wisdom. Wash me with pure virtue. Cleanse the iniquity from this world. Quiet hails the power of water within me."

She heaved Gwydion up into the darkness and then rammed the

blade down into the earth, prying the soil from the ground beneath the grass and breathing in the perfume of the dirt. Harvest me the food of your might. Succor me upon your breast. Nurture me with vengeful solace. Quiet hails the power of earth within me.

Arianna raised Gwydion high, screaming into the wind and the now pouring rain. Guardians of the four corners, I call upon thee. Consecrate me with your gifts and rage them in my blood."

The echo of a single clap of hands broke the sound of the rainfall and as the water ceased to fall from the sky, the voice of Mab finally spoke. "A spell for novices, Priestess!"

Arianna turned to face a shadow near the singular brown stone standing to the right of the Trilithon. Raising Gwydion for battle, she made her way over to the rock. A cold wind and mocking laughter blew around her yet again. *Not this time, witch.* "Show yourself," she yelled into the night.

She could hear the whipping sound of Mab's sword, but Mab remained hidden from her sights. The cold wind rushed by her again, but this time it touched Arianna's face like a slap of anger. Wiping her cheek with her hand, she said, "You plan to fight me this way?" The stones seemed to dwarf her as she yelled, "Show yourself, coward Queen of Darkness."

"Queen of Darkness?"

Arianna spun around to see Mab standing in her human form by the single sarsen, leaning on it. "Is that what they call me now?"

Mab stood five-foot six-inches, clothed in an elegant red and gold dress with long, flowing dark red hair set against porcelain features that showed in the light of the moon. She was a woman of great beauty and in her hands, she carried an impressive, bejeweled blade.

Mab flared her dress folds at Arianna. "Admit what your eyes are telling you," she said pushing away from the stone. "I am more than you can handle."

"I'm tired of your games, Mab."

"Games? I'm just getting started."

"Let's get this over with, ehy? Defend thyself." Arianna thrust her blade and Mab dodged the parry, rolling to the ground. When she came up, a rock in her hand flew at Arianna, hitting her in the side of the head, and Mab followed the stone with the lunge of her sword. Arianna swerved away, darting from the oncoming weapon. In one slick movement, Arianna sidestepped Mab's attempted blow and advanced into her, catching her at the right shoulder, stabbing her deep. Mab screamed in pain and drew away from Arianna, who looked to Gwydion, stained with blood. She wiped her sword with her fingers, seeing the crimson of Mab on her hand. "You do bleed!" Arianna felt her power surge.

Mab struck at Arianna with her sword, but her parry was deflected. Mab screamed and attacked again, pushing Arianna face first into a tall sarsen. Arianna's left shoulder crashed against the stone, pushing her pin into her flesh and spilling her blood onto her blouse.

Arianna turned back around and advanced towards Mab. "I am the high priestess, Mab, and I have come to kill you."

"I live forever," Mab's coarse voice shrieked into Arianna's ears. She unleashed a powerful force of energy at Arianna, but Arianna held out her hand and controlled it, pushing it back to her attacker.

"Give me Gwydion, and I'll spare your life," called Mab.

Arianna held tight to her sword, still surging back the energy of her opponent, "I will never release her to your hands."

"I can give you everything you want. I can give you power, I can give you riches. I can give you Arthur," Mab's voice smiled, tempting Arianna.

Arianna's anger swelled. *Fight this witch on her own terms.* "*Maclyn mor zyll seffen maga amnen maga Mab efwwar dah!*"

"You can't curse me, Christian!" Mab said coyly.

"Curse you? I want you dead!"

The two women continued to fight for control over the energy that was passing between them. Mab incantated, "*Gelfin todd ech moccynn moor! Tud cromber lun magala efwwar dah, Arianna!*"

The earth moaned, and the ground around both women opened like a lion about to feed. The pit was deep and a fire raged at its bottom casting shadows onto the brown of the earth. Roots from the surrounding plants, buried deep in the soil, slithered from the edges of the hole like snakes pushing through. Shadows danced and spirits of hell cried out.

Mab pushed back at Arianna, angling her towards the hole. With one hand surged out towards Mab, still fighting for control over the bolt between them, Arianna raised Gwydion to strike as hands beneath her yanked at her skirt and black wraiths tugged hard at her feet, trying to drag her down into the flames.

Beneath them, Arianna saw muted specters with faces that were nothing but a mass of burned flesh hanging from their jowls. Her stomach felt queasy, and pain surged in her chest. Mummified hands pulled her down—roots that now adopted a skeletal likeness, looking like the organs of the dead whose bones had been eaten away by insects that crawled in the earth.

Arianna managed to dig her boot heel into the muddy soil and push away from the hole. "*Macolatha efende fintorroa Eathera seofel!*" She raised Gwydion and struck fiercely at Mab, throwing her back a good fifty feet. In that moment, the energy between them was released and as Mab hit the ground, the earth around Arianna closed.

"You think visions of hell will scare me?" whispered Arianna as she regained her footing in the again falling rain.

Mab stood there facing Arianna, her red dress drenched and spattered with mud. Arianna's sword was ready for the dark one to advance. In a swift movement, Mab vanished and struck again from behind Arianna, surging a bolt of lightning into her. Arianna fell to the ground on her stomach, hitting the soil so hard that the buckle of her belt cut into her waist. She shot up from the pain, stood on her shaking legs, and wiped the warm liquid that was rolling down her cheek. She was bleeding.

Arianna swung Gwydion, slashing into the black of Mab's wraith. She slashed at her over and over again, only to find Gwydion slice through nothingness. Mab laughed long and loud at Arianna. "What you quest for will never come to pass. I will fill you with lust and greed," antagonized the witch.

"Is that how you controlled Mordred? How you wish to control Merlin?"

"No, it is how I wish to control you!"

In one strike, Mab materialized again right in front of Arianna, catching her off guard. Arianna thrust her sword at Mab, but the witch deflected her parry, bending backward away from Arianna's lunging blade. Mab turned away from her and kicked Arianna to the ground. With one foot, she rolled Arianna through the grass like a ball at play. Adding a surge of light and energy to the mix, Arianna watched the world spin around Stonehenge as though she we were a wheel on an axis until she felt her body lift from the earth below. Suddenly she was thrown through the air, until the altar stone collided with her body. Hitting the earth, she lay there a moment in stillness. The Henge was rotating around her in circles as on a carousel, and in the middle stood Mab. Not a few feet away, Arianna could see Gwydion as the dizziness faded. She rose up slowly, stumbling, but saw Mab already running to her, sword engaged.

Arianna picked herself up and sprinted towards the witch. As she neared Gwydion, she dove into the mud, face first, sliding in the direction of her enemy and retrieving her sword in a single motion. But it was too late, Mab was on top of her. Arianna felt the pommel of Mab's sword thrust into her shoulder blades. She arched backward as the pain cut though her torso and into her breast bone.

Mab again engaged and slashed at Arianna, cutting the forearm that bore her sword. Pain surged through Arianna's right hand as her blood streamed from the gash, and every nerve in her lower arm numbed.

Arianna grabbed Gwydion with her other hand, but Mab was still on the hunt. This time Arianna managed to raise her sword in defense and as they clashed, she pushed Mab back and away from her. Mab fell to one knee and in the brief moment that Arianna had to regain herself, she managed to form a force field around her. Red and blue lights encased her as she took a breath to center herself. She felt her body tiring.

During that second of distraction, Mab cut through Arianna's lights and advanced to her, a fully engaged predator on the prowl. Again, Arianna raised Gwydion high, and the two women volleyed in front of the twin trilithons. The sound of their swords boomeranged off the stones like chimes in the abbey tower. Arianna crossed her weapon to Mab's as though in a draw, locking their next move. Pushing forward, Mab and she were eye to eye, neither giving in. In one fast move, an unexpected electric shock, as if from a socket, ran through Arianna forcing her to retreat, lest she fall. In one slam, Mab struck at Gwydion. The blow of the witch's blade was strong and hard, and Arianna could feel each counterstrike run through her like a dull knife. In a last ditch effort, Arianna shot some of her blood towards Mab and it ignited, exploding into a ball of fire as it sped towards its target. The witch controlled the ball and returned it back to Arianna, who pulled it around her body and speared it to Mab once more.

Mab easily averted the attack and started laughing. "You are a novice witch. Admit it. If you continue, you will lose your life."

"I will defend my Merlin to the death."

"So it shall be." In a swift moment, Mab disappeared from her position fifty feet from Arianna, only to reappear directly in front of her and run her sword though Arianna's side, into her rib under her right breast. Arianna screamed in agony, feeling the blade hit the bone. A sudden rush of fire surged through her body. Her blood soaked her dress, and as its warmth left her body, the cold sting of death draped over her. She shivered and her eyes blurred. Through her hazy vision, Mab stood there cackling as though in a dream.

"You are a fool!" she said mocking and spitting at Arianna The witch reached for Gwydion. "The sword is mine!" Mab yelled, grabbing the hilt in her hand and pulling it from Arianna. Taking the guise of the specter, she flew away with the weapon.

Arianna dropped to her knees, her arms hanging at her sides

paralyzed, watching, in slow motion, as Mab floated away from her with Gwydion hanging from the tails of her black cloak.

Arianna fell to the earth as Mab came to rest on the sarsen. Arianna knew her foe was waiting for her to give into her wound and die.

"Merlin, I am sorry!" Arianna cried.

The rain fell again and Arianna rolled onto her back and looked up to the sky to see the moon peeking through the storm clouds. She looked down at her dress, soaked in her own blood, and smiled through her disparity. *Arthur, we share the same wounds now.*

Glancing towards the moon, she prayed once more. "Mother, light up the darkness. Bathe the circle for your daughter."

The sky thundered and lightning streaked the midnight dome. Droplets of rain pounded her face as a sense of calm passed over her and silence filled her ears. Beneath her, she felt the energy of the earth actually pushing against her body, almost willing her to stand. A wind rushed across her, and her lungs filled with the freshness of the air.

The ground was slimy from the mucky mixture of moist mud and her blood. Turning over, she knelt on all four limbs like a dog begging for life. Pain coursed through her, and all she wanted to do was fall back into the Earth. But in a single burst of energy, she yelled to Mab, "Gwydion is mine!"

Her chest felt like it was on fire, as Arianna pulled herself up on her feet. She stood and stumbled for a moment, but held her legs tight. "Gwydion, my armor and my strength, feel the power of your mistress."

Arianna raised her hand to the moon, taking the energy from Mother Earth's natural satellite, which beamed it's radiance down to her.

"Gwydion, come to your guardian now!"

Arianna extended her hand and a beam of light shot to Mab, who materialized instantly and fell from the top of the sarsen. With a stunned expression, she lay there on the ground, as though refusing to believe that Arianna was still alive.

Gwydion pulled from Mab's hands as though Arianna's beam was a magnet. Drawing the weapon to her, the sword followed the ray of light back to her.

Into the night, Arianna tilted her head back and yelled, "The high king will rise and he will take his life again."

"You think Galahad can guard Excalibur forever? That sword is mine." Mab was struggling to stand.

"Only one man can claim Excalibur, and that is Arthur!" Arianna raised Gwydion to the sky. "I am the guardian of Excalibur, and no one attacks my ward." The sky thundered. "Excalibur!" called Arianna as she pointed the blade of Gwydion into the night. "I, Lady Arianna Lawrence Pendragon, daughter of Avalon, ask the God of heaven and the Goddess Mother of the planet earth to reveal her most precious secrets!" Arianna struck one of the sarsens, sliding the blade of Gwydion on the stone, releasing sparks off the granite. "Excalibur, come forth from the caverns of time. I, your guardian, Arianna, summon you. *Ectoris Blye ephachatta ciaric.*"

The stones shook and the light from the moon refracted on the trilithons, opening a window to the past from which Arianna could see the causeway to Camelot. "Excalibur, can you hear me?"

From the center of the trilithons came a sound that rang like a song from the heavens. Excalibur was shooting forth, surrounded by light that seemed to form a protective prism around the historic blade as it cut its way to the sound of her voice.

Arianna reached out to Excalibur as it came towards her and in a flash before it reached her, she shattered its prism with Gwydion, while in the same stroke, reaching out and catching the hilt of Arthur's sword with her free hand.

Arianna struck the altar stone with both weapons now in her possession, shouting, "Mab, if you want the sisters so much, you come back here and you claim them."

"They are mine!" Mab yelled from across Stonehenge and sprang into a sprint towards her.

"Let us finish this!" cried Arianna as she broke into a run towards the center of the circle. Meeting in the middle, she attacked Mab with a hard blow from Excalibur. Mab struck back, parrying away from Arianna, who counter struck with the hilt of Gwydion and knocked Mab to the ground. Mab popped up and broadsided Arianna with her sword. As the blade came from the left, Arianna raised Gwydion and crashed her steel onto Mab's tang. It vibrated up from the hilt to her hand, and Arianna watched Mab shake with fury. Arianna extended her sword and thrust it at Mab, who jerked away, slipping on the wet ground and finding herself on her hind parts. From there, the dark queen managed to form an energy ball and threw the red sphere at Arianna. It bounced off Gwydion's blade, sending it over the lintel on the right of the circle. Arianna quickly rammed her foot into Mab's chest and placed the point of Gwydion over her heart.

"Tell me why you want me dead?" As Arianna spoke, sweat mixed with blood and poured down from her face onto Mab. Mab clasped onto Arianna's ankle and knocked her to the earth.

"You are the one the ancients foretold of, the one who will unite the houses."

Arianna felt no pain as she raised herself quickly to her feet again, slashing at her enemy's chest with Excalibur and cutting her open. Mab bent over, her blood gushing to the earth, but still she raised her sword again. The two parried, clashing at each other, and the sounds of three swords echoed through the circle.

Arianna crossed her blades, advancing towards Mab, and the old queen ducked to protect herself from beheading.

"Your heart is as impure as Mordred's," shouted Arianna. "The sister swords will never defend you."

Mab attacked Arianna with a blow to her stomach, kicking her hard. Arianna winced in pain doubling over. "Yes, Mab, take me as you and Mordred took Arthur! It will be an honor to die as Arthur did." Arianna advanced again at Mab, banging into her sword.

Excalibur's sharp blade cut Mab's bicep, slashing at the muscle and almost cutting off her arm. Mab fell again.

"Bitch!" called a vicious Mab as she held tight to her wound.

Arianna could see that Mab was trying to cloak herself into the black phantom; she was flickering in and out of view, but exhaustion must have prevented her magic from working effectively and she remained in the flesh.

Arianna raised Gwydion and Excalibur in the air. "Sisters of Avalon, I, your guardian, command the death of this witch!"

Arianna ran toward and lunged into the queen, the two swords penetrating her body. Mab tried to stand but fell to one knee.

"Can you really kill me, Christian, or will your Jesus do it for you?"

"Jesus would not kill you—he would forgive you. But you're not dealing with Jesus. You're dealing with me."

In a lightning move, Arianna pulled both of the blades from Mab's body and scissored them at the witch's throat, severing her at the neck. Her body fell quickly and her head rolled towards the altar stone, resting its eyes towards the moon.

"Domh Ringr, accept the gift that I, your priestess, lay before you. You have sheltered me in my hour of need."

Exhausted, tears rolled down Arianna's face as blood still seeped from her side. "Excalibur, I call you by name, my ward and my defender. The day will now begin, and our quest will come to pass."

Arianna walked over to the altar stone and struck it with the blade of Excalibur. "I call upon the circle to take her forth!" Again Arianna struck the stone screaming, "I, Arianna, Lady Lawrence Pendragon, guardian of Excalibur, daughter of Avalon, beseech the God of Heaven and the Mother Earth, the Goddess. Take custody forthwith this day of Excalibur, sword of Arthur and the Holy Grail, until her king summons her forth." She kissed Excalibur and whispered to her, "We will come for you!" With that she plunged the sword into the stone, and it accepted Excalibur, sparks flying from the blade, the metal chiming like a bell.

CHAPTER FORTY-SIX

Burning

—————◆·◆·————

"We must burn Mab!" The world around Arianna was hazy, and had Brach not come to her aid, she would barely have been able to hold herself upright. She could not leave Mab's body on the grounds of the circle. Arianna stood by the triple bluestones that lay on the ground near the altar stone. She removed her oil lamp and a black velvet pouch from the saddlebag on Brach. Lighting the lamp with a match, she rested the light source on the stone and bowed to Excalibur, "I thank thee, blade of Arthur, for aiding me."

She looked down at her nemesis, Mab, whose lifeless, beheaded body lay on the indigo grass of the circle. Her head, several feet away, lay with her face in a contorted expression. Her blue eyes were still open and bloody drool oozed from the side of her mouth.

Arianna stood over Mab's body and opened the black velvet pouch, her shaky hands pouring its contents out over Mab's blood soaked dress. Before the battle, Arianna had prepared a mixture of mandragora and sagebush.

"I ask the herbs of the Mother to heal the Domh Ringr from the evil that lay upon her."

Picking up her lamp from off the stone beside her, Arianna opened the side cap and poured the lamp oil over the body and around the grass. "I ask the Mother Earth to purify your circle and renew it for the ages."

She lifted the lamp above her head and brought it down hard upon the oil stained grass that ignited around Mab and drew inwards towards the hemline of her dress. Watching the oil ignite with the cloth, the herbs, and the flesh of her enemy Arianna chanted, "*Maclyn moor zyll maga. Amnen Mab dah*!" and backed up as the flames grew.

Arianna carefully folded her right arm to her rib cage, attempting to hold her body together as she bent over and picked up Mab's head by the hair. As she raised it from the ground, blood streamed out upon the grass near Arianna's feet. When the blaze had grown high enough, she tossed the head onto the pyre. Mab's hair singed as it was eaten up by the inferno, and Arianna could smell the stench of it burning in the air. Flames of orange and red crackled, taking on a blue aura at the height of their temperature. The fire burned at Mab's feet, taking to her boots— the leather burning away—revealing her toes as the heat crawled around them. As the fire raged, bits of fabric from the witch's dress flew up into the air, hovering over the site.

As Mab's death mask was burning, it released the odor of cooked grease over a barbeque pit. Her skin was melting and her charred skeleton was all that remained as the flares from the flames licked away at her eyes. The Henge reeked horribly of burned meat and lamp oil.

Arianna stood there, sweating from the roar of the fire. She looked upon the whole of Stonehenge, which was magnificent as the lights of the ritual cast a dance of victory upon the stone icons.

The indigo of the sky and the moon shining brightly beamed down on her. The glow actually gave Stonehenge a pretense of peace. Arianna hoisted up Mab's sword, and though she could hardly hold it, she lifted the Queen's blade and tied it to the pommel of her saddle with some rope from her bag. The wounds she had sustained were taking over rapidly, and Brach must have sensed this, because he bent low to allow Arianna to grab his mane and mount him.

"Take me home, Brach."

She let him lead her through the twin trilithons, and she struck Gwydion on the side of the sarsen as they passed

"Guardians, you may take thy rest!"

Chapter Forty-Seven

The Hill Calls for the Priestess

Arianna rode fast through the valley; her side feeling as though it were caving in, to the point where she was having trouble balancing her torso on the saddle. She came to the hill and halted, peering down in the darkness to the barn, where the lights and the outdoor lamps were glowing. To her right, by the kitchen door, she could barely make out Cynthia and Dr. Marcus waiting for her. She held the pommel on her saddle—beads of sweat and blood pouring down her face. Brach turned to her as though waiting for her signal.

"I need a moment, old friend."

Brach looked back toward the hilltop. She gave him a slight kick on the side, and the two made their way down the hill, with her barely holding on.

Brach's hooves trotted on the hard pavement coming down the causeway.

"Arianna is back!" she heard Cynthia shout. "She is home!"

Brach bent low for her again and Arianna dismounted and hobbled down the causeway, limping her way into the museum. She stood at the bottom of the steps and painfully climbed up to Arthur's room, one agonizing step at a time. At the top of the stairs, she stood and bowed to the portrait of her king, her back and legs aching horribly with every move she made.

"My lord, I thank thee for the aid that you and Excalibur delivered on this, my most highest of hours." She pulled her cross out from her dress. It was covered in blood from the wound on her chest where the pin had stabbed her. Arianna held the symbol to her heart.

"Our blood did mix in battle this night." She took a deep breath, turned and hobbled as best she could back down the stairs, yelling, "Jack, Alexis, I am here!"

Her family was standing at the Museum doorway, and as Arianna screamed, they stepped towards her. She saw George in the background with Cynthia, both wanting to come to her but they stayed back, giving Arianna and her family the first opportunity to reconvene. She looked straight at George and with her tired eyes, she told her friend exactly how she felt. Dr. Marcus came from the foreground, and she put her hand up signaling him to stay away.

Jack was about to embrace his wife when he paused in his tracks and examined her from head to foot. She looked down at her dress and the evidence of her battle. It was torn and tattered at the hemline and shoulders. Her hair was pasted to her face from the blood drying on her cheek and as she attempted to run her hand through it, she could feel that the strands were matted, covered in soil and filth.

Looking up at Jack, she watched his face twist in fear, then caught him again looking at her blood-soaked bodice. His eyes met hers as she touched her side and attempted to cover her wound.

"It's alright, Jack. I am fine," she said as confidently as she could, knowing that life was draining out of her. "Mab is dead."

Tears rolled down Jack's face. He stood almost frozen as he looked upon Arianna.

"Mom, oh my God! Mom, you killed her!?!" Arianna caught a strange look of both pride and disgust in her daughter's expression before Alexis buried her head in Jeremy's chest.

"Please, I need some water, and then I must go to Merlin."

Dr. Marcus ran inside.

Shock coursed over Jack's face. "You're hurt." Jack reached for her, but she put her hands up and backed away.

"I am covered in battle. I must go to Merlin with Mab's death upon me." Jack again stretched his arms out towards his wife, but she pulled away a second time, lifting her hand as a shield. "I am unclean. I must go to Viviane, and she must heal and purify me."

"Arianna please, the doctor is here. He can help you!" Jack desperately pleaded.

"Arianna, let me tend to your wounds before you leave," said Dr. Marcus as he handed her a cup of water. She accepted it carefully from him, not wanting to touch his fingers. After quenching her thirst, she threw the glass down upon the pavement, loudly shattering it into dozens of pieces.

"Dr. Marcus, I thank you for being here, but, I must leave. I must be purified under the laws of the Druids."

"But your wounds—they could kill you," he advised Arianna. Again she backed away.

"I won't let you leave!" screamed Jack as he stepped towards her, but she ran to the causeway as Alexis stepped in front of her father.

"Sir Brach, come now!"

Brach met his mistress midstride, and she mounted him quickly, shouting back at Jack, "Please, my love, I must leave you in order to return to you in peace."

Arianna sat tall on Brach and looked to her daughter. "Hold onto each other for my sake, and love each other."

"Mom, are you sure you cannot stay to let us help you?" asked Alexis as she embraced her father. They were both crying and Arianna cried with them.

George and Cynthia came to Jack and Alexis' aid. George shot a look of support to Arianna, and she smiled at him. He turned to Jack, "My friend, her quest begins here."

Arianna threw a kiss to her family. "I love you," she said. She turned Brach towards the hill and he led her to the twin maples where she lifted Gwydion and held her towards the moon. "I, Lady Arianna Lawrence Pendragon, High Priestess of Avalon, call on the essence of time. Open this damned gate!"

CHAPTER FORTY-EIGHT

Victory

━━━◆◆◆━━━

"*Saffier etyme mor tulun*," said Arianna as she and Brach crashed through the gates of time. The flash of the yellow light sounded like glass shattering as Arianna pointed Gwydion towards the portal and closed it. Sheathing her sword, she felt as though her body could cave in from her wounds. She opened her bodice and tore a piece of the chemise from under her skirt, tying the torn fabric tight around her ribs and tucking it under the bones of the bodice. With all the strength she could muster, she yanked the laces tight around her rib cage and tied them off, feeling some support around the main wound. She sat for a moment and took a breath before pulling hard on the bridal. Brach stood on his hind legs and whinnied, came down on all fours and galloped quickly up the land bridge. Arianna reengaged her sword, as she was unescorted and knew the dangers of the hills of Avalon at night. Thankfully, dawn was rising.

Sir Brach's hooves pounded the land bridge as they neared the exterior gates of Camelot.

"A rider approaches!" shouted the sentry from his watch.

Arianna looked up to the young soldier, who was armed with spear in hand. As she drew closer to the gate, she commanded, "Open in the name of Merlin!"

"Declare yourself, peasant!" demanded another sentry standing opposite the metal barrier.

"I am Arianna, high priestess and mother to your king."

"Mother to the king, are you? Look at you, peasant, you are filth—get on with you!"

Arianna drew Brach as close as possible to the guard and spoke with low intensity. "Soldier, I will have your rank if you don't open this gate."

The sentry leaned in just as closely and responded, "The mistress of this fortress is a lady of fine means. Now go before I order you in chains."

Behind the young sentry, a knight approached. "What is it, man?"

"Look at this wench, Sir Michael. She's calling herself Lady Arianna."

The knight came closer to the gate and drew his sword.

"Michael, it is I," Arianna said as she pulled her hair back away from her face.

Michael raised his torch and looked at her more closely, "Dear God! Has she killed the witch?" He turned to the soldier and grabbed him by the shoulder, pushing him away. "You fool!" yelled Sir Michael. "This *is* Lady Arianna! Lift the gates!" he cried to the sentry above, his voice billowing with authority.

The thunderous sounds of the iron lifting were music to Arianna as she and her steed rode through the entryway.

"Keep careful guard!" she heard Michael command as he mounted his horse and followed after her, catching up to her side.

"Michael," she asked as they rode, "what is the status of Merlin's health?"

"He is not in good form, my lady. He is failing rapidly."

Both riders dashed up the entry passage towards the steps of the castle.

"Is Mab dead, High Priestess?" yelled Michael.

"What do your eyes tell you, young knight?"

She was haggard and tired as she dismounted Brach, her body and soul screaming in quiet agony. Arianna untied Mab's sword and limped up the ten steps toward the main castle entrance with what felt like the last of her strength.

Sir Michael cut her off at the pass. "Please let me announce you!" he begged.

Arianna shot him a cross expression and he looked back at her like a scolded schoolboy. The night guard stood at attention as she ordered, "Open these doors!"

With a hard creaking sound, the doors parted, and Arianna dragged herself quickly into the dimly lit hallway. She passed the drawing room and turned the corner, which led to the entrance of the knights' hallway behind the Round Table room. Michael gestured to the guard, who saw them coming and opened the door.

Arianna stopped under the painting of King Uther. She looked at Michael straight in the face, her heart racing. "Please tell me that Merlin is not dead."

"They hold vigil for him as we speak."

"They who?"

"His Majesty sits with him as High Priest Blaise, his assistant Aaron, and Viviane prepare him for death."

"High Priest Blaise is within these walls?" Her legs gave way, and Arianna held her back to the stones behind her. "Go tell them I have come. I will await you here."

Michael ran up the stairs towards Merlin's room.

Arianna held tight to Mab's sword. "You have not won. Neither Merlin nor I will give up."

"Mother!" a voice Arianna's ears starved to hear greeted her from the top of the stairs. Down came her son Joseph running with Michael.

As he approached Arianna, she stopped him with a wave of her hand. "Please, my son. I am covered in the blood of Mab."

Michael held the torch closely to Arianna, and a sickening look came over Joseph as he saw the outcome of the battle on her. He held hard to his chest. "Dear God, Mother, you are wounded! Please let me help you."

Arianna backed away from Joseph, never leaving the support of the wall. "After Viviane purifies me, I will enjoy the touch of your hand."

Joseph shook his head. "I understand the laws of purification."

"Please take me to Merlin," she insisted.

Joseph led the way up to Merlin's chambers. He approached the door and carefully but quickly opened it.

As Arianna staggered in, all eyes befell her. Nimue looked upon her, stood and cried out, "Is she dead?" and lurched toward Arianna.

Viviane moved in to intercede. "She must be purified!"

Two men, dressed in Druid albs, backed away from the bedside to make room for Arianna as she shuffled further into the room and leaned on the sword of Mab, whispering, "Merlin, it is I, Arianna. Mab is dead. Please tell me that I am not too late."

"I am Blaise," one of the Druids said as he carefully approached.

Arianna looked at the man, "Are you he who healed my sons in the forest?"

Blaise answered, "I am he, Priestess." He was examining her waist, her hair and her face.

Arianna placed her hand over her bloody corset, held her head high and asked, "And what healing laws do you give to the wizard?"

"High Priestess, we have done everything we can within human and herbal medicines."

Arianna wiped the blood of Mab from her dress and held her red stained hands out towards the priest. "Here is the poison that is killing Merlin. She has been put to rest. Her headless body burns at Domh Ringr."

"The power to save him lies in the brooch you wear on your bodice, my lady," said Blaise.

Arianna ripped the pin from her dress "What secret does this carry?"

"Who you are and what this battle was fought and won for."

Arianna looked at Merlin. "I am tired of riddles and spells, Priest. I have not the strength to heed to them any longer."

"Call him out of his sleep," commanded Priest Blaise.

Arianna stood over Merlin.

"Please Arianna," begged a desperate Nimue, "speak loud your voice so my husband may hear you and awaken."

Arianna inched her way to the foot of the bed and raised her hand into the shadows as they danced with the flames from the hearth above the head of the ailing wizard. "Merlin it is I, Arianna. Hear my voice." Merlin lay motionless. "The one who poisoned you is dead. She can no longer lay her venom on you."

Merlin groaned. Arianna watched as his chest raised from under the sheets, heaving with breath.

"Merlin, I call you by name. Come follow my voice from the caves of your sleep."

"Ariannnnna!" called Merlin.

"Remember whence I slept in your arms. You held me and kept me safe. Come to the safety of my voice now."

"Ariannnna!" Merlin shouted.

Arianna held her pin tight, clasping it so hard that the pin drew blood, which dripped from her fingers. As it glowed in her hand, the nearby fire roared and the light from the crescent moon on the brooch met with Arianna's amber eyes. She raised her hand, and the light cast its radiance on Merlin's face.

"Remember when Gresham impaled me and you told me to join Arthur and find peace for my soul? Come, for your peace is waiting hither unto you."

"Arianna!" Merlin cried out as he reached for her.

She stood tall and commanded. "Merlin, come forth now!"

He snarled again and—within the misery—he yelled, "Arianna!" His hoarse voice cut through her heart.

"Ariannnnna!" Merlin howled.

She watched as the blaze of the pin cast rays of light around the room. His walking staff that leaned in the corner waiting for its master to call upon him for service, vibrated against the wall. The red eye of the dragon that headed the staff burned for its master as it met with the blush of Arianna's pin.

Merlin's hand raised to Arianna, and rays of energy from his body mixed with the waves of light streaming forth from her palm. A red and blue ball of light formed in Arianna's hand, and its glow radiated between them. Their faith and devotion to each other was connecting them again as one. She raised the ball and played with it as waves of color emitted from her coiled fingers. Shooting it across the room like a toy, it bounced off the walls, refracting bolts of lightning around the bed. Arianna relished the heat of the beams searing through her, warming her and taking away the pain that speared her side. She could feel the gash actually closing up under her corset but was overcome with the intensity of an exhaustion she had never known.

As quickly as it began, the magic between them faded and the room took on its normal shadowy dance of the fire from the hearth. In the new darkness, Arianna cried out with the last of her strength, "Merlin, I call you, come from your sleep!"

Merlin pulled his head up from his pillow and called out aloud and with clarity, "Arianna!!!!!" He opened his eyes.

"Merlin!"

Nimue ran to her husband as Arianna hobbled, best she could, out the door.

Chapter Forty-Nine

Purification

Arianna retrieved the torch from its sconce on the wall and opened the door to her room. Stumbling through the entryway, she used the flame to light the fireplace. Gazing into the conflagration, she saw Mab's lifeless body burning in the circle, and she could taste the smoke she inhaled. Her body and mind were fatigued, and her legs felt like anvils swinging from her hips. In front of the fire, she gave way and collapsed on the floor.

Eventually, footsteps in the hall awakened her. Startled from her deep sleep, she shouted, "Mab!" and clenched her hand around the jewel Merlin had given her as though she were holding her Gwydion. Seeing the fire in the hearth, she remembered where she was. The heat of battle had not waned, and her heart still beat like a steed hurtling to war.

Picking herself up from the floor, Arianna could hardly stand. Her torso was locked from the impalement she endured during battle, and it required all her remaining strength to pull up straight. She looked at the chair sitting by the door; resting upon it was a blue and white gown, a shawl and a note.

Arianna,
Remove your clothing and throw it to the fire.

Place this gown upon your body.
Come to the circle of the bluestones.
High Priestess, your purification awaits.
It will be my honor to welcome you to the coven.
Viviane

Arianna read the letter twice. Tears of joy, sadness, love and anger came to her as she let the brooch go from her hand, placing it on a bedside table as she undressed. She tried to untie the laces of her bodice, but her hands were too weak to unravel the knot. Spotting a dagger on the table, she took it in hand carefully and cut her way out of the garment, letting her corset drop to the floor. She had trouble removing her dress and the chemise; where she bled out, the fabric stuck to her flesh like dried glue. Her hands shook as she carefully tore the cloth from her skin. Eventually, standing naked in front of the fireplace, she threw the heavily soiled mass of clothing into the flames, placed the clean gown over her head and repinned her broach upon her.

Days of stress drifted from her shoulders as she looked in the hand mirror that was on the dry sink near her bed. She tried brushing her tangled hair but could hardly close her hands around the handle of the brush. Her eyes were swollen from fatigue, and her jaw and brow—which had been scraped in battle—were black and blue. The left side of her mouth was cut, and her lip was puffy. Arianna closed her eyes, still feeling Gwydion in her hand and hearing the sound of clashing swords in her ears.

Arianna slowly made her way out to the verandah. Pain seared through her left leg as she stepped. Moving the gown to one side she saw that the limb was bruised from the top of her thigh to her knee, and the skin was badly scraped from when the creature had grabbed her and tried to pull her into the hole. Her knee was swollen and cut with blood crusted in the folds of her skin. She opened the doors, limped out to the gaping wall and reminisced about her earlier departure from Jack.

What worries he must be having for her. She hoped that he was all right.

Arianna gazed upon Avalon, a hill clustered with green trees of every shade. It was high noon, and the sun was beaming down from directly overhead. A beautiful blue sky with wonderful white cumulous clouds drifting in the distance greeted her, and she stood motionless in awe of the Mother.

A knock on the door interrupted her thoughts. She made her way over slowly and opened it. The young page, Cavyn, timidly stood in front of her, and his nauseated expression let Arianna know how hideous she must have looked to the boy.

"My lady, Blaise and Lady Viviane await your presence down the hall."

Arianna summoned a faint smile for Cavyn and reached for the shawl still hanging from the chair. Purification was about to begin. Though wounded and in much pain, she exited her room, and Cavyn escorted her—with torch in hand—to Blaise and Viviane.

Upon her entrance, Arianna saw that Blaise's aging green eyes had compassion and affection for her.

"How are you standing?" he asked. She closed her eyes for a brief second and then looked straight at the Druid priest. She smiled and he bowed his head to her. Without their hands touching, he handed her a walking stick to help her take her steps.

"Come, child, the Mother waits to clean and purify your spirit," said Viviane in a nurturing voice as she lead Arianna down the staircase.

"How is my Merlin?" Arianna croaked through her hoarse voice.

"He is very weak, but he will gain strength again as soon as my lady and he reunite."

Arianna closed her eyes, thanking God in silence.

Blaise and Viviane continued their lead down the knights' hallway and into the outer courtyard where the circle of the bluestones stood as a place for contemplation and meditation before battle or rituals. High Priestess Lady Igraine, King Arthur's mother in Tintagel where King Arthur was born, originally designed the courtyard. It was shaped in an open horseshoe to welcome all who came to find peace and harmony. The bluestones, cut three feet high and at least four feet thick, were smooth in texture and arched in shape. Each stone absorbed the blue cast of the earth and sky, forming an intricate pattern of what seemed like blue and green water flowing through canals. When Arthur built Camelot, he moved the stones to his court to remember his beloved mother.

As they approached, Arianna was met by twenty of Viviane's novice priestesses standing inside the horseshoe of the bluestones, shoulder to shoulder, forming a circle and waiting for her entrance into the loop. Viviane gave the signal to open the sphere, and Arianna held tightly to her walking staff as they passed through. Around them, the young ladies closed the circle, and Arianna was led by Viviane and Blaise to a large wooden tub in the center filled with water and rose petals of pink and red. Looking up, Arianna saw that each woman was holding part of a white sheet to give her privacy during her purification.

"Do you accept purification of your own will?"

"I do, Priest Blaise," answered a proud Arianna.

"Do you accept the will of the Goddess in peace of body, mind, heart and soul?"

"I accept the will of the Goddess in peace of body, mind, heart and soul."

"What do you ask of the Goddess this morning?"

Arianna thought she might fall before she answered. "I ask for purification and the symbol of my service."

Blaise bowed his head to Arianna and exited the circle. A young novice rang a bell three times, and the sound of its peal quickened Arianna's heart.

"Sister, remove thy gown," requested Viviane.

Arianna dropped the staff and tried to untie the rope around her waist, but her hands would not allow it. Viviane came to her aid, gently wielding a small blade and cutting the knot. The gown fell from Arianna's body to the ground, and she stood in the light of the warm sun. Viviane's motherly eyes examined her. They were immediately drawn to the rib where Arianna was stabbed—seeing skin that was red like raw meat and flesh that had been charred from the healing lights of Merlin's awakening.

Arianna looked down at her own nudity. Her once pure skin was scraped with purple bruises that covered her arms and legs, and blood was crusted over many parts of her body. Tears came to Viviane as she pointed Arianna toward the tub. Arianna turned and held onto the side. With great effort, she placed one leg in and then the other, feeling the warm water upon her sore legs.

Viviane grabbed a bucket of water and poured it over Arianna's shoulders. The warmth washed over Arianna's body and rinsed away her own blood—and Mab's. She cringed as the water moistened her torn flesh. The once clean water looked a putrid brown, and the odor of blood now overcame the scent of the rose petals that floated in the liquid.

A young novice to Arianna's left poured the powder of jasmine and sage onto the hot coals of her primed censor. As the smoke rose, the young lady rocked the censor back and forth and in a circle as an offering to the Goddess. Fragrant herbs cleansed Arianna's nostrils of the stench of death that had remained with her since the battle.

Viviane chanted, "We ask Artemis to come to the aid of her daughter."

"Come, Artemis!" called the young girls.

The novices circled Arianna in the tub.

"We ask Artemis to dwell within our sister and bring her into the coven."

"Come, Artemis, come!" called the ladies.

Viviane pinched leaves of myrrh from a nearby bowl and added them to another bucket of water. "We ask Artemis to cleanse and heal our sister from the evil that has touched her."

"Come, Artemis!"

Viviane and another young lady cupped more water in their hands and poured it over Arianna. The stings of war were leaving her body.

"We ask protection from evil for our sister, Arianna. Shield her in the name of all that is good and righteous!"

"Come, Mother Artemis, to thy servant, Arianna!" the young ladies chanted.

Viviane placed her hands on the crown of Arianna's head. Arianna looked up to the priestess' face as she intoned the Goddess, saying, "I, Viviane of the Lake, ask the Goddess Artemis to heal my sister, Arianna, from her peril. Purify her soul and bring her peace."

Arianna reached up and held tight to Viviane's waist as her friend massaged her at the neck before bending to the ground, kneeling next to Arianna, and using the oils of myrrh and Echinacea on a cloth to gently remove the dried blood from Arianna's breast. Arianna winced where the pin had stabbed her in battle. Viviane kissed her cheek, and Arianna savored the touch of another.

"My sister, how did you bear all this pain?"

"For a friend I love."

Viviane poured more myrrh and Echinacea on the cloth before she wiped Arianna's legs and arms. Arianna's body received the medicines of purification and healing, accepting their comforts with pleasure and pain.

Viviane raised the cloth again and carefully cleaned the wound under Arianna's ribcage. "As you came into Merlin's room, I sensed you were near death yourself. When the lights came from between you, I felt that as you healed the wizard, he healed you in return."

"The Goddess was with us," responded Arianna.

Viviane cleaned the scar on Arianna's left shoulder, where Gresham had attempted to kill her ten years prior, and the scar on her hip from Giles' blade when Arthur was killed in battle.

"I ask Artemis, Goddess of this earth, to nourish my sister in her hour of hunger."

Viviane was handed a cup of buttermilk and honey, and she gave it to Arianna to drink. Arianna sipped the liquid, savoring the bittersweet taste as it replaced the flavor of Mab's ashes in her mouth. The fresh milk mixed with sweet honey awakened Arianna's tongue. She had not realized how parched she was. "I thank the Goddess for this nourishment."

Another novice came to Viviane and handed her an apple. Viviane cut the fruit horizontally, showing Arianna and the sisters the pentagram hidden inside the fruit.

"We ask the Goddess to feed our sister. Give her strength in her hour of weakness." Viviane gave Arianna the piece, and Arianna bit down hard on the fruit to help relieve her from the pain of clenching her jaw throughout the battle.

"I thank Artemis for this meal," spoke a humbled Arianna.

Leaning Arianna's head back and covering her eyes like a child in a bath, Viviane was handed a jug of water and she poured it over Arianna's face and hair. After gently dabbing the water from her features, she massaged Arianna's scalp and brushed her hair, cleaning her of the soil and blood that dried in the strands.

"What price you have paid, my sister," she whispered. "Please, you are not well. You may give yourself a few days to heal before we mark you with your service."

Arianna tearfully spoke to Viviane. "I'd prefer it be today."

"As you wish," replied Viviane, holding out her hand. "Come with me. Let us dry you and dress you."

Lydgia, a young novice of sixteen years of age, came to them with a long blue cloth. The young girl had blonde hair that cascaded down her back and purple eyes that held the future. She and Viviane swaddled Arianna in their tender care.

A dress was set aside for Arianna to wear. It was Wedgewood in color with gold laces at the back and up the arms. The long bell sleeves were cut from the shoulder to the wrist, and gold laces adorned the slit. A gold rope belt was tied around Arianna's lithe waste, and the flares of her skirts were adorned with a gold rose design. Her hair was brushed and braided, and gold sinews were placed in the braids. A garland of wild flowers was laid on her head, and beautiful pastel ribbons were draped over her shoulders.

Escorted out of the circle, Arianna was greeted by Blaise as she came from the coven of her sisters. He reached out his hand to support her. "What symbol do you take as your service to the Goddess?"

She looked into her new friend's eyes. "I ask for the trefoil and the crescent moon to adorn my brow as the symbol of my union with the Mother."

Arianna saw a smile of pride flash over Viviane who said, "Be it done as you wish." She again chanted, "Artemis, give thy daughter strength as she takes the symbol of her service this day."

"Grace her with your wisdom!" chanted the girls.

Arianna carefully stepped to a table covered with a blue and lavender cloth near where the stones curved. On the cloth were the tools of marking: a wooden bowl with the powdered Woad, a charred piece of wood burned in the shape of a scalpel, and a small blonde wood-toned mallet. Next to the tools was a cruet of water and one of vinegar.

Galahad and Joseph were invited to join them now that the purification was over. Arianna staggered to the table, where she greeted her sons in silence, weakly smiling at them, glad that they could be with her this day.

She looked up to Merlin's verandah. He must have still been far too weak to be with her but none the same, she wished that he could help to mark her.

Viviane and Aaron aided Arianna as she was laid on the flat stone table. It felt wonderful to not have to hold herself up any longer. The flares of her skirt draped over the sides of the table, her hands crossed in silent prayer and meditation as she enjoyed resting on the coolness of the stone.

Blaise had removed the pin from the blue and white gown and he must have purified it, because it shone in the sunlight as he held it now in his hand. He fastened it to her blouse.

"Priestess Arianna, do you take of this symbol with peace and reverence to the Goddess?"

"I do, Master Blaise, with all my heart."

Arianna closed her eyes and quietly wept as the young ladies chanted, and High Priest Blaise and Viviane of the Lake mixed the woad with the water and vinegar. Blaise lifted Arianna's head and gave her the sacramental wine of the Goddess. She accepted it, allowing the aperitif to relax her and grace her with its fragrance. Viviane rubbed some of the oil of Echinacea on the area above Arianna's brow where she would be marked, as the women chanted in song.

Blaise picked up the charred, scalpel shaped stick that rested on the table next to Arianna's head and scratched the symbol of the trefoil onto her right under her hairline. Arianna clenched her hands tightly, as the pain of the scraping was intense. The priest made three points of the triangle on Arianna's skin. She could feel him carefully draw the shape of three concentric leaves that entwined together to form the feminine triskelion. A trickle of warm blood rolled down her face near her ear, but Aaron wiped it away before it dripped from her ear lobe. Blaise paused and Aaron gave Arianna another sip of the wine.

As Blaise continued marking her skin, Aaron wiped the blood from the symbol. Viviane soaked a cloth with the woad and pressed it into the open pores, gently banging the blue green dye into Arianna's skin with the mallet. Arianna pinched her eyebrows together as the vinegar in the plant stung at her eyes. Viviane grabbed for her hand, and Arianna relaxed her face, allowing Blaise to continue with the three points of the entwined triangle. With precision, he aligned the center leaf perfectly in the middle of her brow. Again, Aaron gave Arianna wine, and she accepted it willingly.

Arianna drifted off into a daydream in which she was riding Brach near the beach at Aubrey, and Merlin rode next to her. Together they were riding into the horizon. She saw him as he was the day he met her, handsome and muscular of body. Tears streamed down her face. Her heart ached to see him that way again, a man of peace and great wisdom.

Gently opening her eyes, she noticed that Blaise was giving Viviane the tools of implementation and that she took of them with love.

"Goddess Mother, take thy daughter Arianna into your care. Give her insight and right judgment!" Viviane scratched the crescent moon onto Arianna's brow. "Artemis, Goddess Mother, see your daughter as she gives herself to you this day." Arianna felt Viviane's tears drip onto her own face and knew that her friend had waited a long time to welcome her into her fold.

Her trance deepened as the sting of the woad burned at her brow. She recalled being only feet from Arthur as he brutally endured the beating from his son Mordred on the battlefield. Mordred slashed at his father without mercy, opening his chest. Arthur fell to the ground, desperately engaged Excalibur and ran it straight into the body of his son. Mordred fell of this fatal wound. Merlin held tight to his king, and Arthur died in Merlin's arms on the battlefield as Arianna cried on her knees at their side.

The ill Merlin, from his bed, came to her in her dream, taking her hand and lifting her off the ground and away from the death of the battlefield. "It's alright!" he said as he held her in his arms. "Aryanyn, I am proud of you this day."

Merlin carried her back to when she found Excalibur; the sword sang for her that day. Arianna listened to the thrill of her ward's song as it enraptured her heart with pure ecstasy.

"Goddess Mother, accept your daughter Arianna, for today she is yours for eternity."

Arianna felt Viviane and Blaise kiss her on the cheek, followed by each young lady. Blaise and Aaron grasped her firmly by the shoulders and lifted her, making her feel as though she were floating in a dream. She opened her eyes, stood on the ground and the young ladies bowed to her.

"High Priestess Arianna, we welcome you to our circle. Enter with love and blessings."

Viviane escorted Arianna into the sphere of the coven. Arianna stood motionless, absorbing the rights of the day. The young ladies each gave Arianna a small blue colored stone. Smooth in texture, these were the gems of the hills of Avalon and were given as favors in ceremonial rituals to remind a woman that she gave herself in service of the Mother Earth. Each stone was intricate in its own way, and each was a shade of sky blue similar to the stones in the court. Arianna was embraced by each lady as they separately gifted her with a flower of welcome. She accepted their love with joy of soul.

Viviane bowed to Arianna. "High Priestess, come, we have prepared food and drink for thee."

Using the walking stick, Arianna followed them to a blanket upon the ground where fruits and breads were set for a feast. She looked upon the apples, berries, nuts and wondrous grapes. The loaves of bread were still warm from the hearth and smelled of fresh-baked dough as Blaise tore one apart and handed it to her. She accepted the bread and a small portion of grapes. Her body tingled with pleasure as she received the meal. Galahad came to her and kissed her on the hand before looking at the symbol of her service. Tears fell from his eyes as he embraced her. "Arthur would be so honored today, my mother."

Joseph came to her next with a red rose in hand. He caressed the wounds on her face and arms and gently embraced her, whispering, "If I had not witnessed the magic of the morning, I would have thought that I would bury you—not celebrate with you this day. I love you so much."

Arianna held her son passionately. "I love you too, my Joseph."

As everyone ate, Arianna glanced up towards Merlin's verandah. Nimue was standing there, looking down on her. Even from a distance, Arianna could see how frail this ordeal had left her friend.

"Please, good people, I am honored by this ceremony, but I must reunite with Merlin."

Blaise approached Arianna. "May we join you, High Priestess?"

She grabbed the hand of her new friend. "Please give me a short time alone with him."

"Mother, when you wish for us to join you, come to the verandah," said Galahad.

"I will wave my wreath for you to see," Arianna replied as she removed the flowers from her head.

Blaise bowed his head to her. "Go, High Exalted Priestess, in the name of the Goddess."

Arianna turned and walked away slowly with the dignity and grace of the ancients before her.

CHAPTER FIFTY

The Reunion

❖

Arianna, with the assistance of her new walking staff, passed through the garden of the blue stones toward the small court; a twenty-foot by twenty-foot brick and mortar sitting area with a water fountain encased in a white stone wall. With a majestic beech tree in the center, the court was used mainly as a place for the knights to sit and pray, usually before times of battle. She stood by the fountain and let the water drip into her hand, refreshed by its coolness, before moving slowly to the back stairs, still feeling the pain from her ribs. Holding onto the banister, she walked up each step one by one. Her heart was desperate to get to Merlin, but her body was begging for rest, a respite that would have to wait until she and the great wizard connected.

She stood midway to catch her breath and fixed her eyes on the tall columns that held the ceiling high above her head. There were arch-shaped windows to the right with dark blue and red dressings. The soft velvet curtains were closed, but the early afternoon sun peeked through the folds of the drapes. She was home, but suddenly her heart ached for Jack and Alexis.

Arianna mustered up enough vigor to finish her climb and eventually stood at the top of the stairwell and looked down the hall. Merlin's room was four doors down. After a few minutes, she paused in front of it before softly knocking.

In wondrous friendship, the Lady Nimue opened the door and embraced Arianna. The two held each other for a long time and Arianna stared into her friend's eyes, feeling great emotion flowing between them.

Nimue broke the silence. "Tell me that this is not a dream." She looked closely at Arianna's face and caressed the wound on her jaw. It was a motherly touch that comforted Arianna.

She placed her hand on Nimue's face. "I am here."

"Let me help you to his side," Nimue said. Also exhausted, Nimue did her best to support Arianna with one hand as Arianna held her staff with the other.

Arianna looked upon the sleeping wizard. His face, though pink in color, was still fragile in its expression. Merlin's hair was a dark gray when Arianna last left him, but now it was as white as the sheets he lay upon. Arianna bent low to him and ran her fingers through it. "Mab did her work well, leaving marks on both of us." She felt despondent, and her legs finally gave way. She knelt by his side, sobbing bitterly in his blanket.

Merlin heard her cries and lifted his hand to her head. He felt the silk texture of her hair as he curled his fingers in her locks. She placed her hand on his, and Arianna raised her eyes to him. He set his sights on their amber color and swam in them. She picked up his hand and kissed it. "Merlin," she said through her tears.

"Please, take this chair," said Nimue as she placed the wooden armchair near the bed for Arianna. Merlin let go of Arianna's hand; her movements were sluggish and unbalanced. He felt her pain as Nimue assisted her. As she sat in the seat and pushed her body into the chair, Merlin could see how she enjoyed the comforts of the cushions.

"Arianna," Merlin said with a hoarse voice.

"Shush," she replied. "Don't strain yourself. We have a lifetime to catch up. Nimue, what does Blaise say about his health?"

"He will recover, dear friend, but alas, his age will not allow for him to be as he once was."

"As we once were," Merlin said as he looked deeply into Arianna's eyes.

"I will leave, as you both have much to talk about." Nimue kissed Arianna, then Merlin, on the forehead, and Merlin smiled as Nimue quietly walked from the room, leaving them to their privacy.

"Arianna," Merlin reached for her. His hand pointed to her forehead. He smiled so sweetly. "It is done, dear one."

"Dear one. I haven't heard you call me that in a long while."

From his pillow, he looked around the room and at his staff, wishing for the strength to take of it and go for a long walk with Arianna.

"I was there in your sight as you took your service."

"You walked with me on the beach," said Arianna.

Through the blur of Merlin's vision, he gazed upon the brooch pinned to Arianna's dress. He held onto her hand and closed his eyes.

"I think that I will leave you alone and let you rest, and I will do the same."

His eyes popped back open. Arianna was doing her best to pull from the chair. "Prop me up, woman!" he said.

"Merlin, please, you need to sleep."

"Prop me up!"

Merlin knew that she was hurting more than he was at this time, but she managed to take two of the large down pillows from another chair and prop Merlin up in his bed. He reached out and touched the jewel. Arianna looked down as he caressed the pin and again closed his eyes.

"Tell me of the battle," he commanded.

"Tell me what you wish to know."

"What did you feel when your powers came to you?"

Arianna sat back in the chair. "It felt as though my powers were within me all of my life. It was my accepting them that brought them forth."

"Who are you?" he looked at her. "Do you know who you are?" He tried to get comfortable in his bed.

"Who I am?" Arianna looked at Merlin with confusion.

"I need to know something," Merlin stared hard into her eyes. "When you were a child, were there ever incidents or occasions that in your mind you understood, but could never explain to others?"

"Merlin, I have just won the greatest battle of my life—for you and for Arthur." Arianna rose from the bed. "I don't understand the questioning."

Merlin, though weak, yelled back, "Answer me!" He shot a cold glare at her. "My life and the lives of others are at stake here, Arianna."

He noticed that her breath caught in her chest as she spoke, "Yes, there were things that were different about me."

In her voice, he heard the sound of a woman trying to mask her pain—a powerful priestess still hiding from her past. "Tell me what they were."

"Things that I felt were real...things that I perceived as nightmares."

Merlin reached for her, "You must remember specifically."

Her look became fearful. "My childhood was laced with visions—sights that I did not understand."

"What did you see?'

"I knew that my friend would die of an illness before the doctors told her parents." Arianna's head dropped. "Please, I am so tired. Must we do this?" Confusion laced her eyes as she continued. "I could see the fabric of what a person was just by looking at them. There were no secrets held from me."

Merlin nodded his head, "Go on."

"I could walk down a street and hear voices and see things like flashes of memory from the past, voices of people I knew not."

Merlin could tell that Arianna was trying to keep herself from breaking down. "Dear God, Merlin, I remember being with friends at school, and I saw a vision of a fire start down the hall." Arianna held tight to the chair arm. "No one could escape. I tried to tell my friends that something horrific was going to happen."

"Did they heed your warning?"

"My friends thought me a fool and laughed." Arianna covered her face. "I was desperate. I ran and told my priest. He said that it was the work of the devil and that I should banish the visions from my soul." Merlin watched as Arianna traced her finger along the design embroidered on the blanket. "He told me that I was unclean of mind, and that is why I heard and saw such things."

"Did the incident occur as you saw it?"

Arianna continued to outline the pattern on the fabric until Merlin reached for her hand, stopping her. She looked up at him; her hands were cold. She closed her eyes as if contemplating. "The fire consumed the building three days after I saw it. Two of the students were burned alive."

Merlin held tight to Arianna's hand. "How old were you when the visions began?"

Arianna swallowed hard. "I was sixteen."

"How did you feel?"

"I felt like an outcast. My mother didn't understand me and punished me often." Arianna lowered her head. "She beat me for telling lies. I tried speaking to my priest again, but he told me that the devil was tempting me. When I realized that God had no mercy for me, I shut myself off...from everything." Merlin heard a sense of melancholy in her voice. "I was living in a world where I was chastised for being myself, so I focused on trying to be what others thought acceptable."

Merlin pulled himself forward in his bed. "Look at me!" She looked deep into his silver blue eyes. "Can you remember ever calling yourself another name?" Merlin's voice became hoarse.

Arianna rose from the chair and walked to the table to pour a cup of tisane for Merlin. Handing it over to him, she spoke again. "When I returned home after I unearthed Excalibur, I wrote another name." Her stare was blank. "I wrote *Aryanyn* on a piece of paper over and over again."

Merlin could hear the ancient ones cry out in joyful harmony. "Was there a vision with the writing?" he asked.

Again her stare was vacant. "I saw myself in another time, dressed in clothes of another day. A time I am not aware of." Arianna drew away. "What is going on here?"

"Take off the brooch," Merlin commanded. Arianna unpinned it. She looked at the symbol on the jewel, and touched her brow. Merlin smiled, enjoying how they were identical. "Give me the jewel."

Arianna placed the pin in his hand. Merlin shook his head. "Is this the woman from your memory?"

Arianna stared at the woman engraved in the sword on the back of the pin as he placed it back into her hand. He closed her fingers around it and tightened his own hand around hers hard enough that the pin buried itself into her palm. Arianna closed her eyes, as did Merlin and he joined her in her vision of darkness interrupted by flashes of light.

"Ary," a voice said. He could hear it as though it came from a tunnel. "Ary," the voice cried louder this time. "Aryanyn." He could see that she did not recognize the voice as she followed the sound.

"Aryanyn, where are you going?" A man in his thirties, the prime of his life, appeared before them. He was dressed in a long, sky blue alb opened at the chest. A dark blue toga adorned his tall body, and the train of the toga draped over his right arm. He was handsome, with dark blonde hair and blue eyes like the sea.

"I am going to the temple to pray, silly boy," said a young woman. She was dressed in a red and gold tunica cut in the Roman style of the third century. Her hair was brown, curled and tied back in a gold bow. On her feet were brown sandals; her eyes were amber in color like the honey of bees.

"What do you pray for?"

"Tomorrow I take my vows. I pray to Artemis that she accept me in her service."

"Come, I have a gift for you!" he said running off.

The young lady followed the man as he entered the court of the high priestess, a room made of white, tan and gold marble walls and columns. Cream-colored furnishings with multicolored scarves were spread about the room, giving it the texture of the ancient goddesses Ihstar and Cedwynn.

They bowed to the priestess, who was sitting at her desk writing in a white leather-bound tablet with a quill she had made from peacock feathers. The woman, in her mid-thirties, was tall and wore a white and gold tunica. Her long black hair, adorned with gold and red ribbons, bounced around her shoulders, and her eyes were green like the forest.

"High Priestess Élan, I have come for the gift that I prepared for Aryanyn." The priestess opened the box on the table and removed an object from its confines. She placed it in the young man's hands. He presented it to the young lady. "This is for you to wear upon your gown."

The young woman looked at the gift. "Is it the symbol of my service?"

"It is, my dear," said the Priestess Élan, "so that Artemis will always guide you in your travels."

Merlin watched as both Arianna of the Arthurian time and the young woman of the Roman time both held tightly to the pin. Arianna's blood dripped on the Wizard's hand, and Merlin drew her deeper into the trance.

A flash of light came over them, and suddenly the young woman was laying on the stone at the circle in Avalon. Élan was marking her—as Viviane had done to Arianna. Merlin shared the pain with Arianna as his own brow burned. Tears streaked his face and he opened his eyes to see tears falling down her cheeks as the vision ceased.

"Merlin, he is you!" Arianna smiled with joy and threw her arms around him. "You gave me this pin when I was a girl..." There was a pause in her voice. "...in the past where my soul began."

Merlin smiled at her as she pulled back from him, still holding his shoulders.

"In my vision earlier, I heard you call me Aryanyn on the beach as I took my service."

Merlin held Arianna's hand. "Yes, I was with you."

"All these years, I have heard that name in my dreams. I have written it, *Aryanyn*. I thought that the nightmares I had in my youth were catching up to me. Merlin what does this all mean?" Her voice begged him for answers.

"After Arthur's death, my aunt did not just send me looking for the guardian of Excalibur. She sent me looking for you. It is you whose destiny must be fulfilled."

Arianna's face was questioning. "Did I know you in the past?"

Merlin brushed Arianna's hair from her eyes and smiled. "We were close friends, my dear." He cradled Arianna's face in his hand.

"It was easier to believe everyone else and cast the truth away over and over again," she said. She looked lovingly into his eyes. "Merlin, I thought that I was daft."

"No, you are not daft. You are Aryanyn of the Lake."

"Aryanyn, Is that my real name?"

"It is, dear one." He smiled lovingly at her.

"Please Merlin, my name has been Arianna all of my natural life. It will be hard for me to be known as Aryanyn." She looked skyward. "Please, Goddess, help me accept all of this."

"She will when the time is right," he assured her.

Arianna placed the pin back in his hand. Her blood was everywhere— on the pin, on her hand, and on her dress. Merlin received it and pushed its point into his own palm. As the blood of Arianna and the blood of Merlin mixed, strength ebbed back through his body. The poison of Mab was leaving him, and he was reminded of the strength for life he wielded on the day Arianna of New York met Edmund Winters of the Warwick Riding Academy so many years before. For a brief moment, Merlin was sitting with Arianna on horseback in the late twentieth century by the Lake of Avalon where fate had brought them together.

Merlin, the high Druid priest, pulled himself out of his bed and embraced Arianna, High Priestess of the Lake. He kissed her sweetly on the forehead. "I am so very proud of you." Arianna held onto him for dear life. "Now you must know your destiny."

Arianna sat down as Merlin climbed tenderly back onto the bed. She grabbed his hand. "I am listening."

"There is a Christian relic called the titulus of Christ," he said.

"It was the sign above Christ's head when he was crucified." She replied, her amber eyes alive and awake once again.

"Arthur quested for this relic in Judea, but he failed in his search," he continued to explain.

"Élan found this relic for her son Constantine," said Arianna remembering her conversation with George about the coins he had found. "*Hic Iacet Arthurus Rex Quondam Rexque Futurus*!" Arianna swallowed the words as she said them. "He comes now, my brother?" Arianna begged. "Tell me Arthur comes now!" She smiled and paused a moment. "But the hawthorn flowers? Draco foretold that they would grow on his grave."

"You will have to go to him when the flowers grow."

"Where do I step into this quest?" she asked.

"It was foretold by Élan on the day of your service that you and the high king would quest for the titulus and heal the two houses severed by centuries of separation and evil."

"Two houses?" Arianna cocked her head to one side and furrowed her brow, obviously puzzled.

"The house of the Christians and the house of the Pagans are to be united for the love of the man called the Christ and for the woman called the Goddess."

"Who are Arthur and I to be honored for such a quest?"

"You are of both houses, both raised Druid and Christian, a son and a daughter of both God and Goddess."

"Are you saying that when Arthur is raised, I am to accompany him to find this titulus?" Merlin saw confusion turn to clarity. "Now I understand the visions that I had in my youth. I am to go with Arthur. This is why Mab wanted all of us dead."

"Yes, Arianna, that is why you had to fight and had to win."

"Mab wanted Gwydion and Excalibur so that I could not rule the elements."

Merlin reached from his place on the bed and held her firm at the shoulders. "This is a dangerous quest," he said as he placed the pin in Arianna's hand. She was staring at the woman on the back of the jewel. "Priestess, today I tell you, you are destined for greatness, as you will conduct the elements in the course of time yet again. If you can raise Arthur, the two of you will return to the time of Constantine in search of the titulus of Christ."

CHAPTER FIFTY-ONE

The Blessing of Merlin

Arianna rose from the edge of the bed. "I will return in a few moments. I have something for you."

Merlin placed himself in the chair by the window and sat in eager anticipation.

Arianna returned bearing a sword in her right hand. When he saw the weapon he did not need to speak a word. He placed his hands out, and Arianna gently presented him with the sword that belonged to his mother.

Inhaling a deep breath, he could not look upon the blade. He closed his eyes and remembered the day the Christian knights invaded their camp, trying to convert his people. Mab, without mercy, brandished this sword and personally killed at least ten men of the church. And then there was the day Mordred invaded his father's court and the sword was engaged in the young heir's hand. Merlin shivered at the thought.

"This is the sword that brought down my foster son, my King." Tears engulfed him.

Arianna knelt next to him. "She is your sword now, my mentor."

"She is your claim to victory," he declared, swallowing his sorrow.

"It was your teachings and your love and strength that aided me in my victory at Domh Ringr. She belongs to you."

Merlin held tight to the sword, still averting his eyes from it. "I accept this gift, dear one." The two shared a moment without words. "Let us call Nimue in and share our joy with her."

He watched as Arianna hobbled out onto the verandah where Nimue was resting peacefully. Arianna seemed hesitant, but Merlin nodded at her to continue. She smiled at him and awakened his wife from the peacefulness of her nap.

From his chair, he watched as Nimue stirred at Arianna's touch. There was a look of solace on her face as Nimue saw her dear friend over her.

"You are bleeding!" Nimue said as she lifted Aryanyn's hand, already covered with a cloth from Merlin's table.

"It is nothing, my friend. Come. Merlin wants to show you something."

Nimue turned and Merlin saw shock grace his wife's face, followed by joy as she quickly stood from her rest and marched straight towards him. "Dear God!" she said, walking in the room. "You look as though you have not a care in the world."

He stood on his feet for the first time in weeks, and she embraced him wholeheartedly. "I was so afraid that I would lose you, husband."

Merlin smiled and kissed Nimue on the cheek. "Here is the proof of Mab's demise, my wife." He showed Nimue the sword.

She recoiled from the weapon. "Please, I beg you, put that away."

"Nimue, I killed her, she cannot harm us now."

He saw fear in Nimue's face and looked at Arianna. "Please do as my wife requests."

Arianna removed the covering from the bed, wrapped the sword in it, and placed it in the corner of the room.

"I told Blaise and Galahad that I would signal for them to join us after we had been reunited." Arianna kissed him on his cheek, removed her pretty wreath from her head and stepped to the high brick rail on the verandah.

"Please, my love," said Merlin to his wife. "Have Gavin come in and help me walk to the wall. I want to feel the sun on my face again." Nimue left Merlin's side to go to the door. A few seconds later, Gavin came to him, smiling. Merlin placed his arm around Gavin's waist. "Please take me outside."

"Husband, aren't you too weak to walk on those legs?" asked his worried wife as she placed Merlin's slippers on his feet.

"My wife, you know I need light and air to revive my mind and body."

Gavin aided Merlin to his feet. The floor felt strange under the soles of his slippers, as though the wooden boards would give way from under him as he challenged himself to endure one step at a time. They rested a moment before Merlin stepped on the shale tiles laid in the mortar of the verandah. He could feel the cold of the foundation through his slippers as he enjoyed the sun on his face and looked upon the blue of the sky, basking in the glow of the Father. As he approached the wall, he reached for the edge and placed his hands on the terrazzo. Nimue stood next to him with Gavin holding him for security. Gavin's touch was firm, and he knew that he would not fall.

From his watch, Merlin could see everyone following Galahad into the castle.

Gavin opened the door and Joseph ran to Merlin and kissed him on the cheek. "I am so glad you are well."

Joseph turned and grabbed his mother's hand and held it. He said nothing as the mother and son pair held each other close. It warmed Merlin's heart to see.

Blaise clapped his hands with joy seeing them all together. As he approached Merlin, he opened his arms and brought him into them. "The Goddess has surely blessed us this day." Merlin let go of the wall, feeling secure in his fellow priest's embrace.

"Please, Blaise, a chair. My legs cannot hold on much longer."

"Aaron, a chair for the great wizard."

Aaron smiled at Merlin with joy and ran quickly to his room for a chair. He hurried back, and Blaise assisted him in taking a seat.

Merlin took to the support of the settle and looked at everyone in his company. He smiled as Blaise reached for Arianna and kissed her hand so sweetly. "It is my honor to know you, fair Lady of the Lake."

Arianna returned his smile. "Master Blaise, the honor is mine."

Blaise stepped towards Merlin again. "Brother Druid, may I bless you?"

Merlin sat a moment, reflecting upon all of the people he loved in the world. "I have not been blessed in many a year. Please say the prayers of the Mother over me."

Merlin looked up to a tall Blaise, standing over him with encircled hands and chanting in vowel sounds that took on the song of a hymn without words.

Aaron came to him and he, too, joined in the hymn, adding his voice to the chant. Merlin listened to their mantra and let it fill him with the sweetness of life. He could hear the voice of the Mother within the tone of her song.

Blaise placed his hands on Merlin's head, and the tune changed to a low hum, sung deep in the high priests' throats. Merlin felt his soul lift as Blaise intoned the Goddess and prayed, "*Echlynn lunnare finthorena Mammeah julunessa ossena Merlynn ethynn morr!*"

Aaron repeated, "*Mammeah julunesssa ossena Merlynn ethynn morr!*"

Tears fell down Merlin's face, as he knew that the Goddess was with him again in mind and body.

It was now Galahad's turn to indulge in the festivities, and he came to stand near Merlin before kneeling beside him and hugging him. "I was afraid that we would lose you." Merlin wrapped himself in the warmth of his king's embrace. Galahad parted from him, and Merlin watched as he reached for Arianna and ushered his mother into his arms. "I have been grieved with worry," he said to her.

"You have no idea the fear and worry that ravaged me before the battle, my son."

"Young page!" Galahad called to Cavyn, making Merlin's quiet heart skip a beat. The boy walked quickly into the room. "Bring the finest wine we have, for we are a family united again." Cavyn gave Merlin that boyish grin that he loved, and left in haste to do as his king commanded.

Everyone in the room was gathered around Merlin and Arianna when Cavyn returned with a wooden tray in his hands. Merlin noticed immediately that on this carrier was a golden carafe of wine, and silver and red goblets that Arthur had used for his royal occasions. He remembered that the goblets were a gift for Guinevere when he returned from Rome after the Holy Wars. They were shaped, as the chalices are in a church, to represent the Holy Grail; pewter based with silver and gold leaves inlaid in the intricacy of the metal. Red dragons were embossed on each goblet like his king's Pendragon signature and name. Each dragon held the cup for his guest as His Majesty King Arthur revered and enjoyed everyone who took pleasure in his hospitality.

The young page poured the wine into the goblets and gave the first to Merlin, then one to all in the room. Merlin looked upon the chalice and knew that Arthur was with them.

"Raise your cups, my family!" commanded Galahad. "Camelot welcomes her son and daughter with open arms. Let us thank God for their return!"

"Here! Here!" cried Joseph.

"And let us be grateful to the Mother for healing both," added Blaise.

The goblets were raised, and all who drank regaled.

Merlin and Arianna toasted each other and drank down their wine, letting the grapes of the Mother intoxicate their joy.

CHAPTER FIFTY-TWO

The Sword of Mab

———◄◆►———

From the door in the knights' hallway, Merlin heard the young soldiers enter the court and turned as laughter echoed through the mortar and bricks.

"What games are they playing?" asked Arianna.

"Dear one, it is the sound of mischievous young men. Let's listen in and enjoy them, shall we?"

Arianna bit down on her lip. "You have not changed. You are just as bad as they."

"Ehy, they are the sons that my Nimue and I could not have. I enjoy each day with them."

Merlin and Arianna tucked themselves near the door to listen. Sir Peter strolled past them unaware of their presence. Merlin laughed, as he had spied on knights before with Galahad when Arthur was king.

"Majesty!" said Peter sauntering into the Round Table room. Galahad was standing by the table, and Merlin could see that he had poured three goblets of wine. Peter sat at the table as Galahad offered him a cup.

"At last, a chalice of wine!" said Peter. "I am a parched man."

"Brother, you have been parched since the day of your birth," Galahad retorted.

"Ahy, 'tis true," remarked Peter. "My father told me I suckled my mother dry."

"Aha! So the rumors that you do indeed suckle the women of Camelot have merit," Joseph added to the banter.

"My word!" said an exasperated Arianna to her co-conspirator. Merlin laughed at her comment.

"Shush you, I want to hear more," said Arianna.

Peter sipped his drink and smacked his lips. "It is the suckling that brings the sweetness of a woman to a man."

"You are insufferable!" said Galahad as he kicked Peter over in his chair. Merlin cupped his hands over his mouth so as not to bring attention to his laughter as they hid. He continued to watch the fun with Arianna over his shoulder.

Peter looked up at Galahad standing over him, and in a single move yanked Galahad down onto the floor.

"So you wish to play dirty?" taunted Peter, rabble-rousing his king.

Joseph was standing there sipping his wine, enjoying the play fight before him. Laughing at his friends, he kicked Galahad in the butt. The tall king shot up from the ground and grabbed his young brother around the neck and into a headlock.

"You go, Galahad," whispered Arianna as Merlin saw her pretend that she was boxing with her boys.

Peter defended Joseph, tearing him away from Galahad but then turned on him and pushed him to the floor, holding him down with one foot, while nearly doubling over with laughter.

Galahad pulled Peter from Joseph. "Oh, brothers, when will thee grow up!"

The three nobleman laughed together as Galahad helped Joseph to his feet.

"'Tis good to joke again," said Joseph.

"Yes, it is good to feel jovial again," agreed Galahad.

Peter raised the wine carafe and poured more for all of them.

"These boys will be drunk before court commences," said Arianna with annoyance.

She was about to go in and break up the banter, but Merlin yanked her back. "Leave them be, dear one. They are young but not foolish."

The men picked up their goblets, and Peter raised his cup. "To the women in our lives. May they be pure of heart but treacherous in body." The three men clanged their goblets together.

"Speaking of women, where is the Lady Arianna? Or do we call her Aryanyn, my lord?" asked Peter as the men took their seats at the table.

From the south door of the corridor, Merlin watched as the knights and courtiers assembled in the opposite hall. He chuckled quietly as the three young men fixed their attire to look respectable for the proceedings.

"Brother knight, my mother has convened court this afternoon," said Galahad. "I am anxious to speak with her about Excalibur."

"You must confront her, sire," said Peter.

"I shall, my friend, as soon as the opportune moment arises during this caucus. She was taken from my hands without warning."

"I was there," Peter said.

"Since Arianna returned, I have not had a moment of privacy to speak with her."

"I understand, my King."

Galahad signaled to the guard, who opened the doors of the Round Table room. In walked some of the finest knights and courtiers that ever sat in the room of the Round Table.

"I feel badly about not having time to speak with Galahad," said Arianna to Merlin.

"Perhaps later when court has recessed. For now, you have to magistrate."

"I do."

"Go and do your bidding." He handed Arianna Mab's sword. "Can you handle those stairs?"

"I can." She smiled at him, and he kissed her on the cheek.

Merlin watched as she carefully climbed up to the sentry guard's post above the Round Table room. The three guards posted there bowed to her, and she signaled to them to be discreet. Merlin smiled, picked up his staff and made his way into the court. Galahad stood, came to him and embraced him, as did all the others who bid him welcome and good health.

Galahad assisted Merlin to his chair, as Gavin, who was assigned heraldry duties of the day, marched in and bellowed, "Oy yay oy yay! Greetings! The court of Galahad commences this night. Prepare thy weapons."

'Call to Orders' was initated. Merlin watched the knights assemble, not in the name of Arthur or Galahad, but in the name of Arianna, high priestess and guardian of the two most powerful swords in history. Around the table they followed bowing their heads, saluting their king and placing their weapons onto the Round Table.

Sir Peter, first knight to Galahad's kingship, bowed to His Majesty. When Galahad came to live in Camelot as a young boy, Peter was brought in as his roommate to help with the transition. After a tumultuous beginning, the two became inseparable friends and brothers. Peter had many problems learning his lessons but was made head of the stables at the age of thirteen by King Arthur. Peter had a rare gift caring for horses. He was trained by Sir Gawain to be a knight, and when Galahad became King of Camelot at the age of eighteen, young Peter was awarded the title of first knight.

Next to Peter was Sir Gawain Agavene, the first knight to King Arthur Pendragon. Sir Agavene was the first cousin to King Arthur through Arthur's father King Uther. When Arthur pulled Excalibur from the stone and was declared King of England, Gawain protested at the time, not knowing that the young prince was of noble birth and his cousin. Gawain, ten years older than Arthur, was assigned to watch over the king by Merlin, and it was his charge to see that Arthur adopted the duties of his noble lineage with grace and dignity. Gawain took his task to heart and—after years of not knowing of his cousin's birth—was all too happy to enjoy and accommodate the king, and the two became united for the cause. Arthur loved his cousin and elevated Gawain to the seat next to him of first knight. Gawain, Merlin, and Arthur prepared the building of the Round Table, and Gawain assisted Arthur in choosing his knights. When the king left to battle his son, he kept Gawain back in Camelot to guard his home.

Next sat Sir Luke Agavene, knight and head of the armory under Galahad's kingship. Sir Luke was the son of Sir Gawain; he was raised in the court of Arthur and trained there. At fourteen, he became His Majesty Galahad's squire at court the day he volunteered to carry the funeral fire for King Arthur's cremation pyre. Galahad was so impressed by Luke's bravery that he ordered the boy placed in his custody to be raised as a knight in his kingdom.

Sir Martin Borwell, knight and liaison to diplomacy under Arthur's kingship, raised his sword to Galahad. Borwell was the oldest living knight of the Round Table. He started out as a squire during the rule of Arthur's father, King Uther. After Uther's death, Sir Martin remained a knight for the people, guarded the realms of Camlann and stayed true to his church. When Arthur became the King of England and built Camelot, he needed good men to aid him in ruling his country. Sir Martin heeded the call with dignity, guarding Camelot as though she were his own. Martin traveled forward to the twentieth century to aid Merlin and Viviane in the search for Arianna. Though retired, Sir Martin served his king when the time called for it.

Sir William Borwell, knight and head of the armory under Arthur's kingship, placed his sword on the table. William was a faithful knight of the Round Table for thirty years, though at times he doubted Arthur's better judgment, especially when Arthur chose Arianna as guardian of Excalibur. Knight William Borwell was devastated when Mordred murdered his king. William was born and raised Catholic and remained steadfast to the teachings of the Church. At times, he acted as liaison for Camelot and the archbishop. To him, Arianna—the time traveler from another world—was not a suitable Christian. Her Pagan ways, and her friendship with the Wizard Merlin defied everything William believed in, especially when she returned to aid Galahad the king and train in the faith of the Druid arts. William was the youngest brother of Sir Martin, who proudly took William under his wing. He started as a page in Arthur's court, rising in the ranks to knight. He married Helen Moray, a beautiful maiden from the French Alps, and they conceived Peter Borwell, the first knight of His Majesty, Galahad.

Sir Frederick Garris bowed his head, raised his sword, and laid it perfectly on the table, all the while never taking his eyes off his king. Frederick was the youngest of the Knights of the Round Table of King Arthur's rule. As a young boy, he served Duke Marash in his household. When Frederick came of age, the duke brought him to the court of Arthur, stating that the boy needed training in weapons and in becoming a man.

Frederick started as a squire when he came to live in Camelot but showed his king that he was strong and eager to train and rise in the ranks to knighthood. Sir Frederick was dubbed a knight by King Arthur at the age of twenty-five. Sir William was accountable for him, and soon Frederick and he were engaging in the service of knighthood and in service of the Church.

Frederick, though tolerant of the Druids, was against Merlin living in Camelot. When Arianna came into the picture, he struggled with his animosity towards the Pagans. This woman from another time caused Frederick to test his faith, as he was falling in love with her. He was aware of Arianna's marriage and felt that the woman was engaging in some act of sorcery to bring the knights to her side. Arianna's eventual rejection of Frederick cemented his faith in the church and his hatred of the Druids.

Frederick's knighthood to the king was short lived, as he rode into battle with King Arthur and watched as Arthur and his son Mordred battled to the death. After Galahad became King of Camelot and traveled to find the Grail, Arianna was left in charge of the city and the king's son, the Prince of Camelot John Arthur. The city of Camlann was hit by sickness and hard times. Frederick and other Christians thought that the Druids, led by the Lady of the Lake, Lady Viviane, were the culprits behind the illnesses. Merlin was questioned highly by Sir Frederick and accused of standing behind his aunt. Arianna supported the wizard in Galahad's absence.

During a hearing against Merlin in the west wing of the castle, Galahad and his men returned with the Holy Grail to find Merlin deep in interrogation with the judge and jury, the Archbishop Thomas, and the elder knights, led by Sir Frederick Garris. Galahad walked into his court and saw the blasphemy taking place in his home. He unveiled the Grail and placed it directly in Merlin's hands, telling him that he attained Arthur's dream. Frederick looked on with disdain, vowing that no Druid would ever stand higher than those who follow Christ.

Next to Sir Frederick stood Sir Michael Bedwynn, knight and man at arms. Sir Michael was the oldest son of Sir Ralph Bedwynn, who served King Arthur until he died in Arthur's arms on the battlefield where King Arthur later gave his own life. Sir Michael inherited his father's broad stature and red hair, a trait the young knight of twenty-two years was proud to carry on. Michael was born in Ireland when his father was commissioned to lead Arthur's army to protect the territorial borders between the two countries. When Sir Michael was sixteen, he witnessed the assault on Lady Arianna in which she was impaled by Gresham's sword. His heroic gestures saved her life, and Galahad asked the young man to train for high office in his court of knights.

Joining the others, was Sir Daniel Montgomery, knight, and aid to Galahad and Lady Arianna. Sir Daniel was the son of Sir Percival Montgomery who served for twenty years as a knight of the Round Table and was chosen by Arthur to accompany him to Rome when Arthur sought the holy cross of Jesus. Daniel's mother Lorraine died in childbirth, and Percival—having no place to rear the boy—asked Arthur if Catherine and Nimue would help him raise the child. Arthur gladly brought the baby into his home, and Daniel grew under the watchful eye of the king. When Arianna first arrived in Camelot and was acquitted of witchcraft, she was taken to Arthur's chambers for refreshment, where the young page Daniel Montgomery was charged with taking care of her.

Immediately following the call to arms, Squire Gavin approached the bottom of the stairs, stood tall, and shouted into the room, "The High Priestess, Lady Arianna Lawrence Pendragon!"

Merlin watched the knights rise to their feet as they looked up towards the lady making her way down the winding stairs. Blaise and Aaron entered and stood next to their seats, as Arianna neared the Round Table. When she was close enough, she reached out and rested her hand on Merlin's shoulder. Though still weak, he felt empowered by her touch.

The men all bowed to Arianna, and Merlin listened as each man greeted her, calling her "high priestess."

She bowed her head back to them, acknowledging their respects to her. Then with all her might, she hurled Mab's sword into the air. Merlin followed the blade as it spiraled high, twisted and spun multiple times before dropping down towards the cinquefoil engraved into the surface of the middle of the table. When it speared the wood, it buried itself at least four inches deep and shook with a twang that reverberated throughout the room.

"My lords, I give you the sword of Mab."

Merlin could see his reflection in its blade.

"My lady, is this the sword that bewitched Mordred, taking the life of our revered King Arthur?" asked Sir Gawain.

Arianna held her head high, "This is the sword."

"Is the sword bewitched?" asked Sir Frederick.

"Mab is dead. I beheaded her and burned her body on the blades of grass at Domh Ringr."

"You burned her body, Mother?" asked Joseph.

Arianna turned to Joseph. "Mab is no longer a part of this world."

One word came from the mouth of Sir Martin. "Huzzah!" he called out. In unity, every man in the room stood and shouted, "Huzzah!" over and over again. The walls of the Round Table room echoed with the shouts of the knights, and Merlin beamed with pride. His dear one was victorious over an evil that claimed not only Arthur's and Mordred's lives but the lives of many men who once sat in this very court—men of great strength and honor.

Merlin watched with pleasure as Arianna basked in her victory. He reached for her hand, holding tight to her. This was a bittersweet victory for him. As much as he hated his mother for all the wrongs she had done to him in her life, his heart also grieved for her. He closed his eyes and listened to the revelry in the room, sat back in his chair, and remembered the same sounds he heard round the room when a glorious Arthur often stood there and claimed similar conquests.

"My lady, I am glad that you come to us the victor," said Sir Martin.

"I thank you, Sir Knight."

Joseph stepped to his mother's side and lifted his cup. "To my mother, The High Priestess Lady Arianna."

"Long live the High Priestess Arianna!" shouted Galahad. The court lifted high their cups and toasted the priestess.

Blaise pounded his fist on the table, shouting her name, "Arianna! Arianna!" The knights joined him and they, too, pounded their fists on the table, calling out her name. The Round Table room boomed with their words and the pounding of their fists.

Suddenly Merlin's eyes raised to the sword lodged in the wood; a piece of the hilt broke away and fell to the surface. As the men continued to pound the table, another larger piece fell off. Merlin watched what was unfolding as again one more piece fell. His eyes beheld a wonder: under the casing was a stone, a red one, just like the blue stone on Arianna's sword Gwydion. He kept his eyes fixed on the phenomenon, held the table and shouted into the noise of the room. "The sword of Mab shows a new face."

"Please, good people," said Blaise, trying to quiet the knights. "I beg you look at the sword."

"Priest Blaise, do you wish to address this court?" asked Galahad.

"Sire, the sword sheds its casing," said Merlin as Galahad looked upon the table. On the facade were pieces of metal that broke from the hilt and the pommel of the weapon.

"Cavyn, remove the sword from the table," commanded Galahad. Cavyn, young and agile, climbed onto the table and pulled the sword from it with all of his youthful strength. He brought it to Merlin, resting it on the table in front of him. As it came to rest on the table, the silver casing around the hilt completely fell apart.

The noise of the knights lowered to a deafening hush as everyone held their eyes on Merlin and Blaise who now approached him. The priest removed the excess fragments of metal and wire wrapped around the new face of the sword.

"Please, Merlin, what say you?" asked Galahad.

"My Lord, the sword speaks to us."

Galahad ran to Merlin's side and examined the blade. "If I did not know any better, I would think that Excalibur had another sister."

Merlin turned to Arianna. "Dear one, may I have Gwydion?"

Arianna drew Gwydion from her sheath and rendered her to Merlin. She looked at the sword on the table with confusion. "Why did this not happen during the battle? The way we raged our war, this sword should have fallen apart."

Merlin looked straight in her eyes. "We will unravel the mystery."

He and Blaise lifted the two swords and placed them side by side. "Merlin, where was Gwydion forged?"

"She was forged from the waters of Avalon, as was Excalibur."

"Look upon the design on Mab's sword," commanded Blaise. "The design is the crest of the house of Echrrynn, the house of the first Merlin, Medwynn Echrrynn, and his wife Mab of the Lake," said Blaise. "This is the sword Cedwynn, the oldest of the sister swords."

"What are you telling the court?" asked Arianna. She backed away from them and paced the floor.

Merlin quietly examined the swords. The *fleur de lis* engraving was exact except that Arianna's sword carried a rose cinquefoil pattern with three drops of water flowing from the petals of the flower. The intricacy of the floral etching had a blue stone—compared to Mab's red stone in the center of the hilt. Mab's sword was hiding the same design except that the roses were surrounded with three concentric crescent moons.

"This floral imprint is the crest of the Echrrynn house," commented Blaise.

Merlin looked over his shoulder at Arianna, nearly frozen there. She reached for the back of Gawain's chair, holding firm.

"Merlin, I ask thee, friend and mentor, what did you ask the Goddess when Gwydion was forged?"

Merlin looked his fellow priest in the eye and answered, "I asked the Goddess to forge in Arianna's name, a sword befitting a High Priestess of the Lake, one that would protect her as Excalibur protected Arthur."

As Merlin finished speaking, the sword of Mab rose onto its point and his staff vibrated in his hand, the wood turning to ice beneath his fingers. The table shook, and a mournful moan passed around the room, as though a ghost were drifting through the walls in the wake of a haunting.

A red beam of light shot from the red stone on Mab's sword towards the dragon's eye on Merlin's staff. Both garnets glowed, bathing their radiance onto Arianna. The light wrapped around the high priestess and cut across the table and back to the dragon on his staff, tracing the curled talon on the neck of the brass beast. The dragon's head turned to Merlin and what was once a brass sculpted figure became a living and breathing creature. The animal broke free from the staff, spread its wings and climbed a few feet into the air. Turning its head again, now towards the ray, the dragon stretched long and hard and uncurled his talons that had tightly gripped the once brass scroll it held, which now appeared to be made of paper. He let it fall from his claw and as he did, Merlin reached out his free hand and easily caught the parchment. Once in his hand, the winged dragon circled the room three times, and then flung itself back to the staff Merlin held. He grabbed onto it with fierce strength, spun around it twice and then came to settle into his place on the staff, returning to the brass figure he had once been.

Merlin felt all eyes upom the ecru parchment and he slowly unrolled the scroll.

As he did, Blaise spoke, "The swords fashioned in the lake of Avalon belonged to the house of Echrrynn. Medwynn Echrrynn was the ruler of the first tribes of the Druids here in England. He was the first Merlin and the original owner of that staff.

Galahad inched closer to Merlin. "What says the scroll?"

Merlin read the words aloud.

My son,

You know that I have always led with kindness while your mother has appreciated a firmer hand. I fear that she is beginning a descent into darkness. The woman I once loved, a woman of great kindness and gentility is acting as though her place among the Druids has been threatened. The birth of your sister and the prophecy of her power is tormenting Mab, so much so that I fear for the life of our new child. There is an anger in your mother's eyes that I can no longer ignore. I believe that I have to act quickly to save your sister. I will steal her away in the night and bring her to live with High Priestess Élan; she will rear her and bring my sweet daughter to her rightful destiny. My heart aches dear son, as I will never see my child grow to womanhood. A shield will be placed around her that will mask her true identity until the time that Mab leaves this earth. This letter to you shall remain locked away until the secret can be reveiled. When the truth comes to light, find your sister and reunite this family.

Maiyonliovina,
Your Father Medwynn.

Blaise addressed the knights, "High Priest Medwynn wanted unity between the house of the Christians and the house of the Pagans. Queen Mab of the Lake was Medwynn's wife. Where the high priest ruled with virtue, she ruled with tyrannical force. Mab was a time traveler. She had two children: an older son and a baby girl. The daughter was rumored to have died before her first year. Upon her supposed death, Mab became more insane and attemped to gain power over the Pagans and control the destiny of her people. She has been working ever since to build an army so vast that every Christian for miles would perish under her wrath." Blaise turned to Galahad, "Majesty, the royal house of Echrrynn has returned." He clasped Arianna and Merlin's hands in his, uniting them. Merlin was shaking, and his friend held on tight to the two of them. He looked upon them both. "Merlin was many years older than you, my dear lady, when you were born. He was a young man and already a priest of the Goddess."

Merlin felt his heart pouring out to Arianna. He held onto her hand so tightly that his own was going numb. "My father told me you were dead."

"He had to protect her," Said Blaise.

Arianna pulled her hands away. "I am Mab's daughter? Merlin is my true brother?"

Blaise again placed Arianna and Merlin's hands together. "Aryanyn of the Lake and High Priest Merlin, look upon each other, for you both are the heirs to the house of Echrrynn. My dear High Priestess, you are the daughter of Mab, Aryanyn of the Lake."

Arianna pulled the sword from Blaise's hands. Tears shed from her stoic eyes. "I killed my mother at Domh Ringr." Her voice cracked as she said the words.

"I am afraid that it was your destiny."

Arianna lifted her head high. "It was my honor to serve the Goddess and rid this earth of an evil that has held me—held all of us—hostage for over a thousand years."

Merlin closed his eyes, thinking, *I have a sister, and her name is Aryanyn Echrrynn.*

CHAPTER FIFTY-THREE

A Ilew Found Enlightenment

My lady, what name do you wish to be called?" asked Sir Martin.

Galahad watched as Arianna paused a moment before answering. "I will take on my true name, Aryanyn, but I will always remain kindly to Arianna, for it was she who brought me here."

Blaise calmed the crowd. "Know this, Aryanyn Echrrynn of the Lake, it is your sovereign duty to raise King Arthur, as you were given the sight to his resurrection."

"Resurrection?" rebuked Sir William. "You speak this word as though you were God himself."

"I would love nothing better than to see my king rise from his untimely grave," added Sir Frederick, "but only God has the right to do this."

Galahad felt himself building a slow rage as the knights wielded such ignorance of their faith as a weapon against his court. "Yes, he does, Frederick," Galahad said. "I agree with all of you that only Christ can raise a man from the grave, as this is our Christian doctrine. But kind sirs, I was also apprehensive when it was my time to quest for the Holy Grail. Arianna helped me with my course, and showed me my true path to glory."

"Yes, my King, she sent her aid to you," Frederick spouted back to Galahad, "but this Druid speaks of powers beyond our understanding that belong only to our Holy Trinity."

"Frederick, our newfound Aryanyn obviously has more power than any of us knew," said Galahad.

Sir Frederick looked at the lady with distain and spoke with sarcasm that oozed from his lips like drool from a rabid dog. "High Priestess, I have come to respect you and honor you in every way that Arthur wished for us to respect his courtiers. It is with earnest doubt as a true Christian that I impugn your powers and your judgment at this time."

Aryanyn responded respectfully, "I will not fault you for your beliefs. Until I unearthed the sword Excalibur, I thought as you, but I have since been asked to step through another door towards a new found enlightenment."

"A new found enlightenment," repeated Frederick throwing up his arms.

"This is blasphemy," cried William lowering his head into his hands.

Galahad rose, "And what of Excalibur?" he asked above the crowd's roar.

The Knights around the table quieted and heads all turned to Galahad.

Aryanyn bowed to him. "Do I have the king's permission to show these good people the gifts of the Goddess?"

Galahad nodded and let his mother command the elements.

Aryanyn lifted her eyes to the heavens and whispered, "*Kir da laun re leian faul resarius mendan morr.*"

The high priestess raised Gwydion above the table. With her other hand, she placed her forefinger and middle finger to her brow. She touched the stone of the sword to her symbol whispering again, "*Ke'tu fay katur enbow sisieath el.*"

Aryanyn pointed to the fire in the hearth in the corner of the room, flames flared and shot forth, reaching over the table. The knights scattered for fear of being burned. In the middle of the Round Table, a small conflagration raged, glowing red and blue. Galahad watched with careful eyes as his mother placed the point of Gwydion into the flames.

"*Gwydion mendora familia Excalibur secoia epata sempora*." White smoke and ash emitted from the flames, and within the smoke, Galahad witnessed the vision of Excalibur immersed in the altar stone at the circle of Stonehenge.

"Sire, do you not bear Excalibur!" shouted William over the noise of the flames.

Galahad placed his hand on his empty sheath. "Excalibur no longer belongs to me."

Aryanyn placed Gwydion back into the flames and the vision vanished. "Good men of the Round Table, Mab wanted control of the swords. If she killed me in battle and stole Gwydion, she would have opened the wall and not only killed her son Merlin, but Galahad as well." She paused before continuing. "Mab desired to make of the Round Table the puppet she made of Mordred."

The court of Camelot was silenced a moment.

"Tell us, Priestess, how do you plan to raise ashes that have been buried for the past fifteen years?" asked a sarcastic Frederick.

"I must find that answer within the confines of my service to Arthur, to the Goddess, and to the mighty one above us—and his son."

"You are wise, High Priestess," said Blaise, bowing to her once again.

"Here! Here!" shouted Sir Martin.

"I served Arthur and now you. I do not wish to disrespect this court," rebuked William, "but raising Arthur goes against everything that I, as a Christian man, believe."

Galahad walked over to William and looked straight into the Knight's eyes.

"We all must have faith for the good of Arthur and for the good of the cause. Blaise, tell Aryanyn what she must do," commanded Galahad turning to the priest.

"Aryanyn of the Lake, it is within the confines of three worlds that you have been sent to us. Use the sight that has been given to you, and you will see the destiny of the high king and your own as well."

CHAPTER FIFTY-FOUR

Aryanyn and the Stableman

———❖———

Aryanyn awoke the morning after her day in court and decided to dress. Standing in front of the full length mirror, she stared at the new symbol that adorned her brow. With some oil of Echinacea she cleaned the tattoo, and the mark stung a bit as she applied pressure to it. She looked hard at her trefoil, still unaccustomed to the blue green color that now graced her forehead.

A yawn came over her, she had not slept very well. Her mind kept her awake as she thought about her past and what she had learned about her family. How would she call upon her sight to raise King Arthur?

She opened the door to her room. The knight posted outside bowed to her. "Lady, may I assist you?" he asked as she passed him and walked down the hall.

"No, good knight. Thank you. I can help myself."

"Madam, please, His Majesty commanded me to keep guard on you."

Aryanyn turned and studied the strong physique of the tall gentle knight standing behind her. She drew Gwydion forth. "My lord, do you see this blade?"

The knight looked at the weapon and answered, "I do, my lady!"

"I do not need you this day to be at my side," she coyly smiled.

The knight stood at attention and gripped the hilt of his sword.

"Madam, I cannot go against the request of my king!"

"Sir Knight, I appreciate that you honor the orders given to you, but I will deal with my son accordingly." Aryanyn walked away.

She felt the knight follow her to the top of the stairs, before he cut her off from descending them. "My lady, it is not fit for a woman to travel alone."

Aryanyn looked at the knight standing in front of her. "Move, sir, or it will be me you fear."

The knight respectfully backed away from the stairs.

"Tell my son I am going to the circle to contemplate."

Aryanyn walked into the stables, passing the stableman, Marc. Marcus—or Marc, as he was lovingly called—lived alone in the city of Wiltshire. She remembered what Catherine had told her about the boy when Aryanyn first met him years ago. He was a boy of poor means who, during a local joust, was caught trying to steal a loaf of bread from a baker's wagon at the festivities. Sir Gawain was in town for the tournaments and noticed that the boy was in chains by the horses' stalls. He asked why a young boy should receive such punishment. When told of Marc's crimes, Sir Gawain addressed the boy and found out that the child was stealing out of the desperate pain in his belly. Sir Gawain insisted on an immediate pardon and hired the boy to work for him in the stables. Marc worked hard for the knight, and Gawain kept him on. He brought him to Camelot for Sir Peter to train in the knight's tack shed. Marcus now served the knights and their horses.

After watching Marc care for his animals, Aryanyn stepped into the tack shed, taking her horse's saddle and preparations. She began to outfit Brach for the day.

"I can do that for you, my lady," Marc said.

"I have taken care of Brach all these years without the aid of a stableman. He is my companion, and we have learned to mind one another." Aryanyn placed Brach's blanket on his back and retrieved the saddle from the floor. She placed it on the steed's back, belting and securing it to his body.

"I never saw a lady of the manor take care of her own animal."

Aryanyn turned to see an amazed look cross the young man's face. "Well, now you have."

She clenched the bridal in her hand and mounted the steed slowly, as the pain of the battle had not yet left her body. "Sir Brach, Domh Ringr awaits. Yah!"

CHAPTER FIFTY-FIVE

Galahad Confronts Aryanyn

————◆◆◆————

Horse and rider cantered out of the stables, taking to their stride, galloping freely through the back route of the castle grounds. They passed the archery yard where the knights and squires practiced their swordplay and battlement strategies. As they rode through the lofty oak trees, Aryanyn could see Joseph teaching the young boys how to use the javelin. Joseph took his stance and advanced the spear high, flying it to its target—a tree across the yard with a large red X painted on its trunk. He did well as the lance hit its mark right in the center.

Remembering the day when Peter taught Joseph to use the weapons, Aryanyn smiled as she continued on her way. She came upon the back gate of the archery yard used by the squires during practice sessions and ordered the Guard to open it.

"My lady, you are unattended!" proclaimed the squire.

"Kind sir, do I look like a woman who needs attending?"

The squire looked at Aryanyn, then at her sword. "No disrespect, my lady, but I advise you to find a lady in waiting to ride with you to your destination."

Aryanyn looked up to the sky. *To be in my time where I can come and go as I please.* "Guard, open this gate!" The guard stood at attention and opened the gate immediately. Aryanyn gave Brach a mild nudge on the side, and the two were on their way. "Finally, some freedom," she said to herself.

The pair took to the sights of Camlann. Aryanyn could feel her body relax as she gazed upon the greenery around her. Elegant foliage opened her senses as she allowed the colors to grace the depths of her spirit. Hills of the country literally bellowed their welcome home as the cool winds brushed her face. She allowed the chill to refresh her.

They arrived at Salisbury Place and then onto the Avenue of Stonehenge, and horse and rider rode straight up, passing the heel stone and slaughter stones on their way to the monolith. Aryanyn stopped for a minute and remembered that here in this time, she did not need a key to open the gate. It was a shame that modern progress, and the ignorance that came with it, elicited rumors of Stonehenge being a place of evil. Such rumors caused this temple of the ancient ones to be barred from humans who only wished to respect it and pray there.

"Brach, look at her. What a disgrace that the citizens of England in our time cannot appreciate this circle as we can here. Shall we invite ourselves in?"

Aryanyn pulled on the reins and horse and rider rode over the land bridge built over the mote cut around the Henge. It was just five days ago—more than fourteen hundred years into the future—that Aryanyn fought the battle of her life here.

She dismounted Brach and walked over to the altar stone. There in all her splendor, mounted in the reddish brown boulder, was Excalibur.

"Mighty sword, I bow to thee!" Aryanyn caressed the blade as Excalibur stood unyielding in the granite. Again, Aryanyn looked around. A chill ran through her as she remembered the battle and Mab's body burning near the trilithons.

She walked back towards Brach and removed her Wicca sack from the saddlebag. Aryanyn unrolled the purple blanket and rested it on the ground near the stone. She placed the runes of the Moon, the Trefoil and the pentacle on the blanket and primed her censor, striking a match to heat the small coals within the compartment. Brach whinnied, probably from the smell of the jasmine burning off from the last time it was used.

"I agree, my friend, the fragrance is most pleasing." Aryanyn knelt down on her blanket facing Excalibur. She inhaled deeply, taking in the fragrance of the jasmine and the Mother Earth. As she placed her hands in prayer, she looked towards the avenue and noticed that Galahad and three of his guards were approaching the circle.

She could see His Majesty signal to his party to wait for him.

Galahad came down the avenue alone, and as he approached, Aryanyn could see the angry expression on his face.

"Mother, what right have you to go against my better judgment?"

"My son, I cannot have ladies in waiting and guards posted around me every moment of the day."

Galahad silenced himself as he fixed his eyes on Excalibur immersed in the stone. He swallowed hard. "So this is the handiwork of your powers, I see."

Aryanyn stood and looked to her deed set in the stone. She stretched to caress the king's face, but he backed away. "I remember the day when Father James blessed you and Excalibur."

"I was ordained King of Camelot that day."

"It was bittersweet. Camelot buried one king and took to her breast another," said Aryanyn.

Galahad stared at the sword. "When Excalibur was placed in my hands, I felt as though Uncle Arthur would never leave me. Now I feel as though he is gone forever."

"You have just as much faith in me as the rest of your honorable knights."

"William is right, Arthur's raising goes against every Catholic teaching there is."

Aryanyn looked into the face of her king before fixing her eyes on her ward, Excalibur. She drew Gwydion from her sheath and fixed the tip of the blade in the grass, leaning on the weapon.

"Mother, only one power in this world has command over life and death. It is our God in heaven. No one else."

"Galahad, do you not understand that until my vision comes to me, neither you nor I will know the truth about how Arthur will return?"

"I see that you have disavowed your Christian beliefs."

"I am still a Christian first, as my heart will always belong to Christ. He alone gave me the very life that stands before you now."

"Then why go on with this?"

"Before I came here," she answered thoughtfully, "every day of my life was nothing but abuse and tolerance. Until I fought Mab, I did not know who and what I was. God has made this life for me, and I must accept it no matter what the cost."

"The cost, Mother, is your soul."

"It is my soul that taught me how to fight all these years. It is my soul that held me steadfast, and it is my soul that helped me fight an evil that no man or woman should have beaten! When you have looked into the evil that I have, my son, you can have all the claims to heaven you wish. But until then, do not talk to me about losing my soul!"

"Mother, I'm afraid that losing your soul will be your price for not just trying to raise Arthur, but for the love I see in your eyes every time you say his name."

Aryanyn stared at her son, caught off guard. "I do love Arthur. From the day he placed his kiss on my cheek before he battled Mordred, I have held a special place in my heart for him."

Aryanyn held tight the cross that she and Arthur shared. Galahad reached for it and rubbed Arthur's blood stain on the gold. It was evident that his heart ached for his uncle. He grabbed his mother's hands. "Please leave well enough alone, and let God keep Arthur with him."

"It is God that put this wheel in motion—not I," Aryanyn said with anger. "Do you remember the words on his grave? Who wrote them, Galahad?"

Galahad spoke the words, "*Hic Iacet Arthurus Rex Quondam Rex Que Futurus*," and approached Excalibur. Aryanyn could see his heart beating from within his chest. "God wrote them!"

"What are you so angry about?"

"It's not anger that I feel, it's panic. After all of these years of faithful service to Camelot, I am fearful that my knights will no longer look at me as their king." Again Galahad's eyes found Excalibur. "I'm afraid that they will prefer to serve Arthur again."

Aryanyn placed her hand on her son's chest. "Arthur is no longer of this world. When he returns, he and I must leave, and your place will still be here as it has been."

"Worlds. Reincarnation. I am sick of these words. Since this all began, my world as I know it has been threatened and I, the one that God chose to find the Grail, does not know how to perceive all of this." Galahad pushed Aryanyn's hand from his chest, "Resurrection non gratis. What are the heavens thinking?"

"You, above all, should know this. It was you who looked into the face of God."

"Yes, it was my destiny to find the Grail and drink from it. It was my honor to look into the face of Jesus and be touched by him."

"You are about to look into the face of our Lord again. Accept the miracle!" Galahad raised his eyes up to the heavens. He gazed at the blue of the sky and the white of the clouds. She asked him, "Are you afraid that if you believe in this, your own soul will be in peril?"

Galahad shuffled his feet and cracked his knuckles. "This goes against everything that Father James taught me since I was a boy."

"Priests are men and know not all that God has planned for us."

"Priests are men, but they are men of the cloth."

"Cloth that has been torn for years, wracked with false power and personal gain," she added.

"And what have you to gain, Mother, by believing the way you do?"

"The freedom of my heart and my soul." Aryanyn looked to Excalibur again. "And a friend that my heart has ached for since the day I watched him die."

"Do you really believe that God will give you the sight to bring Uncle Arthur back?" Galahad asked.

Aryanyn closed her eyes. "Until I see what God and the Goddess wish for me, I will not know the might and power of God."

"When your voice cut through Merlin's window the night of your battle with Mab, it was as though the hills of Camelot raged with you." Galahad now retreated from Aryanyn and held fast to the sword in the stone. "I felt Excalibur vibrate on my leg, and her temperature flared in her scabbard. I had to pull her fast from her covering, as she was burning my leg. Mother, your voice called her and she sang for you as she was pulled from me, into the light that came through the doors. There was no stopping her. She yanked out of my hand so fast that she burned my palm." Galahad showed Aryanyn the marking on his hand. "I remember hearing you shout again, 'Excalibur, I call you by name!', and she was engulfed in the prism and vanished from my sight." Tears fell from Galahad's eyes, and Aryanyn wiped them with her finger. He looked down at her meditation blanket. "I am afraid to believe in this, Mother, for I admit it is beyond my understanding."

"My son, king and ruler of Camelot, we will find the answers together."

CHAPTER FIFTY-SIX

Aryanyn Calls Upon the Constellations

Aryanyn stood on her verandah. Dusk was approaching. Her eyes fixed on the wonder of the night sky above Camelot. The grounds of Galahad's kingdom were spread out before her—hills that kissed the sky and mountains that stretched for miles. The North Star was just beginning to twinkle in the night, and Aryanyn concentrated on its splendor. She basked in the miraculous nature that only the mighty one and his bride, Mother Earth, could give to their children. Aryanyn and Galahad had visited Arthur's grave that morning to find that hawthorn flowers had not yet begun to grow where his ashes were buried.

Respecting Galahad's wishes, she was remaining close to home. Riotous affairs plagued the country before she had returned, and Galahad was afraid for her, even knowing that she could fight for herself.

She knelt upon the Wicca blanket that she had prepared on the ground of her balcony and placed her sword Gwydion, Mab's sword Cedwynn and Merlin's staff together side by side as she studied the intricate details of each weapon. Picking up Mab's sword, she ran her fingers over the roses etched on the hilt and the three crescent moons. Looking at her hand, she remembered the blood of Mab that she had shown Blaise; the crimson still on her dress—mixed with her own blood.

Aryanyn wiped one hand with the other as though she could cleanse herself of the memory. Again, she looked at Mab's sword. *Mother, why did you hate me so?* Her chest heaved with sorrow as she wiped away her tears, then stared at Merlin's staff, denying the lost child within her. Shaking her head, she sneered back at the sword. "We were your children!"

Aryanyn picked up the staff, held it close to her and looked into the face of the dragon. "Father, you made this for my brother, Merlin. Please tell me what I must do!"

Aryanyn doubled over in pain from the anguish, holding her mid-section. It felt like a hot knife was gutting her as she laid on her bed crying bitterly in her pillow, "Father, I needed you."

She threw the pillow across the room, "Why do I have to face this alone?" Her stomach felt as though she would purge. "I am tired of facing my life alone."

Aryanyn felt lightheaded, as though the top of her skull was no longer connected to her body. She moved to the chair across from her bed and stared out the window toward Avalon.

Memories flooded of the day Draco came to her at Arthur's tomb, telling her of the high king's future. Moving to the dry sink, she raised the water pitcher and poured cool water into the wash bowl. She washed her face, allowing the liquid to cleanse her of the pain she felt.

Aryanyn rolled up her sack, sheathed Gwydion, and picked up Mab's sword and Merlin's staff. Opening the door, she looked at the knight posted down the hall. "Knight, come here, please!" He came quickly, bowing his head to her. "I must go to Arthur's tomb," she explained. The knight smiled as Aryanyn was letting him do his duty. "What is your name?"

The young man stood tall and answered, "I am Daniel, High Priestess."

Aryanyn looked at the young man dressed in the dark blue and red uniform of Galahad's court. He stood proud as Aryanyn examined his black knee high boots, dark blue tunic, and brown leather vestment embossed with the red and gold Celtic cross. "Daniel?" She was surprised to see how the passing years had changed his features. "I had not recognized you in court a few days back. You were the young page who brought me a tray of food and drink in King Arthur's chambers after I was acquitted of witchcraft when I first came here."

"I am he, my lady," he said with pride. "His majesty placed me in charge of you."

"May I ask how old you might be?"

"I am twenty-six, my lady," said the stately knight.

Again Aryanyn looked at the young man. "I am pleased to have you watch over me. I request that you post yourself at the base of the sarsen stone opposite Arthur's tomb."

The knight bowed. "It will be done as you wish."

"Now let us leave these walls. They are blocking my sight." The two walked down the hall and straight to the stables.

"Marc, make ready the high priestess' horse!" commanded Sir Daniel.

The stableman looked for approval from Aryanyn, and she gave him a nod.

He saddled Brach with bridal and effects and brought him forward. Aryanyn caressed her steed and gave him a bit of apple from the bucket on the post. She removed a horseman's scabbard from the tack shed and slid Mab's sword into it before mounting her companion. Marc handed her Merlin's staff. Sir Daniel came from the knight's tack shed, mounted and ready to leave with his lady.

Aryanyn gave the signal, and the two left for the tomb of Arthur. They reached the gates of the court square, and Daniel gave the gesture to lift the huge iron rack. The gate thundered as it rolled up the towers.

He led Aryanyn up the land bridge and the ramp away from the castle grounds.

"My lady, may I speak?"

"You may."

"When I was a boy, I remember seeing you sleeping on a comfortable chair in King Arthur's chambers. I recall looking at your attire and wondering why you were wearing such ugly clothing."

Aryanyn smirked, "You thought my trouser riding costume ugly, ehy?"

"I mean no disrespect, but a woman who dressed like a man looked out of place in my eyes. I prefer my women to be dressed as elegant as you are now."

Aryanyn looked down at her attire. She was wearing her brown riders skirt and hunter green cloak with a lovely ecru laced blouse. She admitted to herself how in her time, only for special affairs, would her attire be formal. In this world, it was an everyday occurrence, one in which she felt comfortable.

They approached the gate of the cemetery. Sir Daniel dismounted and opened the iron gate, allowing Sir Brach and Aryanyn entrance to the tomb. The chivalrous knight assisted Aryanyn from her horse, but seemed to stop in his tracks as she walked over to the grave. Aryanyn looked back. "Are you just going to stand there?"

Daniel stared at the tomb, his eyes hypnotically fixed on Arthur's name and the words written on the stone.

"What is it, Daniel?"

He removed his hood and bowed his head.

Aryanyn gently walked over to the young knight. "You may go and pay your respects to the king, Sir Daniel."

His chest heaved as he shuffled his first step towards the tomb. He made the sign of the cross and knelt down on the grass, striking his chest with reverence to His Majesty Arthur. Aryanyn joined him as she, too, made the sign of the cross and bowed to her friend.

"My father, Sir Percival, is buried over in the knight's cemetery. He died with King Arthur on the same battleground. I have not been to this sacred place since my father and King Arthur were buried."

"Come, let us go to your father."

The pair took the bridals of their horses and walked next to them the half mile to the path of the Avalon cemetery grounds, and another acre's length stroll to the main entrance of the knights' cemetery. They were greeted by a tall grey stone Celtic cross and two high grey stone towers, holding within their fortress a four-foot-tall brass bell.

Aryanyn read the names on the stones. She could see the faces of these men of honor, remembering Sir Ralph as he died in Arthur's arms that horrid day, and Sir John and Sir Percival, two more brave men who gave their lives on the same battlefield; it was their bodies that Brach carried away from the bloody ground.

Daniel bowed to his father before kneeling down with Aryanyn to say a prayer.

Aryanyn placed her hand on Daniel's shoulder. "Sir Percival would be proud of you."

Daniel took a hard breath as he read his father's name, "Sir Percival."

A gust of wind wrapped around the two as they prayed, and Aryanyn felt her symbol burn on her brow. She placed her hand on the trefoil and could hear a voice echo through the tombstones. "I call you by name. Arthur Pendragon, come from your sleep." Aryanyn's stomach tightened and her body shook. She looked to Daniel, who—continuing to pray—obviously was not privy to the voice.

"Daniel, please bring the horses."

Daniel stood quickly, walked over to the two horses and brought Brach to Aryanyn. The two cantered quickly back to the king's grave. Aryanyn jumped off Brach and took her Wicca sack, Mab's sword, and Merlin's staff with her to the foot of Arthur's grave while the young knight, along with the horses, made his way toward the sarsen that stood directly in back of the plot. Aryanyn directed her eyes to the words *Hic Iacet Arthurus Rex Quondam Rex Que Futurus.*

She laid her purple blanket on the grass three feet from the tombstone and sat down. "*Saffier Ciariac mangor lynn ethynn etymen mor lun.*" Aryanyn raised Gwydion's hilt and placed the blue stone to her symbol. Aryanyn cried out to the moon above, "*Ethynn eblur entone' vas mor lun!*"

She closed her eyes. "Hail almighty symbols of the house of Echrrynn. Show me the sight." A burning sensation coursed through the small of her back, and she welcomed the heat and the perspiration that accompanied it.

Opening her eyes, she stood and backed away from the blanket. "Gwydion, I command you to bring forth your secrets." Aryanyn took her sword by the hilt, holding her firm, and impaled her blade into the soil over the tomb. She could feel her temperature swell, and a trickle of sweat rolled down her face as she picked up Mab's sword in her hands. "Cedwynn, I Aryanyn, daughter of the house of Echrrynn, call upon the will of the Mother. Show me the path to the high king." She stabbed the blade into the soil facing Gwydion.

The taste of bitter root formed in her mouth as she grabbed hold of Merlin's staff and glared hard at the dragon. "I, Aryanyn of the Lake, command the elements of night. Cast down your stars and show me the path of Arthur called the Pendragon." With great force, she thrust the point of the staff into the ground, using it to head the symbols in the shape of a triangle. Encircling the weapons, she examined the leaves inlaid on the hilt of Gwydion, the roses and the water droplets dripping from the petals; and Cedwynn, whose roses were surrounded by the three crescent moons.

Aryanyn removed her pin and held it in her hand as her eyes followed the intricacy of its design; the red moon, the gold trefoil and the sword itself were shaped like Gwydion. Turning it over, she looked at the woman on the back of the brooch.

"Aryanyn of the Lake, look upon the emblems of your family. Call upon their clandestine knowledge and bring forth the destiny of the high king. *Ethynn entmyne vas mor anglynn lunneare ciaiac amnene mor tu lun!*" Aryanyn cried into the night. "*Vas mor anglynn ciaiac. Vas mor anglynn!*" The pin radiated, the trefoil blazing yellow in her hand. "*Vas mor anglynn!*" Aryanyn shouted. The earth quaked beneath her as she commanded the night, and the eye of the dragon glowed crimson. It shone with brilliance, shedding its light on Cedwynn, whose blade illuminated, her hilt burning hot with silver lights bolting in the dark. Cedwynn's moons heated as they absorbed the glow of the rays, shining out white above the lights coming forth in three-dimensional forms from the body of the sword. Wind whipped through the cemetery, billowing cold vapors over the tomb, and the crescents of the moons formed a perfect circle. They spun around, twisting themselves like the cone of a tornado, gyrating and pulling at the roses on Gwydion.

Aryanyn's sword shook as the funnel pulled at her. Her roses shimmered in scarlet and reflected the sparkle of the white moons. A bolt of light cut through the cone and onto Arthur's tombstone as the roses at the base of the stone grew tall, accelerating in speed, climbing towards the canopy of the trees. They wound themselves through the branches of the trees to form a shelter over Aryanyn and the sight of Arthur's grave. She waved her hand and commanded, "*Espherac risases lun artess!*" Listening to the priestess, the flowers formed a perfect sphere that opened to the ceiling of the great Elysium. The circle of the moon separated into the three crescents forming a natural trefoil around the area of the grave.

Aryanyn dropped her brooch in the middle of the triangle of weapons, and the earth quaked again as three beams of light shot up towards the heavens, casting their rays onto the constellations.

The lights drew the triangle of the dragon's head in the night sky, igniting Draco's dim stars that were watched over by the guardians of the North Star and headed by Polaris, the North Star in Ursa Minor. Polaris shone brightly and woke up Thuban, the star at the end of the dragon's tail, which slithered like a snake, casting down upon the earth along the trail of lights from the triangle. It swung so hard that it rang the bell in the knight's cemetery.

"Draconian!" cried out Aryanyn. "Draconian, King of the Constellations, I call you by name. In the name of the High King Arthur Pendragon, come to my aid!"

Storm clouds hovered around the triangle of the dragon's head and a loud frightening roar shrilled into Aryanyn's ears. From the center of the clouds, the lady could see Draco, in all his glory, cut through the basket of the Little Dipper and fly with the wing span of at least three block's length. Soaring overhead, he commanded the sky, swooping down with the wind streaming over his reptilian reddish-brown skin. His descent was perfect as he landed within the circle of the roses.

Draco stood at least twenty feet high. His head was wide and crowned with four short spikes. His snout was long and square with large almond shaped nostrils, and his eyes were green with a catlike black pupil in the center. They were fierce and intimidating. Protruding from his neck were five longer spikes. He had four limbs: two shorter limbs with retracted raptor hands holding three digits coming from his wings, and two elongated legs with raptor claws. He thrust out the brown-gold scales of his chest, showing Aryanyn the power of his body and the passion of his strength. To Aryanyn, he was frightfully beautiful.

"High Priestess Aryanyn of the Lake," said Draco as he bowed his massive head to the lady.

"Draconian, Lord of the Constellations," Aryanyn bowed in return.

Draco's eyes fixed themselves on the symbols in the ground. "You have been victorious over the evil queen."

"It was your letter and your warning that told me to beware of her."

"Mab was a powerful entity in this world. It took the will of an iron maiden to cast her down."

"My Lord Draco, it was my honor."

"Now that you know your heritage, do you still feel the same?"

Aryanyn's eyes veered toward Arthur's tomb, and she held them on the words. She raised her head with pride and looked at Draco, high in the canopy. "My lord, I gather by your words that you have been watching my performance."

"I have had my eyes on you from the day that you left these grounds years ago."

Aryanyn looked to the dome of the night sky and onto the triangle of stars in the constellations that formed the head of the dragon in the dragon realm above her.

Draco smiled and nodded, "Yes."

"My lord, you knew who I was the day you foretold of Arthur's coming?"

"I knew who you were the day you were born." Draco opened his wings at the sight of Arthur's grave, bowing to His Majesty's name. His wings were wide like the length of the lake, scalloped at the ends and spiked by the long bones that held his leathery skin to them. They were mahogany red with veins like spider webs running through them. The fluttering of his wings sounded like the drum of a beating heart.

Draco lowered his winged hand and pulled Merlin's staff from the ground. "I call upon the flowers of the Grail gates. Grow fruitful upon the grave of your servant, Arthur Pendragonous."

Draco struck the earth with the staff and again the earth shook. From the grass sprouted the hawthorn flowers of the Grail. They were white like the fresh fallen snow with red pistols in the center. Arthur's grave now carried a blanket of these flowers. Aryanyn shuddered as they grew beneath her feet.

"Lord Draco, it was you who foretold the coming of Arthur. How does one raise ashes from the soil?" asked Aryanyn.

"My lady, Arthur's blood comes from an ancient line of kings born under the sign of the dragon realms. It will be their gift to bring blood to flesh burned long ago."

Aryanyn replied, "The God above carries the gift of life to his people. Only he can raise ashes from dust and return life from death as he did his son."

Draco bowed to the lady and lifted her hand, which looked like a baby's in his massive claw. "Look upon Orion." He pointed to the belt of the three stars.

Draco inhaled showing the massive strength of his lungs. He exhaled and his nostrils blasted out a flame that rose to the heights of heaven. The flames drew the shape of a bird, one with large wings as large as his own and raptor claws. Aryanyn watched with amazement as the wings blazed and fluttered in the sky. White ash fell like snow, and Draco scooped some into his hand, shaping it into a sphere and again blowing his breath upon it. He threw the ball of ash up to the flaming bird and roared out, "*Apheoniexas Anastasious efecias dominicuas!*"

A caw came from the Elysium. Out from the fire flew a phoenix that was as red as the scarlet rose. He sailed into the night, his wings wide like the canopy of the trees. He descended from the constellations, his body ablaze as he flew down into the circle of roses.

"Anastasious!" said Draco as he greeted the phoenix.

The wondrous bird stood at least sixteen feet tall. His blue eyes—the color of a morning sky—were dotted with deep amethyst pupils, and his beak was long and golden, reminding Aryanyn of the sun on a summer day. Anastasious' wide body was covered with orange and red feathers in shades of the sunset. He was bold and beautiful.

Aryanyn stood among these great mythical birds of prey as the phoenix and the dragon bound wings in greetings.

"So the legends of the house of Echrrynn and the high king have come to pass," said Anastasious.

"The prophecy will be fulfilled by midnight of the third day's moon," commanded Draco.

"My lady," Anastasious bowed his head. "It is with honor that I, Anastasious Apheoniexas, will be of aid in raising Arthur Pendragon, High King of both Pagans and those who follow the Christ."

"How do you know of me?" asked Aryanyn.

The phoenix raised his head. "On the day of your vows, Élan called to me. She requested that I be here at the hour of your need."

"How will you be of service, Lord Anastasious?"

"It is within the ash and the dust that I assist the high king." Anastasious grasped Aryanyn's brooch. He thrust his chest wide, showing Aryanyn the mark of the red crescent moon upon his plumage. Placing the pin to his chest, it connected with his mark as a blaze of golden flame emitted from the phoenix. He propelled his enormous torso, and fire bolted from his stigmata, casting its mark on Arthur's tombstone.

The top of the stone glowed, cracking it from the crown through the words and to the earth, burning itself into the roses at the base of the grave. The earth moaned, and Anastasious pulled back the flame to his chest. He removed the pin from his body, holding it in his wing. He walked over to Aryanyn and handed it back to her. "I believe that this is yours."

She looked at the pin as tears shed from her eyes.

"The dye is cast my lady," he looked at the tomb.

"As Draco commanded, I ask you to assist us at midnight of the third day's moon." The phoenix bowed his head to Aryanyn before ascending to the Elysium from whence he came.

"High Priestess, beware of those who are non-believers," said Draco. "Take heed and bring only those with honor, for Arthur's rising will be in peril."

Draco reached over the top of the roses. He stretched his wing and pulled Daniel, who was hiding behind the sarsen, over the wall. Daniel looked horror-struck after being witness to this miracle of the sky. He kicked his legs and flailed his arms as he was lifted through the air by the great dragon.

Draco placed Daniel on the ground next to Aryanyn and the boy fell shaking.

"I command you to stand, son of a knight of the Round Table!" said the dragon.

Daniel pulled himself together.

"Do not fear me, son of Percival. It is you who will tell the non-believers what transpired this night."

Daniel bowed to Draco. "I will do as you command, King of the Dragons."

Aryanyn lifted her head to Draco as she pulled Gwydion from the ground. "I will heed to your wisdoms, Draconian."

With those words, Draco took to the skies. He roared, casting his tail down on the earth, ringing the bell in the cemetery. "Arthur Pendragon, prepare thyself," Draco shouted before he found rest in the constellations of the night.

CHAPTER FIFTY-SEVEN

Beware of Those Who Do Not Believe

———◆———

Aryanyn came quietly up the land bridge to the gates of Camelot with Daniel by her side. She looked up at the tower to where Gavin and Marc had already begun raising the barrier.

Michael greeted her at the defensive structure. "His Majesty entreats your company in the west wing!"

"Caucuses! Can I just get on with my work?" she scoffed. "Come, Daniel, there is much to do!"

The two rode quickly up to the castle steps where Marc waited to take their horses to the stables. Aryanyn dismounted Sir Brach, giving him a loving kiss on the snout and let Marc lead him and Gallant away.

The night guard opened the door for the pair, and Aryanyn and Daniel walked straight towards the back of the castle. Aryanyn was about to make the left turn when she stopped short, almost tripping Daniel, and the two bumped into one another.

Aryanyn covered Daniel's mouth with her hand, telling him to stay quiet. "I want to hear what they are saying before we walk in," she whispered. Daniel acknowledged the gesture and stood behind the column.

The hall smelled like a brewery with the smoke of the fireplace and the pipe tobacco mixed with the scent of ale as it came through the doorway. Daniel smacked his lips.

"I agree, Daniel, I could use a tankard myself."

"Please, after the visions I have just witnessed, I could use the spirits to calm me down."

Aryanyn turned her attention to the voices from the room.

"Majesty, please, I understand that the lady is your mother," came William's voice from around the corner. "But we cannot, in good conscience, defend the thought of her raising King Arthur."

"William, please. I, too, have had some trouble understanding Mother's powers, but I do know that Mother and King Arthur have a special bond. It is within the ties of that union that we will be blessed to see this miracle unfold."

"Miracle? Is that the word they are using for heresy these days?" she heard Frederick ask.

Aryanyn grabbed Daniel and entered abruptly. Galahad looked shocked as he watched his mother dragging the knight in with her. She also noted that Sir Peter, Sir Martin, and Sir Gawain were in the room as was her son Joseph.

"So you think me a heretic, Frederick?" yelled Aryanyn as she stormed into the room. The knights stood at attention as the high priestess came in unannounced. "Please, sit down. Why stand in respect for a heretic?" she added. "The church would have all your heads on a silver platter."

Merlin, who was sitting hidden in the back of the meeting, stood and walked forward, smoking his pipe.

"Has he been there all the while?" shouted William upon seeing the wizard.

"Ehy, William, I have!" Merlin said with pride. "Were you successful?" he asked turning his attention to Aryanyn.

"We were, High Priest," said Daniel with a grin on his face that seemed to speak volumes to the room.

"And what has your sight shown you, sister?"

"My brother, your foster son will rise on the third day of the midnight moon."

Merlin inhaled a long drag of his pipe and sat back down in his chair as Frederick cried out, "Midnight moon, hah!"

Daniel's face twisted in knots. "Majesty, may I speak?"

"The room is yours, Sir Daniel."

Daniel stood at attention. "It was my honor to accompany Lady Aryanyn this evening. She and I not only visited King Arthur's grave, but my father's as well."

"Get on with it, man!" yelled Frederick.

Aryanyn was proud of the young knight as he ignored the pressure from Frederick and continued. "The lady's powers were high this night as she called upon her family's heirlooms to show her the sight."

"Sight!" William coughed out the word.

"Father, let the young man speak," suggested Sir Peter, and William backed down.

"I felt like I was in a dream when the stars in the sky descended for the high priestess." Daniel eased in his stance and blurted, "Dear God, Draco and Anastasious are a sight to behold!"

Merlin blew out a cloud of smoke that looked like the wings of the dragon. "So it begins!"

"Draco came to visit you this night?" asked Galahad.

"Yes, Majesty, a dragon the size of this castle stood majestically over the tomb of our king!" declared Daniel.

"Dragons, powers beyond that of mortal men... Majesty, please, I cannot hear anymore!" interjected William again.

"Quiet, Father!" Peter dashed from the fireplace and walked over to William. "It was at the Grail that Draco escorted Jesus down the stairs of heaven, and it was Draco that assisted Jesus in giving us the Grail from the hands of our Lord himself."

"Yes, yes," impugned Frederick. "We've all heard your version of the grail story with your mythical dragon and your run-in with our lord and savior."

"How dare you question the story of the grail find!" shouted Peter.

"But my son, there is no proof to the story," cried William in return.

"I want to believe all that we've been told, but it is all so far-fetched."

As the men continued their shouting match, Galahad poured ale for Daniel and Aryanyn. Aryanyn sipped and enjoyed the drink and the argument.

"Who is this Anastasious?" asked Martin as he, too, came out of his silence.

"Anastasious is the high phoenix!" answered Merlin.

"This is pure witchcraft!" yelled Frederick.

Aryanyn could remain quiet no longer and stepped forward. "It was in this room fifteen years hence that I was accused of witchcraft by an angry mob! I was acquitted if you recall. This is no witchcraft!"

"Mother, I am sure that is not what Frederick meant," said Galahad.

"Majesty, it is exactly what the knight means," said Joseph in defense of his mother.

Frederick filched a piece of bread from the table and bit down on the dough, ripping at the loaf. "High Priestess, I know the powers which you command. I apologize for the insult, but only out of respect for my king."

Aryanyn clenching her hand behind her back. "If it were not for the respect I hold for my sons, I'd show you what powers I command." Aryanyn was rubbing her brooch and whispering words under her breath. She caught herself and willfully backed down, holding her powers at bay.

Cavyn came into the room pouring ale for all as Galahad followed up on Martin's earlier question. "Mother, what is this phoenix you speak of?"

"He is the key to the laws of resurrection by the rites of Elysium. He is the phoenix who will aid us in the raising of King Arthur."

William drank his ale down fast and pounded the goblet on the table, wiping his chin of the drops that fell from his beard. "Elysium? And what of heaven's voice in all of this?"

"Sir William, the phoenix is part of the heavens," said Daniel.

"Please, boy, keep your devil worship opinions to yourself," commanded Frederick.

"I am the son of Sir Percival Montgomery," Daniel continued. "He stood in battle with all of you and shed his blood for the cause of King Arthur. Today I stand here listening to two men who King Arthur loved, and I am ashamed of you."

"Ashamed? Listen to the boy, William. He is ashamed of us," snarled Frederick.

"Yes, this is exactly as Draco predicted."

"What did this *dragon* say?" said Frederick in a sarcastic tone.

"To beware of the non-believers."

"Have you seen battle, young knight, where men's bodies lay torn and mangled beyond reckoning?"

"I have battled the Saxon army, Sir Frederick."

"Have you killed your enemy in battle?

"I have for the good of my king and country."

"Well, did any of them rise up and live again after they were slain?

"No, sir, they were dead."

"See, now the boy understands," said Frederick. "Please, Majesty, how can you stand there and let this woman try to bewitch this court? Obviously she has bewitched the boy." Frederick stepped forward, examined his king from head to toe and looked him square in the eye. "Or maybe she has already bewitched and beguiled you?"

"That's enough!" commanded Galahad. "I won't have this kind of talk in my court lest you will find yourself in chains, Sir Frederick."

"Well, at least they'll be chains I carry for the good of my God, not this blasphemy you allow in your home," said the knight staring past Galahad and straight into Aryanyn's eyes.

"Daniel, arrest this man!" commanded Galahad.

"Not to impugn your judgment, my lord, but that's what he wants," said Martin stepping between Galahad and Frederick. "Majesty, if you put him in chains, the church will come banging at those doors, taking you and your crown."

"What would you advise?"

"Keep him here, under scrutinizers' eyes and let him see the powers of God. Let him go back to that church of his and tell all the world what he has witnessed."

"All I will witness is witchcraft, heresy and the devil himself," rebuked Frederick.

"The church has become like the apostle of Christ," yelled Daniel. "Doubting Thomases!"

CHAPTER FIFTY-EIGHT

Escape from the Castle

———◆———

Galahad seized a torch from off a nearby wall and hurriedly ran to his mother's room. "Mother, are you ready?"

There in her red and gold dress stood the high priestess; he recognized her attire as that she wore in the portrait he painted years ago. Behind her, in his traditional black and purple cloak, was Merlin, high priest and Druid wizard.

Galahad felt anxious to leave. As he waited for Aryanyn and Daniel to make their final preparations, he thought of how he longed to see his Uncle Arthur once again, while in his heart and mind he could not deny that what was about to transpire was unnatural. *Does God have his hand in this?* he wondered silently. "Mother, please make haste. There are those who would wish us harm, and I want to be underway within minutes."

"Daniel, please carry this sack for Merlin," requested Aryanyn of the young man.

"I am honored," replied the knight as he accepted the purse from Aryanyn and placed the black leather strap across his shoulder.

Joseph picked up his mother's Wicca sack and personals as Galahad lit another torch and gave it to Daniel. "Make haste, but keep watch on Merlin, as he needs your strength to get him to his horse."

"Ehy, sire."

The group made it down the brownstone corridor and outside to Sir Martin. Galahad passed him and led the group through the courtyard. He turned and saw that Martin had closed the door behind them and was now following to see to their safety as both Aryanyn and Daniel aided Merlin. From the corner of his eye, Galahad caught sight of Aryanyn's pin bathing Merlin in a ray of light as they approached the gate to the archers' field.

"Mother, stifle that thing lest we draw more attention to ourselves. There are some who would trade their lives to prevent the second coming of Arthur."

Seeing the glow, Aryanyn threw her cloak over the pin.

Gawain, who had gone on ahead, opened the wooden side gate to the archery yard. He bowed as Galahad led the group down the path to the archers' area. There, hidden among the trees, already mounted and ready to leave, were Blaise, Aaron, Lady Viviane and her novice Lydgia. Marc stood in the shed, holding the reins of Sir Brach. Gawain stepped in and helped to lead the other horses out to the path. Merlin's horse Sir Bennett and Daniel's steed Gallant awaited their riders. Galahad grabbed the reins of Ryker, his stallion of twenty years. To the left, coming from the knights' tack shed, were Luke and Peter—mounted and armed, leading Joseph's horse to him. Silence was of the essence, and everyone moved with care.

"Daniel and Michael, go ahead and secure the area through the south. We will take the northern route and follow the crescent of the moon to where the North Star opens the entry of the hill."

Both Daniel and Michael struck their chests before riding away.

"Luke, you head to the left, and Peter to the right. Keep at least ten tree lengths close." Both knights bowed and galloped off.

Galahad waved his hand and with the assistance of Gawain and Martin, led his mother and her entourage out of the archers' field through the back gate.

"My lords, guard the keep this night."

CHAPTER FIFTY-NINE

The Resurrection of
Arthur Pendragon

The quiet was filled with apprehension; all Galahad could think about were Frederick and William's dissention. He looked back at the group behind him and forged on, riding at a quickened pace.

Out of the quiet came Aryanyn's voice. "Galahad, when we reach the tomb, please ensure that I have time to contemplate before beginning the ritual."

"I understand, Mother."

"Look at the dusk, Galahad," said Merlin as he sat back on Bennet and pointed to the sky. "See how the red of the setting sun is bouncing off the lilac of those clouds."

"I see, High Priest."

"What magic might this night bring?"

It was evident by the glow in Merlin's eyes that he was glad to be alive to see such a radiant sky. Galahad looked up towards the darkness and saw the North Star, shining as always, the constant navigator of all men on earth or at sea. The long ray of her terrestrial body beamed down on the valley below, lighting up the path that Galahad followed.

A little over an hour later, they arrived at the Avalon cemetery. There, as Galahad had ordered were Michael and Daniel, standing sentry outside the fence. In front of them was the sight of the roses. The sphere climbed up at least thirty feet and was so intricately entwined in the branches of the trees that the red of the roses almost made the trees appear as though they were bleeding. When Merlin came to the foot of the iron gate and saw the spectacle, he lost his balance, and Galahad quickly grabbed him and prevented him from falling.

"Dear Goddess!" said Merlin as he placed his hands over his mouth aghast. "What powers has my sister wrought to conjure such wonders?"

Galahad stared at the enormity of the sphere, wondering how powerful his mother really was.

Aryanyn raced ahead of them, riding towards the gate.

"How do we enter?" asked Galahad.

"Daniel, cut a doorway through the stems of the roses when last we were here," Aryanyn answered as she dismounted her horse and passed through the gate.

"Peter, Luke and Joseph, spread out," ordered Galahad. "Go surround the circle and keep watch. Let's give her a moment."

The three knights bowed to him and took to their sentry.

Galahad and Merlin followed Aryanyn, continuing to give her the space she needed. About fifty feet behind her, they dismounted. Daniel aided Merlin and they waited near Michael, who was guarding the entry.

Galahad walked away from them and examined the intricacy of the entwined roses; it seemed as though they were braided together like the locks of a young girl's hair.

Through the roses, Galahad could see the spark of a fire as he heard his mother begin to pray.

"*Ke tu fe sinseath soliana. Mammeah*, if it is your will for Arthur to walk this earth again, return the high king to me. *Eriale entus enlovina.* If it is your will that his soul remain forever with you, keep him safe in your loving embrace within the ash and the dust. *Soeesnna emmeore' sinaatha eathera. Kor sool endor inventa.* Give me the peace of mind this night to accept your decision."

With a heavy heart, Galahad spoke to himself. "Yes, Lord Jesus, if it is your will, bring him home to us. But God, my Father, if this is not your plan, send me a sign and I will end this—I serve you and you alone."

"Let us begin," said Aryanyn exiting from the roses.

Daniel gave Merlin his wizard's purse and Galahad and his mother led Merlin, Blaise, Aaron, Lady Viviane and Lydgia inside the circle of roses. In the center were the most wondrous hawthorn flowers, white like the clouds and buttoned with red pistols that made the grounds look as though red confetti had been thrown about.

"The flowers of the prophecy," said Merlin with tears of joy in his eyes. "Oh, Mother Goddess, I am unworthy of such a vision." Merlin tried to bend to touch the flowers. Aryanyn picked two from the ground and placed one in Merlin's hand and one in Galahad's.

Galahad cupped the flower in his palm and held it a moment as Aryanyn spoke to Merlin. "Yes, brother, the day is here. Come, let us sanctify the ground to make the passage easier on our king."

"My lady, look at the sky," said Blaise.

Galahad looked up with Aryanyn and saw the crescent moon beginning to phase in the high dusk of the evening.

"Yes, Blaise, I know there is much to do," said Aryanyn as she grabbed her Wicca sack and walked to the foot of the tomb. Galahad watched her spread her purple blanket on the ground as Merlin walked over to the tomb and placed his hand in the burned crevice of the marble, following it to where the Latin word *Hic* began.

"Is this the work of the phoenix?" asked the wizard.

"It was his birthmark and my pin that created the blemish."

Galahad approached the marble stone, and he, too, placed his hand in the fissure, knelt and touched the burned roses at the foot of the tomb. He turned and in front of him was Merlin's staff and Cedwynn, standing firm in the soil. His eyes fell upon the crack in the tomb, and again he felt his angst taking over.

Above him, Merlin raised his hands and head up to the Elysium, shifted to stand near his sister, and palliated the blade of Cedwynn. "*Ech tu rescente eth Echrrynn.*" Galahad remained on his knees, close to the tomb, as the wizard withdrew his staff from the ground and looked into the face of the dragon. "*Ethynn morr ciarac Angor offor lorn.*" Merlin raised the staff and thrust it back into the ground. Galahad felt a cool breeze brush over him, sweeping the scent of the hawthorn flowers into the air; they carried the aroma of blood within them, like that of a women's menses. He nervously inhaled hard, and the fragrance drew down his throat, tasting like he bit his tongue and swallowed his own blood. His entire body wanted to run away. *This is all wrong,* he said to himself.

Suddenly, he was distracted from his thoughts as the sound of his mother drawing her sword from its sheath pulled him from his trance. He watched her raise the hilt to her brow, meditating and connecting the blue stone with the symbol on her forehead. She thrust Gwydion into the ground across from Cedwynn. "*Ethynn morr ciarac Gwydion offor lorn.*" A gust of wind encircled the sphere, and the sweet fragrance of the roses overcame the site again.

The high priestess took of her censor, opening it. Viviane grabbed the torch that Aryanyn had placed in the ground, and lit the stones. The small black rocks burned and emitted smoke into the air. Aryanyn waved her hand, bringing the smoke to her face. Viviane swung the censor around Aryanyn as she prayed.

"*Wyn ethynn synsaeth envitas orlunda ka fasna dah!*" Aryanyn was rocking back and forth on her knees now. "*Wyn ethynn synsaeth envitas orlunda ka fasna dah!*" she rocked again. "*Ka fasna dah!*" Aryanyn stood and placed her hand on each of the heirlooms of her family and yelled "*Ka fasna dah!*"

Galahad's heart quickened as he heard his mother shout her prayer into the trees. He stared as Merlin pulled out his wizard's purse. He knew that Merlin kept his most potent herbs and potions there— the remedies he used for his strongest spells and conjures. The purse matched his cloak, bearing the dyed plumes of both the raven and the crow, black as the night and purple as the dusk. Within the plumage, painted in white, were the symbols of the crescent moon and the sun. A queer twinge ripped through Galahad.

Merlin opened his wizard's pouch, and as his sister prayed to the Mother, he spread the dried leaves of mandragora and sage while murmuring, "*Wyn ethynn synsaeth envitas orlunda ka fasna dah!*"

Blaise and Aaron joined him and placed their hands in the purse, taking more of the mixture, and encircling the tomb, spreading the sage around the area. "Sanctify this land *Mammaeah leinarea zool*," prayed the priests.

Again Merlin pinched the dried herbs, cupped them in his hands and gave some to Galahad. "Crush them, sire, and pray with me." Galahad felt the herbs in the palm of his hand and looked at Merlin before clenching his nervous fingers around them. He watched as Merlin allowed the breath of the Mother to take the dried leaves of the plants into the breeze.

"*Ka fasna dah!*" the wizard chanted.

Galahad opened his own hands and let the contents blow freely. Sweat poured down his face and it felt like a stampede was crushing down on his chest. He had heard the prayers before but never in the full language of the Druids. *What did the words mean?* He remained steadfast near the stone as the great magician joined with his sister; locking their hands together and raising them, they turned and faced each other.

There was a glow about his mother as she and Merlin prayed, "Mother Goddess, take of the herbs and sanctify this ground for thy servant Arthurus Pendragonous. *Ka fasna dah!*"

"And so be it," he said to himself, bowing his head. He caught the words in his throat, wanting to choke them down. *Could he stay there and take part in this ritual?*

When Galahad looked up again, Aryanyn's brooch glowed brightly upon her chest. Merlin placed his right hand on Aryanyn's chest, and the light came through his fingers. Aryanyn opened her eyes at her brother's touch, and they concentrated on one another, their eyes meeting. Something told Galahad that all was ready.

"Look, my lady, the North Star shines its beacon in the sky and Polaris and Ursa Minor show themselves," said Aaron. "The dye is cast!"

"Come, Galahad, come join us," commanded Aryanyn.

With one foot, Galahad wanted to go to her; with the other foot, he wanted to run. Aryanyn looked back at him, waiting. He chose to keep his feet on the same solid ground and remain the objective observer. She shook her head at him and gave him a supportive smile that let him know that while she disagreed with his choice to keep his distance she also understood.

Blaise passed by him and brought in the wood for the pyre that Daniel and Aaron had prepared earlier that day. Aaron quietly helped him tie the pieces of wood together to form X-shaped table legs. They picked up four flat slabs of oak that had been notched by Aaron's hand and weaved them into each notch with rope, joining the tabletop to the legs. The two young men turned the table pyre over and stood it on its supports. There was a bale of hay near the side wall that Daniel must have prepared earlier that day, and Blaise, Aaron and Viviane placed the hay upon the top of the pyre and beneath it, as the final step, preparing it for Arthur.

Galahad's mother, the high priestess, was now silent. He could see by the stoic look on her face that she was high in mediation. Coming out of her contemplation, Aryanyn seized a blue velvet blanket and placed it over the hay. Lydgia came to her aid and laid the runes of the Mother at each corner: the sun rune at the right upper corner, the crescent moon at the left upper corner, the trefoil on the bottom right, and the rune of Gwyn ap Nudd—the hollow figure of a man holding a scepter of fire— on the bottom left.

"Gwyn ap Nudd, protector of the underworld, I ask thee to guide Arthur into the light," prayed Viviane.

Blaise and Merlin pressed the mandragora and sage together and the two cupped the herbs in their hands once again before spreading them upon the blanket, chanting, "*Ka fasna dah!*"

Aryanyn, Viviane, and Lydgia joined hands and beckoned quietly for Galahad, Blaise, Merlin and Aaron to join the circle around the pyre. Galahad still could not bring himself to join in the ritual, and—by the look on Aryanyn's face—he knew that she was disappointed. The high priestess broke the circle and crossed to the table, caressing the blue of the velvet.

"*Ios Arthurus envitas ka fasna dah!*" She lifted her hands to the sky. "*Ios Arthurus envitas Draconiuos ka fasna dah!*" She again caressed the blanket and said, "*Ios Arthurus envitas Apheoniexas Anastasious ka fasna dah!*" She rejoined the circle and they all chanted "*Ka fasna dah!*"

"Aaron," called Aryanyn.

"My lady, what is your wish?"

"Please take the shovel over there and dig for the urn."

Aaron left Aryanyn's side, rushed to the bale of hay and picked up the shovel. He approached the foot of the tomb and commenced his digging. Blaise darted over and as Aaron dug the hole, Blaise pushed the soil from the area with a branch, clearing the way for the young priest to continue his work.

"High Priestess, I think I have uncovered His Majesty's remains!" said Aaron with a reverence in his voice that split into the fibers of Galahad's heart.

Blaise and Aaron lay down on the ground and carefully cleared away the dirt to exhume the box. The coffin that held the urn was four feet long and two feet wide. To Galahad, it looked like a casket made to hold a child. He shivered. Together, the priests carried the box over to the pyre, and Blaise held the torch high above it so that everyone could see clearly.

Galahad was finally motivated to move and walked over to the pyre. This was his last memory of Arthur's death. There in the wood, burned on the cover within the engraving of a crown, were the letters A.P., the very letters that Galahad, the newly ordained eighteen-year-old king, branded on his precious uncle's casket. "I am here, uncle, to protect you." He stared intently at the box. "Send me a sign if this is not your wish," he whispered.

He placed his attention on Merlin, who opened the latch of the box and lifted its lid, revealing a black and red velvet pouch, which he removed. Opening the strings that held it closed, he pulled out a marvelous gold urn from inside. On the face of the metal was a dragon with wings spread, its raptor claws extended to protect the remains of the king. The dragon bore the same red eye as that of Merlin's staff. Aryanyn removed the urn and carefully laid it down on the table.

"Aaron, I ask thee to call Joseph, Luke and Peter from their watch."

Galahad interrupted, "Mother! They belong at their posts."

"My son, I need them here to guard the pyre. Stand one at each corner with swords drawn so that Arthur will see their faces as he comes from the other side."

Galahad drew forth his weapon defiantly and looked straight at Aryanyn. "They will remain at their stations."

"My lord, please. What fears do you have?" asked Merlin.

"I am here to guard my mother and you, High Priest, from those who might wish you harm this night." Galahad turned to Aryanyn again. "Know, Mother, that I am the knight of the Grail quest. If God indeed allows you to raise Arthur, I will consider that the sign that I am to accept this ritual and protect the reborn king." Galahad knelt before the urn and struck his chest. "My king and my liege."

When Galahad looked up from the urn, he found his mother standing over him, giving him a look that cut through him. "You do not believe in me," she whispered to him.

In a low voice, he responded, "I believe in you my mother, Aryanyn, High Priestess, but I must also keep to the beliefs of my heart and what I have known the whole of my life. Until I see what comes to pass, my heart and soul are telling me that this is wrong. But that is not for me to judge. Now go and do what you came for. If it is the will of God and the Goddess, it shall come to pass."

"Yes, Your Majesty!" she said through clenched teeth before bowing to him.

Aryanyn picked up the torch by the tomb with a blatant anger that

Galahad had never seen directed at him before and walked about the sphere. She approached the empty tomb and read the words out loud, "*Hic Iacet Arthurus Rex Quondam Rex Que Futurus.*" She placed her hand over the symbol on her brow. "I call on the guardians of the four corners—come to the aid of the king." A bolt of lightning lit up the night and claps of thunder followed. The winds picked up, and a warm breeze filled the circle. Aryanyn removed her cloak and placed it over the broken tombstone.

"Merlin, come join me now!"

Merlin ran as best he could towards his sister as the high priestess removed her pin. Holding it in her hand, she reached for her brother and firmly held the jewel between them. Galahad watched as Aryanyn's blood trickled upon the white hawthorne flowers beneath them in the center of the weapons of Echrrynn.

"Emblems of the family Echrrynn, I call upon your clandestine knowledge and upon the dragon and the phoenix. I, Aryanyn, High Priestess, and my brother Merlin, High Priest, command their presence!"

Aryanyn opened her hand, releasing Merlin's, and held the brooch open to the sky. The trefoil on the pin radiated a lavender light up to the heavens. She dropped it to the ground and shouted, "*Vas mor anglynn! Vas mor anglynn!*"

The pin shined its light upon the symbols of the Echrrynn family, illuminating the eye of the dragon on Merlin's staff, which cast its light upon the three crescent moons on Cedwynn's blade. The winds gusted hard and cold through the circumference of the sphere, calling upon the roses on Gwydion that turned black in color and mixed with the red roses around the grave to climb high up the trees.

Galahad looked up at the colors of Arthur, and could hardly draw breath as he watched the miracle unfold. He made the sign of the cross on himself.

"*Risases arteras!*" cried out Aryanyn.

The moons from Cedwynn rose up into the night, casting their light into the triangle of the dragon in the constellations of the sky. Galahad knew this part of the skies well, as Arthur and Merlin trained him to find his way in the forest by navigating the sky. He watched as the three points of the dragon's lair lit up, and the guardians of the dragon blew their horn of revelry calling on the dragon king.

Galahad's eyes lifted to the lights of Polaris as he heard Aryanyn call out, "I Aryanyn, call Draconian to come to the aid of Arthur Pendragon!"

The star Thuban slithered upon the tail of the dragon, waking him, and Draco roared. He gazed upon the moon as it was coming to its phase.

"I, Draco, heed to your call," boomed a voice from above. From the center of the triangle, Draco opened the skies.

"Anastasious!" called Draco. Out from the black hole of night came a caw so spine tingling it spread chills from Galahad's head all the way to his toes. Merlin placed his hand over his ears to shield himself from the piercing sound.

Both the dragon and the phoenix roared together, taking flight in the sky. Draco flew around the moon, and although he was high in the sky, his wings seemed to cover the eye of the Mother. Anastasious flew under him; the bird screeching loudly and fluttering his massive wings. Even from this distance, Galahad could see that Draco's wings were scaled and boned, and the light of the satellite moon pierced through them.

Anastasious's wings were dense with layers of feathers that the light of the moon could not pass through. They seemed to reflect a red haze over the lunar circle. Both mythical creatures flew around, commanding the stars and marking their space, before descending together towards the center of the sphere of roses and landing on each side of the pyre. Draco's spiked head stood high into the canopy, and his green eyes shone in the torch light. Galahad stood mesmerized at the size of his rib cage and the width of his hands. He could crush the earth in those.

Galahad, seeing the dragon king, dropped to one knee. "Majesty, Draco."

Draco acknowledged the gesture and bowed his head, "So we meet again, knight of the Holy Grail!"

Galahad turned and saw Peter, Luke, and Joseph running towards them followed by Michael who drew his sword as he approached.

"Lower your weapon!" commanded Galahad to Michael.

"Majesty Draco!" shouted Daniel, charging in after them..

Peter, Luke and Joseph bowed to the Dragon King.

"It is I who should kneel before the Grail knights," said Draco, lowering his head to the earth. Anastasious followed suit, bowing to the group.

"Knights, go back to your posts. I will call you forth when I have need of you," ordered Galahad.

"Why do you send them away?" asked Draco.

"Draconian, many men would wish harm to members of this party. It is my wish that these soldiers remain steadfast."

"My lord, your knights would better serve you and Arthur if they were present at his rising."

"Ahy, but it is those who do not believe that would bring us down," explained Galahad.

"I fear that you may be one of them, my friend," commented the dragon.

"Why do you say this to me?" asked Galahad feeling a rush of blood to his chest.

If you had faith, you would know that this night is destined to be."

The dragon turned his eyes from Galahad and looked to Daniel. "So we meet again, son of Percival."

Galahad looked at Daniel and at Draco. Daniel's words from back in court haunted him: *all of Arthur's men were doubting Thomases.* Galahad took a breath and again looked at the sarcophagus on the pyre. He turned to his mother. "Let us proceed."

"I give you my friend, Anastasious," said Draco to the crowd in the sphere. He, too, stood tall in the trees, his head crowned with plumes of red and orange like raging flame of a fire. His eyes were pure ebony as though Galahad were looking into a glistening black hole. The beast stood erect, thrusting his chest and showing off his crescent moon tattoo. He was surely a remarkable sight.

Merlin approached Draconian, who spoke to the wizard. "High Priest, it has been many a season since we have had the pleasure."

Merlin bowed. "Ahy, my friend, 'tis been too long."

"Priests of the forest, I am glad to be in your company again," said Draco.

"As are we," said Blaise, bowing his head to the dragon.

"Enough with pleasantries, my friends of Arthur," said Aryanyn, stepping forward. "The phase of the moon is upon us, and we have much to do."

Anastasious soared to the crown of the sphere, perching himself atop the roses. "I am with you."

Galahad watched as Draco placed his massive foot near the pyre and glared into the eye of the dragon on the urn, igniting a fire within it that shook the ashes it kept. Aryanyn picked up the vessel, and the eye shed an orange light on the high priestess as her hands shuddered from trying to hold tight to it.

"Open the urn," commanded Draco.

Aryanyn obeyed the dragon, pulling at the lid of the urn, opening it and carefully laying it on the table. "Your majesty, it is I, Aryanyn. Hear me call you from your sleep."

"Pour the ashes on the pyre," boomed Draco.

Aryanyn lifted the urn, holding it firm. Without compunction, she obeyed the dragon, pouring the charred remains of Galahad's Uncle Arthur onto the blanket.

"Spread the ashes, Merlin, but be gentle," requested Aryanyn.

Merlin's hands trembled as he touched the grey matter. He pinched some of the ashes between his fingers, feeling them, and sifted some into Galahad's palm. They were fine like flour before it turned to bread. Tears shed from the wizard's eyes and rolled down his cheeks wetting his beard. "I remember the day of my foster son's funeral, watching his precious body burn hot upon the pyre," he said in a mournful voice as he gently spread the ashes back upon the blanket.

Aryanyn chanted again. "I, Aryanyn Echrrynn, call the High King Arthur from his sleep."

Draco stepped back from the table and drew air into his lungs. His shoulders lifted as he inhaled deeply several times and with all his might, exhaled his breath in a blaze that lit the pyre. The dried hay on the table ignited in a burst, and the pyre burned.

"Aryanyn, take up your brooch," Draco demanded.

Galahad retrieved her pin from the ground and passed it to her. She smiled at him as the light from the trefoil cast a triangle upon the flames.

"Call the High King," Draco called out to Aryanyn.

"I, Aryanyn, call Arthur Pendragon. Come forth from your sleep."

"Anastasious!" cried Draco. The phoenix cawed loudly and descended down into the rising flames, which hungrily consumed his body. As he burned, his ashes dripped and crumbled onto the blanket below and mixed with the remains of Arthur.

"I, Aryanyn, call Arthur Pendragon from your sleep," shouted the high priestess again.

"My lord Galahad, for this miracle to come to pass, I ask thee to take of thy sword and cut me here." Draco pointed to his left rib right under his heart. Galahad stared at the massive beast above him, unaware that he would be requested to participate in the ceremony in such a way. After a brief hesitation, he unsheathed his sword. "Draconian, this is not Excalibur, but an ordinary sword from the armory. It is unworthy of such a request."

Draco stared down on him. "It is you, Majesty, who found the Holy Grail, and it is your faith that allowed Aryanyn to claim her destiny. For Arthur to breath this air and rise again, he needs all of your faith and love."

Galahad could feel his face flush with fear. *Could he cut the dragon? Could he play a role in this resurrection? Could he remain a bystander any longer?*

A vision appeared above the pyre, and Galahad's eyes rose to a cloud of white. Within the cloud was the image of Galahad and his men at the Grail gates, standing upon the very hawthorn flowers they stood upon now, with the Great Draco above them guarding Jesus. Jesus raised his precious cup from the well of the Holy Grail that was formed by a rose bush of scarlet cinquefoil roses like those that now surrounded the tomb. After drinking from it, Jesus passed the cup to Galahad, who shared in his body and blood. As the vision faded, Galahad looked around him, feeling the peace of Jesus' face looking down upon him.

"Where do I cut thee, dragon?"

Draco brought his winged hand to his chest, and Galahad took up his blade and slashed at the rib of Draco. The dragon roared loud as his blood poured from the wound and soaked into the fine mixture of Arthur and Anastasious's ashes.

"Call him, Priestess."

"I, Aryanyn Echrrynn, call upon the king to rise from his sleep!"

A flash of light bolted from the pyre, and the fire moaned. Out from the ashes came a new phoenix—this one the size of an adolescent bird—who squawked in piercing shrieks that grew louder and deeper with every caw he released.

Another spark of light now radiated from the ashes and, as if by the hand of God, the light cracked like a whip upon the pyre and sketched the figure of a man in the ashes.

Galahad watched as the spark drew the shape of a head and a neck. The flare followed with the form of broad shoulders coming down into a torso and a waist. A new burst of light flickered from the foot of the pyre and drew two feet. Coming up, burning its way up the blanket, the flare formed two legs and two arms that joined with the other ember.

In a thunderous clap, the two bolts of light weaved together, forming one, and cracked down upon the outline of the man they had just drawn. Draco took another breath and blew his fire hard upon the figure. Anastasious cawed until his eyes teared, and two drops fell into the middle of the fire. The wet tears sizzled as the fire burned them away, and the fire moaned again as it back-drafted under the pyre, quaking the ground beneath them. As quickly, the fire was reborn and engulfed the pyre, wrapping its flames around the makeshift table and crackling in the night.

Draco yelled, "Aryanyn, call to Arthur!" as Galahad was forced to back up a step by the intensity of the heat.

"I, Aryanyn, High Priestess of Avalon, call Arthur Pendragon. Hear me, my King. Follow my voice."

Galahad was consumed with pride as he heard her scream to him. "Call him with me, my son."

He stepped back towards the flames. "Arthur, come. It is I, Galahad. Hear me, my King and uncle."

"Call him good priest," Aryanyn shouted to Blaise beside her as the wind picked up around them.

"Arthur!" yelled Blaise.

"Arthur!" cried Merlin. "Come from your sleep!" The wizard shouted his words above the others.

Viviane and Lydgia raised their hands to the sky, calling, "Arthur, come to us! Hear our voices!"

Again, the earth quaked and flames surged upon the table.

Galahad beckoned his fellow knights guarding all within the sphere to come to his side, "Knights of the Round Table, come join us and call for your king."

Daniel, Michael, Joseph, Peter, and Luke all ran quickly towards the pyre. Aryanyn grasped Galahad's hands, leading everyone in joining around the circle. "I call the guardians of the four corners, hear me. Come earth, and raise him from your bosom. Come water, and wash him with renewed life. Come fire, and sanctify his soul. Come wind and air, and breathe within his lungs." Storm clouds hovered above, blowing wind and air over the site, bathing the earth with cool refreshment.

Galahad felt the coolness on his face and the wind at his back. The high priestess let go of his hand, joining his to Joseph's. She walked around the circle and drew the swords of the knights from their sheathes one at a time, thrusting them into the soil at each corner of the pyre, rocking them into the ground and calling aloud, "These are the swords of the Holy Grail standing ready to defend their king." With her hands raised, Aryanyn walked around the circumference of the pyre and came to stand near Galahad again. "Gwyn ap Nudd, protector of the afterlife, call the king and waken him," she shouted into the arboretum.

The ground quaked from under Galahad, and the table on which the form of Arthur rested swayed back and forth like a cradle with a babe.

Gwyn ap Nudd, the faceless warrior, appeared next to Arthur's grave—half in the light from the fire and half in the world of the dead. The mythical dark knight of the underworld was dressed in the blue robes of Avalon. On his chest were the trees of the Mother, surrounded by the waters of the lake, and the armor of Avalloc, the God of Avalon who ruled the underworld since time began. "Arthur!" his low and gravelly voice called with force. "Come from the dark!" He held up his torch, a scepter of brilliant golden rays of light. "I release your soul."

The world around him fell silent for a moment as though the entire Mother Earth had exhaled a deep breath and paused. The only movement was the flickering of the flames. Galahad felt his legs nearly give way as he looked up at the pyre. There lay the body of a man upon the table.

"Anastasious, drown the fire!" commanded Draco.

The phoenix soared above them and shed his tears upon the pyre. He ascended to the hovering clouds and pulled one of gray and one of white under each wing. Clapping them both together, they thundered hard, giving up their moisture to the earth and calming the flames of the fire. A steamy white vapor rolled out from the lowering blaze and hovered over the pyre and around all who were present.

A coughing sound seeped out from within the fog as though from a man who was fighting for his last breath. Galahad lurched towards the table, followed closely by Aryanyn. The body of a naked and somewhat emaciated Arthur lay upon the pyre. Aryanyn placed her hand upon his chest and lifted Galahad's and placed it next to hers. He felt the warmth of Arthur's body as she placed her ear to his left breast.

"His heart beats."

Galahad could see the rising of his chest as Aryanyn's head lifted from his torso. His body was long and broad, but no longer chiseled like that of a God, as Galahad remembered him at his time of death. The hair upon his head and the beard upon his face were no longer graying, but were long and brown and youthful. He breathed but he did not move.

Galahad removed his own cloak and covered the king.

"Call him, High Priestess," said Draco again.

After a moment's hesitation, she spoke, "I, Aryanyn Echrrynn, call you by name. Arthur Pendragon, awaken and live!"

His body convulsed as he gasped for air once more. Aryanyn reached for his face and caressed his hollow features. It was a loving caress, one that confirmed to Galahad that Arthur lay before him."

She whispered in his ear, "I, Aryanyn, call you, Arthur Pendragon. Harken to me."

Arthur's eyes opened, and he appeared to be trying to focus on Aryanyn.

"It is I, my lord."

Aryanyn beckoned her brother to come to her, and the wizard rushed to her side and looked upon the face of his foster son.

"Arthur," said Merlin, his voice cracking.

Arthur tried to pick himself up, but quickly fell back to the table.

Galahad felt paralyzed with fear, as he stared into the face of his uncle, wondering how this withered man could ever fulfill the powerful destiny that lay before him.

"Help us!" said Aryanyn, breaking Galahad's trance. He immediately reached under Arthur's shoulders and aided him to a sitting position.

Draco cried out, "Arthur Pendragon, stand on thy feet and take strength from all who welcome you."

Arthur looked into the face of Draco and at Galahad, his eyes seeming to be empty of vision. He turned back to the dragon king and with all his strength shifted his shriveled legs, hanging them over the side of the pyre.

"Stand firm, High King!" commanded Draco.

Galahad wanted to help but knew for the sake of Arthur he had to keep his distance. Arthur again veered his eyes to the dragon king as he pushed himself from the pyre, stood on his legs for a brief moment, but collapsed into Galahad who caught him as Aryanyn and Merlin rushed to his side. Slowly they rested him back on his own two feet and though unsteady and shifting, he remained standing and, after a few breaths, raised one foot and took a step away from the remains of his burning bed.

Draco called out, "Arthur, look into my eyes."

Arthur obeyed the dragon king, his eyes still vacant and confused.

"I, Draco, lord of the constellations and the realm of the dragon lines, command you, Arthur to take thy life again. The worlds of the high king and the high priestess await thee."

Galahad watched as Arthur straightened his back, straining to stand tall. The veins on his legs protruded as they pumped life up his body, filling his shrunken chest, down into his arms and eventually up towards his neck. As the blood reached his head, Arthur leaned back and screamed, his shrill voice filling the night. When he came back up, he inhaled the air of the wind, and Galahad suddenly saw a sparkle in his eyes and knew that though he was weak, his king had returned.

In a hoarse voice, Arthur spoke, "I hear thee, lord of the skies, and obey thy wishes."

Anastasious flew overhead and bathed the king in his tears. The water flowed and Arthur basked in the cleansing as the phoenix baptized him. An aura of light formed around the awakened king, and his eyes connected with Anastasious.

"Who are you?" asked the gentle bird.

Arthur stared with strength at the beast and heaving to catch his breath replied, "I am Arthur Pendragon."

Anastasious cawed loudly, "Arthur Pendragon, you are reborn

today." Raising his wings, he took flight.

Draco bowed to his king. "Within this new birth is the key to your destiny. We leave you in peace."

Draco bowed to Galahad before thrusting his chest forward and releasing a thunderous roar. With wings spread, he launched into the sky.

CHAPTER SIXTY

Come From Your Sleep

———◆———

Galahad held his eyes to the skies as the dragon flew in his magnificence. Turning, he saw his Uncle Arthur standing in a kind of trance, staring off into space. To Galahad, he looked nothing like the pictures in the cathedrals of Christ after he rose from the dead. *Is it a sin to compare the two?* he thought to himself.

"Please, Daniel, help Merlin and Blaise dress the king," said Galahad.

Luke and Joseph came to their aid taking off their cloaks and holding them in front of Arthur, giving the man some privacy. Daniel picked up the clothing that rested on Aryanyn's Wicca blanket and dressed Arthur, placing the shirt over Arthur's head and draping it on him. Galahad stood in front of the king, gazing into the man's incredible blue eyes.

"Uncle, 'tis good to have you here again," said Galahad.

Arthur stared back at Galahad, saying nothing. Arthur's body was acting like that of a puppet; his arms and legs were weightless as Daniel placed the last of what now appeared to be oversized garments on the king; a brown leather vestment that held the red and gold Celtic cross on the left chest—the emblem that Galahad had taken as his mantra. Daniel fastened the belts on the jacket, but Arthur could not stand, as the weight of the leather was too much for his new his body to handle, and he looked as though he would topple over.

"Daniel, take it off!" Galahad commanded.

Daniel removed the piece and hung it across his arm. Arthur pointed to the symbol on the chest of the garment and closed his eyes, whispering to himself, "Arthur Pendragon, come out of your sleep."

Galahad threw his own cloak over Arthur again, and Daniel tied the laces.

Arthur reached for Daniel's hand and Galahad saw Daniel wince in pain as Arthur placed a lock around his knight's wrist. Daniel was trying to free himself but could not. Galahad reached over and pried Arthur's hand from the young man. Daniel looked at his king a bit shaken as Arthur asked, "Where is Arianna?"

"I am here, my lord," said the priestess, stepping forward.

Arthur glared at her and reached out a finger to touch the symbol that graced her brow. Trembling, he fell to the ground. Galahad bent low to help him as Arthur again spoke to himself, "Arthur Pendragon, come out of your sleep." Arthur raised his head to Aryanyn and spoke the name he knew her by aloud. For a moment, Galahad wondered if the king was blind.

"Yes, Arthur, it is I." Aryanyn knelt down on the ground and caressed his face, curling her fingers in his beard.

Arthur grabbed her shoulders, holding on tight for dear life. "Where am I?"

"Do you not remember?" Aryanyn asked. Tears formed in the lady's eyes as she reached for her brother Merlin. "Look, my lord, it is your foster father, Mer—"

"Merlin?" questioned Arthur. He was reaching out, but in the wrong direction. Galahad placed Merlin's hand in Arthur's.

Merlin smiled. "Yes, my son, it is I."

Daniel dropped to one knee, trying to help Arthur stand on his feet. Arthur pushed the young man away, but Daniel stayed there dumbfounded, and Galahad gave him a nod to speak to Arthur.

"I am Daniel, Majesty, son of Percival Montgomery."

There were so many questions written on Arthur's face—and Galahad saw Daniel's expression turn from pride to fear.

"Go on, speak to him," prompted Galahad to the young man.

"My lord, it was I who was your personal page."

Again Daniel tried to aid Arthur, but Arthur shoved him away.

"Arthur, it is alright. You can trust Daniel," said Merlin.

The king glared hard towards the young man. "Where is Percival?"

Daniel looked at Galahad and Aryanyn, as tears formed in the young man's eyes. "He is dead, sire," he replied with trembling hands. "How could he not know me?" Daniel asked Galahad. "Sire, I spent half my life with him." He shook his head.

"Can you walk, my lord?" asked Galahad.

Arthur looked right past him at Aryanyn, and Galahad noticed that his face relaxed when his eyes fell upon her.

"Daniel will not harm you, Arthur," said Aryanyn.

Arthur was hesitant at first, but placed his arm around Daniel's shoulder, and Daniel aided the king to stand.

"Where do we go?" asked Arthur.

To the castle so you can rest, my friend," said Aryanyn.

"Go bring back the steeds," shouted Galahad.

Joseph, Luke and Peter ran quickly to the iron gate. Within minutes, they were back with horses ready. Daniel and Michael aided Merlin to mount Bennett again. A horse was not provided for Arthur, so Galahad helped his reincarnated king to mount Ryker. Arthur held tight to the pommel of the saddle, trying to adjust himself to the feel of the animal beneath him. Galahad sat bareback behind him and wrapped his arms around Arthur, holding him firm to the horse. Galahad gave Ryker a kick on his side, and the group followed his lead. As they galloped onward, Galahad could feel Arthur's restless heart beat straight into his own chest within the rhythm of the horses canter. For a moment it was as though he were a young boy again, except that when he was young, Arthur rode behind, holding him on the saddle and teaching the young Galahad how to use his sword and the spear while riding a steed.

"Which way Sire?" asked Michael riding ahead with sword engaged, taking guard.

"Through the cemetery, make haste! The night may have eyes."

Aryanyn heeded to Galahad's caution and drew forth her sword as did the other Knights around them.

The cemetery was about a half mile's ride away from Avalon. Galahad kept his arms taut around Arthur who seemed to be having trouble balancing on the saddle. They came upon the cemetery and galloped quickly past the bell tower. The bell emitted a light twang that reverberated in Galahad's ears. Arthur turned his head to the sound of the bell. Galahad watched as he looked to the side and whispered under his breath "Camelot" reading the word on the main Sarsen that headed the entry of the cemetery grounds.

They continued on and again Arthur spoke. He uttered the word "Uther..." Arthur pushed Galahad's hands from around his waist. "Stop! I want to see."

"Hault!" commanded Galahad.

The riding party came to a speedy stop, and Aryanyn pulled Brach up alongside Ryker. "Arthur, please, dear friend you must regain your strength."

He shot a look at her and at Galahad, and she nodded to him that she understood.

Galahad jumped off the back of Ryker and helped Arthur dismount. He raised his hand up to the others to remain at their positions. Arthur held onto the side of the horse gripping the stirrup strap. His eyes scanned the area. To Galahad, his uncle looked as if he were in a maddening trance. Arthur endured one painful step at a time. There in front of him was the graveyard where more than one hundred tombstones stood—those of men who not only served Arthur, but his father King Uther before him.

Arthur remained silent, staring at the stones from a distance for a while, before he whispered, "Ralph" and dropped down to his knees.

Aryanyn quickly dismounted Brach and ran to him. "Come, we will go to them," said Aryanyn.

Arthur paused a moment and tried to stand. Galahad stretched out his arm and Arthur grabbed hold of him and stood, with Aryanyn close behind.

"Come, Majesty," said Daniel leading the king.

Arthur followed again, with Aryanyn taking his hand as though a child being led by his mother. Galahad watched his uncle continuing to read aloud the names of the knights buried there. "Sir Percival Montgomery, Sir John, Sir Ralph." He again fell to his knees, pulling Aryanyn down with him, tears suddenly streaming down his face. "Please tell me they are not all dead. Please tell me all is not lost to me."

"I'm sorry my king. Some is lost, though some remains," said Galahad.

"Where am I?" Arthur appeared panic-stricken.

"Do you remember this man?" asked Aryanyn, beckoning Galahad forward.

Galahad felt Arthur's stare examining him.

"Who are these people?" His face still had not achieved its full coloring; he was white as a sheet, and his skin absorbed the lilac hue from the sky.

"Majesty, do you remember how you died?" asked the high priestess.

Galahad saw a vague look in Arthur's eyes. He waved his hand to Daniel who dismounted quickly and came to them. Galahad whispered, "Stay with him."

He pulled Aryanyn away from Arthur and the group. "Mother, he is not the great high king. That is some fallacy. The man I knew is dead." He paused a moment. "What the hell have we done?"

"That man is Arthur," she replied. "He needs something to jolt his memory."

A morose laugh came up from Galahad's belly as he replied, "A jolt you say! The man needs an army or a long swift kick in the buttocks."

"Galahad, that is Arthur you are talking about."

"No, that is some puppet." He scanned the man again. "Right now I feel like a grave robber. But I have not stolen a body, I have stolen a soul. I should rot in hell."

"Please, my son, you are a good man!"

"I don't feel like a good man right now."

Aryanyn walked away from Galahad. He could see by the way she folded her arms and tugged at her earring that she was trying to find some recourse for the situation. The minutes felt like hours.

"There is a way he might remember," said Aryanyn.

"What mother?" asked Galahad following her. "Please reveal your plan."

"Joseph, please bring Brach and Ryker over. We must go to the lake."

"What can the lake do for him?" asked Galahad.

"Please, ask no more questions of me until we are there—trust me."

"My lord?" questioned Joseph looking to his brother.

"To the lake then," Galahad replied.

CHAPTER SIXTY-ONE

A Time of Awakening

It was still dark and Luke held the torch high to light the way. The lake was about an hour from the cemetery, as it was on the other side of Avalon. Daniel stayed close to Arthur and Galahad, never leaving their side.

The lake came into view as the party emerged from a thick stand of trees. Galahad lifted his eyes to the moon as the light of the Mother fell upon the water, and the Isle of Avalon reflected itself at the water's edge. Daniel came to them and helped Arthur dismount his horse after Galahad dismounted Ryker. The young knight then rushed to the aid of Merlin.

Galahad contemplated the aftermath of the battle, fifteen years ago, when Arthur perished on these grounds. Where the grass was now green and pure in nature, it once held the blood of many men.

"Mother, we are all tired. Do you not think that we should return home, as Arthur needs his rest?"

"I'll not have Frederick and William mock this man," replied Aryanyn. "He takes back his life tonight!"

There was determination in his mother's eyes. "I agree, but look at him. He needs time to address his past."

Aryanyn fixed her eyes on the reborn king and circled him while Galahad assessed his weakened stature. Aryanyn reached for Galahad's shoulder and said, "Son, look at him. He knows who he is but his mind is still asleep. If we don't finish what Anastasious started tonight, Arthur's quest—and mine—will falter."

Galahad looked at his uncle and felt a sense of sadness overcome him.

"Son, no—" Aryanyn shook her head. "Do not pity him now. The great bear, the warrior king needs to be strengthened. W must bring him to the Round Table, but first he must remember who he is."

Galahad was not convinced, and his mother must have sensed this, as she grabbed him by the clasp of his cloak and shook him. "None of us ever showed him a day of pity when we followed him." Aryanyn looked out to the others in the riding party. "Our belief in him gave him strength to lead. Our loyalty gave him courage. Don't back down now, friends. He must be stronger than he ever was."

Galahad looked at Merlin when he heard him speak. "I agree that Arthur cannot return to Camelot in this sorry state." Merlin reached for his sister's hand, his chest heaving. "How may I help?"

"The moon is taking rest in the east." Aryanyn unsheathed Gwydion and called upon the blue stone. "Merlin, take Arthur to the place where his blood left his body."

Merlin looked around the bend of the lake and appeared to shudder as though remembering the event., but obeyed and grabbed hold of Arthur. "My son, come with me."

The two walked to the edge of the lake. Aryanyn hung her hand on her sheathe belt and held the buckle tight. Then she placed her hands in prayer before she rubbed her palms together and pressed her fingers to her lips. "Knights of Arthur, it is now time to give back to Arthur everything he gave to you. Viviane, Blaise, come here please. Majesty, Daniel. You, too."

Galahad beckoned all who were called to join him at her side and Aryanyn led the group to Merlin and Arthur.

"Sister, we must make haste, as he is weakening."

"Who are these men?" asked Arthur turning and looking at the circle that had formed around him.

"Do you remember why you are here?" asked Aryanyn.

"I cannot remember, Arianna."

"Do you know who I am?" asked Galahad.

Tears shed from Arthur's eyes as he looked around as though trying to find something or someone. "Lancelot," he whispered and Galahad felt his heart ache for his father, a pain he thought he had forgotten.

"Can you remember what this is?" Aryanyn siezed her cross from under her blouse and showed it to Arthur. He gazed at it and held it in his shaking hand for a moment.

"Why are you wearing it?" A cold sweat poured down Arthur's face.

"You *gave* this to me."

Arthur looked around again, "Why does this place look familiar, and why am I afraid of it?" Galahad could hear despondence in his king's voice.

Aryanyn grabbed Arthur's hand in hers. "You will remember shortly, my King."

The high priestess unsheathed Gwydion. Galahad's spine tightened into his neck, as he anticipated what he was about to witness.

"Merlin, take hold of thy son."

Merlin grabbed Arthur's arm.

"Galahad, Daniel, hold onto the wizard's cloak."

Galahad and Daniel obediently grasped Merlin's cloak tails.

Aryanyn lowered her blade into the water at the edge of the lake. She stirred the water counterclockwise, allowing the reflection of the moon to follow the flow of the water's path.

"*Entmyne orlunda lunnare magoria*," she chanted. The water in the lake spun like a whirlpool, taking the moons with it into each phase. "*Entmyne orlunda lunnare magoria!*" she chanted again. The waning of the moon showed itself as it shifted from the full moon, to the new moon, to the three quarter moon, the half moon and the crescent moon—and back again all the way to the full moon that haunted Galahad, the moon that Arthur died beneath. The North Star, escorted by the Big Dipper, showed itself in the sky. Down on the lake, its lower ray connected with the hilltop on the Isle of Avalon.

"Take cover in the twin maples!" cried Aryanyn as she pulled Arthur towards the trees. Galahad and Daniel led the rest of the party as arrows began to shower down from above.

"What is happening?" yelled Galahad over the hiss of the attack as Merlin followed him with bated breath. "She is delivering Arthur to the scene of his own demise," said the wizard. "Living through this once was enough for me!"

Galahad looked to the bottom of the hill and watched a younger Merlin ride down to greet Sir Ralph. Around them, knights were battling with swords, with fists, on horseback and on foot. The banging of metal crunched all around.

"Forward, south of the embankment!" cried the vision of Arthur on the battlefield as he commanded his knights.

From the safety of the trees, Aryanyn directed her party's attention to Mordred, Arthur's son, who stood by the lake watching Arthur's men take cover. Percival advanced with sword engaged at Mordred.

"Traitor!" screamed Percival.

"I would rather be a traitor than my father's slave!" yelled Mordred as he lunged at Percival, cutting his arm at the elbow. The knight cried out in pain, grabbing at the wound.

"Percival? Where's Percival?" asked the reborn Arthur, looking down at the battle scene in a stupor. His eyes were searching.

Mordred lunged again at Percival. Ralph, seeing the attack, ran from behind, knocking Mordred to the ground. Percival took advantage of the situation and leapt down at the prince, trying to stab him with his sword. Mordred stood, turned defensively and ran his sword through Percival's shoulder, weakening him badly.

"Father!" screamed Daniel from the trees.

Galahad held him back. "He cannot see you."

Percival, surprised by the turn of events, held tight to his wound and fell to the ground. Ralph attacked Mordred, only to be slashed at the leg. Percival again tried to stop Arthur's son; crawling on the ground, he grabbed at Mordred's ankle, but the prince pulled away and ran his sword straight into Percival's chest.

"Father!' screamed Daniel with horror, and again Galahad had to restrain him.

"Mordred!" yelled Arthur from the field below, coming to the aid of his men.

"No, my King!" yelled Ralph as he lunged at Mordred from the left side, gashing his arm.

One of Mordred's henchmen ran to protect his prince. He used his sword as a spear and shot it straight into the back of Sir Ralph.

"Ralph!" yelled both the battling and the reborn King Arthur.

Ralph fell straight down to his knees with the sword held taut in his back. Arthur drew the sword from Ralph's body, and blood gushed everywhere. He placed his friend on his lap and removed his helmet. Ralph lay back in his king's arms and died.

Tears fell down the reborn Arthur's face. "No, please, I cannot remember this!" he begged, grabbing for Galahad with terror in his eyes.

"You must, my lord, if we are to carry on!" said Aryanyn.

Galahad pushed his uncle and faced him towards the battle scene again.

"Father!" yelled Mordred as he attacked from the back with a branch. Arthur wrenched in pain, pushed Ralph's body off his lap and stood. Mordred again attacked his father with a blow to his face.

"Mordred," whispered the new Arthur.

"Accept your rebirth," said Galahad choking back his own tears.

"You lie again, Father!" yelled Mordred as he lunged at Arthur.

Arthur counterattacked his son, and their swords banged at one another. They began a volley of rounds and the thunderous sounds of their angered weapons bounced off the surface of the lake and into the forest. The exchange ended with a cut into Mordred's forearm, his gauntlet falling to the ground.

"Excalibur," whispered the reborn Arthur.

Mordred scooped up the blood that gushed from his arm and threw it into his father's face followed by repeated sword attacks as he tried to bring the king to his knees. Arthur fought Mordred off, refusing to strike the young prince down.

"Why didn't you take him?" asked Galahad. The reborn Arthur stared at the battle saying nothing.

The sound of horsemen broke the group's attention as a younger Merlin rode to the aid of his king.

"Stay out of this!" yelled the battling Arthur.

"But, sire—'" the younger Merlin tried to distract the prince.

Mordred struck at Merlin, and Arthur used the opportunity to stab Mordred, opening a gash in his shoulder.

The young Merlin was speaking at Mordred now, but his words could not be heard in the distance. Galahad looked to the older wizard standing with him in the trees and heard him whispering under his breath as though back on the battlefield. "Mordred, your mother wanted nothing to do with you or me. Dear God, Morgana was under Mab's spell. Mordred, please! Mab could not control me or my magic, so she put lies in your head!"

"Shut up!" yelled Mordred in the distance, pushing the young Merlin to the ground.

As Arthur ran to aid his foster father, Mordred leapt onto his back. Arthur fought the young prince off and jumped back to his feet—but without his breastplate that had given in to the various blows. Arthur grabbed and pushed his son's face into a tree.

Galahad heard both the Arthur on the field and that of rebirth speak in unison. "I have had enough. I am your father, and you will hear me."

"Hear you, Father?" Mordred's nose was bleeding down to his mouth. "No, Father. Now you hear this!" Mordred lunged at Arthur, burying his sword in his chest. Galahad could feel the pain of the blade spear his own heart for his king. As the battling Arthur pulled the blade from his chest, blood poured from the wound.

The older Merlin covered his face. "I cannot watch this again."

"Arthur, noooo!" young Merlin cried out, watching his son fall to his knees.

The reborn Arthur spoke. "I never meant any harm to my son. I never knew he existed until he was ten, and by then he already hated me."

The battling Arthur pulled himself up with the aid of Excalibur before Mordred attacked for the last time, slashing him at the shoulder.

"I do love you," whispered the reborn king.

"Mordred!" the bleeding Arthur screamed on the battlefield with his last ounce of energy.

Mordred turned toward his father, laughing. Taking the advantage, Arthur slashed at his son, cutting into his upper chest. Mordred fell from his wounds, but still he laughed at Arthur. Arthur ran Excalibur straight though his son's body. Excalibur squealed as the sword withdrew from the cracked armor. Mordred's life spilled all over the ground. He died instantly.

Arthur fell, too, giving into his wounds.

The young Merlin ran to Arthur, picking him up and rocking him gently.

"Tell Galahad that he is my joy," said the reborn Arthur under his breath, "and tell Arianna that I love her."

Merlin continued to rock his son, trying to cover his bloody wounds until Arthur gave up his spirit, turned his head and laid his final sight upon his dead son.

The resurrected king suddenly ran full speed down the hillside, stopping over the young Merlin and his own body. Reaching for his sword, his hand passed through the vision, which disappeared completely, leaving him alone on what was once the battlefield of his death.

"Excalibur!" shouted the reborn king, turning back to the riding party above. "I need my sword."

"Let us make haste," yelled Galahad, "for Camelot awaits her father's return."

Chapter Sixty-Two

Camelot Welcomes Her King

A horn from the tower blared as the riders neared the city. Arthur's hands were tightly wrapped around Aryanyn as they rode on Brach towards home. He could feel her pushing back against him, holding onto him, caring for him as if she knew that he was still weak and needed her support.

"Gavin," cried Galahad who was leading the pack. "Blare welcome to our king and father, for he is home again!"

All around them, the subjects of Camelot castle gathered to see Arthur ride through the gates. Shouts of revelry were heard, and Arthur's heart leapt in his chest.

From the distance, Arthur recognized Nimue and Martin standing at the top of the steps. He looked up to the gaping wall of the mezzanine verandah atop the main castle doors and saw Sir Gawain and his wife Lady Catherine, as well as a young woman, with a somewhat familiar face. Everything was coming back to him quickly now—and though it was overwhelming, Arthur felt himself welcome the new challenge.

The riding party dismounted, and a young man came to gather the horses.

Arthur stood at the bottom of the stairs with Galahad, his eyes fixed on the aged night, Sir Martin Borwell. Martin looked back at Arthur, struck his chest and bowed.

"My old friend, Martin," said Arthur grabbing Martin by the shoulders, pulling him up and staring into his shocked face. Arthur grabbed his friend in a tight embrace, and the two laughed together heartily.

When Arthur released him, Martin inspected him and spoke in a low whisper. "It is you, isn't it?"

"Yes, Martin. The Lady Aryanyn called me from my sleep and Gwyn ap Nudd released my soul. This has been a whirlwind, but all is coming back to me."

The two shared a quick smile as the Agavene Family came through the great doors of Camelot Castle. Arthur looked into the eyes of his cousin, Gawain, who bowed his head and embraced him, kissing him on both cheeks. "My lord and my liege," he said, and Arthur felt the emotions of his words.

Lady Catherine bowed, as well, and Arthur in turn met the notion by taking her hand and kissing it. "I see you have kept your promise, my lady, for my cousin is well, as are you."

She looked back at him, her face narrowed with suspicion. Slowly a smile crept across her lips and she stared deeply into his eyes as though searching to see if it was really him inside.

He squeezed her hand and leaned in a bit closer to her. "Your sight does not betray you. I have indeed returned."

She leapt at him and threw her arms around him in a bear hug. He tried to spin her, but found himself too weak and nearly dropped her before Galahad stepped in and caught the pair. As they landed, they all broke out in laughter and others joined in their revelry.

Arthur looked around at his knights, both young and old, and at the groups of people who were slowly gathering on the balcony and in the square to see their reborn king. There were blacksmiths, cooks and servants, tailors, milkmaids, and bakers. Children and their parents climbed upon the fountain steps. Up on the mezzanine that looked over the square stood a hundred and better of his subjects. Fathers of small children hoisted them over their shoulders to see him. The fort wall above them held within its confines at least two hundred young soldiers and squires not yet knighted. Arthur's heart heaved with emotion as he looked straight into the village square and saw a thousand or more streaming in through the gates like human pigeons gathering to find drink at a well. They were all pointing to him, and he heard one woman say, "Look 'tis Arthur come home to us." Another shouted, "It's a miracle! King Arthur has returned!"

He could see the worry on some faces as they looked upon him and also saw the change that overcame them as they realized the truth of what they saw. Some of them came close enough to reach out and touch him, not trusting that he existed until they felt him for themselves.

Arthur felt a crushing anxiety come over him as the crowd drew nearer. He turned to Galahad, telling him, "I want so much to be with them, but I need more time."

Martin brought Gavin up to the center of the landing, and the young squire blew his horn over the masses, directing the attention of all in the square. Standing next to the boy, Martin shouted, "Good people, our father has returned, but Arthur needs time to regain his strength. Go back to your business, and tomorrow we will hold a feast in honor of your returned king."

"Huzzah!" they shouted in revelry. "Huzzah! Huzzah!"

Arthur silently cried and bowed his head humbly to those who graciously welcomed him home.

"Come, noble people," said Galahad to his court, "to the Round Table room for food and drink."

The two guards opened the large wooden doors of the castle keep. They creaked as Camelot welcomed her king. Arthur placed his foot through the door, and it was as though the ancients whispered, *Welcome home.*

He walked into the entry corridor and past a young page who met the party with torch in hand. Arthur had never seen him before in his castle and noticed right away that the boy appeared intimidated as he led them through the dimly lit entrance.

"And who might you be, young man?" Arthur asked the page as they walked.

Galahad gave him a reassuring nod and Cavyn swallowed hard before answering, "I am Cavyn Josephson, sire."

"Josephson? From whose house are you?"

"Sire, I am cousin to Sir Peter," replied the young boy. "Son of Lady Margaret."

"And how old would you be?" asked Arthur.

"I am twelve, Majesty," said the page.

Arthur smiled at the boy. "Lead on, Page Cavyn."

Cavyn held his torch all the higher as he led the group through the great halls and on to the revered doors of the Round Table room. Arthur's eyes raised to the dragon etched in gold that guarded the room. He silently read the single word branded into the wood below the dragon: *Excalibur.*

He stared at the name of his ward, whispered her name, and looked down at Cavyn, who gawked with amazement while standing in waiting. Galahad gave him a signal to continue, and the page led the group through the doors.

On the table was a simple breakfast of finely churned buttermilk, fruits and nuts to nourish the belly and freshly made bread that filled the air with an inviting aroma.

Arthur stood at the doorway of his Round Table room and fixed his eyes on his pendragon signet tapestry that hung over the room. He looked to the finely embroidered Celtic cross to the left of the pendragon.

Galahad led the others in silence, giving him room to reacquaint himself with this place where so much of his history had been written. Arthur gently placed his hand on the chair of each knight who was no longer with him. He shook his head. *What price have you all paid?* he whispered under his breath.

"Come, good people, let us nourish ourselves," said Catherine, snapping her fingers. The young servants came in, taking up the trays and offering the food to all in the room.

Arthur reached for a small loaf of bread and broke it in two. He dipped half in the buttermilk and placed it in his mouth, savoring the flavor. As soon as he swallowed, he felt the reawakening of his appetite for both food and life. "Majesty Galahad, this bread and milk tastes like creamed velvet upon my tongue. I appreciate that you remembered what I enjoy."

"Perhaps you would like to sit down," Merlin suggested.

"I would indeed."

Arthur looked at the table for his seat. It was not there. Looking to the back of the room, he spotted it in the corner. Galahad coughed, and Arthur looked to him, noticing his cheeks had turned red hot. Galahad ran to the back under the guard's post, and Gavin assisted him in picking up the chair and bringing it back to where it rested fifteen years ago.

"My lord, your chair awaits."

"Nephew, this chair does not belong here. You are now king, and I will not take your place."

"Perhaps 'Call to Orders' would be a good way to take your place at this table," said Galahad. "My lord, please sit here on my chair."

He grabbed Galahad's hand and placed it on the chair that carried Galahad's name. "This is the Siege Perilous, and only one man can claim her. On the day of your coming, it scribed your name. Only the chosen can sit here in the place of honor. You honor my home, as it has become yours."

"And his home it shall be until the day of his death!" interjected William as he and Frederick barged into the room from the knights' hallway with their swords drawn.

Daniel guarded King Arthur, pushing him to the side, using his body as a shield to protect him.

"Father! Lay down your sword!" ordered Sir Peter.

"We have come to see the imposter!" shouted Frederick.

"Stand down those weapons in this room! Are you mad?" shouted Martin.

"Mad! Nay, I think I am not the madman. This woman has you so bewitched that you would think this man our king," said Frederick as he pointed to Aryanyn and to Arthur with his sword.

"Sir," warned Galahad as his guards closed in behind the intruders to secure the room, "I would sheathe your weapon quickly or suffer under penalty of law."

Frederick advanced upon Arthur, but Daniel, with sword drawn came to his defense and lunged at the elder knight. Frederick easily parried his blow and sent him to the floor. Gawain and Martin interceded though and pushed him to his knees. Martin pressed the point of his sword to the man's throat. Frederick knelt, holding on to his own sword with one hand and the floor with the other. William made a countermove, but Peter swerved to his father, cutting him off.

"You cannot believe that this man is King Arthur," Frederick laughed.

Arthur came from behind Martin, who disengaged his sword.

"Arthur, please!" warned Galahad.

"Frederick, lay down your weapon," commanded Arthur who stood two feet away from the knight, staring him down. "Frederick," he repeated with the gentle baritone sound that was his signature, "lay down your weapon."

Without fear, Arthur stepped closer, standing only inches away from Frederick. "No man shall enter these halls armed with intent to harm one of his own."

Frederick rose to his feet. "You have not yet proven to be one of our own."

"And how do you propose he do so, sir knight," said Gawain.

"Merlin was Uther's Druid guide as he was Arthur's," said Frederick. "Excalibur was given first to Uther, but Uther mocked the powers of the sword, so Merlin and Viviane locked the sword in the stone until the rightful heir took of her."

"We know the tale, Frederick," interrupted Martin.

"We have been made aware that once again the sword rests within the confines of the stone, Majesty," said William, "and that many men have tried their hand at setting her free—to no avail."

"And I'm certain you were one of them," added Martin.

"Indeed I was and the sword would not release for me. If this man is the true Arthur, let him prove it at the stone," Frederick finished.

Blaise stepped forward. "Only Arthur can remove the sword."

"Arthur, will you allow us to take you to the stone?" asked Galahad.

"Frederick was and always will be a faithful knight in the service of his position. I take the challenge willingly."

"Cavyn, come forward. Tell Marc to prepare the horses." The young page left the room and reentered seconds later. "Majesty, the beasties are ready."

Galahad clapped his hands acknowledging Cavyn. "Come good people, the Domh Ringr awaits the king. Michael and Daniel, place Frederick and William under arrest for drawing their weapons in this place of peace. I want them in chains, then bound to their horses, where their treachery will bring them shame."

CHAPTER SIXTY-THREE

Excalibur Reclaims Her King

Marc stood outside at the end of the steps with horses ready. Arthur drew from the castle, escorted by Galahad and accompanied by Aryanyn and Merlin. He stopped on the landing for a brief moment looking at Julius, his prized steed—older, but standing just as black as midnight and as majestically as he was the day Arthur died. Arthur gently walked down the steps and over to Julius. The horse backed away for a moment.

"I can imagine how spooked you must feel my friend," said Arthur to his mount. "As though you are seeing a ghost."

The horse neighed and Marc handed Arthur some apple bits to give him. Arthur cupped the pieces of fruit and held them out to his horse. Julius grabbed them and ate with gusto, while Arthur carefully patted him on the neck. "Yes, you remember me, don't you, boy?"

A few moments later, Julius bent low and allowed Arthur to mount him. Both horse and rider needed a moment to gain their balance. "Yes my friend, neither of us finds ourselves in the body we once treasured."

Sitting high in his saddle, Arthur felt the hard leather under his hind parts and the heartbeat of the steed through his thighs. He looked toward Galahad, Aryanyn, and Merlin who sat atop their horses. Behind the main riding party were the other knights of the Round Table including Frederick and William who were shackled to the pommels of their horses and guarded by Michael and Daniel. "Let us away," he said.

Daylight lit the path to Stonehenge, and the monolith stood in the glory of the sunlight, casting its shadows on the backdrop of the landscape. The riders came to the avenue of the circle. Arthur, Galahad, Aryanyn and Merlin's steeds were the first to place their hooves on the trail. As the group made their way up the passage, Arthur heard the caw of three crows overhead. He raised his eyes to the sky to see the black birds flying above them, as though they were leading the way, not he.

The priestess, the wizard and King Galahad joined him in passing the heel stone, followed by the others. A gust of cool wind blew around the base of the boulder, pushing the riders toward the circle. He again gandered up towards the sky; flying overhead alongside the black birds now were three eagles. As Arthur came to the outer circle of the sarsen, the eagles screeched loudly, encircling the stones with the crows and landing atop the lintels to take watch over the group at the face of the monolith.

Arthur dismounted first, followed by Galahad, who assisted Merlin from his horse. Daniel and Michael forced the chained prisoners from their horses as Aryanyn dismounted Brach and led him towards the brown sarsen, dropping his reins. The high priestess guided Arthur, her son and her brother into the stone temple followed by the other knights.

Arthur looked around, it was many years since he was privy to the magnitude of the Henge. The ancients' voices in the stones were calling to him as his eyes caught sight of Excalibur sitting obediently in the altar stone. He approached the massive brown sarsen and touched it, feeling the vibration of the earth's core, and his blood flowing with the rhythm of the planet.

He continued on to the smaller bluestones and rubbed his hand over the smooth granite of each, allowing his mind to wander as he viewed the landscape around him and felt the pulse of Mother Earth.

Arthur turned to Aryanyn, guardian of the sacred sword. She mirrored his stare and said aloud, "Excalibur, I am no longer your guardian. Go to Arthur, for he has need of you now."

The wind gusted as if whispering encouragement into Arthur's ears. He said a silent prayer, asking the ancients that built the Henge to unlock the sword from her grip and motioned to Galahad who nodded in return. Then Arthur advanced towards the stone. With every step he took, the eagles screeched and the crows cawed long and loud, taking to the sky over the monolith and orbiting around the circle. As Arthur drew closer, the bird's cacophony echoed off the stones and filled the air.

He gazed at the pendragon signet that graced the pommel of Excalibur: the gold and silver leaves inlaid on the hilt and tang, the red ruby heart incased in the hilt of the sword, and the rose design that graced the blade—forged when magic ruled the earth. Arthur thought of his father, a man of great power, and he remembered his son, a young man gone astray by a bloodline that sought to make him a madman. His eyes teared as he remembered the battle and envisioned this magnificent blade ramming through the body of his son. *Mordred*, he thought, *what I would have done to have you by my side.*

Arthur looked around the ancient circle and focused on an eagle that was perched on the north sarsen stone. The eagle looked down at the king, spread his wings, and screeched loudly as though saying, "Take her, she is yours."

Arthur coiled his fingers around Excalibur's hilt, held her firmly and staring at Frederick said, "*Ebehtas Anonexias Embialosos Safieiera Ambyntha Solandina Excalibur Exhumena megaria.*" He pulled at the blade, and the ground quaked, swaying under his feet. He heaved at the sword again and the blue green granite reddened with heat. Excalibur shook in the stone, and Arthur could feel a warmth surge within him.

He became one with the earth again as the Mother and he shared the beat of a single heart. He cried aloud, "*Ebehtas Anonexias Embialosos Ambyntha Excalibur Ka fas nah!*" The sword grew hot and red as Arthur shouted. "*Ephphata!*" He yanked at her with all of his might and felt the blade release from the stone, a babe born to her mother. As Arthur raised his relic blade, the noble sword of Avalon, her steel sang like the abbey tower of Glastonbury's church bells on a wedding day. *Excalibur reclaims her king!!!*

Frederick fell to his knees and spoke aloud, "She has bewitched us all. Even me."

CHAPTER SIXTY-FOUR

Galahad Celebrates the Return of King Arthur

The castle was abuzz with the return of Arthur, who tossed and turned in his bed, unable to sleep. Visions of his death—and now his rebirth—plagued him and he pulled himself from the bed. In front of the mirror, he passed his hands through his hair and stepped closer to the reflection, looking for the gray that once peppered his sandy-brown locks. Untying the laces of his shirt, he lifted it from his body and examined the vessel of his rebirth. It was not the body from where he left this world. It was more like that of his younger years, before it was strengthened by hard labor and the toils of war. He dressed for the day and rested on the verandah, setting his sword at his side and looking out into his kingdom. *But is she really mine?* he wondered to himself.

Arthur picked up a quill and tablet and wrote the events of the past day in a private journal, an age old tradition he kept since he was a boy in Merlin's care. A knock on the door interrupted his solace. He pushed himself from the chair and opened the door to Galahad.

"My lord, your people await you in the great square."

Arthur raised Excalibur, kissed the heart of the hilt, sheathed the sword, and draped his cloak over his shoulders. Following Galahad through the halls and out the main doors of castle Camelot, he was immediately met with shouts from the gathering crowd.

"Arthur! Arthur! Arthur!"

In the middle of the great square were the cooks, and they had a huge wild boar on the skewer atop a raging fire. One turned the charred beast as another basted it. Arthur inhaled the aroma of the pig, and his tongue longed to savor the taste.

Tables were set on the landings, and spread out upon them were fresh baked breads, trays of vegetables, potatoes, mutton, roasted corn, and fruits and nuts. Everyone scurried about as Camelot's citizens lined up for food and drink. Arthur was glad to witness this celebration, as it was he who—as a young king—brought his subjects from all walks of life to this square to celebrate with him.

Two strong looking men dressed in tattered brown leather and long black cloaks broke through the mob, driving a wagon that carried at least ten large wooden kegs of ale. Arthur licked his parched lips; a good drink of Camelot's brew would be a grand start to the day. One of the men dismounted and opened the hatch in the back of the wagon. He wrenched a metal tankard from a hanging hook, pulled on the spigot and let the ale pour. It ran down the cup and produced a foam that cascaded over the rim.

Galahad descended the steps and accepted the cup from him, shouting to the masses, "To Arthur, our King and Father! Heaven has brought you home to us!"

Galahad reached high, and Arthur took the stein from him. Drinking the bittersweet liquid of barley and corn that grew in his fields was like sipping the lifeblood of his homeland. He licked the froth from his lips, smiled and said, "Heaven has brought me home to you. Let us rejoice, for I am rejoined with Excalibur as the humble servant of God and the Goddess this day."

He unsheathed his sword and raised her high as the crowd chanted his name over and over again.

Arthur enjoyed another sip. "Good sir, please share this with everyone here, for my people are all parched."

"The great bear has returned!" said Michael as he knelt on the ground and made the sign of the cross. "Majesty Arthur Pendragon!" he joyously shouted as he struck his chest, saluting Arthur.

"Remove your helmet, Knight!" commanded Arthur.

Michael kept his head down and obeyed.

Arthur looked down upon Michael's crown of sunset red hair. "Knight, lift your face so that I may see who honors me this day."

The young knight glanced up towards Arthur. His green eyes were luminous with what Arthur assumed were bittersweet tears. Arthur placed his hand on the knight's shoulder. "Son of Ralph Bedwynn, I order you to stand in the presence of your king."

Michael stood to meet Arthur face to face and Arthur embraced him. "You honor your father." Arthur struck his chest in memory of his knight, Sir Ralph Bedwynn. Michael bowed his head to the gesture.

Daniel, Peter, and Luke came to Arthur, bowed, and knelt before him.

Arthur looked to Galahad for assistance in identifying these young knights.

Galahad seemed to pick up his queue. "My lord, do you not remember these fine men?"

At Arthur's request, the young knights stood, and Arthur looked them over.

"Peter," said Arthur. "Was it you who stood up for me just yesterday?"

"Ehy, my lord."

"You honor your king," Arthur commented as he turned and looked at the other young men. Studying their older faces, memories flooded him of the boys who once played in his courtyard. "Luke? Daniel?" asked Arthur.

Their youthful smiles revealed their delight at his recognition. Arthur hugged the young knights. "You are all men now."

"I beseech you, good knights," interrupted Galahad. "Others wish to greet our King Arthur."

"You are your father's son, young du Lac, always constant in your watch."

"Ehy, my King, that I am!" said Galahad as Arthur saw a grin of pride wash over his face.

Arthur turned to see Aryanyn approach him with a young man by her side that bore some resemblance to the high priestess. She came to stand near him and Arthur lifted her hand and gently kissed it.

"My lord, I wish you to meet my son, Joseph Lawrence."

Joseph bowed to Arthur. "It is an honor, Your Majesty."

Arthur examined Joseph from head to foot and smiled. "So you are the boy I heard much about so many years ago."

"Hopefully good things," smiled Joseph.

Arthur turned to Aryanyn and said, "Like all mothers, some were words of pride and others of concern." He could see that he embarrassed the young man. "I hear from Galahad that Leonora is betrothed to you."

"We are to be married on a midsummer's day, sire."

"Go and join with your lady, as we have a lifetime to speak of such matters," said Arthur with finality. Joseph bowed to him and walked off, leaving Arthur with Aryanyn.

"I remember being young and foolish," he said as he looked into her fiery eyes.

"A lifetime to speak of such matters," repeated Aryanyn. "Those words bring happiness to my heart."

Arthur opened his arms. "Come, let us find remedy in a long embrace." Aryanyn seemed to crumple within his arms, and he held her as close to his chest as was possible, their breathing joining as if in a single breath.

Merlin approached, clapping his hands, followed by Blaise, Viviane and Aaron. "My heart beats like a drum in the pulse of a dance," Merlin said. "My sister and my son are together again."

He wrapped his arms around the pair, laughed and kissed them both on their foreheads.

Arthur looked at Aryanyn and at the wizard. He felt home again.

CHAPTER SIXTY-FIVE
A Gift and Bitter Reckoning

King Arthur exited to the verandah from Galahad's chambers. Aryanyn, Galahad and Joseph, were already seated and Arthur realized that he was interrupting a moment between a mother and her two sons.

"Majesty," Joseph stood at attention as Arthur came towards the trio.

"Please, Joseph, take thy seat."

"Uncle, would you care for a cup of mead?" asked Galahad.

"What mead has our winery fermented these days?"

"This is loganberry, Uncle," said Galahad.

"Please."

Galahad poured a cup and handed the goblet to his uncle. Taking it, Arthur noticed the ring on the smallest finger of Galahad.

"Guinevere's ring?" Arthur inquired as he grabbed hold of Galahad's hand. A peculiar chill passed through him.

Aryanyn stepped over and joined her hand with Galahad. "Speaking of rings—" she said.

Arthur looked down and beheld the sight of his pendragon signet on her forefinger. He rested his cup upon the table and held both the hands of Aryanyn and Galahad.

"I thought that these rings would have been placed in a cedar chest after you took the throne, nephew."

"After your death, they served a higher purpose," said Galahad. "I saw fit to place a promise on them both."

"A promise?"

"Uncle, after your death, Aryanyn nearly refused to leave Camelot. She wanted to aid me in my newly established kingdom. Merlin knew that she had to leave, or her life and the destiny of her son would be in danger."

Arthur held their hands even tighter.

"She was afraid that our young Joseph here," Galahad placed his hand on Joseph's shoulder, "would become another Mordred."

Joseph stood and Arthur thought he saw a look of embarrassment shrouding the young man's face.

"I don't understand, Mother. How can you compare me to Mordred?"

"Joseph, my dear son, you and Mordred suffered under the same rage—hateful, vengeful and defiant to the end. I knew that if I could not get to you, I would lose you to the anger, just as Arthur lost Mordred." Aryanyn placed her hand on Joseph's face and kissed his cheek tenderly. "I love you so much. You know this."

Arthur looked to Joseph with a newfound respect.

Galahad continued. "I decided to place two promises for both Mother and I to keep. One, that she would not give up on Joseph, and two, that she would return to me when I had need of her."

"So the heavens planned the prophecy of my raising as soon as my body began to burn?" asked Arthur.

"I guess it did, my uncle," Galahad said with a bright smile.

Arthur turned to Joseph again. "I am glad that you have grown by the love she gave you so freely." Arthur looked into Aryanyn's amber eyes. "I wish that Mordred would have accepted my love in the same manner." With humility, Arthur bowed to Joseph. "Son, I thank you for showing me what Mordred could have been. You have inspired me this day."

Aryanyn stepped forward, removed her ring and handed it to Arthur. "The prophecy has been fulfilled. This ring belongs to you again."

Arthur placed the ring back on Aryanyn's forefinger. "The prophecy goes well beyond my returning to this earth. Wear it now, as I have no claim to it." Arthur placed a gentle kiss on Aryanyn's hand.

"Cavyn is waiting in the hall," said Arthur to Galahad. "May he come in?"

"Is there something he needs, Uncle?"

"He carries a gift."

Galahad gestured to the guard to open the door, and Arthur smiled as Cavyn entered the room with a long white cloth that flowed over his arms. The page stood next to Arthur, who seized the article from the boy.

"This is for you," said Arthur, placing the item in Galahad's hand.

Galahad's face wrinkled with confusion as he opened the ties that held the cloth together. He placed his hand beneath the sheet, and Arthur felt him grasp the pommel of the sword within the encasing. With the whisper of angels, he drew out a magnificent rapier and examined the weapon.

"As you can see, nephew, the pommel holds the Grail cup within the confines of the crescent moon. On the hilt is embossed the pendragon; his hands behold a ruby red knight's cross." Arthur felt Galahad's hands shake as they touched the markings of the sword together.

"The tang bears the same gold and silver inlaid leaves that Excalibur and Gwydion are encrusted with—and on the blade, look, my nephew, the roses of Avalon are symmetrically engraved down the silver plating of the steel."

"My uncle, what a treasured weapon."

"Her name is Anwnn. She is the sister to Excalibur, Gwydion and Cedwynn. She bears the pendragon, and she is the last of her clan. Today, my nephew and my King, I, Arthur Maximus Constantine Pendragon, welcome you to the fold of the priory of the pendragon. It has been a long time coming."

Galahad held the sword to his chest and heaved with labored breath. "I am humbled by this gift."

"It was planned by Merlin and me years ago that when you came of age, you would receive this honor. My death served to prevent you from your rightful place at my table. If I should have lived, you were to be knighted in my court. When Aryanyn chose you as the heir to Excalibur, Merlin knew that some of the elder knights may not support your office, as you are the son of a transgressor. Merlin hid this sword until the day came that you, Majesty Galahad du Lac, son of Lancelot du Lac, my friend and brother pendragon, would follow in your father's footsteps and join him as a Knight of my Round Table." Arthur paused a moment before continuing. "But as we all know, God had other plans."

"My father was a good man."

"And a great warrior. In part, I, too, was responsible for Guinevere's adulterous act, as I was more the king and not the husband she needed. My regret was banishing Lancelot and my wife. I should have kept them here and let forgiveness flow to both of them."

"Uncle, after your death, Guinevere left my father and entered into the nunnery of Glastonbury Abbey."

Arthur could not believe what he was hearing.

"It is my regret to tell you that she died there after taking vows. She is buried in the abbey cemetery."

"She took vows?" A sadness filled Arthur's heart.

"In penitence for her adultery."

"And your father?"

"I know not his whereabouts."

"One day, my nephew--when the time is right--we will look for him."

Arthur embraced his nephew, stood back and unsheathed Excalibur. Aryanyn followed Arthur's lead and drew forth Gwydion. The sisters met in camaraderie as Galahad struck the swords with Anwnn. As the steel of the blades collided, they glowed, releasing the power of their unity.

The swords were sheathed and Arthur made a request. "Please, I beg indulgence here. I need to speak with Galahad over a private matter."

"I agree, Uncle, there are matters we need to discuss," said Galahad.

"Joseph, please join Mother for something to eat in her chambers. We will speak of things later."

"I understand, brother."

Aryanyn kissed Galahad on the cheek, and Arthur heard her whisper in his ear, "Remember who and what you are," before she and Joseph walked from the verandah.

Arthur lifted his goblet and sipped the loganberry mead. It was sweet and smooth going down his throat. He knocked back another sip and continued. "I speak now to my king and not my nephew. Have you thought about what proceeding you will take with Frederick and William?"

"I have to uphold the law—a law that you and Merlin saw fit to instill in your own court and one that I hold dear."

Arthur finished his mead and turned to his nephew. "Galahad, I understand and respect your position, but Frederick and William served me well and I wish you to reconsider."

"They are dangerous men whose intentions cannot be trusted, Uncle."

Arthur looked towards the bell tower. "William has proven himself to me time and again." Arthur paused, contemplating. "When Guinevere looked to Lancelot for love, it was William who knew about the affair, and it was he who tried so hard to keep it from me and the rest of the kingdom. While I do not agree with his choice, I recognize that he did so in an effort to save me pain. More importantly, before Mordred mortally wounded me in battle, he revealed that William sent Merlin to the north side of the embankment, keeping him far away from Frederick to spare the wizard from Frederick's sword."

"I appreciate and understand your desire to be lenient with Sir William, but why is it you wish me to pardon Sir Frederick?" asked Galahad.

"Believe me," started Arthur, "Frederick was always a rebel in my court. He did intend to kill Merlin that day on the battlefield to rid the castle of his Druid ways. He was delighted by the evil spread by Mab and Mordred. I know that had it not symbolized a departure from the church, he would have joined them in battle against me. That being said, I have known Frederick since we were both young men. He may appear misdirected, but his intentions are good. His faith in the Christ is strong, sometimes almost fanatical. Though I have not been a member of this court for some time, I still believe that with the proper guidance, there is hope for Frederick."

"Had I been privy to this information years ago, I probably would have had him beheaded, and deservedly so," responded Galahad.

"Do not be so quick to judge young king. It is the ruler who has the responsibility of redirecting the misguided." Arthur raised Excalibur in the air in battle mode. "Do you think that I wanted my son's blood to stain this blade? This is the blade of the Mother Goddess and of God the Father in heaven. She was given to me to uphold the laws of heaven here on earth. Yet in battle, I had to decide who would live—my son or my people. Do not think for one moment that killing those who disagree with you is the right choice or an easy task."

"I hear your argument, Arthur, but both of these men struck out against you," said Galahad.

"William only did so when his family was threatened by the church," revealed Arthur.

"Can you be certain of this charge?"

"Nephew, I have been gone from this earth for more than fifteen years. There is not much I can be certain of or prove any longer."

Arthur turned and looked out at the great land before them and Galahad followed his lead.

It was high noon, and the sun shone over the hills of Avalon when Galahad said, "Your wish will be considered, Uncle."

CHAPTER SIXTY-SIX

Aryanyn and Arthur take their Quest

Galahad entered the Round Table room quietly, anticipating the request he would make of Arthur and Aryanyn. He delicately placed Anwnn on the table and daydreamed of battles to come. He shook his head at thoughts of Frederick and William while he sat, resting back into the cushion of the chair.

He, who took over this seat of power so many years ago, could not relax. He glanced around the table remembering his boyhood days, hiding behind the door of the knights' hallway, listening to the caucuses regarding the governing of Camelot. He vividly recalled the knights drinking their ale and arguing for the betterment of the country. He wanted to be one of them, but never thought that one day he would be king.

Today, Galahad had the honor of asking his fellow king and uncle to take on the quest of his lifetime. He would soon be saying goodbye to Arthur once again.

Galahad focused on the five petals of the cinquefoil that graced the Round Table. A knot like a ball of lead shot laid in his stomach as he thought that he, the boy known as Galahad of the Lake, could have William and Frederick beheaded before dawn. His heart sank. These men raised him and taught him how to rule a nation. Thinking of them, his eyes sought the crucifix that hung across the room.

"My lord, I see you are ready for the affairs of this evening," said the sullen voice of Peter, interrupting Galahad's thoughts. "Father and Frederick are in the knights' hallway under the guard of Michael and Daniel."

"Do you know if your father and Frederick ever had ill words with one another?"

Peter's expression morphed from sullen to angry. "Frederick often angered my father over government and church issues."

"Did you not ask him to confide in you?"

"I did, my lord, but you know my father—always quick to protect his family from troubles."

Galahad looked toward the hallway door. "Keep them in chains until I summon them into my court."

Peter's always steady hands were trembling for his father. It was evident to Galahad by the way he gripped the hilt of his sword that his first knight tried to cover the disparity, and Galahad could not help but empathize with the pain he felt at his father being locked in chains. "I suggest that you leave me and go to your father. I am sure that he is in need of his son at this hour."

Peter stood at attention and clicked his heels in obedience before leaving. Passing him on the way out were Merlin and Lady Nimue, who entered the great room. Galahad stood for the wizard and his wife. He embraced Merlin and lifted Anwnn. "I hear that this was of your making, High Priest."

Merlin smiled. "It was my pleasure."

"I thank thee for such a treasured gift."

"If I had my way, the circumstances would have been different."

"Still, I will honor her all the days of my life."

"Anwnn is in good hands," said Merlin with a hint of pride in his voice. Galahad bowed his head to the wizard, and Merlin and Nimue took their seats.

Sir Joseph, Sir Luke, and Page Cavyn entered the court. The young knights bowed to Galahad before taking their stations. As always, Cavyn stood to the left of Galahad, awaiting orders.

The door guard announced the arrival of Sir Gawain who, accompanied by Lady Catherine and Lady Leonora, entered the room, followed by Blaise, Aaron, Viviane and Lydgia.

From the knights' hallway, Galahad could hear the voice of Martin resonate into the room. He could not tell exactly what was said, but Galahad knew by the sound of the elder Borwell brother's voice that he was not pleased with William. He entered alone and walked over to Galahad, bowing humbly to him. Galahad noted the gesture, nodding his head, and Martin sat near the younger knights.

"King Arthur and the Lady Aryanyn, sire!" Squire Gavin cried out in revelry.

The Camelot family stood for the pair as Arthur and Aryanyn entered the court. Galahad was pleased to see that Aryanyn's hand was cradled in the folds of Arthur's arm. The two walked into the great Round Table room dressed in the finery of the day, Arthur in his signature red and black armed with Excalibur in her sheath, and Aryanyn in her gold and red dress armed with Gwydion. Arthur bowed to Galahad, and Aryanyn curtsied, before the chivalrous Arthur assisted the lady to her seat.

Galahad held Anwnn firmly in his grip, and raised her point to the ceiling. The others bearing swords lifted high their weapons.

"Uncle, please grace my table with the words of the pendragon. This day they should be spoken by the man who brought them here long ago."

Arthur bowed his head humbly. He crossed Excalibur with Anwnn. Aryanyn added Gwydion and Merlin drew forth Cedwynn, the sword of his lineage. The four blades clashed, and their song filled the court. The sister swords of the lake were unified once more.

King Arthur spoke, "*Abethynn Arianhrod ech osfynnlor gwileth mangor osfor Draconian essafor osforlorn.*" His baritone voice echoed through the room.

Galahad followed, "*Osfor Draconian essafor osforlorn!*" and felt the station of his kingship for the first time—he was now truly a member of the priory of the pendragon.

Galahad lowered Anwnn, kissed his sword and placed her at bay on the table. Arthur, Aryanyn and Merlin followed suit. The other knights bearing swords disengaged their weapons, each laying them down in line with the custom to not be armed at the table of brotherly peace.

"Thank you, Uncle Arthur. The blessing of the pendragon shall forever more be a call to orders in my court."

Arthur bowed to him.

Galahad took his seat, leading the others to do the same. He glanced at each sword lying in its place, all pointing to the cinquefoil rose intricately carved into the center of the table. He thought of the face of the Goddess holding within her embrace the rose of the Mother and the symbol of the Holy Grail that protected the blades of the pendragon.

Galahad clapped his hands. "Cavyn, bring wine."

Cavyn left the room in haste, bringing back goblets and carafes. He placed the tray on the table and poured the gift of the Goddess for Galahad and the others. Galahad swirled the wine round in his goblet. He enjoyed the aroma, letting it intoxicate him before he drank it down and slammed it on the table with a hard thud, drawing all attention in the room.

"My lord, Arthur Pendragon, please bring forward the Lady Aryanyn, once known throughout these lands as the Lady Arianna." Arthur assisted the lady from her chair. The two approached Galahad who stood facing them, placing his left hand on Arthur's right shoulder and taking one of his mother's hands in his own. "Lady Aryanyn Lawrence, it has been a long road for us since we first met fifteen and better years ago. We have seen both good and bad in these times. You have brought a joy to my life that I did not believe could be reignited after Uncle Arthur left this world.

"Today I speak to Aryanyn Echrrynn, the woman who found her mortal soul within these walls and the woman who—by prophecy—is bound to fulfill an impressive destiny."

The amber eyes of the priestess shed quiet tears that dripped down her cheeks and onto Galahad's hand.

"I ask the gatekeeper of Avalon and the guardian of Excalibur to lead Arthur Pendragon back through time and to protect him on his quest to find the titulus of Christ and bring peace back to the divided houses of the world."

Aryanyn squeezed her son's hand, and Galahad felt her pulse begin to quicken. She smiled and kissed him on both cheeks. "My King, and my son, it is my honor to accept your invitation. I will fulfill the prophecy of Élan as it has been foretold."

Galahad turned to his uncle. He felt a radiance burst within as he looked into Arthur's eyes, the brilliant blue eyes that were taken from him years ago and now returned to him by a merciful God. He bowed his head to Arthur. "Arthur Maximus Constantine Pendragon, son of Uther Pendragon and Lady Igraine of Avalon, by lineage you are the son of Rome and of Briton. It is the destiny of your soul that you travel back in time to the Rome we have forgotten for it is your destiny to bring back the true symbol of Christianity––the titulus of Jesus Christ––to join it with the Holy Grail and bring the houses of the world together in lasting and mortal peace."

Arthur bowed his head. "With your permission, sire."

Galahad gestured to Arthur, and his uncle bowed his head once more before walking over to the wall. "May I take this cross from its nail, Majesty?" Galahad nodded and Arthur reached up to remove the religious symbol from the wall. He kissed the feet of Jesus, venerating the man, and walked back over to Galahad, placing the cross in his hands. With his forefinger, Arthur traced over the letters I.N.R.I.

"When I was a boy, I learned about this man from Sir Ector, a knight in my father's army," said Arthur. "I embraced Jesus, telling myself that although I was raised a Druid and would never disavow my Pagan roots, I would pledge my life to quest for this man called the Christ and follow in his footsteps. When the one God and the Goddess made me King of Camelot, I vowed my allegiance to both of my faiths, and I took on the dragon and the crescent moon as my royal signet. I promised to find out who Jesus was."

Arthur bent his head and again kissed the feet of Jesus. "When I returned from Rome after fighting the Holy Wars between the Christian Roman legions and the Pagans, I returned without the Grail or the relic cross upon which the Christ died. I realized that God had found me unworthy of either, as I had done nothing in my court to uphold his presence in my house. In my humbleness, I carved this cross in thanksgiving to Jesus for a safe return." Arthur placed his hand on the crucifix, weighing it down in Galahad's grip. "It was my way of bringing this man called the Christ into the house of pendragon."

Arthur placed his hand on Galahad's chair. "I told him that if I was unworthy, I would rest a chair of honor in my court and would wait for the man who would be worthy of the Grail. That day, Christ showed me your destiny, nephew." Arthur retrieved the cross from Galahad and placed it in front of Aryanyn, who kissed the hands and feet of Jesus. Galahad smiled at her show of love for his savior.

"When Mordred came to live here, he taxed my being, and I wondered what God wanted from me. After your father—my friend Lancelot—and my wife Guinevere betrayed me in my home I asked that question often. When Arianna came and we spoke of her son Joseph, I realized I was not the only distraught parent in this world."

Arthur moved from Galahad, stood near Galahad's young brother and rested his hand on Joseph's shoulder. "I am glad that you did not become another Mordred."

Joseph bowed to Arthur.

"Your mother raised you well."

"She did, sire," said Joseph with pride.

"Arianna gave me a friendship and the faith to move forward," continued Arthur. "On the day of my battle with my son, she gave me a cross to wear."

Galahad turned to look at his mother, who pulled the cross from under her blouse and hung it in front of her bosom.

"It still bears my blood stain," said Arthur.

Aryanyn swiped her finger on the nick where Arthur's blood stained the gold.

"Her gift told me that Jesus was with me in battle and that whatever the outcome, I was doing his will."

Galahad saw tears begin to quietly tumble down his uncle's face.

"I had no idea that it was God's will that I kill my son, but the reasons were made clear to me after I died that day. Élan came to me on the battlefield and told me why I succumbed to a sleep that only God could give an unworthy soul and why Aryanyn, then named Arianna, had come to me."

Galahad saw pride turn to a distant stare in Arthur's eyes.

"Coming from behind the trees was a beautiful woman dressed in the attire of a Roman princess. Startled, I bowed to the woman and asked her if she was the Angel of Death. She told me she was sent by God as the caretaker of my soul—that God knew of my love for my son and of my love for my people, and that everything was as it should be. She also told me that I had been chosen to search for the titulus of Christ with the high priestess, Aryanyn, and that it was God's will that I await rebirth."

Galahad watched Arthur as he came back towards him. He was still the same Arthur, commanding the attention of all in the room, and he grabbed Aryanyn's hand, and kissed it gently. "It took immeasurable time for me to find peace for not only Mordred, but for myself." Arthur turned back to Galahad. "My lord, though my body is not yet in readiness to accept the challenge of my lineage and my birthright, on behalf of my heart, mind and soul, I accept this quest that my rebirth has delivered to me." Galahad raised his wine. "The two houses are joined for the service of the body and the soul."

"Huzzah!" cried out Joseph, and the court raised their cups in unison, regaling them with a hearty, "Huzzah!"

Galahad looked to his hand at the two rings he wore. One was the ring that he gave Miriam as her royal signet on the day of his marriage.

The other was the ring on which he and his mother held their promise

He removed Miriam's ring from his left hand and approached Arthur. "Uncle, as Aryanyn and I have kept a promise on your rings, today I ask a promise of you. In the coming months, rejuvenate your body to prepare for your journey, quest to Rome and return safely. Bring home to this land we call Camelot, not only the mother of Joseph and myself but also the titulus of Christ."

Arthur bowed to Galahad, who placed the ring on the smallest finger of Arthur's right hand.

"I send you and Aryanyn off with the blessings of Camelot and the Christian and Druid houses."

CHAPTER SIXTY-SEVEN

The Trial of William Borwell and Frederick Garris

"Knights Bedwynn and Montgomery, escort William Borwell and Frederick Garris into this court," said Galahad, standing at the east side entrance of the Round Table room. Both young knights raised their swords and pulled their captives in front of the doorway. William stood quickly as Michael pulled the chains that bound his hands and pushed him like a criminal through the doorway, followed by Sir Peter, his son, who carried with him an anxiety that was written on his face.

Frederick remained on his knees.

"Up with you!" shouted Knight Daniel Montgomery, but the man would not budge. Daniel pulled him up to his feet, chains and all, and dragged him into the court.

William was the first to kneel before Galahad. Frederick was pushed to his knees by Sir Daniel.

Galahad lifted Anwnn and stood over the accused knights. William kept his head down, as though not daring to raise his eyes to Galahad.

Frederick, however, boldly raised his head and stared directly into Galahad's eyes for several seconds, without expression, before turning his dark gaze to Arthur.

Sir Luke Agavene acted as magistrate. "Sir William Borwell, you stand accused of high treason. What say you?"

William raised his head slightly and answered, "I plead guilty, my lord."

"Sir Frederick Garris, you stand accused of high treason. What say you?"

Frederick lifted his head and said smugly, "I accuse my king and my countrymen of heresy." The accused dared to stand, and Daniel shoved him back onto his knees. "That is not Arthur," he continued, "but an apparition."

"My liege, may I speak?" William asked.

"You may speak, Sir William," answered Galahad.

William remained on one knee and struck his chest with both fists. "My liege, my lord and my king, Galahad du Lac. I, William Borwell, beg for the mercy of this court. Majesty Galahad, I have fought too long and too hard for the service of this land I call my home. With sorrow, I apologize to King Arthur, my former king and my brother, for my failure to understand the power of this table and the kingdom for which Arthur sacrificed his life. Majesties, forgive an old man whose fear clouded the judgment of his heart."

William changed his position from kneeling on one knee to kneeling on both and prostrated himself in front of Galahad. He took a deep breath. "It is not Arthur that I am against, but his raising."

"If it is not Arthur you are against, William, why accept treason as your fate?" asked Luke.

William looked directly at the cross on the wall. "I am an adjutant to the church and stand proud of my office. If I accept Arthur and his so-called rebirth, I disavow my beliefs as a Catholic and betray my pope and the office I uphold in my service to Camelot and the church."

Galahad looked down at the elder knight, taking account of his defense, and stood in front of Frederick. "What say you in defense of your status, Sir Frederick Garris?"

"I will not beg for mercy or explain who and what I am. I am a Catholic, and I do not believe in rebirth or reincarnation. There is only one life and one soul. This is the biggest mockery to God and man that our lifetimes will ever see!" Frederick looked at Merlin. "Or is it the biggest illusion of magic that you fools have all fallen to on bended knee?"

Arthur stood from his chair. "Majesty, may I speak?"

"No, Uncle, you may not speak!"

Arthur sat down quickly, anger twisting his features.

Galahad circled the accused and looked down into Frederick's eyes. "What makes you so sure that this is not Arthur?"

"There is only one God; he alone has power over life and death. This man is a fallacy wrought by witchcraft and heresy--one that I will not recognize as a life at all."

"What gives you the right to call this witchcraft?" questioned Luke.

"The patriarch of Rome, Gregory the First. I am his liaison and the liaison of my lord, Jesus Christ," spat Frederick.

"Yes, we all know that it was you who wanted Merlin and the Druids banished from Camelot." Galahad stood tall over Frederick. "You would place your country in danger for these church coins that fill your pockets?"

"My payment will be to see *our* friend Merlin here and his Pagan ways banished from *my* home and country."

Merlin lifted his head, "You have never been a friend, sir," he said with contempt.

"You are the voice of the devil himself, and you lead these people," Frederick pointed to Blaise, Aryanyn and Viviane, "to wreak evil upon this Camelot that we Catholics call home."

Frederick stood and tried to walk over to Merlin, but Michael yanked hard on his chains, wrapping the cold metal around Frederick's throat and dragging him back down to his knees.

Frederick sneered at Galahad and shot a look of disdain in Merlin's direction before he spat across the floor at the wizard.

"I beg your pardon!" yelled Merlin, standing.

"Druid, you are the fabric of this poison." Frederick wiped the spit from his lips.

"Hold your tongue, Frederick!" shouted an angry Galahad as he placed the point of Anwnn to Frederick's throat.

Hate for the wizard was written in Frederick's eyes. "I'll hold my tongue when you use your balls, sire."

Several audible gasps resonated from the walls and into Galahad's ears as he turned to see many of the knights lower their heads, ashamed of this infidel they once called their brother.

The silence was deafening as the court awaited the king's decision.

Galahad recalled the day when he heard of Arthur's death. It was William and Frederick who stood in this very room, bloodied and cleaved with the evidence of their battle, reporting the deaths of Arthur, Sir John, Sir Percival and Sir Ralph. Galahad sat and listened, overcome with the reality of a banished father and a dead king. In his grief and anger, he had thrown his dagger across the room, knocking it into the stone below the crucifix that Arthur carved.

Today, Galahad stared at the same cross and remembered the man who died upon it. He read the titulus: I. N. R. I. *Jesus the Nazarene King and Redeemer of the Jews.*

"Redemption," he whispered under his breath. *Remember who and what you are.* He looked at King Arthur, the man who gave his blood to save his home and the country he loved from a madman—Mordred——who would have had them all put to death to claim a throne to which he had no right.

By law, these men should be beheaded. *God allowed Arthur's rebirth. Can I stand in right judgment and take these lives in his place?* He looked at Arthur, remembering their recent conversation.

"Sir Luke Agavene, what does the law state in reference to the charge of treason to this court and to the table of the Round?"

Sir Luke approached the accused and struck his chest, saluting his king. "Majesty, the laws of this court state the punishment is death."

Galahad looked at the accused. "Do you hear what your crimes have brought to you this day?"

William stood in horror and Galahad read his fear. "Peter, come to my aid!" William reached out his hands, and the chains rattled in front of him as though calling for the first knight to remove them.

"Weakling!" yelled Frederick knocking William out of the way, and lurching at Galahad. Michael ran to Galahad's side and forced Frederick down, holding him at bay. Unruly commotion took over Galahad's court as Martin rose quickly from his chair and held his younger brother, William, for dear life. Daniel, Michael, Luke and Peter now held down a laughing Frederick. "You're all doomed men." His words were muffled under the knights' bodies.

Galahad stood over William, "William Borwell, is it true that for the past years you have played the pawn from threats by the church against your king and family?" Galahad heard his own voice echo off the stones at the opposite end of the room.

Frederick screamed from beneath the pile of men holding him back. "Go ahead, dig your grave, William."

Peter rose up from the mound of men to stand near Galahad. He looked at his father, who appeared too horrified to speak.

"Father, please, it means your life," begged Peter.

William hung his head in shame and answered, "It is with regret and sadness that I confess to my king that for the past twenty years I have lived under pain of threat not only from the church but from my fellow knight of the Round Table, Sir Frederick Garris."

"Coward! You have always been the coward!" shrieked Frederick as he writhed in his chains.

"I would rather be a coward and see my family live than have the church and you take everything I hold dear." William looked at his son and teared up in his revelation of the truth. "Forgive me, Peter, but it was your life that was in danger."

Peter stood frozen in fear until Galahad gestured to him to go to his father.

Simultaneously, Frederick was brought back to his knees by the younger knights as Galahad approached William and placed Anwnn's point to the floor, leaning on her tang.

"William Borwell, I understand the pain of fear that you have suffered under these many years. It is a shame that you could never come to me willingly, knowing that your king and fellow brothers of the Round Table would serve you and your family the protection owed to you. William, it pains me to strip you of rank and vesture, and place you in Affalon Tower until this court sees fit to pardon you—if that date should ever come."

Galahad leaned back and raised his sword to the throat of Frederick.

"Frederick Garris, today you are stripped of your rank and removed forthwith from Camelot and all of England. You will spend the rest of your life banished from the country you called your home. You will be escorted to the dungeons of Versailles, where you shall live out your remaining days."

CHAPTER SIXTY-EIGHT

Jack and Father Wallace

Jack Lawrence stood at the foot of King Arthur's grave, where two weeks ago the beautiful memorial to the king stood tall and proud—unstained by the thousand and better years that the king had laid in his slumber. He ran his finger through the new fissure in the tall gray marble stone. The break ran through the king's name and cut into the words: *HIC IACET ARTHURUS REX QUANDOM REX QUE FURTURUS.*

Jack laughed as he read the words, spitting them out, "The once and future king." He removed Arianna's will out from his pocket. "I wonder who really owns her heart...you or me."

He unrolled the paper he was holding tightly in his hand, reading 'The Last Will and Testimony of Arianna Lawrence.' Cynthia had found the will in his wife's drawer. As he read the loving words she wrote to him, he noticed that Arianna did not sign her name Arianna—on the paper, it read Aryanyn.

He thought back to the passage about the woman named Aryanyn in a book about St. Helena, a book his daughter Alexis proudly cherished when she found out this true identity of her mother.

"Did you know who my wife was when she came to you? Was it then you planned to take her from me?" Jack looked up to the heavens. "What right did you have to take her away?"

Father Wallace was coming towards him from the distance. Taking a handkerchief from his pocket, Jack wiped his face before the priest arrived.

"George told me where to find you."

"Is there something you need?"

Father Wallace lowered his backpack from his shoulder, opened it, and removed an old brown velvet sack from the bag.

"Last night during the storm, the winds were so violent that they broke a branch off the tree on the left side of the chapel. The branch broke the stained glass window bearing the symbol of the Trinity." Wallace placed the sack in Jack's hand. "A bolt of lightning must have shot through the open window and cut through the base of the statue of Saint Helena. I found the remains of the statue this morning on the floor; the base was burned along with the curtain behind it. In the broken base was that purse you are now holding." Jack looked up at the priest. "It is a miracle that the chapel did not burn down," said Father Wallace.

Jack snickered as he looked at the pouch. It bore the initials A. E. An eerie feeling came over him, reminiscent of the early years of his illness. He opened the pouch, and as dust from its casing fell over his hands, coins spilled out into his cupped palm.

So he could see the coins more clearly, he placed his glasses upon his nose and raised his head with question, to the priest.

"They're Roman," said Father Wallace.

In Jack Lawrence's hands were the relics of days gone by. He read the names on each coin: Pilate, Crispus, Emperor Constantine and the Empress Helena herself––the revered saint of the church. Another coin bore a familiar face, and the name Aryanyn was etched upon the surface. Looking up at him was the face of his wife with her hair long, down around her shoulders. Above her, he saw the symbol of the trifecta, also known as the Trinity; and below her was the crescent moon. He folded the coin tight into his palm.

"So what the books say about Arianna is true. My wife is this

Aryanyn. It is she who has raised the king and who will go back in time to find the titulus of Christ."

The priest held out his hand for the coins, but Jack held onto them. "Father, how do I handle this?'

"My son, you must find faith in God."

"My faith in God ran out a long time ago."

Father Wallace placed his hand on Jack's shoulder.

"Please don't play the priest right now," Jack pleaded. "I need answers. Isn't there some rule that states that Ari is committing some sort of sin by staying away from me?"

"Do you not think that Arianna has been a loyal and faithful wife since the day of her vows to you?"

Jack could not look the priest in the eyes. "I am afraid that Arthur will be the strong man that I have not been for Ari."

"Your wife has been divinely chosen. If she had not the strength of heart and mind, she, Aryanyn Echrrynn, would not have been honored by this quest."

"I feel as though I have been married to a stranger all these years." Jack pulled his wallet from his pocket and looked at his wedding picture. He caressed the image of her face, pulled the coin from his pocket and looked at the woman on the patina.

"Father, these two women cannot be one and the same."

"They are, Jack."

"I miss her, Father. My bed and my heart have an emptiness in them."

"Know this, Jack. You are giving her to the world right now. It is heaven that controls this destiny, not us."

"So I have no one but God to blame for my failing marriage?"

Father Wallace grabbed Jack by both shoulders. "Did you not tell me yourself that despite everything she endured for you and your son, Arianna never once failed you or your family?"

Jack held his head down, answering, "She has always been my strength regardless of what was placed before her."

"My friend, it is time for you to be strong for her. Do you not think, that maybe she is just as afraid as you?"

Jack looked at the priest trying to comprehend what he was saying. "I remember that when I was sick, Arianna came into the hospital room. She knew that my illness was killing me, but she stood there and held my hand." Jack looked at the trees around him. "Ari does not feel fear."

"She is just as afraid now as she was then," the priest explained, "but she does not want you to worry for her. All she wants is to fulfill her destiny so that she can come home to the safety and security of your loving arms."

Jack walked over to a tree stump and sat down, overwhelmed with emotion. "What if she dies in some far off land and I cannot be there to say goodbye? How can I live with that?"

"These coins came to us in the statue of the saint, who is telling us that Aryanyn will be safe and will return to us. We have to find comfort and faith in this sign. Come back to the house with me. We'll have a mug of ale."

The idea of sitting around a table drinking nauseated Jack. "I'd prefer to be alone right now."

"Jack, you cannot find answers being alone. You need your friends with you at these times."

Hearing footsteps from the causeway, Jack looked up to see his daughter coming towards them. He pulled himself up quickly, embarrassed at his outpouring of emotions, and tried to hide his face from Alexis.

"What are you doing here, Lexy?"

"I came to see if you're alright. You left in a bit of a rush."

"I'm fine." Jack knew that his daughter could see right through him.

"Your father has a lot to absorb, Alexis. Your mother is traveling around with a powerful king."

"Is that what this is all about, Dad?" Alexis stepped towards her father. "If Mom really wanted out of her marriage, it would have happened a long time ago." Alexis kissed her father lovingly on the cheek, and Jack felt the support of that kiss. "Mom loves you Dad. You should see how she looks at you."

Jack managed to crack a smile, grabbed his daughter's hand for strength and walked away. He looked back briefly, wanting to believe that Arianna was faithful to him but unable to reconcile that his competition was a revered king. *Was he not a fool for believing that once this was over, she would still be his?*

CHAPTER SIXTY-NINE
The Release of Madness

Archbishop Arimborgo exited his finely crafted horse drawn coach in Paris, one of the most beautiful cities in France. Yet today, his precious carriage did not stop in front of the marbled and mosaic *Sainte-Croix-et-Saint-Vincent* but proceeded to the entry to the dungeons of the city. He walked down the dark path and into the main entry, a long narrow hall made of dark brown wood and cold grey floors.

A well-armed man in ebony leather, full torso armor and a black cloak greeted him. Arimborgo placed a parchment in the man's hand. The guard looked at the seal and simply read, "Rome." He broke the red seal that belonged to the first bishop of the Catholic Church, and read the words on the parchment. He laughed, "*Viens*," he said in his French accent, and Arimborgo followed him a few steps.

"Why don't you release him and bring him up to me?" Arimborgo asked.

"Oh no," laughed the guard with a sneer. "This one is for you."

Archbishop Thomas Arimborgo of Rome belonged to one of highest conclaves of cardinals and bishops that ruled the papacy and the Roman Catholic Church. He was not prepared to drag his red satin cassock through these halls, but he seemed to have no option.

The floors were filthy from mud and dirt that tracked in on the boots of the guards for what looked like decades or more. Dark wooden doors made of oak housed the prisoners. The smells coming from behind them were so vile that the archbishop had to focus intensely on his mission so as not to lose the delicacies of fresh bread, churned butter, smoked cheese, apples and strawberries that he had enjoyed that morning.

"Father, forgive me!" shouted a man from behind a nearby door as he tried to reach beyond the small window through which his scant meals were served. The prisoner's disfigured, three-fingered hand groped at the priest. His open lesions, smeared with blood and dirt, touched the priest's own uncovered hand. Arimborgo was yanked away from the doorway by the guard who struck at the hand of the prisoner fiercely. The man shrieked in pain, and the priest picked up his pace as he attempted to clean his hand on his cassock.

After climbing down a few steps, they stopped near a cage of metal and barbed wire where two men were shackled, tossing their heads back and forth on the fence screaming vicious obscenities. Arimborgo turned away as one man shouted, "*Merde*," and spit in his direction. The other man tried to pull from his shackles, rattling the cage around him. He kicked the other prisoner and shouted, "*Va te faire enculer.*"

The guard entered the cage, grabbed the prisoner by his hair, and pulled his head back. "Est-ce que tu te moques d'un prêtre!"

Staring back at him, the prisoner shouted, "Filthy prick!"

The guard smacked him in the face and walked away, relocking the door again behind him.

Arimborgo's heart pounded all the way up to his temples. He wanted to complete his business as soon as possible and run from this heinous place. "The high bishop of Rome sends me to hell to do God's bidding," he said, looking over to the guard, who bit down on a loaf of bread as they walked through the mildew-ridden halls. Approaching a smaller stairwell, the man threw bits of bread to the ground as he grabbed a torch from the wall. The combined smell of the fresh bread and aged mold passed by the archbishop's nostrils and he thought of a rotting pig on a platter of delicious smoked cheese. *How vile.* The archbishop looked back while they descended and watched several rats run from under the floorboards to devour the crumbs. He yanked up his cassock, held it close to his body and fled quickly down the stairs after the guard.

"Where is the prisoner?" he asked, attempting to peer further down the shaft. The man seemed to ignore him. "Down there?"

"*Oui*," replied the guard with distain as he continued down the steps.

The archbishop stopped short as the intense odor of human waste wafted from the woodwork. Unable to refrain any longer, he doubled over and purged his breakfast, hearing the guard laugh at his plight. Arimborgo stood and wiped his mouth with a white cloth from his pocket as the guard continued his belly laugh.

At this level of depth, less light and air were available, and Arimborgo felt faint. He brushed his hand on the wall for balance but pulled away quickly, as though the wall were a living animal waiting to strike. He backed up a few steps, feeling that the walls were caving in on him, but the guard pulled on the cross around Arimborgo's neck and dragged him further into the dank dungeon. "Let's move."

"Bless me, Father," Arimborgo prayed as he looked to the ceiling, made the sign of the cross on his chest and followed the guard. Prisoners continued to assault him with maddening screams as they passed the locked doors.

"Food. You must feed me. Have you anything to spare?" begged a woman with her lips pursed to the floor beneath one doorway.

"Let me out! Please! I'm innocent. You have to let me out!" shrieked a man from behind another. They kept walking. "Let me out of here!" he shouted again and for a moment silence crept into the hallway followed by a massive thud against the door as though the man had run at it with all of his strength. Soft, painful whimpers followed from behind the wood.

"We keep moving," shouted the guard, obviously keying into the archbishop's hesitation and fear. At the end of the hall, they were welcomed by a piercing cry that had the hairs on Arimborgo's neck standing on end.

The guard inserted his key into the lock and opened the door. As he threw what was left of his bread on the floor, the archbishop heard the squeaking of mice from underfoot. He jumped to the side as the guard placed the torch in the room.

A voice from within the cell screamed, "Get behind me, Satan!" as the guard pushed Arimborgo into the tiny room. The stench of urine, mold, and body odor hit his eyes and nose, and he grabbed the tail of his cassock and wrapped it across his face.

"That's what he says always," claimed the guard, poking at the man with his boot.

The prisoner huddled against the wall as though trying to claw his way out of the cell.

"I came here for a knight of the Round Table. This is some half-crazed beggar," said Arimborgo.

"This is the ward you come for."

The archbishop stared past the guard at the man huddled in the corner mumbling to himself about the devil and God. "This is what has become of Sir Frederick Garris?"

"*Oui, évêque*. Garris. He is for you now."

Arimborgo stepped forward slowly. "I'm here, Frederick," he said, noticing that the knight's once sandy brown hair and beard were tangled and matted, hanging well past his shoulders. He still wore the clothes from the day he was incarcerated; they were filthy, torn and practically falling from his body. Garris' pants were shredded to his knees, and his skin was infected and purple from mice and rat bites.

"What have they done to you?"

"*Évêque*," said the guard from over his shoulder, "you speak to an idiot—he's mad."

Unexpectedly, Garris crawled on his knees and pulled hard on Arimborgo's coat, yanking him down to the floor. His back hit the ground, and he was immediately overtaken by the aroma of feces. Garris jumped upon him before he could raise himself from off the ground and he sniffed Arimborgo—much like a dog investigating a newfound friend. The guard stepped over the pair and kicked Garris off the archbishop.

Frederick screamed back at the guard, "Be gone, Satan, leave me alone."

"The pontiff sends me to collect a madman. What in the name of Christ is he thinking?"

"Christ?" Frederick threw himself against the wall, "No! I cannot look on him!"

Archbishop Arimborgo stepped toward the man. "My friend, I am here! Do you not know me?"

Frederick eased his grasp on the wall and slowly turned around to face his visitor. After several tense moments, a peacefulness seemed to wash over Frederick. And then a maddening smile flashed across his face before he kneeled to kiss the crucifix that hung from Arimborgo's neck.

ANGELICA HARRIS

Angelica Harris was born April 23rd in New York City from a diverse European family. She attended William Cullen Bryant High School where her love for writing was ignited by her schoolteachers before she attended Hunter College where she majored in Liberal Arts, History and Theatre. As a young woman, Harris interned at the *Roundabout Theatre* Off Broadway in New York City. She acted at her Community theatre and lent her Cosmetology talents doing hair and makeup and creating designs for many of the local shows. Harris also worked on the Sci-Fi Soap *Dark Shadows*. Angelica has always had a passion for Medieval History, especially the Arthurian Period. She is the author of titles *The Quest for Excalibur* and *Excalibur and the Holy Grail*. Harris had her first book revised in 2005 with her editor Andrea Howe. In 2004, Angelica partnered with *Corey Blake*, literary development director with LA Film Lab Entertainment and Chairman of the Dream; Writers of the Round Table Inc., and Writers of the Round Table Press for the development of her third book, *Excalibur Reclaims Her King*. Harris and Blake were invited to speak about their work at the Virginia Reading Conference in 2006.

In addition to her novels, Angelica was commissioned by the *Titanic Experience* in Florida, the *RMS Titanic Museum* in Nova Scotia, and the *RMS Titanic Maritime Museum* in Southampton, England to further develop a short story/historical piece for display in the museums. Angelica's first two books were accepted into the *Royal Library* in North Kensington and Chelsea, London, England for their historic accuracy of King Arthur Folklore. Harris is the creator of her own inspiring coaching program called *Success for Authors*, a unique series, designed to help aspiring and established writers transfer their love for words to excellence on the page.

Harris is the Producer/Director of the *Hall of Imagination* at Frankie's Playce. She was interviewed on *Blog Talk Radio* in September 2008. She is a member of the Queens Chamber of Commerce and the

Glendale Kiwanis Club, and has spoken at *Reading Across America Day* at St. John's Lutheran Elementary, presented her *Titanic* short story for the *97th Anniversary of the Foundering of the Titanic* at the Maspeth Kiwanis Club, and presented her books and reading program to the Glendale Kiwanis Club. Harris was invited in 2008 and 2009 to attend *Author's Night* in New York to benefit The East Hampton Library.

Ms. Harris enjoys fencing and belongs to the *Society for Creative Anachronism* and the *Tourette Syndrome Association*. She teaches 5th and 6th Grade religion in the CCD Program and is a Lector and a Eucharistic Minister at *Sacred Heart Roman Catholic Church* in Glendale, Queens, NY. Though she was raised Catholic, Angelica has thoroughly studied the Wicca faith to bring out the true essence of the religion to her readers. In this, her third book, Harris has invented a Pagan language using the Druid language she studied from Celtic mythology to create the linguistics of the speech. She is most proud of her studies and promises that this book will be an adventure to her readers both historically and magically. Angelica is married to John LoCascio, and has two grown children, a daughter, Andrea, and a son, John.

COREY BLAKE

Corey's writing and visionary work has been published in *Writer* Magazine, *Script* Magazine, and on *StartUp Nation* and has been featured on Fox News, NBC5, Sacramento and Co, Adelante (WGN Chicago), and in print such as *Young Money, Hoy, La Raza, Hispanic Executive Quarterly, MovieMaker* Magazine, *Dance* Magazine and *Hollywood Screenwriter* Magazine. He is the co-author of *EDGE! A Leadership Story* (finalist, National Best Books 2008 Awards) with Bea Fields and Eva Silva Travers, *From the Barrio to the Board Room* with Robert Renteria, and *The Family Business* with Dr. Kay Vogt.

Prior to writing, Corey worked in Hollywood as a commercial and voice-over actor starring in campaigns for McDonalds, Mountain Dew, Pepsi, Wrigley's, Hasbro, Miller, Mitsubishi, and the infamous Yard Fitness, where Corey plays basketball naked. Corey also appeared on shows such as The Shield, Fastlane, Buffy the Vampire Slayer, Diagnosis Murder, Joan of Arcadia, and Sabrina the Teenage Witch before he produced The Boy Scout and directed and produced Gretchen Brettschneider Skirts Thirty and Unsuitable for Elevation 9000 Films.

An avid speaker, Corey has keynoted at the Society of Southwestern Authors 2008 Wrangling with Writing Conference and the 93rd Annual Missouri Writers' Guild Conference, and made guest appearances at the Virginia Reading Association (with Angelica Harris), Screenwriting Expo 4 (LA Convention Center), Cinespace (Hollywood), Avalon (Hollywood), The Ivar (Hollywood—The Make-A-Wish Foundation of Greater Los Angeles), Spring into Romance Writing Festival (San Diego), and the Midwest Literary Festival (Chicago).

Corey is proudly married to Dr. Dawn Blake, a Psychologist. They make their home in the suburbs of Chicago and Corey travels frequently back to Los Angeles.

www.ingramcontent.com/pod-product-compliance
Lightning Source LLC
Chambersburg PA
CBHW020932020726
47495CB00002B/468